"YOU'RE . . . NOT A GOD?"

Golden Hand rocked back on his heels and rested his forearms on his knees. He stared at Green Eyes Blue some more and finally said, "No, dear, I'm a man. My name is Golden Hand. What's your name?"

"Green Eyes Blue."

She couldn't explain why, but suddenly she felt painfully shy.

"Green Eyes Blue. That's a nice name. Very fitting. Very descriptive."

Something in his tone gave her the idea he was laughing at her. In her village the chief's proudest possession was a small mirror made of highly polished silvery-gray stone. It reflected her face almost as clearly as a puddle of still water. The chief had let her look at it once, and she'd seen how her eyes were different colors than those of all the other children, who had made fun of her. Now this secret breath of humor brought all those jibes back again.

"Don't laugh at me!" she said sharply.

He started back, his eyebrows arching. "I'm not laughing at you."

"Yes, you *are*. I want to go home. *Please* let me go home. . . ." And then, unaccountably, she burst into tears.

She felt his warm hands take her shoulders and pull her close. Her head rested on his chest as she sobbed.

"It's all right," he murmured, stroking her hair. "It will be all right. . . ."

Sister of
the Sky

Margaret Allan

AN ONYX BOOK

ONYX
Published by the Penguin Group
Penguin Putnam Inc., 375 Hudson Street,
New York, New York 10014, U.S.A.
Penguin Books Ltd, 27 Wrights Lane,
London W8 5TZ, England
Penguin Books Australia Ltd,
Ringwood, Victoria, Australia
Penguin Books Canada Ltd, 10 Alcorn Avenue,
Toronto, Ontario, Canada M4V 3B2
Penguin Books (N.Z.) Ltd, 182–190 Wairau Road,
Auckland 10, New Zealand

Penguin Books Ltd, Registered Offices:
Harmondsworth, Middlesex, England

First published by Onyx, an imprint of Dutton NAL,
a member of Penguin Putnam Inc.

First Printing, January, 1999
10 9 8 7 6 5 4 3 2 1

Dedicated to

Tan Mong Seng
The folks of misc.writing

I have been greatly aided by Dr. Paul Pettennude, an archaeologist who has been doing work in the Mayan area for over thirty years, most recently in the Teotihuacán area we now know the ancients called Tollan. His help and advice have been invaluable. If, then, anything in this novel conforms to current archaeological knowledge of Teotihuacán, it is Paul's doing. Errors and simple fancies are plainly my own.

—Margaret Allan

"You rebel—and yet you want them: those obligations, those penalties, those debts!—Man wants to serve!"
—*Ugo Betti*

"There is neither mastery
nor slavery
except as it exists
in the attitude of the soul."

—Don Marquis

"Servitude debases men to the point where they end up liking it."
—Vauve-Nargues,
Reflections and Maxims

Chapter One

I sit on my high place and watch dusk weave blue webs along the tops of the mountains of Tlaloc. Those enduring peaks hold us in a mighty grip. Even the stones, the dark and bony ribs of this great valley, are infested with Gods. But why not? This is the Place of the Reeds. This is Their home. And buried beneath the House of the Plumed Serpent, upon which my eyes turn at this very moment, is the birth passage of the Mother, the dark cave where the World came from beyond the World. Men dance and sing upon that womb, and the time of retribution approaches, but not yet. If I'm lucky, not until I've departed this valley and Tollan, the City of Gods, forever.

I am old. My bones creak now, and I drink too much pulque, and not only after the sun has hidden his face from us in darkness. Sometimes I drink the fire liquor with my tea in the morning, to find enough ease to rise from my bed. And sometimes I chew the bitter green leaves the traders bring from the mountains far to the south, to take away the pains I have collected over a lifetime that my few remaining friends say has been much too long. But they are old and as jealous as I am. They have not been touched by the fingers of the Great Ones, as I have. Yet had they felt those awful caresses, they would regard me with pity rather than jealously. They spite me for my fate, and I, equally, spite them for theirs. So I forgive them.

Anyway, as the time of my end approaches, I find it

hardly matters at all. I shall welcome the darkness gladly, and bid the World and all within it a loud farewell. The night cannot come too soon for me.

I have but one task left, though unlike too many others, this one was not laid on me by holy charge. My debts to the Great Ones are paid twice over, and I will be sure not to entail new obligations. Rather, I take this on myself, as others in the long line of my predecessors once did, not knowing how their words would work on the looms of time. Nor do I, but the story must be told to its end. And so I will do that.

I owe her that much.

I am too old to do this properly. My ancient knees crack and burn if I try to do the right steps, or the dances that should accompany the words I sing. So now my son is Chief Scribe and Singer, and I am an old man. But I can still write the tale. I can still shape the beautiful pictures that paint the secret Language of Hands, the language in which the Gods whisper Their dark secrets. I can still use the inks and the shell pens to inscribe them on the thin wooden boards.

I do miss the dance, though. And if I could, I would rise from my seat atop the House of the Moon, where I now sit beneath the altar and huge visage of the Goddess Herself, and I would dance. I would dance for Her, and sing for Her, and my hands would shape the tale in Her own language, high above Her city.

For this is Her city. We forget it sometimes, and when we do, She reminds us. As She did once upon a time.

In that time, spring had come upon the south land with great heat.

It was the time of the rains.

It was the time of the brown floods and the bright new leaves.

It was the time of rebirth. . . .

BOOK ONE

—◦◦◦—

Captivity

"A cat pent up becomes a lion."
—Italian proverb

Chapter Two

1

Green Eyes Blue stared up at the green leafy canopy above her head. The forest around her seethed with heat. She had crouched here waiting for the afternoon rains to end, and now they had. The hard blue sky was visible only as small rents in the thick leafy roof above her. The foliage was so dense it took many minutes for the last of the water to make its way to the earth below. It fell drop by crystalline drop, from cupped leaf to cupped leaf, and trembled in tiny jewels from the tips of the lowest leaves.

High above, a troupe of monkeys screeched and chattered. Green Eyes looked for them but only saw a few fleeting shapes that leaped quickly away.

She sighed, leaned back against the smooth trunk of the tree, and looked down at her belly. She saw nothing of interest there and raised her gaze a bit, to the dark aureoles that covered the swelling bumps on her chest.

Thoughtfully she tweaked the nipple on her right breast and felt a small twinge of pleasure. With her head bowed, her hair fell across her face in shining black curtains. She wore only a simple skirt colored with red dye and ornamented along the hem with her mother's stitchery. It cupped her slim waist smoothly. Her legs, drawn up, showed the first rounding of thighs, and the taut, muscled calves of a natural runner. On her callused feet were plain sandals made of twisted rope.

She had worn something similar as long as she could remember. These were the clothes of childhood, the sort of things boys and girls alike wore every day. But that would change soon, for her childhood was ending. Her mother had told her so.

She raised her head and stared out across the clearing. There the trees were somewhat less dense, for only the small-

est could find purchase for their roots in the jumble of dark
stones and lumpy hillocks. Straw grass nodded in shafts of
sunlight, like hair on the great shapes that protruded from the
earth like the tops of dark skulls.

She wondered if once she became a woman she would still
be able to come here. She hoped so, but she was still confused
about what her new role would be. Nor did it help that her
own body seemed determined to do everything it could to
keep her confused. Every day seemed to bring some new
thing. Breasts suddenly appearing on her smooth chest. The
odd urges that rushed over her in hot, prickly flashes. The
jumble her thoughts sometimes became. And the daylight
dreams, when it seemed her mind floated away into the high
blue sky, humming softly.

She got her feet under her and stood in a single smooth motion. Something had moved on the other side of the clearing.
Perhaps a rabbit. The way the sunlight pierced the leaves in
bright, standing columns amid the steaming shadows made it
hard to see. She raised one hand to her forehead and shielded
her eyes.

There it was again. A flicker of motion, barely caught at the
edge of her vision. With utmost care, she reached behind herself and lifted her most prized possession from where it
leaned against her shoulder pack.

Her eldest brother had made the bow for her in secret. He
hadn't wanted to. "A bow is for a man," he'd said in his high,
squeaking voice, and she'd laughed at him. Then she'd kissed
him on his cheek and stared at him with her strange eyes and
he'd relented. He loved her. He would do anything for her,
even break the taboos.

But he had not taught her how to use the bow. That was a
sacrilege he could not bring himself to swallow, though she
didn't mind. She'd taught herself. She'd cut the reeds and
smoothed them into arrows, and hardened their points in secret fires she kindled here, in the Old Place.

She knew her weapon so well that she slipped an arrow

from her pack and nocked it against the fish gut bowstring
without interrupting her intense watch on the clearing at all.
Then, crouching down, she held the bow ready as she
moved slowly out into the grasses, her odd, two-colored
eyes glittering.

Again . . . there!

She leaped forward, her feet light as a wild dog's claws as
she bounded across the slick top of a half-buried mound of
rock. And . . . there!

A flash of twitching ears, the bright glint of beady eyes. She
raised the bow and drew it with a single smooth motion. Her
breath stopped for an instant as her fingers relaxed. The bowstring twanged and she fancied she could hear the hissing
flight of the arrow.

A soft, startled squeak.

"Hah," she murmured.

It took her a bit of hunting to find her prey, for her shot had
been good but not perfect. The brown rabbit had managed to
hop a few yards before collapsing. She found it still alive,
pierced through the belly, quivering in a puddle of blood. Its
black eyes stared up at her, slowly glazing.

It had fallen partway into a crevice beneath a huge outcropping of dark stones. Without a thought she bent down and
pried a rock of suitable size from the damp earth, raised it, and
brought it down in a single savage movement.

The rabbit ceased its struggles.

Carefully, she pulled the arrow from between its ribs and
cleaned it on a hank of wet grass. Then she grasped the soft
ears and tried to tug the dead beast from the crack in the
stones, but it had managed to wedge itself in and it wouldn't
come loose.

She rocked back on her heels and let out an exasperated
sigh. Then she stood up and peered around until she saw
what she was looking for a few feet away. A nest of parched
brambles with a few larger stalks protruding. She walked
over and yanked one of the stalks from the earth, then

snapped it across her knee. She went back to the rabbit, slipped the thick end of the branch between two likely looking stones, and began to pry.

After a few moments of work the bottom stone loosened and she was able to hook her fingers around it. When she lifted it away the top stone fell in a shower of dirt that spattered the rabbit beneath. As she returned her efforts to the rabbit, something else, loosened by her efforts, fell down into the hole and struck the back of her hand.

"Ouch."

She saw a thin trickle of blood. The shape, whatever it was, had sharp edges. She pulled the rabbit the rest of the way out, then reached down for this new thing. It was a little longer than her hand from wrist to fingertip, covered with impacted dirt, a few sharp glints showing through.

She brushed away the dirt and stared at it.

It was a stone knife. Her eyes glittered suddenly with pleasure. It was the most beautiful knife she'd ever seen. The chips used to shape it were so wonderfully worked they were barely visible. In the sunlight it had a beautiful green tinge. She had seen stone like this, though not so perfectly crafted. The chief of her village had a spear tip that was similar. It was his most valued possession, for it had come from the quarries of Tollan, the City of Gods, a gift from a band of priestly traders as a token of the chief's authority.

She felt a sudden thrill. What to do? If she showed it to anybody, they would surely take it from her. Such things weren't for girls. But as she balanced it in her hand she marveled at the way it perfectly fit the smooth curves of her palm. It seemed to have its own warmth. It didn't feel like cold stone at all.

It . . . spoke to her.

It was crazy, but the knife seemed to hum softly against her skin. Its sleek green curves drew her gaze and held it. She squatted for a long time, not noticing how the minutes flowed by.

It was the most beautiful thing she'd ever seen. It was hers. She would not give it up.

She felt a pang of loss as she hid it in the bottom of her shoulder pack, beneath the limp body of the rabbit. It was as if her hand and the knife somehow called to each other, and ached with dumb loneliness when they were separated.

She hoisted the strap of the bag over her shoulder and picked up the bow. The columns of sunlight had begun to slant. She could hear the farmers who worked their plots along the river singing their afternoon prayers as they planted for the spring season.

She was surprised to discover how much time had passed. Maybe she'd held the knife longer than she'd thought. Her mother would be worried.

She set off across the clearing with brisk, easy strides. The secret place where she hid her bow and arrows was deeper in the forest, and she would have to hurry. But the rabbit would be good for dinner, and her mother would be glad of that.

She had no idea she would never see her mother again.

2

Old Big Nose nudged his son, Young Big Nose, in the ribs. Old Big Nose was scarred and gnarled and darkened by the sun. His black eyes danced with dark merriment as he watched the girl stride along, her head high, her dark hair flowing like wings.

Young Big Nose, his first son from his second wife, was tall and thin and smooth, though his skin too had been burned nearly black by years on the endless trading trails that criss-crossed all the world like spider's webs. He licked his lips and nodded. "She's a pretty one," he whispered.

Old Big Nose glanced at him, his grizzled eyebrows arching in surprise. "You want her? You've already got three wives."

Young Big Nose smiled. "Who said anything about a wife?"

Old Big Nose grunted. "She'd bring a good price in the markets. Young and juicy like that. She might even still be a virgin. Those tits on her are just budding."

"She looks like a wildcat. Did you see her with that bow?"

"Country people. Bumpkins. They're half savage anyway. Bring up their kids like animals." Old Big Nose nodded to himself. "And even that might raise her price. I know men who like them like that. They like to tame the wild ones."

Young Big Nose let out his breath softly. "Do you want to take her then?"

"Why not?"

His son shrugged. Silent as ghosts, they moved off.

3

Green Eyes Blue approached the great mound of stones piled in the center of the Old Place. Here the trees found purchase, and the light was always shaded and gloomy. The stones themselves seemed to exude a chill, and when the rains fell, they were cold and slimy to the touch.

She climbed carefully. Near the top she found the tiny cave, barely large enough to fit herself into. Here she kept her secret treasures, such as they were. Her bow, her arrows, a few trinkets of shell, a scrap of cloth colored a particularly pleasing shade of green. Even her brother didn't know of this place. It was hers, perhaps the only thing she possessed that was hers alone.

She crawled inside, found the soft hide wrapping, and bundled up her bow and arrows in it. She sat cross-legged and still had to lower her head to keep from scraping against the ceiling.

One slab of black rock was marked with deep scratches. Leaping animals and men dressed in fantastic costumes. She had stared at these magic pictures often, trying to decipher their meaning, but she couldn't.

The Old People had carved these images in the living stone, in the deeps of time when the Gods had lived here. But the Gods had grown tired of men, and moved on. Or so the priests taught. She wasn't sure. Maybe the Old People had grown tired of the Gods and left them behind.

She knew such thoughts were sacrilege of the worst kind, and so she only indulged herself in such malign musings here in the cave. For some reason she had the idea that the Great Ones could not see or hear her within these sheltering walls. Perhaps she was right. Certainly no bolts of lightning had struck her down yet.

She settled her pack in her lap, opened it, and withdrew the knife. It settled into her hand as if it had been made to fit there. Her fingers closed around it naturally, feeling its sensuous weight. It felt heavier than its size warranted. She wondered if the green stone was different than other rock.

She closed her eyes and hummed softly to herself. The knife seemed to exude a feeling of immense age. Perhaps the Gods had made it when the Old Place was new. She liked that thought, though it frightened her somehow.

It was the same way she felt about the Old Place itself. She liked it, and it scared her a bit. Maybe that was *why* she liked it.

Most of the villagers avoided the Old Place because they said it was haunted. She'd never seen anything untoward, though at times she *had* felt the strange pull of the place. All those broken stones, half buried, some of them marked with strange pictures. The Old Place was well back from the river where the villages now clustered along its wide banks.

Here, deep in the woods, it was impossible to farm, and the trees grew thick and tall beneath the brooding peak of God Mountain.

She had even once committed the ultimate sacrilege and climbed God Mountain all the way to the top. There she had

stood and looked out upon the world and saw a great green
ocean. The tops of the trees stretched green and unbroken
eastward into the mists. She imagined she could see the misty
blue of the ocean, though of course that had to be an illusion.
The ocean, it was said, was many days march away. Somewhere in that gauzy distance was the great city of Pital, the
largest in the region, a mighty port where the huge trading canoes from City of Gods docked. Or so went the stories. She
had no idea if they were true. She'd never been an hour's
march beyond the boundaries of her own village.

Once again time drifted away as she held the knife. She
woke from her reverie with a start. The wise thing would be
to wrap the knife with her other things and leave it here. But
when she reached for the bundle, something stopped her. The
thought of leaving the knife twisted her belly with an aching,
lonely sensation.

After a moment's thought she sighed and put the knife back
into her bag. It was small. She would be able to hide it with
her personal things. It would be safe.

Or so she told herself.

When she was ready, she crawled out of the mouth of the
cave on her hands and knees. As she emerged she blinked
at the late-afternoon light, now slanting down directly into
her eyes.

A rough hand slapped across her mouth and squeezed hard.
Strong arms yanked her the rest of the way out of the cave
mouth like a cork from a bottle.

4

It was like trying to wrestle a young panther bare-handed.

Old Big Nose yelped through gritted teeth as the squirming
she-cat sank her sharp fangs into the soft flesh of his palm.
His son grunted softly as the knot of her heel slammed into
the tender eggs at the jointure of his crotch.

Blood leaked through Old Big Nose's fingers as he tried to keep a grip on her gnashing jaws. His lumpy features contorted in pain as she chewed at him. Some small part of him noticed that she fought like a jungle animal, writhing and twisting, clawing and snapping . . . but in silence.

It was her soundless ferocity that frightened him more than anything. He clouted her as hard as he could on the side of the head, once, then again.

Her body went limp as a rag. A crimson trickle leaked from her right ear.

"Gods," Young Big Nose whispered. "You killed her."

Old Big Nose raised his right hand and stared in disbelief at his palm. The flesh there hung in shreds, and he could see the white glint of bone in the pink and bleeding meat.

"Tie her up," he instructed shakily. "Make sure she can't get her hands or feet loose." He paused, watching the blood drip from the edge of his hand. "She tore me up," he said with shuddery disbelief.

Young Big Nose placed two fingers in the soft hollow of her throat. "She's still alive," he said.

"Of course she is," his father said. "She's an animal. Gods. Go on, tie her up, and then help me with this." He swallowed hard. "Look at it bleed."

His head came up. The woods had gone utterly silent. The flesh at the back of his neck crawled. The great stones, leaning this way and that, cast long, eerie shadows. His ears popped. Terror suddenly welled up in him like dark water. It was all he could do not to leap up and run as fast as he could in any direction at all. It didn't matter, as long as it was *away*.

"Hurry," he said. "This place makes my bones creep."

Young Big Nose nodded. He felt it too, the undeniable sensation that unseen eyes were watching *him* with an inhuman chill—as he would watch a bug. This place was a spirit trap. The thought burped into his mind that something terrible had happened here long ago. He inhaled sharply and shook his head. After a long moment when all he could hear was the rapid, insistent beating of his heart, the feeling began to fade. He took a length of rope from his pack and got to work.

The crickets began to sing.

5

She woke with a pounding ache in the side of her head, queasy and sick, conscious of dizzying motion. She groaned, turned her head to the side, and emptied her belly of what remained of the gruel she'd eaten for breakfast.

The world turned upside down as she landed with a thump on her side. In her dazed state she automatically tried to break her fall, but her hands wouldn't respond. She rolled over on her back and stared up at the sky, trying to understand what had happened to her.

A face covered with scars, framed by a cloud of gray-streaked hair, swam like a moon into her vision. Eyes that seemed cruel and laughing at the same time regarded her coldly. Thick lips moved. She knew that mouth shaped words, but for some reason the sound was slow, deep, and sludgy. She shook her head and gasped at the sudden lance of agony that nearly burst her skull.

". . . be puking on me, you little savage," the man said. "Or I'll plug that blow hole of yours up and let you drown in your own spew."

"Hurts . . ." she said weakly.

His grin grew wider and more nasty. She saw that two of his yellowed front teeth had rotted away, leaving only putrescent black stumps.

He leaned closer to her. "Of course it hurts. I meant it to hurt. Look what you did to me."

His breath was hot and smelled like a dead animal left too long in the sun. He raised his right hand. It was bound in scraps of rags, which covered some noxious poultice that leaked from beneath the edges of the crude bandage.

She had no idea what he was talking about. The last thing she remembered was getting ready to leave the cave, after she'd put the green knife away in her bag.

The knife!

She tried to move her hands again, to no avail. The face above her kept on grinning. "Won't do you no good, girlie. Those are good knots. Same as I'd use to tie up any other cat. Or a bitch coyote."

She closed her eyes. "Hurts . . ." she whispered again. "Mama . . . help me."

Someone laughed harshly.

"You hear that? Now she wants her mama. Isn't that sweet?"

More greasy, knowing laughter. This time it sounded like two voices.

The world swam away. When she woke the next time, the stars were in the sky.

6

"I don't know," Old Big Nose said. "It burns like fire. There's a demon spirit in there for sure." He stared at his hand by the light of their small campfire and shook his head. "Something's wrong with my fingers. They don't move right. Look how swollen it is."

"Well, my balls don't feel so good either. She got me a good one right between the eggs."

Old Big Nose glared at him. "You're young. Your balls will survive. But what if my hand rots? The only thing then is to cut it off. Gods."

"You need a healing priest," his son told him.

"Of course I do, you ninny. But we're still in her part of the country. You think word won't get back to her people if we walk into one of these stinking villages with her trussed up like a turkey?"

"I thought it was a bad idea."

"You say that now. But I don't remember you saying it then. All I remember is you sweating and your dick getting hard. Don't think I didn't notice."

Young Big Nose didn't answer. After a moment his father shifted a bit, raised his head, and looked across the campfire. Green Eyes Blue was sprawled there, still bound. Every once in a while she made a soft, sputtering sound. "She doesn't sound good," the older man observed.

"We don't have to haul her into a village. We don't have to take her anywhere if we don't want to."

Old Big Nose spat into the fire. His sputum sizzled and popped on the coals. He raised his wounded hand and waved it at his son.

"Listen to me, you worthless shit poke. I paid in blood for that little bitch, and by the Gods I'm going to get my money out of her."

"I don't know. She's a monster. Who'd pay anything for her?"

"Somebody will. She's still a pretty one." He raised his head. "And I don't want you poking around with her, understand? If she's still a virgin, that makes her all the more valuable. So keep your dick under your shirt." He laughed softly. "Or I'll cut it off myself. And then what will your wives say?"

"I still don't like it. Better to slit her throat and have an end to it. We've done all right on this trip. Best profit I've seen in years. Why do we have to take risks with a piece of country trash like her?"

"Because I say so, and that's all you need to know." Old Big Nose fell silent for a moment. "Do we have any of the mountain chewing leaf left?"

"A little."

"Good. Get me some. It will help with the pain."

Neither of them noticed that the small girl across the fire was watching them through slitted eyes.

7

Her mind seemed to be working again. She still couldn't re-member what had happened or how she'd ended up here, but she was composed enough to make a few guesses.

The two men were traders. That was obvious enough. They spoke with the curious, lisping accents of the north. Not quite the pure sounds of those native to City of Gods. She'd heard the priest traders speak like that, and this was different. These men looked rougher and poorer than the priest traders, too. But there was nothing unusual about them otherwise.

Such men were a constant in the life of the villages. They came and went like the wind, appearing with bags of glitter-ing things, trading them for other things, and moving on. She knew such men were dangerous, because her father had warned her about them.

And her brother had told her hideous stories about how sometimes children disappeared when the traders moved on, never to be seen again. He told her the traders ate them, roasted them over fires and cracked their little bones to suck out the marrow.

She thought about the rabbit in her shoulder pack. Maybe if she offered it to them they wouldn't eat her. But as soon as she thought of that, she remembered what else was hidden in her pack.

The . . .

She wouldn't allow herself to think the word. Maybe these men had some magic that would let them hear her speak it, even in the silence of her own thoughts. The older one, the one whose hand was bandaged, had rolled himself up in his blanket. She felt a savage thrill of satisfaction when she thought about his hand. She must have done that.

Good!

The old one suddenly began to snore. It was a raucous, bubbling sound. Without moving or opening her eyes all the way, she tried to get a better look at the other one, but all she could see was the dim shapes of his legs stretched out toward the fire. Nevertheless she sensed that his gaze was on her, slow, cold, calculating.

She held herself very still for what seemed like an endless amount of time. Finally she heard a rustle of movement out of the shadows. The fire burned down to dull embers. The feeling of being observed slowly leaked away. Finally she heard the whisper of deep, regular breathing, rasping in counterpoint to the older one's honking snores.

They were asleep. She could let herself think again. Slowly, she tried to move her hands. They had dumped her on her side like a bag of meal and she had lain there unmoving so long that her muscles had congealed. Her first attempt at movement sent a cramp raging through the thick upper muscles of her back. She only barely managed not to cry out, but even so the pain tried to drag her away to its own dark place. Eventually the shudders in her back subsided and she tried again.

The pain this time was bad, but not as bad as before. A finger's width at a time she inched her hands up and to the side.

She could feel the rough strap of the bag still over her shoulder and when, moving equally carefully, she shifted her weight, she could feel the soft lump of the rabbit inside.

So they hadn't checked. Which meant that maybe the (don't say *knife*) thing was still in there too. She remembered how the mere weight of the . . . thing . . . had been enough to cut her own skin. It would be more than sharp enough to cut through the ropes that bound her. If she could reach it.

Grinding her teeth against the agony that coursed through her body as her tortured muscles finally began to respond, she worked her bound hands closer and closer to the flap that covered the top of the bag.

A night bird shrieked, its unearthly cry so close it startled her. The pouch fell away from her numbed fingers. She listened to the bird flap away, the sound of its wings like wind whipping at clothes drying on the rocks along a riverbank.

The old man's snores stopped. She froze. If he looked over

and saw her now, sprawled on her side, her skirt hitched up over her hips and the bag riding against her thigh, he would know.

She held her breath and silently breathed a prayer to every God and Goddess she could remember. Oddly enough, just as she whispered the words, "Mother, help me now," the old man snuffled softly and began to snore again.

It seemed to take forever, but finally she was able to work both hands beneath the flap and into the pouch itself. Then the rabbit, now stiffening with rigor mortis, became a problem. Every time she tried to get her hands around it to reach the knife, the stubborn dead thing would shift just enough to block her.

Unconsciously she gnawed at her lower lip, not even noticing when the coppery taste of her own blood suddenly coated her tongue. Beads of sweat bloomed on her wide forehead and began to drizzle into her eyes.

She blinked at the salty sting, clamped her teeth hard, and forced a final twisting lunge. The rabbit slid aside. Her fingertips touched something cool and smooth.

In silence she worked until she had it caught in a shifty cradle between her fingers. Her wrists were tied so tightly she couldn't get any real grip on the smooth surface of it. And she remembered too well how sharp its edges were. A single slip in the darkness might be enough to nick one of the blue veins on the inside of her wrists. Then her blood would pour out and she would die, only moments from freedom.

A large body crashed through the brush. Wild pig, she thought to herself. She waited several beats to see if the sound had disturbed the sleep of her captors, but nothing changed. After a while she allowed herself to breathe again.

When she finally was able to work the knife free from the pouch, the relief that bloomed in her was as cool as the breeze that suddenly touched her sweating skin.

She inched the blade around until one sharp edge stood out

at an angle to her wrists. Now, if she could just reach the ropes that bound her ankles together . . .

Thankfully all her exertions had loosened her muscles a bit. She bent her knees as far as she could, and slowly arched her back. As she moved she scraped her cheek across a broken stalk. It stabbed at the corner of her eye. She ignored the pain. More . . . more . . . just a finger's length more . . .

There.

Carefully she sawed at the ropes, working by feel, a stroke at a time, hoping she wouldn't slice through one of the veins in her ankle either. It was slow, grinding effort, but when the first of the turns of rope separated, the joy she felt was fiercest emotion she'd ever experienced.

Silently she strained her ankles against each other, stretching the coils of the rope wider and wider until at last she slipped free.

I can run now, she thought. But it would be better if my hands were in front of me.

Can I kill them?

The thought blurted out of nowhere, blank and frigid and deadly. It shocked her. She had no idea where it had come from. It was as if something were inside her mind, something she'd never known was there, and now it reared its dark head in bloody curiosity.

The thought was ridiculous. And ridiculously seductive. For a moment she imagined plunging the sharp blade into them, into their eyes, into their soft bellies. Laughing as their blood exploded up her arms, hot, dripping, and vigorous.

She shuddered. The thought, just as a questing snake sometime will do, poked its head higher, looked around, and then slithered sinuously back into its hole.

Every one of her nerve endings was on fire. Keeping as good a hold on the knife as she could, she bent at the waist, tucked herself into a ball, and brought her wrists forward, passing her bound hands around her feet.

Now she was free. Free to leap up and run like the wind.

They would never catch her in the dark. It didn't matter if she lost herself, she could always find a way back in the daylight. This was still her country. All she would have to do was seek the river and follow it back the way she'd come.

She rolled over, got her knees under herself, and balled her hands into a single fist around the knife.

Thank you, Mother, she thought.

A huge weight fell on her and smashed her flat.

"Where do you think you're going, bitch kitten?" Young Big Nose said.

8

It was the regularity of the sounds that had awakened him. The slow persistent scratching of her movements, like nothing in nature, had invaded his sleep and lifted him out of his febrile dream of her.

He'd drifted off with a dull, throbbing ache in his groin to give him something to remember her by, and when the fitful dream-sleep had finally taken him, he found her again in the half world between wakefulness and death.

And, oh, my, how happy he was to see her there. She'd been an itch and a flame and a goad in his thoughts ever since he'd first seen her running like a young goat across the slick stones.

Now she stood before him, her strange eyes glowing with familiar heat. He felt the same heat overcome his aching balls, felt his organ engorge and rise until it stood straight up and across his belly, quivering at attention.

He looked down and realized he was naked. When he looked up at her he saw she was naked too. He raked his vision across her like a whip, touching those softly mounded breasts, tingling the pink nipples to hardness, then drifting slowly down to rest at last on the hairless, childlike rise of her secret place.

In his dream he stretched out his arms and she came to him, the swell of her belly pressing softly against the rigid heat of his penis. She made soft mewing sounds as she moved against him, her hands reaching around to settle tiny fingers on his buttocks, stroking gently.

He groaned and pulled her tighter to him, feeling the hot white fire begin to bubble at the base of his own belly. Her hair brushed against his chest like the finest fabric. Her teeth, sharp as broken shells, nibbled with infuriating gentleness at his chest.

Scritch, scritch went her teeth.

Scritch, scritch.

Scritch . . .

His eyes popped open. He lay confused for a moment, still gripped by the passion of his dream. Then her movement, a swirl in the shadows beyond the fire, caught his attention. He blinked.

What . . . ?

He flung off his blanket just as she rolled to her knees. Somehow she'd gotten her ankles free. He got his own legs under him and launched himself across the nearly dead coals of the fire.

His weight crushed her to the ground. His organ, still inflamed, was caught between her buttocks and his belly. He pressed harder.

Maybe his dream would come true after all.

9

All the air slammed out of Green Eyes's chest. His weight pressed her lips against the earth and filled her mouth with dirt. Blinded, she kicked out at him and, still holding the knife, twisted and slashed upward. She hit something, felt a short, sliding movement, and then the knife was free.

He screamed.

The sound of it sent birds shrieking into the air. He lurched away from her and she lunged forward, scrabbling on all fours like a crab toward the high brush that surrounded the camp.

"*Hoooooo!*" he wailed.

I hurt him, she thought. I *hurt* him.

10

Old Big Nose woke with a start, his son's cries mingling with the screeching of the birds. He jerked reflexively upright, feeling a twinge in his lower back, his thoughts muzzy with sleep.

What?

He blinked. There was only a sliver of moon in the sky, but the stars were hard and bright. After a moment he got his bearings and turned toward the altercation on the other side of the fire. The light was just bright enough to make out Young Big Nose rocking back on his knees, both hands clamped over his face. His mouth was locked wide, a dark pit below his fingers, and as he rocked he kept bellowing out those strange hooing cries.

Old Big Nose stared at him in astonishment. Then he saw the smaller shadow scuttling away, and he leaped to his feet. He bounded across the fire ring, passed up his son with one giant step, and kicked the smaller shadow as hard as he could.

The dull, meaty thud of his blow drowned out her muffled groan. But it slowed her and gave him a chance to aim his second kick more accurately. He slammed the side of his heel into her skull and she dropped like a poleaxed goat. Quickly he knelt next to her, and slapped her face. No reaction. She was either unconscious or dead. At the moment, either was fine with him.

He turned around and went back to Young Big Nose, who had toppled over on his side, hands still clamped across his face as if he was terrified to let go. Old Big Nose had seen it

before. He'd been a soldier once, and even as a trader he'd
seen his share of brawls.

His knees crackled like dried-out hides as he knelt beside
the boy. He took Young Big Nose's hands in his own and
began to pry them away.

"No, no," he soothed. "Let me see. It's going to be all
right."

But it took all his strength to wrench those fingers apart,
and even then for a moment he wasn't sure what he was looking at. A lot of blood, obviously. His son's eyes bulged
whitely in the starlight.

Where his nose had been there was now only a bloody
gash.

11

The morning sun burned hard into her eyes, but all she
could do was close her eyelids. She couldn't turn her head.
She sat flat on her rear with her legs straight out in front of
her. Old Big Nose had bound up her ankles again, this time
even more tightly. The last thing she'd felt in her toes was a
soft electric tingling, but that had been a while ago. Now her
feet were turning blue.

Her hands had been retied as well, jerked cruelly backward
around the trunk of a young tree and cinched so far up, her
arms had no play of movement at all. Like her feet, it had
been some time since she'd felt any sensation in her fingers.

He had stripped her naked, of course, and as a final indig-
nity, he'd run another length of rope tight around her neck,
pinioning her entire upper body against the trunk. He told her
that if she struggled he'd just tighten the rope and watch her
strangle to death. She believed him. The noose was already so
tight she could sip only tiny breaths of air, barely enough to
keep herself conscious.

The thought came without warning: *I'm going to die.*

It was only there for a flash, and she wasn't quite sure what it meant, and it vanished as quickly as it had come. She thought it would be back, though.

The grasp of her own death was beyond her reach. She was still too young. All she could think of was sleep. Sleep must be like death. You closed your eyes and didn't move. The only difference was that with death they threw your body in the river and let it float away, if you were poor. Or they burned it on a fire or hid it in a brightly painted tomb, if you were rich.

Many times she'd wondered about that. What if you woke up in your tomb house and couldn't get out? Some years before, when she was little, that thought had preyed on her mind so much that she stood close to one of the old tombs down the river, her ear pressed against the stone, imagining she could hear thin cries within.

Young Big Nose lay on his side. A huge dirty bandage covered his face below his eyes. His skin was pale as a fish's belly, and his eyes were closed. Green Eyes was glad of that. When his eyes had been open, they'd remained locked on her with a red fury that made her belly shrink and her skin grow bumpy with terror.

Not that the older one was any better. He squatted on his haunches before her, his eyes twinkling with the laughing evil that made her want to look anywhere but at his face.

His seamed mouth slid up into a demonic smile. She saw another flash of his rotting teeth. He was close enough that a blast of his fetid breath scoured the insides of her nostrils whenever he spoke.

In his left hand he hefted the green knife. He looked down at it, then up at her. "Pretty thing," he said. "Just like you. Pretty."

He sighed. "And worth ten of you, little bitch. You're too stupid to know it, but this is God-work, from the Old Times. It's very rare. When I get back to the city, I'll sell it and maybe make enough to retire." He flipped the knife into the air and caught it neatly.

"I'd been saving you to sell in the city market, without even knowing you had a chief's ransom in your bag. Too bad for you."

His grin slowly widened. "It doesn't matter about you now, so if I take a loss on damaged goods, why should I care?"

Suddenly, with the speed of a snake, he leaned forward and slipped his left hand between her thighs.

She gasped as his fingers roughly penetrated her, moved inside her for a moment, then withdrew.

"As I thought," he said. "You're a virgin still." He tilted his head toward his son. "I won't let him kill you. Even damaged you're worth something. Anyway, when he's better, he can have you."

He stood up, and dusted his good hand on his skirt. He lifted his swollen right hand and stared at it. He shrugged. "He can take your flower. Who knows? You may even find you enjoy it."

Chapter Three

1

The Lord Golden Hand listened dreamily to the sounds of the caravan as he strode along at the head of his party. Behind him stretched a column of retainers almost a hundred strong. About half of these were bearer-slaves, men whose muscles had been warped by a lifetime of labor into bulging shapes that left them looking barely human.

Golden Hand's family owned hundreds of such men. He thought of them as pack animals, and he treated them as well as he would any other valuable possession. Somebody had to carry the goods that were the source of his family's wealth.

And as far as wealth was concerned, this had been a particularly good expedition. He'd been on the trails nearly three seasons, traversing the long routes between Tollan and the southern city the Dog Ears called Copan, and the trading had been rich and profitable. He'd carried down to them a host of articles worked out of the famous green obsidian of Tollan, including some pieces specially ordered the previous year by the noble families and the priests of Copan.

The Dog Ears were a strange people, Golden Hand mused. They built beautiful cities, but they had a streak of cruelty in them prodigious even by the standards of a savage world. As a consequence, they waged such ferocious wars among themselves that sometimes entire peoples were exterminated.

And that was a waste indeed. Golden Hand had no visceral objection to violence. But he much preferred trading. Sack a city and you own its wealth, but there will be no more. Trade with a city, and you partake of its wealth forever.

So while his own home city of Tollan could field mighty armies in self-defense, and if necessary send powerful troops to enforce its will, its true strength rested on the twin foundation of its Gods and its vast trading networks.

He smiled as he thought of this, for those networks—at least a part of them—were in his care. Tollan was the greatest city of the Middle World, a seat of enormous power nestled in the long valley beneath the Tlaloc Mountains, but without the wealth its traders gathered, it would shrink and die.

Golden Hand understood this on the most basic level, because he'd been trained from birth to assume the role he now enjoyed. His father, Prince Long Fingers, was chief of the Clan of the Water Moon, which was one of the Eighteen Families of Tollan that made up the Joint Council of the city.

The origins of the Eighteen Families stretched back into misty time. From their ranks had come kings, and still did. Golden Hand's own great-great-grandfather had been a king of the city, though because of internecine squabbles and the resulting murders, he'd died without legitimate male issue. Unable to establish a dynasty, his place had been taken by the Clan of the Summer Moon, whose chiefs had ruled as kings ever since.

Golden Hand had some thoughts about that situation too—the Summer Moon was growing weak and decadent—but he could wait. He was in his twenty-second spring, and time was still a glittering bauble to him. Tollan was a rich fruit ready to be plucked by a strong hand, but not yet.

He looked down at his own hands and flexed his fingers. Heavy gold rings gleamed on every digit. The gold had been hammered out of raw nuggets mined from rich veins in the earth. It was a relatively new art, and his family had been instrumental in bringing it to the north from the Dog Ears who practiced it in the south. Of course the old conservatives still preferred jewelry made of shell or polished stones, but the younger generation liked new things. Golden Hand was trying to establish a fad for golden decorations among the young aristocracy, and so he draped himself with as much gold as he could bear. He'd even taken the name Golden Hand officially, as a token of his intentions. His father had not approved of the name change, but the new market had his complete blessing.

In fact, Golden Hand had taken a trip of several days' duration south of Copan, while his factors stayed in the city to complete the usual negotiations. With only a small party he'd journeyed into the southern mountains and made contracts with the hard and dusty men who worked the gold mines there. He'd seen wonders: there was a single nugget of amazing purity as large as his own head riding on the back of one of the slave bearers trudging in the column at his rear.

And there were a lot more nuggets of more normal size filling other bags. But the gold itself was not his greatest prize. The agreements with the mines were. The Dog Ears had agreed to supply their entire output to the Clan of the Water Moon. And they had given him two families skilled in the workings of the soft, bright metal. In Tollan a host of artisan clans owed their fealty and livelihood to the Water Moon. Golden Hand intended to retrain some of them in the art of working gold as soon as he arrived home. He understood something else: Tollan's strength lay not simply in its traders, but in the fact that the city was a gigantic factory, sucking in raw materials like its famous greenstone, and reworking them into valuable artifacts.

He saw the city as a great, living thing, gulping down raw wealth and shitting finished goods. His father thought the image crude, but Golden Hand liked it well enough. He liked crude, earthy images. He thought them more truthful than the high-flown pleasantries certain of his more effete friends used to cloak the harsher realities of the Middle World.

"My Lord, will you be wanting to break our journey for midday soon?"

"Um?" Golden Hand turned and saw the round, cheerful face of his Chief Factor, a bull-shouldered man named Twisted Tooth, who acted as his second-in-command and oversaw the day-to-day operations of the expedition.

Twisted Tooth gestured toward a dark line of trees approaching perhaps half a mile away. "We've been marching in the sun most of the morning. The bearers are tired and thirsty. Once we reach the shade, it would make a good stopping place. The map says there's a stream there for water."

"See to it," Golden Hand said.

Twisted Tooth bowed his head, turned, and headed back down the column to give the orders. Golden Hand yawned and stretched, enjoying the way his back muscles popped beneath his tanned hide.

He'd been lost in his own private musings, but now he raised his head and scanned the countryside with interest. He had not traveled this particular trail before, though Twisted Tooth had. They'd come down far to the east, detouring to make a visit to Pital, a great city by the sea, and a principal port for the long canoes of the Tollan water traders.

The column had been moving along the tops of a ridge of low hills all day. Evidently these hills had suffered a fire years before, because the forests that covered everything else didn't extend here. The shrubbery was dense and green, interspersed with wide meadows of grass and flowers. It made a pleasant change from endless marches beneath the gloomy canopies of these southern jungles. Tollan was an open city, basking in the clear sunlight of the high valleys, and Golden Hand missed that openness and light terribly at times. These forests were constricting, mute and green and silent. And he thought they were probably haunted.

This part of the world, not far from the Great Blue Water, was a hilly jungle interlaced with hundreds of rivers. The land seemed poor. What human life there was was clustered next to the rivers, scraping a meager living out of fields irrigated by river flooding.

It was hard to imagine anything great ever having lived here, but in the jungles Golden Hand had seen the remnants of something larger and finer than the huts of simple farmers and fishermen.

Hidden away, half covered by damp mulch and thick,

creeping vines, he'd seen great stone heads, their shapes strange and wondrous. Some he could recognize: the visage of the Plumed Serpent, even oddly altered, was unmistakable. But the heads of vanished warriors or kings represented peoples he knew little of: squat and morose, with thick, heavy lips, they bore some resemblance to those who still farmed the regions. But how could such a degenerate people have once been great enough to sculpt those heads, or the huge, intricate altars, or the long walls that now lay crumbled in ruin, their ancient carvings cracked and mutilated?

At one site he'd gazed long upon a fallen face. The massive stone carving had revealed an expression so serene, and yet so powerful, that he'd felt an unaccountable urge to weep. Once there had been a mighty people hidden in these jungles. What had they done, how had they offended their ancient Gods, to bring themselves to such irrevocable ruin?

It made him shiver to think about it. And he was sure the spirits of these ancient dead lived on, wandering the dark forests they had once ruled, moaning softly of loss and sadness and regret.

Ah, well. The Gods could be capricious, and Their hands strong. They struck where They would. It was a good thing to keep in mind, never to take anything for granted. This dead people must have been full of pride once, too.

Like Tollan.

Though surely there was no comparison. Even the greatest of these heaps of moldering stone had covered only a few hectares, less than the space of a single small neighborhood in the City of Gods. What was once mighty in the Old Times was less than a drop when placed against the glory of the modern world.

He snorted. He was letting his thoughts run away with him again. His father said he was too deep, that he thought too much, and maybe his father was right.

He stretched again and filled his lungs with fresh, crisp

air. Soon enough they'd be back under the trees, and their nostrils full of the stink of unceasing rot.

He looked off toward the east, out across the green ocean of trees below. About a half mile from the base of the hills ran a bright river. It was relatively clear along its banks, and Golden Hand could make out a thin brown trail alongside it. He squinted, then raised one hand to shield his good eye.

Three figures down there, crawling along. Mildly interesting. This was a desolate stretch, so they were probably small-time traders of some kind. He wondered if they were from Tollan.

When Twisted Tooth returned, Golden Hand pointed. "Send somebody down to invite them to travel with us if they're traders. Especially if they're from the city. I could use seeing something besides your ugly face every day."

Twisted Tooth laughed. "Maybe, Lord, if you had more than one eye, I'd look better to you."

"Twisted Tooth, even if I had four eyes, you'd still look ugly as sin."

2

Water.

It was all she could think of. She staggered along, rasping her parched tongue repeatedly across cracked lips. The sun was a blaze in her eyes. Off to the right she could hear the sound of the river, a low, hissing roar. She could *smell* the water. She could almost *taste* it. But they wouldn't give her any.

The sweat had stopped running in her armpits and down the insides of her thighs long ago. Now her skin felt dry and feverish. Her head was swollen and light, as if it were floating on her shoulders like a big bladder.

"Agghaa . . ."

A great knife of pain ripped from the joints where her

arms met her shoulders as Old Big Nose yanked hard on the rope that ran from his hands to her wrists. She stumbled forward, her breath clogged in her throat, and only barely kept her balance.

"Hurry it up," the old man growled. "We ain't got all day."

Young Big Nose stopped, turned, and peered at her above his ragged mask. She could see thin red lines beginning to extend out from underneath his bandage, a patchy crimson spiderweb, and knew that fever demons had gotten into his wound.

It gave her a little satisfaction, but not much. The only good thing was that he was still too sick to wreak the vengeance on her his father had promised. She knew it was true because he'd tried the night before, but his sex-snake hadn't gotten hard. He'd tried for quite a while before rolling his stinking weight off her.

They'd even taken her sandals. And they hadn't given her back her skirt. She stumbled along behind them naked as an animal, sunk in shame, feeling the sun burn blisters on her white bottom. Even the tough callused soles of her feet weren't enough to protect her from the random stones. She'd seen the thin tracks of blood she left as she walked.

"Water . . ." she croaked.

Old Big Nose grinned. "Water? What do you need water for? You should have thought of that . . ."

He shook his head and glanced at his son.

"Knnggg hnnnggg!" Young Big Nose hooted.

"Kill her? Oh, no. We have much better plans for her, don't we? You just wait, boy. You'll see."

"*Kngg hngg!*"

"Oh, shut up. Here, let me look at that bandage."

He turned his attention from Green Eyes and she moved forward a little, taking the slack out of the tether rope. Even that much was a relief. Just to stand aimlessly instead of stumbling along on this journey that was nothing more than an extended kind of torture.

While Old Big Nose poked and prodded at the bandage on his son's face, Green Eyes unconsciously wrapped her fingers around the tether rope. The old man was holding it loosely in his bad hand. One good yank and she could run.

Until they caught her, of course. It was open grass out here, ten paces to the riverbank, thirty or so across thick green meadowland to the apron of the forest. If she was her usual self, healthy and fed, it could be a race. Young Big Nose was weakened, and she might manage to outrun his father.

But she was half-starved, weak from lack of water, dizzy from the hammer blows of the sun, naked, unshod, and bound. It would be no contest. Even a baby could run her down.

And when the old man caught her again . . .

She closed her eyes. She didn't want to think about that. She scraped her tongue across her lips. It felt as if the skin there had turned into one big scab. If only they would give her a drink, even one little sip.

Suddenly the smell of the river filled her nostrils with overpowering seduction. It wasn't just the smell of the water, it was everything that sweet odor represented.

She'd grown up along the river. It had been a part of her world as long as she could remember. Some of her earliest memories were of toddling along behind her mother, her and her sisters, laughing and shouting, as Mama hauled clothes and blankets down to the river to wash them. Or, on other days, going to check and repair the nets and fish traps the women used to harvest shining silver fish for the village's larders.

She could almost taste those fish, rich and juicy. She could remember wading out with her sisters and grabbing them from the nets with both hands. How they'd wiggled and flopped, surprisingly strong for something so small.

She'd loved to watch them caught in the woven weirs,

swimming back and forth in the clear water like streaks of light, so smooth, so quick.

And she could swim almost as well as the fish could. For the people in the river villages, swimming came as naturally as walking or running. Oh, the thought!

She began to shake slightly, remembering the clean joy of it. The sensation of sliding her fevered, aching body into the cool waters, feeling the pores of her skin open wide to the balm of the river.

"Hnnkkk . . ." Young Big Nose moaned forlornly.

Green Eyes glanced up, her puffy eyes narrowing. Old Big Nose was still paying no attention to her, concentrating instead on adjusting the bandage across his son's face. And Young Big Nose wasn't paying attention to anything but his own pain. His eyes were shut, leaking bright tears.

Could they swim?

She had no way of knowing about them, but she recalled something that had happened a couple of summers back. A small party of northern traders had come through the village, four or five of them. They'd spent several days there, discussing the possibility of the villagers planting a few fields in different crops. She remembered her father scoffing— they'd suggested bananas, and everybody knew bananas wouldn't grow along the river.

Two of them had gone out to look at the fields. She and her father had tagged along. Strangers, while not uncommon, were not so usual a phenomenon they couldn't excite a little girl's curiosity.

One of the traders had strayed too close to the bank. It was a soft spot, one the villagers knew well, but the trader hadn't been a water man. He'd gone right over, splashed into the fast-moving stream before anybody could do a thing.

Green Eyes had watched with mild interest. There really wasn't much to see. If you fell in the water by accident you swam back to shore, and everybody laughed. The river was running a little fast, but that made no mind. You just let the current carry you downstream while you stroked for the nearest bank. Everybody knew how to do that.

Everybody, it seemed, but the trader. As soon as he hit the water he began to thrash around and shout. The farmers laughed. They thought it was some kind of joke. But the other trader began to jump up and down and scream, and by the time the man in the water had sunk for the third time, a handful of the village men were diving into the swift currents.

Too late. They never found the trader's body. The other trader had been very angry. It took a while before he understood the explanations: since everybody here knew how to swim, nobody had realized the trader was in any danger until it was too late.

The trader had gruffly replied that not everybody lived by a river, and where he came from hardly anybody knew how to swim.

Did these two know?

Slowly she turned her head back and forth between the river and her captives. Well, what did she have to lose? They were going to kill her anyway.

Several hundred paces up ahead, the path they were on angled to the left and plunged into the forest, leaving the river behind. If she was going to do anything, now was the time. There would be no escape for her through the dense jungle underbrush.

She began to take deep, slow breaths, trying to hold the air in as long as possible. It was a technique she'd learned when diving for shells and turtles. You breathed in and out deeply for a minute or two, and when you finally held your breath, you could keep on going for an astonishing length of time.

She felt the faint electric dizziness that meant she'd soaked up as much extra air as she could. She tightened her grip on the tether rope.

"Hallooo!" a deep voice shouted.

Young Big Nose and Old Big Nose turned, startled, to see

a group of three men emerge from the forest about a hundred paces ahead.

Green Eyes jerked the rope with all her strength, turned, and ran.

3

Twisted Tooth liked Golden Hand, in some ways even loved him, but there were times he thought his young master was crazy. And this was one of those times.

"Go invite them to travel with us," he'd said. Easy enough to say. And take no notice that there wasn't any kind of path between the two trails, and so even with a pair of husky guards to break a trail, there was still a deal of hot, sweaty, gnat-blown jungle to get through before issuing his kind invitation.

Let alone thinking about whatever sort of slimy, God-cursed brigands he might be inviting into his party. Twisted Tooth knew Golden Hand was much smarter than he was. But he felt no jealousy. He was smart enough himself, and he had a lifetime's greater experience. And that experience told him much about the probable quality of these presumed guests.

The trading trails were long and went many places, and many kinds of men traveled on them. There were the great caravans out of Tollan, led by men like his lord, and there were other caravans run by the traders of the temples. These were powerful forces, powerful enough to be civilized. Then there were the smaller private companies, some of whom were legitimate and behaved in a proper manner, and others that were little more than bloodthirsty brigands who preyed on whatever they could find.

And there were the one- and two-man operations, usually a pair of brothers or a father and son, who lived entirely by their wits and whatever they could steal or murder for. Like wild dogs they tended to be thieves and skulkers, lurking along at the fringes of trade, snuffling at the leavings of the great predators like his master.

He paused to wipe his brow as his two guards hacked and slashed with axes at the underbrush ahead. A cloud of tiny, stinging bugs settled around his ears, whining thinly. The humidity here was so thick it was like standing in a hot pool of water.

After a moment the guards broke a way through the thicket and they continued. It seemed this went on for hours, but when they finally saw the bright edge of the forest up ahead, Twisted Tooth realized they'd actually made pretty good time. A moment later when they clambered out onto a patch of meadow, the relatively unchanged position of the sun overhead confirmed his guess.

About a hundred paces away was the small party he'd been sent to fetch. He squinted, getting his bearings. Two men and, a few paces behind them, a young girl. Something odd about the girl, but . . .

He waved his arms. "Halloooo . . ."

And watched in astonishment as the girl suddenly leaped away, light as a gazelle, and flung herself into the river.

4

She hit the water with a satisfying splash, ducked her head under, and let the strong fingers of the current carry her farther toward the center. She didn't want to take a chance on Old Big Nose being able to snag her back with a branch or something.

She scissored her legs powerfully, trying to push herself along with the current. If she was lucky, she might not surface until she was out of their sight.

But she'd not reckoned on the air in her distended lungs. The green water was a swirl of bubbles around her. When she opened her eyes she could see the surface of the water not far above, a shining pane of light shimmering in the sun. With her hands bound she had no way to keep herself under and a moment later she popped out of the water like a stick of dry wood.

She expelled a gush of stale air and gasped in a fresh lungful, twisting around to see where she was as she fell back. When she saw her two captors, along with three strangers, standing on the bank almost thirty paces distant, well out of reach, her heart almost exploded with joy. Then, because she was still hampered by her pinioned wrists, the water tossed her in the other direction and they slid out of sight.

She didn't care. If she never saw them again, that would be something to make grateful sacrifice to the Gods for all the rest of her days. She turned her head to the side and gulped in more air, then concentrated on keeping herself afloat. She flashed her legs again. If she worked with the current and let it guide her, she might be able to make certain she came ashore on the opposite side from her kidnappers. After that it would only be a matter of finding a bit of sharp shell or a jagged outcropping of rock she could use to rub through the ropes, and she would be free.

She had just reached the swiftest part of the current when the trailing tether rope, sodden and sinking, wedged itself between two buried stones and stuck fast.

The shock traveled up the rope and stopped her immediately, with such force it dragged her under. But the current immediately tossed her back up, and then the rope pulled her down again.

Up, down. It would be funny, if she wasn't drowning.

5

Twisted Tooth stood on the riverbank with the other. It was as he'd expected. The two men were of the lowest sort, and in terrible condition to boot. The older one's wounded hand was a festering mess, and the younger one looked as if someone had cut off his nose.

The older one screeched, "Catch her. She's my slave. She's getting away."

"Well, swim out and get her yourself. Hey, what's the matter with her?"

Old Big Nose squinted against the river glare. The girl kept bobbing to the surface and sinking back down, but not moving from the spot. Suddenly he realized what must have happened. Damn it, if he could only swim!

"She escaped, good sir. She's our slave. We had her on a tether rope when she ran off. The rope must be caught in something. Oh, she'll drown. Good sir, I can't swim!"

Twisted Tooth shaded his eyes again. The old bandit looked to have it right. Something was holding the girl in place, yanking her under repeatedly.

"Pig turds," he said, stripping off his kilt and sandals. He slapped one of the guards on his shoulder. "Give me your knife."

Gripping the handle of the weapon firmly between the snaggled teeth that were his namesake, he put his head down and dived cleanly into the water.

6

Green Eyes thought, *So death is like falling asleep . . .*

The terrible contest between the cord that bound her to the earth and the endless power of the river continued unabated—up, down, up, down—but she knew for her it was coming to an end.

Her arms felt separated entirely from her shoulder sockets. They dangled without any more sensation than the rope to which they were attached.

Somewhere in the enormous buffeting she'd endured, she'd lost the rhythm of her breathing. Now there was a cool weight expanding slowly in her chest, and she felt so heavy, so heavy . . .

Her thoughts began to drift away. It really was like falling asleep. That calm, slow time before everything faded away, when you hung warm and dozing, and the oddest thoughts percolated through your mind.

She was still aware of her body, but as a distant thing, hardly connected to her now, a mindless thrashing weight at the end of a long silver cord.

It was very strange. She no longer cared about that far-off husk. Abruptly an even stranger vision appeared before her. Somehow the waters had become still, had turned into airy crystal. Light glittered everywhere. Before her stood a woman. Her dark gaze bored deep into Green Eyes's face.

"It's not your time yet, daughter," the woman said softly.

"Who are you?" Green Eyes replied.

"I am . . . Mother."

"No. My mother doesn't look like you."

"Nevertheless, you are one of my daughters. Just as I am a daughter of many other Mothers." And now Green Eyes could make out the shadowy figures ranged behind the woman, an endless line of forms stretched far, far away. She could tell nothing about them, those shadowy ones, except—

"They have eyes like me," Green Eyes Blue said.

"Some of us bear the mark," the woman said. She raised her hand, and in it was a knife. Green Eyes gasped. "That's mine . . ."

"It is now," the woman agreed. "I took it from another One, and now it is for you to use."

This made no sense at all to Green Eyes. "Who are you?" she whispered again.

"When the time comes, you will know," the woman said. Then her hand flashed forward, bringing the blade of the knife through the silver cord with one clean stroke.

Light and water exploded around her.

7

Green Eyes saw a dim flash of a different knife, and then suddenly the rope that was killing her was gone. Strong arms enfolded her. She saw a snaggled grin and began to choke. Something rumbled in her ear. She felt strong, purposeful movement around her, and had a fleeting thought of when she'd been a child, and her father had carried her snuggled against his huge chest.

Then darkness.

8

The girl was a mess, Twisted Tooth decided as he worked on her. He had laid her on her belly on the grassy bank and turned her head to one side. Now he squatted across her and pressed down rhythmically on her shoulder blades. He worked slowly and calmly, but for a few moments he thought he was too late.

Then she gave a sudden jerky heave. Her jaws twisted and she belched out a gout of bloody water. He redoubled his efforts and was pleased to find them rewarded with more eruptions.

"What are you doing?" the old man demanded. "She's our slave. Don't damage her!"

"Shut up, you old fool," Twisted Tooth said absently.

"Now, see here!"

"Coil, do something with him," Twisted Tooth said without looking up.

Chain Coil glanced at Long Stroke. The two soldiers each clapped one hand on Old Big Nose's shoulders and dragged him kicking and spluttering away. Twisted Tooth heard agitated honking in the distance.

Somebody ought to put that one out of his misery, he thought. If he doesn't shut up, maybe I will.

9

"How do you feel?" Twisted Tooth said.

She lay on her side, her knees drawn up, and stared at him with the most amazing eyes he'd ever seen. Her right eye was a bright, shining green, like one of the Godstones from the south. Her left eye was as blue as a deep well beneath a high summer sky.

The right side of her head was badly swollen, and that eye ringed by a purple-yellow bruise, only the faintest slit of green showing through the lumpy flesh. There was a deep scratch along the side of the other eye, now bleeding freely, though it looked to Twisted Tooth as if the river had ripped off a scab that had been there.

Her lips were blue and her skin pale, though a bit of color was coming back to her cheeks. She regarded him silently, giving no indication she'd even heard his question, let alone understood it.

He stroked her sodden hair away from her face. She flinched hugely at his touch.

"Oh?" he said. "No doubt your fine masters treat you well, since a man's fingers are so pleasant to you."

He sighed, then leaned down, put his shovellike arms beneath her, and scooped her up as if she were made of feathers. His blunt features were thoughtful as he carried her back toward the others.

Coil and Stroke were grinning at each other as they watched the old man hop up and down.

"What do you think you're doing? Put her down! She's ours. Our slave!"

Twisted Tooth glanced down at his limp burden. She'd passed out again, but she was breathing smoothly and regularly. The color in her cheeks was stronger, too. She would live.

Suddenly she began to shake.

"What's wrong with her? What have you done to her?"

"Saved her life. She almost drowned. It's a normal reaction."

"Well, put her down and be on your way. Thanks for your help. Good-bye."

Later, Twisted Tooth would never be quite sure exactly what had made him decide the way he did. He knew it had something to do with her incredible eyes, and the childish beauty he could see clearly beneath her injuries. Perhaps it was the way she quivered against him, touching him with pity. Maybe it was the strong suspicion of how she'd sustained all those bruises and cuts. Or maybe, now that he understood her wild plunge had been an escape attempt, it was admiration for that kind of spit-at-the-demon bravery.

And maybe it was that this stinking, low-born, sputtering slime of a so-called trader just angered him beyond his limits. Whatever it was, he made his decision.

"No, she needs to see a healing priest. We have one with our caravan." He glanced at Old Big Nose's hand. "Looks like you could use one too. Is that your boy?" He tilted his head toward the spot where Young Big Nose was hunkered down, bony arms wrapped around knobby knees.

"Yes."

"What's wrong with him?"

"He had an . . . accident."

"Well, he looks like he could use some help too. Oh. I'm sorry, my manners. I am Twisted Tooth, Chief Factor to the Lord Golden Hand. Are you from Tollan?"

Because of all the excitement, Old Big Nose had not really been paying attention. But now his native shrewdness snapped to the forefront. The accent was what did it.

This burly man standing before him didn't speak with the liquid trill of the high aristocracy, but he was certainly Middle-Born, and . . . Chief Factor?

"You said . . . Lord Golden Hand? Of the Water Moon?"

Twisted Tooth nodded. "I take it you are from the City of Gods, then."

"Yes . . . yes I am," Old Big Nose said, his tone suddenly turning greasy and unctuous. "I am from the Holy City." He essayed a smile, though he could have no idea of the effect his rotting stumps had on Twisted Tooth.

From the worst slums of it, I'd guess, Twisted Tooth thought, but he only nodded gravely again. "Very well. My master bids me to offer you the sanctuary of our caravan. Are you returning home?"

"Yes. As you can see, we've had a fine trip. Our bags are full, and a good slave for the markets besides."

"Well, come along then."

An uncertain, sly expression crossed Old Big Nose's face.

He's afraid of something, Twisted Tooth thought. I wonder what it is.

"Well, ah, perhaps it would be better if we continued on our way. We wouldn't wish to put your master out with our humble presence."

Twisted Tooth stared at him. "Perhaps you misunderstood me . . . trader. My master, *Lord Golden Hand*, bids me extend his hospitality to you." He raised his eyebrows. "So let me be certain I understand. After my Lord Master does you this great favor, you wish to offer him the deadly insult of turning him down? My. You must be a very brave man."

"Well, since you put it that way . . . I see you misunderstand me. I only meant that . . . of course my son and I would be delighted!"

"I thought you would be," Twisted Tooth said.

10

Because of the various delays, Golden Hand had decided to halt their march for the day at the edge of the woods. There was, as Twisted Tooth had promised, a fine stream there. Besides, there was no particular rush. He'd seen his factor bring the other traders into the camp. Twisted Tooth had put his kilt back on again, but he still carried the small pale form of the girl in his arms.

The two traders were a scruffy-looking pair, and they smelled like the pigsties from whence they undoubtedly had sprung. He felt a twinge of regret at seeking their company. Oh, well, if they displeased him, he could always have them whipped from camp.

He met Twisted Tooth as the factor passed the ring of pickets he'd set around the stopping place. "What's this?"

"They say she's their slave," Twisted Tooth replied in a low rumble, raising his eyebrows in the direction of the two traders. "More likely kidnapped from one of the local villages. She almost drowned herself trying to escape from them."

"Oh? That sounds like a story. You'll have to tell it to me later. In private. What about them?"

"They need the priest to look at them. I think somebody cut off the young one's nose." He glanced down at his burden. "And after seeing how this one had enough bravery to fling herself bound into the river, I'd even make half a guess as to who did the cutting."

Golden Hand reached over and touched her cheek gently. His rings flashed dully in the gloomy light. "Soft . . . I think if you cleaned her up and let that swelling go down, she'd be very pretty."

Twisted Tooth nodded. "She doesn't look like the locals in these parts. Her lips are a bit thick, but look how scabbed and swollen they are. And her eyes . . . well, I don't want to wake her. You'll see."

"Yes," Golden Hand said. "Take her to the priest first. Let the other two wait."

Twisted Tooth grinned. "Whatever you say, Lord."

Golden Hand grinned back at him. "While they wait, they can take a bath in the stream. Make sure it's downstream from camp, though. I wouldn't want to drink any water they'd been splashing in."

11

When Green Eyes woke, her first thought was that she was dead and this was the Underworld, the dark Place of the Dead. She sat up suddenly, and was rewarded with a chorus of sudden pains and aches. She gulped. Surely the pain didn't continue *after* you died?

But the sound of her movements attracted attention. A shadowy form loomed over her. She shrank back, her eyes wide.

"There, there," a soft voice whispered. "You're fine, little girl. I am a priest of the Plumed Serpent. I've dressed your wounds and performed the proper spells. You needn't think I don't know the right prayers, either. Are you thirsty? Would you like some water?"

It wasn't the words so much that soothed her but the soft and reassuring tones in which they were spoken. Healing priests always talked like that, even the ones that came upstream occasionally to visit her own tiny village. And . . . water?

"Yesss . . ." she sighed. "Water . . ."

A moment later she felt the hard rim of the water gourd at her lips. She gulped greedily, but only for a moment before the gourd was withdrawn."

"You can have more later," the voice said. "Too much will make you sick. Sleep now."

A gentle hand stroked her brow. She drifted away.

Chapter Four

1

Green Eyes sniffed softly, and then relaxed. The aromatic smell of dried grasses filled her nose. She shifted against the mattress, and sweet odors rose around her. It was pleasant to lie like this, eyes closed, on her blanket spread over the grasses, listening to the morning sounds.

Somewhere men cried out to each other as they worked. Now she could smell the cook fires, the sudden rich spatter of hot grease intermixed with the tang of charred wood.

In the distance monkeys gabbled and parrots shrieked. All familiar sounds. Soon her mother would come, calling cheerfully, chivvying her silly girls awake, and the day would begin . . .

She blinked. She opened her eyes.

Overhead, instead of the familiar thatched roof of her cottage, was the top of a brightly colored tent. She lay still for a moment, staring at the strange patterns. Then it all came back, and her whole body clenched in a reflexive spasm.

After the sudden shudder released her, she was still afraid to move. Perhaps this was all a bad dream, and she really was lying on her own bed, and in a moment or two she would awaken fully and everything would be as it always had been. As it should be.

Shadows passed along the tent walls, and she heard the muffled clank of pots ringing against each other. A dull ache filled her head, and she realized she was looking out of only one eye. The other one felt as if it were stuck shut. Tentatively she raised her hand, and felt a similar ache course through her shoulder. But all these pains were distant, shrouded, as if something was standing between her and a sharper agony.

When she tried to touch her eyelid, her fingers found an

unfamiliar lump of swollen flesh. Something was wrong with her eye. She dropped her hand and lay still again, listening to the humdrum sounds of a camp waking up for the day.

She had no idea where she was. The last thing she remembered . . .

She blinked again. Then, as if a curtain in her mind was slowly drawing aside, the bits and pieces began to return. It had begun with the rabbit. And then the knife, and then the two men, and . . . terrible things.

Then the river.

After that things faded out again, except for . . . the woman. The Mother. And all the shadowy Mothers behind her, and the knife. The silver cord.

Then nothing. And now here. Wherever here might be.

She didn't think she was dead. She was pretty sure the Underworld would be less . . . solid. As she thought this, she gripped the edge of the blanket on which she lay. The fabric felt soft and rough at the same time, and it felt entirely real.

But what had *happened*? She remembered the water, the terrible force of it, and something yanking her beneath the surface again and again. And then the Mother had come, and then . . .

She shook her head. The gesture reawakened the pain that slept in her skull, but it wasn't bad. Not nearly as bad as it should be, she thought.

In a thousand ways she was still a child, but she was teetering on the edge of womanhood, and she had grown up in a hard world of inconstant Gods, malign spirits, and uncertain tomorrows. In the forests and the rivers lurked a hundred different dangers. Tiny jeweled river snakes whose white fangs brought horrible death with a single snap. Larger snakes within the forest, biters that rattled, or the Great Snakes that squeezed. Lord Jaguar Himself, who ruled the night and took His prey without mercy. Or the Sky Snake, Lord of Storms, who sizzled from the clouds and brought death to the unwary with a blinding, flashing stroke. And, not least, the lesser invisible demons who invaded the body with fevers and swellings. She'd seen two sisters and one brother taken by such things, spirits of such force that even the village shaman had been powerless against them.

She lay on her back with her eyes wide and thought of death. But she didn't think she was dead. And once she reached this conclusion, the resilience of childhood smoothed away the rest as if it had happened long ago, perhaps to someone else.

"I want to go home," she whispered.

She knew that wherever she was, it wasn't home. The sounds and smells and sights, on first observation familiar enough, were strange and alien when she examined them again. Men shouted and cried morning greetings to each other, but their accents were strange. And no women joined in.

The roof over her head was cloth dyed with strange colors and patterns, not familiar poles covered with thatch. Even the smells of the cooking fires were indefinably . . . other.

But unless everything she'd ever been told about the Underworld was a lie, she wasn't dead. So that clarified things. If she wasn't dead, then she was just in an unfamiliar place. And it didn't really matter where. What she needed to do was get away from this place and get back to her village. Her usual hopeful, cheerful personality suddenly bubbled up. It was a problem no different from learning how to use the bow or make arrows for it.

So, methodically, she put her mind to it. She was still chewing it over when soft footsteps sounded outside the tent, and the murmur of hushed male voices.

The Big Nose men!

She squeaked, hoisted herself on her elbows, and kicked out with her feet, automatically readying herself to run or fight. But she got tangled in the blankets and was frantically trying to fling them off when the tent flap opened, admitting a shaft of sunlight and the stooping shapes of two men, one holding the flap for the other.

2

She cowered back as the two men came farther into the tent. The first was hugely shouldered, corded with muscle. His face was round, and when he smiled, he showed a wealth of crooked teeth, almost too many for one mouth.

"Now," he said. "Don't be afraid. Nobody's going to hurt you."

She stared at him wide-eyed, her heart pounding.

The second man leaned over the first man's shoulder, and that was when she knew for sure she wasn't anywhere near her own village. In fact, for one panicked instant she wondered if she hadn't been wrong after all, and this truly was the Underworld.

The second man was a monster.

Her teeth began to chatter as he loomed over her. He was taller and more finely formed than the first man. His expression was calm and distant and curious. Where his right eye should have been was a black patch held in place by a red cord. On the black patch was imprinted the shape of an open yellow eye. His other eye was like a polished ebony shell glittering in the perfect setting of its socket. His head was completely bald except for a patch on the top, from which erupted a fountain of black, shining hair that fell to the side and trailed away down his back. His cheekbones were sharp, his nose straight, his lips thin. He smiled at her, and she saw how white and even his teeth were.

He wore a blue skirt that came to his knees, and soft leather boot moccasins, heavily beaded, that rose halfway up lean, muscled calves. On his fingers were heavy yellow rings that flashed and gleamed in the dim light. Necklaces and bracelets of the same stuff adorned his chest and his arms. A great red-and-blue tattoo of a firebird rose from the top of his belly and spread its wings across his chest.

He was so unlike any man she'd ever seen before that she knew in an instant he must be a God. And there was only one way she could find herself in the presence of such a being. She must be dead after all, and this was the Lord of the Underworld, come to claim His prey.

She whimpered and closed her eyes.

"What's the matter with her?" a soft, clear tenor voice said. The accent was liquid and warbling, and reminded her of birdsong.

A deeper voice, the accent somewhat rougher—yet oddly familiar, almost reassuring—replied. "I think she's frightened of you, Lord."

"What? Ridiculous. She doesn't even know me."

"My point, Lord. She doesn't know you. Remember where she comes from. One of these villages. She doesn't know you, and I doubt she's ever seen anybody who looks quite like you. And she probably doesn't have the slightest idea what's happened to her."

"Do you think she understands us?"

"Maybe. Tollan trades all up and down these parts. And the native tongues aren't so very different."

Green Eyes had begun to shake. Her teeth chattered, though she tried to keep her jaw clenched tight. She was aware of movement close by, and then a soft fingertip stroked her cheek.

"Pretty girl, don't be afraid of me," the clear voice trilled. "I won't hurt you."

Her eyes flew open.

She found herself staring deep into his single black eye. For a moment their gazes locked, and something sizzled between them. He was smiling at her, but as this happened his smile vanished and he jerked back a little.

"My," he said. "Look at your eyes." He seemed a little shaken.

Inside her skull, her mind made whirring sounds like bats exploding from a hidden cave. As he spoke, soft puffs of his breath touched her cheek. It smelled sweet and fresh, not at all like . . . Old Big Nose.

"Please don't take me, Lord . . ." she managed. Her voice shook so badly she could hardly understand herself.

He blinked. It was disconcerting to see that one bright black eye wink at her, while the other one, the yellow one, remained blank and staring. That one must be his God-eye, she told herself, and wanted desperately to hide from its unwavering scrutiny.

"Take you?" he said. "What on earth are you talking about, girl?"

Slowly, she realized she was actually having a conversation with a God. And he hadn't eaten her or blasted her with his God-eye, or, really—he hadn't done anything. Anything except talk.

Some of her terror leaked away, almost without her realizing it. When she spoke again, her voice was a little stronger, a little more steady.

"Don't take me to the Underworld. To the Place of the Dead."

His eyebrows arched. "To the Underworld?" His good eye found her again, and then he burst out laughing.

"Twisted Tooth, she thinks she's dead. She thinks I'm the Lord of the Dead."

Twisted Tooth nodded. "I told you, they don't see much of your likes in these parts. And she's obviously had a hard time of it. What did you expect?"

Golden Hand laughed again. "Well, I've never been mistaken for a God before."

Twisted Tooth grinned. "How does it feel?"

Golden Hand ignored him. He turned back to her. "Here. Give me your hands. Yes, that's fine."

Gently he drew her forward. He placed her fingertips on his own hands, then her palm flat on his chest.

"There. See how solid I am? I'm not a God. I'm a man. Here. Feel my face, my nose. Feel my hair. It's real."

Her lips moved, but no sound came out.

"What? My eye? Here, touch it if you wish. That's a patch over it. I had an accident when I was a boy. The priests weren't able to save it, and I keep it covered. It's ugly underneath. You wouldn't like it, I can tell you that, but there's nothing Godly about it."

He let go of her hands. "If I had pretty eyes like you do, I wouldn't cover them at all."

He rocked back on his heels and rested his forearms on his knees. He stared at her some more and finally sighed. "Has anybody ever told you how pretty you are? You're going to be a beautiful woman. Don't worry. Those scratches and bumps will heal."

"You're . . . not a God?"

"No, dear, I'm a man. My name is Golden Hand. What's your name?"

"Green Eyes Blue."

She couldn't explain why, but suddenly she felt painfully shy. Almost childish. She wanted to put her thumb in her mouth and turn away from him.

"Green Eyes Blue. That's a nice name. Very fitting. Very descriptive."

And now, something in his tone gave her the idea he was laughing at her. In her village the chief's proudest possession was a small mirror made of some highly polished silvery-gray stone. The chief said it had been made in a far place where the Gods lived. It certainly possessed a kind of magic, for it reflected her face almost as clearly as a puddle of still water.

The chief had let her look at it once, and she'd seen how her eyes were different colors than those of all the other children. When she was little they'd made fun of her, but eventually the play grew old, and nobody paid much attention anymore. Now this secret breath of humor brought all those jibes back again. If he wasn't a God, then he was just a man. And she'd just about had all she wanted of men being nasty to her.

"Don't laugh at me!" she said sharply.

He started back, his eyebrows arching again. "Goodness, little one, I'm not laughing at you."

"Yes, you *are*. I *hate* you. I want to go home. I want my mama. *Please* let me go home . . ." And then, unaccountably, she burst into tears.

She felt his warm hands take her shoulders and pull her close. Her head rested on his chest as she sobbed.

"It's all right, little one," he murmured, stroking her hair. "It will be all right . . ."

What a strange, strong heat rose in his belly.

3

"Well," said Golden Hand, "that was a tale, wasn't it?"

The two men were strolling along the edges of the camp, inspecting the outposts, greeting the guards who responded with jokes or cheerful waves. Twisted Tooth paid particular attention to the heavy bags piled off to one side, in a guarded area. Now he knelt, untied one of the bags, and peered inside.

He stood up and dusted off his hands. "The weight looks good," he said. "Nobody's swallowing nuggets."

Theft was always a problem, and the penalties for it swift and harsh. The last man who'd swallowed a meal of gold had given it back up screaming, when Twisted Tooth had cut it from his living belly.

"Do you think her story is true?" Golden Hand said.

"Why not? There's nothing very odd about it. Did you get a good look at those two brigands? Men like that take what they can, wherever they find it. A young girl, a girl as pretty as that one is, would seem a fine prize. She'd fetch a good price in the markets of the city, and the old one, at least, would know it. And they'd think her fitting prey, one they could master easily. Two grown men against a girl. They'd like those odds."

Golden Hand's mouth quirked. "If what she said is true, they were mistaken. She chewed a hole in the old one's hand, and bit the young one's nose. And was well on her way to escaping when you intervened."

"No, she was well on her way to dying by the time I got to her. But she had escaped, and if that rope hadn't gotten snagged, she probably would have gotten clean away. She's an amazingly resourceful child."

"Did you notice how quickly she got over her fright of me? As soon as she realized I wasn't some monster come to suck her bones, she settled down and started chattering."

"Lord, do I detect an interest beyond simple mercy here?"

Golden Hand stopped. "You mean in a virgin who hasn't even begun to bleed yet?"

Twisted Tooth shrugged. "What difference does that make? Anyway, she can't be far from womanhood. Those little breasts won't stay little much longer."

Golden Hand remembered the soft feel of them against his chest. And the hard, pointed nipples . . . He sighed. "There's some things about her story that interest me."

"Oh?"

"Yes. She told us the old one let the young one rape her, though he failed. But the old one must be shrewd enough to realize her virginity would add to her value in the city. So he must have been telling the truth when he told her that knife she found was valuable enough he didn't care what happened to her."

"Hm. I missed that."

"That's why I'm the leader of this caravan, and you're only the Chief Factor."

"No, Lord, you're the leader because you were wise enough to have Prince Long Fingers of the Water Moon for a father."

Sometimes Twisted Tooth's tongue was just a bit too sharp for Golden Hand's taste. Especially when he spoke things that Golden Hand privately considered to be rather more truthful than he wished to acknowledge, even to himself. He frowned.

"Yes, well, I think I want to look into this more thoroughly."

"Are you going to keep the girl?"

"I haven't decided. Those eyes of hers."

"Yes, I wondered when you would get around to them," Twisted Tooth said, his voice complacent.

"My dear factor, I may be only the stupid son of my glorious father, but I'm not a total idiot. She bears the Godmarks—both of them. I've never heard of that before."

"And she's quite pretty, and may well turn out to be a beauty. Her sons might bear the marks too. And that would be . . . very interesting as well, wouldn't it, Lord?"

Golden Hand stopped, placed his hands on his hips, and stared at Twisted Tooth in exasperation. "What, exactly, are you trying to say?"

Twisted Tooth spread his hands and smiled disingenuously. "Why, nothing, Lord, nothing at all. Just musing along, saying whatever falls out of my poor mouth."

"You'd do well, then, to watch that poor mouth of yours. My plans are my own. For the time being."

"Of course, Lord. And whatever those plans might turn out to be, you know you can count on my support."

"Oh?"

"Certainly. Shall I go strangle those two traders now, as a token of it?"

"Hmph. No, not yet. But you still have your whip, don't you?"

"In my pack, Lord. Do you need it now?"

Golden Hand flapped his fingers. "Perhaps later. But I do want to look into the matter of the knife more closely. She says she found it buried in an Old Place. And the old man thought it was valuable enough for him to forgo the price of her virginity. Do you suppose it might be . . . ?"

Twisted Tooth shrugged. "She said it was very smooth, and green in color, Lord."

"Ancient Godstone," Golden Hand mused. "It could be. Stranger things have happened."

"Well then," Twisted Tooth said, his tone flat and practical, "let's have a look, shall we?"

4

Old Big Nose rolled out of his blankets at the first gray hint of dawnlight. He sat up and sniffed the cool air. The day would grow hot soon. The days were always hot in these damnable jungles.

He glanced over at the gurgling lump of his son. He loved the boy, but he wasn't sentimental about him. His mother had been a common prostitute, though Old Big Nose had married her anyway. She'd borne him six other children that lived, none of them much smarter than she was, and all a trial to him. Young Big Nose was the best of the lot, and he'd even shown occasional flashes of real intelligence. But now, watching his troubled sleep, Old Big Nose thought that the girl might have ruined him permanently.

Damn her. He rued the moment he'd ever seen the devil, let alone come up with the bright idea of snatching her. From that moment forward, his luck seemed to have turned.

Well, he still had his own wits, and they might yet be enough to see him through. He sighed and hitched himself up and back until he was resting against the trunk of the tree under whose branches they'd spent the night. The gray morning mists were beginning to thin out. He saw dim figures moving sleepily through them. Somebody was kindling a fire. The sharp aroma of new smoke tingled in his nostrils. It smelled fine.

He looked down at his own wounded hand. At least that was a little better this morning. They'd taken him and his son before their healing priest after darkness had fallen. And that experience had told him more than anything else what sort of camp he'd stumbled into.

Like anybody else who lived in the city, he knew of the Water Moon. It was one of the three richest and most powerful of the Eighteen Families. Rumor had it that in truth it might be the strongest of them all, though the Winter Moon still ruled in name.

At any rate, this fancy Lord Golden Hand traveled only with the best. The healing priest hadn't turned out to be some country shaman or root doctor. He wore the rich, dark robes of the Temple of the Plumed Serpent itself. He brewed up teas and unguents that smelled awful—as all good medicines should—and when he applied them, the fitful heat immediately began to drain out of Old Big Nose's hand. The priest had changed their bandages too, though Young Big Nose had hooted mournfully throughout the whole proceeding, and Old Big Nose had felt like slapping the boy. Then he remembered he couldn't do that anymore.

Most amazing, the priest had then raised the magic pipe and puffed it till his eyes bulged with holy red fire and then, with a single bounding somersault, he had taken the spirit of the Jaguar into his body.

Old Big Nose had sat frozen with terror as the God made His unmistakable appearance, dancing around them, hissing and shaking the rattle of His power over their wounds.

It had been very satisfying. When the priest finally sank back into himself and sent them away, Old Big Nose had no doubts his powerful magic would do the job it was supposed to do.

Only the highest of nobles could bring such mighty magic on the trail for their own use. That Golden Hand could do so as a matter of course made his position far clearer than any boastful bragging on the part of his factor.

Of course, the doings of the nobles were as far above him as the stars. He'd only seen them at a distance, on great ceremonial occasions, and then so bedecked with their holy garb they weren't recognizable as human at all.

He'd never had any personal dealings with such men. They might stoop, if they felt it in their interests, but they didn't wallow in the muck of his world. They paid others to do it for them. Men like that factor, Twisted Tooth.

That one worried him. And then he thought of something that worried him even more. That damned *girl* again. He didn't know what had happened to her. The factor had carried her away. What if he'd talked to her?

Old Big Nose wasn't too fretful about her telling the story of her abduction. She was only a piece of country trash, after all, and no matter how low his own station relative to a great lord like Golden Hand, he was still a trader of the city. Such things happened. Nobody would blame him for taking a juicy little prize along the way. As far as it went, maybe he could even sell her to the factor. It wouldn't be a bad outcome at all if he could spare himself the dreary task of dragging her all the way back to the city, especially since the real treasure was still in his heavy pack, cool and gleaming.

But what if she'd told Twisted Tooth about *that*?

He closed his eyes and set his mind to clicking off the possibilities. First, she might not even mention the Godstone blade. Or if she did, the factor might not understand what she was talking about, and miss the potential value of the thing.

But that was asking for a lot of good luck, wasn't it? And his luck had been particularly horrible as far as anything involving that little bitch, hadn't it?

A flicker of red rage gripped him. By the Jaguar and the Plumed Serpent, *why* hadn't he killed her when he had the chance?

The thought subsided quickly. You did the best with what life and the Gods handed you.

He pulled his pack closer and stuck his good hand deep inside. He'd wrapped the blade in a soft scrap of skin, to protect it, and to keep himself from slicing his fingers by accident. He drew it out and stared at the small package. Amazing how much wealth could be wrapped up in something so tiny.

Best to make sure all that wealth remained his and his alone. Cramps clutched at his bowels. He climbed stiffly to his feet, looked around, then slipped the package beneath the belt of his kilt. Sighing, he trudged off into the brush to do his morning business.

5

Golden Hand and Twisted Tooth sat in front of Golden Hand's tent, eating a breakfast of fried wild pig, boiled roots, and very tough cornmeal tortillas.

Twisted Tooth spat. "Lots of rocks in this flour," he muttered.

Golden Hand, who didn't much care what he ate on the trail, as long as it filled his belly, nodded absently. "It must be from that last lot we bought south of here."

Twisted Tooth looked up. "What have we here?"

Still chewing, Golden Hand looked up to see the two traders approaching, half stumbling under the weight of their trading packs, being goaded along by the butt of Chain Coil's spear.

"Gentlemen, good morning," Golden Hand said graciously. "Sit down and take your breakfast with us."

He thought they both looked improved over his first sight of them. The older one's shoulders were straighter, and the hideous patchwork of scars disfiguring his face no longer stood out like a writhing nest of white worms. As for the younger one, his eyes looked clear above the fresh bandage, and his face didn't seem as swollen as it had been earlier

"Thank you, Lord. You do us great honor," Old Big Nose

replied smoothly as he seated himself cross-legged on the other side of the fire. They waited silently while one of the cook's slaves brought them their food, and then dug in with a will. The flap of Young Big Nose's bandage extended down over his mouth, and he presented the strange impression of shoveling his meal up under the bandage.

"Well," he said eventually, "my name is Golden Hand, of the Clan of the Water Moon."

He saw the old trader seemed unsurprised by this, for though he bowed smoothly from the waist, he made no other sign. But it was evidently news to the younger one, for he goggled stupidly, one hand dripping with food poised before his bandage, until his father rapped him sharply on the back of his skull.

"Show respect," the old man hissed, which sent the youth into a paroxysm of bobbing and gobbling. It was all Golden Hand could do to keep from falling off the log on which he was seated.

But he allowed none of his sardonic inner merriment to show on his solemn features. "And you are called?"

"I am Old Big Nose," he said. "This is my first son and my heir, Young Big Nose."

Golden Hand acknowledged the introductions with a gracious nod. "Have you been treated well? I directed that my own healing priest be sent to treat your wounds."

"For which we are forever in your debt, Lord. He did treat us, last night, and I feel much better this morning. So does my son."

They chatted of inconsequential things for a while, until Golden Hand said, "I have spoken with your slave girl this morning. She also seems to be doing well."

"Ah. Excellent, Lord," Old Big Nose said. Golden Hand thought he detected a tremor of anxiety, but it was well concealed. If what the girl had told him was the truth, the old man was playing a desperate game, and playing it well. Reluctantly, he raised his estimation of him a notch.

"Indeed," he remarked smoothly. "May I see the Godstone knife she told me of?"

"Knife, Lord? A Godstone knife? What are you talking about?"

It was very smoothly done. Golden Hand could detect no hint of hesitation, only the proper amount of honest incomprehension.

"She told me of a knife she'd found, that you took from her. A Godstone knife, perhaps one from the Old Times. Such a thing would be quite valuable, and I've never seen one. I was hoping you would show it to me."

Old Big Nose spread his hands. "Lord, I would be happy to show it to you. I would be even happier if I had such a thing, so I *could* show it to you." He sighed heavily. "But, sadly, I do not."

Golden Hand allowed a puzzled expression to drift across his features. "I don't understand. She was quite explicit. She described it clearly. A small greenstone knife, very sharp, very smooth, about the length of her hand from the base of her palm to the tip of her middle finger. She seems quite young. Too young to have made up such a tale."

Old Big Nose's eyes remained soft, bland, and unconcerned. "Ah, Lord. She is our slave. We bought her from one of the villages, though if I'd known what a wildcat she would turn out to be, I wouldn't have spent a single bead for her." He sighed again as he raised his right hand. "See what she did to me with her teeth."

"How terrible," Golden Hand observed politely.

"Yes, it was. We had to discipline her, I'm afraid. You saw the bruises. Perhaps we were too . . . vigorous in our discipline, after all. Your factor can witness that demons had stolen her mind. When he came upon us, she had just thrown herself in the river to drown. Who knows what strange visions she may have seen? No doubt this nonexistent knife is just another one of them. A fever dream, Lord. Nothing more."

This old spawn of wild dogs has taken some time to think about things. So let's cut right to the meat of it, Golden Hand thought.

"Then, of course, you won't mind if my factor inspects your packs? Just to be sure who is lying?"

An expression of vast hurt spread slowly across Old Big Nose's features. "My lord," he said softly, "I am but a humble trader, not a great lord like yourself, but we are both traders together. It gives me pain you cannot imagine that you would doubt me."

Twisted Tooth glared at him, and Old Big Nose hurried on. "But of course I would be happy to set your mind at ease. Here are our packs. Search them as you would."

Golden Hand nodded at Twisted Tooth. "Go ahead."

The factor grunted and got to his feet. After a few minutes it quickly became evident the contents of both packs consisted only of goods of marginal profitability that would justify their travels when they returned to the city, but only barely so. How did these men live on such meager profits? Golden Hand wondered.

There was certainly nothing with the kind of value that a Godstone knife would represent. There was, in fact, no knife at all.

"Their belts," Golden Hand said.

The old one sniffed angrily, and the young one honked, but neither resisted Twisted Tooth's fingers. He held up a pair of blades crudely chipped from brown obsidian, the cheapest kind of work. "That's all," the factor said.

"Well, my sincere apologies," Golden Hand said. "You must be right. The girl probably dreamed the whole thing."

Twisted Tooth took back his seat next to Golden Hand. For the next few moments nobody said anything. Finally, Old Big Nose raised his head. "Lord, about our slave. When will you return her to us?"

"Hmm? Is there some hurry? She seems quite weak. I've already given orders we'll rest here for a few days, until she is better able to travel. And both of you look as if you could use a rest yourselves.

"Ah, that is true, Lord. We thank you. Could we see the girl, though? After all, she is our property."

Once again, Twisted Tooth grimaced at the old man's temerity.

But Golden Hand seemed entirely unmoved. "No, I think it best if she continues to rest. I believe she's frightened of you, and I don't want to upset her. As for her being your property, who knows? I may even consider doing you the favor of buying her. What do you say to that?"

He saw the old trader's eyes flicker involuntarily. Ah. It was the first thing he'd yet said that surprised the ancient snake.

But Old Big Nose only bowed his head again and said, "That would be a great favor indeed, Lord."

They passed the next few minutes in idle conversation, and then Old Big Nose got to his feet, bowed, and said, "With your leave, Lord, I believe my son and I will leave you be. I'm sure you must have much to keep busy with, and we surely wouldn't want to get in your way."

Golden Hand smiled up at him. "You are too kind," he said.

When they were gone, he turned to Twisted Tooth.

"Well?"

Twisted Tooth rubbed his blocky jaw thoughtfully. "I wonder where the old bastard hid that knife."

6

Two days later, deep into the night when the mists curled like languid ghosts over the dying campfires, and even the guards doing picket duty leaned against their spears and dozed, Old Big Nose crept silently to the back wall of the dark tent.

Squatting behind him, his son made a soft, indeterminate snuffling sound, and Old Big Nose raised a finger to his lips. All around them the camp slumbered.

It had been an uneventful two days, except for one thing. Early this morning the factor, Twisted Tooth, had come to him with a small cloth bag. He'd opened it and dropped into Old Big Nose's shaking palm a heavy golden ring.

"This comes from the hand of my master," he said. "Now it is yours."

"Ah," said Old Big Nose, hefting it, his dark eyes suddenly glittering.

"It is gold, the new metal from the south," Twisted Tooth added.

"I know what it is."

"Yes. Then you know it is of great value."

"Very great, Your Honor. What is it for?"

"The girl. My lord has decided to buy her from you."

Old Big Nose eyed the gleaming bauble in his hand. It was valuable. Even before he'd left the city, he'd noted that the younger nobles were starting to wear the stuff, and in the back of his mind he'd intended to see if he could find any on his journey. He'd had no luck, but now he had this.

"Your lord is too generous," he said. His hand moved, and the ring vanished.

Twisted Tooth eyed him coldly. "You mean you're not going to argue? To bargain? You surprise me."

Old Big Nose grinned without mirth. "As you once pointed to me, Your Honor, it would be very foolish to refuse the wishes of Lord Golden Hand. I am grateful. Please thank him for me."

"You can thank him yourself. He's gone hunting for the day, but he'll probably want to see you when he returns tomorrow."

"Oh, yes, to be sure," Old Big Nose said.

But he had no intention of thanking Golden Hand for anything. He'd had two days to think and plan. Young Big Nose was recovering nicely, and seemed to have most of his strength back. It was the golden ring that decided him. It, together with the Godstone knife, would make this the most profitable trip he'd ever made. There was no point in waiting any longer. That the girl had been taken from him didn't bother him at all. The price he'd been given was far more than he'd expected to get in the city market.

But the girl herself did bother him, every time he looked at his torn hand, and every time he looked at his son's ruined face.

Now, the Godstone knife once again in his hand, he waited at the back of the tent, listening for any sound from within. He heard nothing.

Carefully, he raised the knife and made a cut in the fabric, until he had a slit wide enough for him to slip through.

"Wait for me," he whispered. Young Big Nose nodded.

The knife had cut through the fabric like a spear through a spiderweb. It would cut through tender girl flesh just as easily.

Then they could slip away into the night, richer than they'd ever been, and all debts paid. Maybe when the high and mighty Lord Golden Hand returned, he would take a moment to reflect that even he couldn't do whatever he wished, whenever he wished it.

Old Big Nose smiled to himself. It would do the young Lord good. Perhaps he might even come to think of it as a favor.

Still smiling, he slipped into the tent.

Chapter Five

1

Green Eyes woke with a clot of dread clogging her throat. She couldn't breathe. The darkness inside the tent was so absolute, she couldn't see the fingers on her hand when she brought it up to her face.

She lay on top of her blanket in the stifling heat, her heart pounding, trying to figure out what had awakened her. Maybe a bad dream she couldn't remember any longer . . .

Then she heard it: outside the nearest tent wall, a soft, liquid sound, like somebody with a cold trying to breathe through his mouth. A moment later she heard the edgy whisper of blade slicing fabric, and felt a soft billow of cooler air.

Terror spread in sickening waves up from the base of her spine. She heard the faintest of clicks as somebody shifted his weight, and then, as she rolled silently off her bed, she saw the slit in the tent wall fill with hazy starlight as the tear was slowly pulled wider. A moment later a shadowy form blocked the dim glow, and a familiar stench wafted in.

She bit off a soft moan as she rolled farther away from her bed. She felt more than saw the shadowy presence penetrate farther into the tent. Now she could hear the guarded breathing, hot and muffled.

She reached the far wall of the tent and stopped, paralyzed with fright. Her mind whirled. She couldn't *think*.

As she lay quivering, her thoughts scattered, she heard a soft grunt, then another. Even with the feeble light drifting in from the slit in the tent, she couldn't make out any details. Unconsciously she curled into a small, trembling ball, her knees at her chest, and waited.

"*Damn* it . . ."

The voice was a guttural whisper. It was the old man, not the boy. That made it worse. She'd bested his drooling son, but not him. He'd hurt her. And she knew with absolute certainty that now he'd come to kill her.

The grunts and the breathy curses ceased. She imagined him crouching over her bed, head raised, every sense tensing to find her, to put his filthy hands on her. And when he did . . .

She squeezed herself tighter, and as she did, her head bumped into something round and hard. A picture floated up in the darkness of her mind: the sides of the tent, weighted down with rocks half the size of her skull.

She heard another soft, shifting movement in the dark. He was in the tent with her, squatting on her blankets, looking for her.

And he had a knife. He'd cut the skin of the tent open, hadn't he? And she knew with what. Abruptly she could *see* it, its deadly green shape fitted in his palm. Those soft grunts—she could picture his arm rising and falling, rising and falling, as he slashed at the lumpy blankets on her bed.

Now he was waiting. He must sense her presence too, in the same way she did his. The instant she did anything to give herself away, he'd be on her. If she screamed, she'd only do it once.

She felt a slow, hopeless exhaustion seep into her muscles. It wasn't *fair*. She was only a girl. She hadn't hurt anyone. Why was this happening to her?

But that blurt of petulance quickly faded. It didn't matter; what mattered was finding a way to stay alive. Slowly, inch by inch, she raised her arms until her fingers found the heavy stone. Across the tent the rip he'd cut still gaped open, admitting a hazy wash of starlight. If she could get him in front of that dim glow, she'd be able to see him. But how . . . ?

How was easy. But doing it would be the hardest thing she'd ever done. She made sure she had a good, double-handed grip on the rock. If her fingers slipped, she wouldn't get another chance.

She whispered, "Go away . . ."

His response was immediate and terrifying. She felt more than saw a swirl of shadowy movement, and then his hunched form slithered into the light, rushing toward her.

She had her knees under her by the time his rancid breath burned into her nostrils, and she brought the stone forward with every ounce of strength her terror-charged muscles could muster.

The moist, hideous crunch of the blow she struck would haunt her dreams for the rest of her life. She felt something hot and wet gush down her forearms. A bitter smell filled her nostrils.

Then she was past him, scuttling for the rip in the tent wall on her hands and knees, suddenly remembering to breathe again. She burst through the hole, the cooler air on the other side bathing her sweaty face like a benediction. Vaguely she sensed something lurching toward her, and heard a soft honking sound.

She rolled away from it, gulped in great waves of precious air, and began to scream at the top of her lungs.

2

Because it would be a solemn moment, Golden Hand had ordered his folding chair unpacked, and now he sat on it with his arms crossed over his chest.

The chair was a folding stool carved of the finest wood, its four legs inlaid with colored stones and polished shells. Its seat was soft leather, dyed bright scarlet and marked with signs of authority. Strings of white feathers dangled from each corner.

The seat was one of the sigils of his power and authority. He had arrayed himself with others as well. On his head he wore a wide dressing made of the skull of a Jaguar, covered with white feathers, from which depended shoulder-length wings made of the finest beadwork. Over his eyes he wore wooden goggles stained black, which gave him a fearsome appearance. And in his right hand he bore a war club encrusted with precious gems, its swollen head studded with perfectly chipped points fashioned from the finest greenstone the city artisans had to offer.

Down on one knee, at his right, Twisted Tooth crouched, his bulging muscles oiled with sweat. Behind him stood the priest of the Plumed Serpent, wearing his blood-colored robes of judgment. And on his left hand, seated cross-legged on a blanket, was the girl.

He glanced down at her. The swelling on the side of her head had lessened, and the full glory of her green eye was visible, a perfect match for the jeweled blue translucence of her left eye. Her hands rested demurely on her lap. Her features were still, her expression empty. She had not wanted to see this, but he'd made her come. This was about her, and the law was clear: the Big Noses were citizens of Tollan, City of Gods, and even in the jungles, far distant from Tollan's great valley, if the power of Tollan was there, so were her Gods, and the rule of Their laws.

He leaned over and stroked her shoulder. Reflexively she flinched away, and he felt a pang of sadness. How long before she could stand the touch of any man without shuddering in horror? The thought hardened him—as if he needed any hardening—for what he was about to do.

They had lain Old Big Nose's corpse on a blanket in the cleared space before Golden Hand's chair. Death had leached all the color from him. The scars on his face were visible only as pale traceries. With the life gone out of him he looked younger, the seams and sockets of time relaxing, melting from his features.

Golden Hand could imagine the old man was only sleeping, though he knew the life had gone out of him. As for the rest, his priest assured him that Old Big Nose's spirit had already departed his flesh, though that spirit still hovered nearby, chained to the Middle World by the sin of the old

man's treachery. Among other things, what they would do
now would free that spirit, so it couldn't remain to cause further harm.

From Twisted Tooth's fist ran a thick rope that ended in a
noose tied around Young Big Nose's scrawny neck. He cowered like a beaten dog, squatting next to the blanket on
which his father's body lay. Above his filthy bandage, his
eyes were wide and wild.

Golden Hand sighed. He gave the scene a final look, then
raised the club in his right hand. "Let it begin," he said.

A stray gust of wind, smelling of greenery and ancient rot,
wafted from the woods and stirred the campfires. Golden
Hand felt the hairs on the back of his neck itch and curl as
the jungle's breath passed over him.

The priest stepped forward, passing Golden Hand's chair
to take up station next to Old Big Nose's corpse. His acolyte,
a young boy garbed in a simple white robe, followed him,
bearing the various implements and magical talismans the
priest would need.

They had moved out of the shade of the forest onto the
edge of the long grasses for this rite. Off to the left, the forest rose smoothly against a distant range of hills, dark and
silent. Above the peaks the sun was sinking toward the horizon, guarded by great bands of clouds tinctured with swaths
of red, gold, vermilion, and purple.

The priest made a signal, and three drummers began to
pound freshly hollowed logs in a slow, insistent beat. The
sound vanished quickly in the vast space below the sky, but
it brought an agitated upwelling of black, screaming birds
from the jungle canopy beyond.

An omen? Golden Hand wondered, a thrill of unease
whispering across the skin of his forearms. The priest began
to chant, and Golden Hand settled back.

The priest—whose name Golden Hand didn't know, for
the priests never revealed their true names to any but their

temple brothers—began the complicated steps of the Dance for the Dead.

As the drums slowly increased their tempo, Golden Hand let his gaze wander. It would be a while yet before he had any role in these rituals. He glanced down and saw that Twisted Tooth had closed his eyes, and that his skull was bobbing lightly in time with the pounding of the drums.

On his other hand, Green Eyes was riveted by the spectacle. She leaned forward a little, her mouth open, her eyes glowing with childlike wonder.

What a strange, brave girl, he thought. He hadn't learned of Old Big Nose's murderous assault until he'd returned to camp about noon with the other hunters. Twisted Tooth had given him the tale as best he knew it. It was somewhat garbled, since the girl was still stuttering with terror, and the old man wasn't talking to anybody.

Nevertheless, the shape of it seemed plain enough, and Golden Hand berated himself for not anticipating the danger to the girl. It is my own pride, he told himself as he watched the priest call for the sacred pipe. I presumed that my own will was paramount, and did not imagine that once I'd made my decisions, anybody else would dream of gainsaying me. Yet I forgot that even the lowest snake may still possess a pride so tender it must strike back at any injury. I didn't realize Old Big Nose was such a reptile. Thank the Gods the only life he spilled had been his own. It could have been different.

As he thought this, a pang of relief coursed through him. The poignancy of the unexpected emotion shocked him. Unbidden, his gaze slid toward Green Eyes again. She was only a girl. She was only his slave. He thought he had vague, partly formed plans for her—enough to trade a bauble for her body—but now he realized there was something deeper and stronger at work.

The beat of the drums pounded in his ears as he slowly, almost reluctantly, gave thought to what that thing might be.

3

Green Eyes stared raptly at the vision of the priest. She remembered his gentleness, but saw none of that now. He was a tall man with a powerful build, and in his crimson robe, his features concealed behind a snarling, painted mask from which protruded the white fangs of the Sky Snake, he made a frightening apparition. And the drums scared her too. Their ever increasing tempo seemed to stir the rhythm of her heart to a faster and faster pace.

She felt lost and alone, trapped in a world of strange men and terrifying Gods, and she would have given anything she had for the comforting feel of her mother's arms.

She looked up at Golden Hand and saw his set, blank expression. He frightened her too, though she sensed he meant her no harm. His arms had been warm too when he'd held her sobbing at his chest. Yet there had been a difference in his embrace from, say, her father's. They were both men, but . . . She chased that thought, but it eluded her. Something was different. And whatever that difference was, it tantalized her. And it frightened her at the same time. She sensed mysteries she'd never encountered before. But she had no one to guide her. Once again a wave of grief and loss and yearning swept over her.

In the west the sun had fallen farther, and its colors had fused into a hundred shades of crimson. The clouds riding above looked dark and bloated, their bellies painted with bloody light. A sharper wind was blowing from the west, bringing the bleak scent of distant, naked stone.

There was no blood on Old Big Nose. The dent in his forehead was huge and ugly, but it was clean. She'd seen death before, but this was different. She'd caused it herself. She'd *done* it herself. Her stomach contorted suddenly as she thought about that.

She hadn't even realized it until later. Her screams had brought a quick reaction. She'd hardly found her feet when massive arms scooped her up. She'd struck out blindly, but her blows had bounced harmlessly off that tough hide, and then he'd shaken her until her senses returned.

"Green Eyes, be still! You're safe. Everything's all right!"

Gradually she realized it was the man with the snaggled teeth. Somehow, resting in his arms brought back vague, ghostly memories.

"Are you all right?" he asked her. She felt his hands run roughly over her body, reach her forearms, and stop.

"Blood?" he said. "What happened? Who cut you?"

Then, before she could answer, he roared, "Grab him!"

She heard a distant scuffle, and then a cascade of frantic honks.

"We need light!" Twisted Tooth yelled. "Strike a fire! Bring torches!"

Within a few moments somebody dumped an armload of dry kindling on one of the smoldering coal beds, and bright flames began to leap into the sky in showers of snapping sparks. He carried her closer, knelt down on one leg, and inspected her arms.

"I don't see any cuts . . ." he said finally.

Her voice was a strained, constricted chirp. Even in her own ears it sounded like somebody else.

"He didn't cut me," she whispered. "He tried, but I hit him with a rock."

"You . . . what? Hit him with a rock?" His chest heaved silently against her shoulder.

"Good work, then," he rumbled at her. "Can you stand? Sit?"

She nodded.

He upended her and set her gently on the ground next to the fire. "Chain Coil! Over here. Keep an eye on her."

With that he stood. She realized he was chuckling. As he strode off, she heard him repeat, "Hit him with a rock, eh? Hit him with a *rock*. Well, let's go *see*."

The whole camp was awake and stirring. She watched

shadowy figures gallop past, heard cries and shouts, saw new fires blaze up. After a while it all started to blur together, and the fear drained away, leaving her feeling weak and sick.

Eventually her eyelids became too heavy and she drifted off, shivering in the night chill. She woke in his arms again, and realized he was carrying her back to her tent.

"Put you back to sleep, little girl," he whispered.

"No . . ." she said muzzily. "No . . ."

He stopped. "Very well. What am I thinking of? He tried to murder you there, didn't he?"

Her last recollection was of him wrapping her in a blanket and setting her back down next to the fire. The light and warmth made her feel safe again. And then it was morning.

Lulled by the drums, overwhelmed by the events of the last few days, and numbed by a fantastic ritual she didn't understand, she'd drifted away again for a moment. Now she felt a curious hot prickling sensation, as if ants were crawling over her skin.

She raised her head and looked across the still and silent husk, directly into the raging eyes of Young Big Nose. He sat with his knees drawn up to his chin, his gangly arms wrapped around his calves, the bottom half of his face hidden. But the eyes were plainly visible, catching the final scarlet light like cups full of blood, and they were focused on her with unblinking intensity.

She whimpered and dropped her gaze. But she could still feel the horror crawling on her flesh, molten with murder lust.

4

The sun had become a vast ball half sunk below the dark teeth of the distant hilltops. The priest had finished his exorcism, the Jaguar had come and gone, and now the priest was only a priest again. He handed his pipe and his rattle, dripping with white claws, back to his acolyte, and came forward to stand before Golden Hand.

"His spirit is clean," the priest said. "Now it must atone, and be released into its final journey."

"Very well," Golden Hand replied. "Let it begin." He stood up, and felt Twisted Tooth rise at his side. Out of the corner of his eye he saw Chain Coil take up the leash Twisted Tooth had let fall. Twisted Tooth had something else in his hand, long and sinuous.

The two men moved solemnly forward until they stood over Old Big Nose's corpse. Golden Hand looked down and, after a pause, began to speak. His voice was normal, as if he were holding a conversation with the dead man. In a way, he was.

"Old Big Nose, you have committed treachery in the eyes of the Gods and in the eyes of men. Your spirit wanders lost in the darkness, trapped within the net of your sins. You must atone, and then you will be free. Do you wish this?"

The drummers beat their sticks fiercely and shouted, "Yes! Yes!"

Golden Hand nodded at Twisted Tooth, who sank to his knees next to the body.

"I sentence you to lose all your possessions, and go into the darkness naked, with empty hands."

Twisted Tooth pried open the dead fingers. In the last rays of the sun, the knife lay there, green and gleaming. He lifted it up so that the dreary dusk light glimmered along the sharp edge of the blade.

Golden Hand heard a collective sigh. The thing was strange and beautiful, its power far out of proportion to its size. Suddenly he understood why the old man had been willing to risk everything to possess it. Yet as he watched it glitter in the light, a chill crept up his spine. The ancient stone possessed a haunting—and haunted—quality, and for a moment Golden Hand wondered what, exactly, had driven Old Big Nose to his final act of murder and madness.

Golden Hand saw Young Big Nose lurch halfway to his feet, his arms flapping wildly, his eyes the size of saucers.

His cry was cut off abruptly as Chain Coil yanked savagely on his leash, spilling him into a pile of thrashing arms and legs.

"Light the fire," Golden Hand said curtly, turning away.

Off some distance to the right, men thrust torches into a great mound of kindling and logs. The logs had already been soaked with oil. They caught immediately. Within a few moments eager fingers of fire leaped up against the darkness of the eastern sky.

Twisted Tooth stood and handed the knife to Golden Hand. He took it and looked down at it, startled. It was the first time he'd touched it. It felt smooth and cool, and somehow warm at the same time. He imagined it throbbing in his palm, like something living, instead of dumb stone.

Quickly he placed it in a pouch inside his robes. He straightened and looked at the corpse again.

"You must pay your debt to Gods and men before you are free to go," he announced in ringing tones.

Once again Twisted Tooth moved forward, this time bringing up the long whip he'd held in his left hand. He switched it to his right, raised it, and snapped it experimentally.

"Scourge the thief," Golden Hand said.

Twisted Tooth brought the whip down hard.

When Golden Hand whispered, "*Enough . . .*" Twisted Tooth stepped away. "You have paid all debts," Golden Hand intoned sonorously. "You are released to go."

He stepped back as four strong men came up.

"Bear him to his fire," Golden Hand said. At least he would get an honorable burning, despite his many sins.

Golden Hand returned to his chair, wondering why he felt so shaken. As he seated himself, he felt a small prodding sensation from the knife he'd secreted in the inner pouch.

He had the sudden urge to take the blade out, look at it, hold it, fondle it.

He heard a small sound and turned, just in time to see Green Eyes Blue keel over in a dead faint.

5

At the edge of the vast meadow Young Big Nose looked up at the hard blue morning sky and shivered uncontrollably. Huge, regular ranks of clouds marched overhead, raking the earth with soft, billowing walls of shadow. The sun was a hot spark stinging in his vision. His eyes began to water and he lowered his head.

They were standing there, all his tormentors. The demonic, God-cursed Lord stood there, his face like a flint, his arms folded across his chest. His eyes were cold as death.

Not like the eyes of the brute at his side. There was a knowing heat in those eyes, a lust that frightened Young Big Nose.

And the girl. The murderer of his father. She stood, pale and silent, at the demon Lord's side, clutching his skirt as if it were a staff. He wanted to stare into her eyes, those horrible, miscolored eyes, and somehow make her know how much he hated her, but she wouldn't look at him. She was afraid of him.

That thought gave him the tiniest quiver of satisfaction, but it didn't last long.

"By the actions of your father, you forfeit my hospitality," the demon Lord said coldly. "And by your acts as his accomplice, you earn a portion of his penalty. I expel you now from my camp and my protection. Go, and never return, either to me or to the City of Gods, on pain of death. You are banished forever. Go!"

The monster raised the terrible whip he bore, a grin tickling at his jumbled teeth. Young Big Nose began to run. Fire sprayed across his naked back.

Twisted Tooth struck twice more, and when he was done, Young Big Nose was shambling across the meadow as fast as he could go.

They listened to his agonized cries until they finally faded and vanished in the distance.

Lord Golden Hand sighed. "It is done," he said.

Twisted Tooth nodded and coiled his whip. Golden Hand took Green Eyes's fingers in his own. Together, they turned and went back to the camp. Four hours later, the caravan was on the trail again. Within an hour, even the sound of their marching dwindled and died, and little remained to mark the spot but the wind, and the empty cries of birds.

6

The third time she tried to run away, Golden Hand lost patience with her and had her brought to him with her wrists tied before her.

"Well? Do you like it?" he asked her.

She stood before him, her head defiantly up, her lower lip pouting. Her expression was so concentrated and rebellious it was all he could do not to laugh out loud, though it wasn't a laughing matter. Somehow, he needed a way to get through her stubborn exterior.

"Answer me, Green Eyes Blue. Do you like being tied up?"

She glared at him a moment longer, then shook her head vigorously back and forth. Her midnight hair caught the sunlight like crows' wings, rippling with iridescence.

In the past several days the priest had continued to apply his magics to her, and all of the swelling had leached from her face, revealing the beauty Golden Hand had suspected was there. It wasn't yet true beauty, of course, because her features were still unshaped by experience or time. Nevertheless, the potential was there. She was like a perfect doll. Life itself would paint the fine details on the empty places.

Golden Hand sighed. "You must say, 'No, my lord,' " he told her gently.

It seemed impossible that her lip could bulge any farther, but somehow she managed it.

"Go on, say it," he urged again.

She stamped her foot. They'd found makeshift sandals for her, but they were a little too big, and this one flew off and landed in the dust. His gaze followed it, then drifted back to rest a moment on her chest.

Stop that, he told himself.

"Green Eyes, you have tried to run away three times now. If I can't trust you, I'll have to keep you tied up like this all the time."

Her eyes flickered. For a moment a blink of uncertainty peeped through.

"I'm not running away," she said suddenly. "I'm running *home*. Why won't you let me go *home*?"

They'd been over it before. He'd thought she'd understood, but maybe not. Maybe he had spoken too gently, used too many sweet words to explain hard truths.

"This is your home, Green Eyes. Well, not this caravan, but me. You belong to me, so wherever I say is home, that's your home. You must forget about the village where you grew up. That's gone forever."

She stared at him, her eyes growing wider. "What did you do to my village? Did you burn it down?"

"No, no," he said hastily. "I haven't even seen your village."

"Then it's still there. It's not gone forever. And it's home. Where Mama and Papa are, and my brothers and sisters. That's where I live. Not here. Not with you. I don't belong to you. I don't belong to anybody. I'm Green Eyes Blue."

As she said this, her eyes flashed, and he thought, My Gods! She's magnificent!

"Child, I bought you from Old Big Nose. You do belong to me, and the sooner you get used to it, the happier we both will be."

She stamped her foot again. "I didn't belong to him either! Not to him, not to you." She pointed her chin at him and glared down her nose—where did she come by that nose? Those cheekbones?—and then, suddenly, her eyes filled up and spilled over.

Slowly she crumpled to the ground, her movements made awkward and graceless by her bound hands, sobbing as if her heart would break. "Wh-wh-why won't you let me *go*?" she wailed miserably.

It was pathetic, and at the same time it irritated him almost beyond endurance. Why was she so stubborn? He knew she wasn't stupid. Why couldn't she accept her new life? He could think of hundreds of girls who'd give almost anything to be in her place. To be loved by the wealthy, powerful Lord Golden Hand.

Loved?

He stepped forward, bent down, scooped his hands under her armpits, and hoisted her up. She didn't protest, said not a word, but merely stood there before him and sobbed silently.

"If you persist in behaving like a child, I'll have to treat you like one. Until you give me your promise not to run away, you'll stay as you are."

He snapped his fingers. Twisted Tooth handed him a length of rope. Golden Hand looked at it, then looked at her. Hands tied together. Tethered to a rope. Was he no better than—

He sighed in exasperation. "Tie the leash to your wrist."

"Me, Lord?"

"Yes, you. Until I think of something better." He stalked away, his stomach churning.

7

Some hours later, as the head of the caravan approached the mouth of a small valley between two worn hills, he was still mulling over the problem.

Behind him, Twisted Tooth marched along, Green Eyes cradled in his arms. Her tether rope was draped across his shoulders like a necklace, and his normally cheerful features bore an expression of irritation—directed, Golden Hand suspected, not at the girl, but at him.

And why not? It was ridiculous to expect his Chief Factor to act as a nanny to a little girl. He couldn't allow it anyway. Who would oversee the myriad details necessary to keep the caravan functioning smoothly?

Oh, he could let one of the traders, or a junior factor, or even one of the guards lead her by her tether. And he could tie her up every night and roll her into her tent. But he suspected that if he did that, by the time they reached Tollan, she would hate him as deeply as she did the Big Noses, and he didn't want that.

He had plans for her. Shifting and inchoate at the moment, but plans nonetheless. Even if she hated him he might still carry through with some of them—but he didn't *want* her to hate him.

Damn it!

Preoccupied with his thoughts, he glanced up the trail toward the valley mouth, and saw a brown, indeterminate figure far ahead. He squinted, concentrating suddenly. These hills were known for bandits.

He pushed his worries about Green Eyes away without another thought. "Twisted Tooth. Put her down. Look up ahead."

"I see, Lord. One moment."

The factor shook Green Eyes awake and quickly set her down. He handed her leash to a junior factor and said brusquely, "Watch her." Then he turned around and waved for the guards.

Golden Hand had temporarily halted the column. "Take
the girl to the rear," he ordered. When that was done, and the
guards were gathered around him, he gave the order to
march again.

A moment later one of the slaves pounded up from the
rear and handed him his great war spear. It was an arm's
length taller than the top of his head, and bore a huge, sharpened point made of the finest greenstone. A bouquet of white
feathers dangled from just below the point, together with a
pair of fleshier, more grisly trophies.

Up ahead the figure had stopped and was standing quite
still, waiting for them.

Golden Hand, who had the eyes of an eagle, saw it first.
He relaxed and said, "It's only an old woman."

Twisted Tooth's voice remained tense. "So what? It could
still be a trap. Keep your spear up!"

In some cases Golden Hand didn't mind taking orders
from his servants at all. Twisted Tooth had been traveling
and trading in distant lands for almost thirty years. That he
was still doing so, and still in possession of all his parts, testified to the effectiveness of his advice.

Golden Hand straightened his shoulders, gripped his
spear tighter, and began to nervously scan the valley mouth
and the back-sloping, boulder-strewn hills that led down to
it. He saw what had Twisted Tooth worried. You could hide
an army in that terrain.

"Scouts," Twisted Tooth said behind him. He heard a
whispered conversation, then the soft pad of sandaled feet as
two of the guards rushed past them toward the valley mouth.

"Archers to the front," Twisted Tooth said. Immediately a
half-dozen bow men sprang forward and arrayed themselves
before the head of the column. They spread out in a fan for-
mation, each one with a heavy-tipped war arrow nocked
against his bowstring.

Up ahead, the two scouts had reached the old woman.
They spoke with her only a moment. Then they turned off

the trail, each one taking a side, and began to scramble up the hillside like goats.

"Halt the column," Twisted Tooth called out.

The archers half drew their weapons, their eyes focused on the two scouts. After what seemed a very long time, the scouts clambered to the tops of the hills. They stood there, scanning the rock-strewn slopes below, then turned and waved their arms.

"All clear," Twisted Tooth breathed. "*Now* we can relax."

The scouts began to climb down. The archers fell back toward the main column, unstringing their bows as they went. Two minutes later, Golden Hand reached the old woman and said, "Well, Old Mother, how goes it for you this fine day?"

8

She stood at the side of the road, dressed in a shapeless brown sack, a large straw bag slung over her right shoulder. She stood as if she'd been waiting there for years.

Her skin was seamed and bronzed by the sun, her nose flat, her eyes obsidian buttons nesting in a deep web of fine wrinkles. She wore a shapeless, wide-brimmed straw hat, from beneath which trailed long strands of unbraided gray hair. Her bushy, high-ridged eyebrows were pure white. She was built like a boulder, short, thick, and squat. She looked as if she'd grown from the earth, or was rooted in it. As she stared at him her eyes sparked with bright, sharp intelligence.

Suddenly he knew why she seemed so familiar. She reminded him of those ancient faces, half buried in the earth, their shapes and forms thrown down and unmoved since the beginnings of Time itself.

He swallowed, suddenly feeling ill at ease. He bowed slightly. "I am Golden Hand," he said. "I'm a trader."

"A great lord from Tollan," she said suddenly. She sounded immensely unimpressed. Her voice was surprising—clear and low and very youthful. For a moment he had a vision of the young woman she must have been, now embedded forever in the wrinkled flesh of age. "I am Mama Root," she said.

He noticed she didn't bow.

"I've been waiting for you."

"What?" Now he was completely disconcerted.

Behind him, Twisted Tooth said sharply, "Old woman! How did you know we were coming? Who told you?"

Her eyes shifted, a glint of laughter showing in their blankly translucent depths, like a silver fish rising to the surface of a shaded pond. "Fear not, mighty warrior. I am no goat staked out for ambush. I saw you in my dreams, and knew you needed my services."

Golden Hand stared at her in astonishment. "What? I need your services? What are you talking about?"

She raised one gnarled, blue-veined hand and pointed. "There," she said.

They turned. Standing several paces away, staring at them, stood the girl, her green and blue eyes glinting in the sun.

Slowly, Golden Hand swung back to face the old woman. Mama Root grinned at him. It was a memorable grin. Most of her teeth were gone.

"It will cost you," she said.

He sighed. "Yes, I suppose it will."

Chapter Six

1

"Take those ropes off her," Mama Root said briskly. "Untie the poor girl. Quick, now! What do you think she is, an animal?"

Twisted Tooth stared at her, nonplussed. "Old woman, I do my master's bidding. He tells me to tie her up, I tie her up. And I don't untie her until he says for me to do so."

Mama Root eyed him as if he were something she'd just found stuck to the bottom of her sandal. Twisted Tooth felt the strangest urge to squirm. Mama Root tapped her broad chin thoughtfully.

"I see," she said. Then, without taking her dark gaze off him, she let out an ear-shattering yowl: "Lord Golden Hand! Come here at once!"

Golden Hand, still at the head of the column, talking with the two scouts, looked over his shoulder, startled. Then, to Twisted Tooth's astonishment, he came hurrying over, as chastened as any schoolboy summoned to his mother's skirts.

"Yes, Mama Root?"

Mama Root gestured at Twisted Tooth. "This big, ugly man of yours refuses to untie the girl. He says you ordered it, and only you can order it otherwise. So order it now, if you will."

"Oh. Why, yes, of course. Untie her, Twisted Tooth."

A brick-red flush began to burn on the back of Twisted Tooth's bull neck. "Lord . . . this old harridan . . ."

"And another thing, Lord. We might as well get it settled now. You have given the girl into my care. So explain to this one, so he can explain it to everybody else—if he can explain anything, which I doubt—exactly who has the girl in charge, and who makes the decisions regarding her." She folded her arms across her chest and stood waiting.

"Ah . . . uh . . . certainly. Twisted Tooth, I've—"

Twisted Tooth spat on the ground in disgust. "Say no more, Lord." He reached into his belt, withdrew his knife, and sliced through Green Eyes's bindings with two quick strokes. The ropes fell to the dusty ground, and he left them where they lay.

"Maybe you'll give this ancient hag my job, too? She's certainly bossy enough for it." Then he spat again, turned, and stomped away.

Mama Root watched him go, an amused smile tugging at her lips. "Thank you, Lord Golden Hand," she said demurely.

"You should be careful of him," Golden Hand said. "He's a good man. And he's in charge of this caravan. You should keep that in mind."

"Oh, I have no designs on his authority, Lord. But the girl is mine, as we agreed. Is that not so?"

"Yes. That is so. I'll go talk to him. Mama Root, don't go out of your way to make him angry. As he says, he does what I tell him to do. Not what you tell him."

"Don't worry," she replied. "I know how to handle him." Again she flashed that secretive half smile.

A startling thought came to Golden Hand. "And do you know how to handle me as well, Mama Root?"

Her smile broadened. "Of course, Lord. You're a man, aren't you?"

Then, before he could think of any reply, she took Green Eyes's hand in her own, said, "Come, girl. It's time for us to get to know each other." And led her away, leaving Golden Hand standing there with his mouth open.

2

Green Eyes couldn't understand exactly why walking along the trail with Mama Root felt so comforting, but it did. On the surface there was not much comfortable about the old woman. Her gaze was sharp and piercing, and Green Eyes guessed she wouldn't be able to hide much from her. And when she talked, she sometimes sounded just like the chief of Green Eyes's village, barking orders and expecting them to be obeyed immediately. But underneath that gruff, harsh exterior, Green Eyes sensed something else, and it was to that she found herself responding, even against her will.

Mama Root made her feel safe.

They strolled along near the middle of the column, easily keeping pace. As soon as they'd taken up their position, Mama Root had turned to Chain Coil, standing nearby, shrugged off her heavy straw bag, and handed it to him.

"Here, boy," she said. "Make yourself useful."

To Green Eyes's astonishment, the big soldier lifted the bag with no protest at all. "Yes . . . mother," he said, a bright flush rising in his cheeks.

"Call me Mama Root," she told him. "Everybody does."

Green Eyes's small fingers were still wrapped in the rough brown warmth of Mama Root's hand. For some reason she didn't want to let go.

"Mama Root, can you explain things to me?" Green Eyes said.

"I can try, dear. What do you want to know?"

"I don't understand," Green Eyes said, her tone thoughtful. "Why are you here? I saw you waiting at the side of the trail for us. Were you waiting for me?"

"In a way, girl. In a way."

"Well . . . why?"

Mama Root sighed. "Let's just say that your . . . mother . . . sent me to look after you."

"My mama? Oh, you know my mama? Can you take me back to her?"

She looked up eagerly, and saw that Mama Root's eyelids had dropped somewhat, covering her gaze and giving her a distant, shaded look. As if she were seeing something far, far away. She sighed again, and spoke without looking at Green Eyes. Though she gripped the girl's hand more tightly for a moment.

"No, I don't know your mama. Not exactly. But your mama would be glad to know I am with you. I think she would. Since she can't be here to guide and protect you herself, she would want me to do it in her place. Do you understand?"

Green Eyes puzzled over it for a moment. "You mean . . . like you would be my mama too?"

"In a way, yes."

"But you're not my mama."

Mama Root tugged her gently to the side of the path, stopped, and hunkered down before her, so she could look the girl in the eye.

"Dear girl, I am not exactly your mama. But I think of you as my daughter. I will care for you and protect you as if you were my own. I will love you as if you were mine."

Green Eyes peered into her dark, warm gaze and knew Mama Root was telling the truth. The sensation of absolute knowledge filled her so completely she didn't even question it. She bit her lower lip, then nodded. A smile spread across her face.

"You will love me?" Green Eyes said.

"Dear, I already do. Now, come. We will fall behind."

They rejoined the march. After a while Green Eyes began to sing in her high, piping voice, and a moment later Mama Root joined in.

3

It took most of the day to negotiate the valley, and they made camp just on the other side of it, near a spring that bubbled noisily from denuded rocks.

As the bright heat of the day slowly melted into the cooler shadows of dusk, Mama Root supervised Chain Coil while he set up their tent, built them a neat fire ring, and then brought a load of wood.

Mama Root told him, "If you're any kind of a hunter, and you stay with me, I can guarantee you will eat very well, boy. I know how to cook."

As it turned out, she certainly did. Chain Coil left and returned shortly, bearing a brace of rabbits. While he was gone, Mama Root took Green Eyes's hand and led her into the edge of the forest. In the last of the light, Mama Root examined various plants, and poked in the ground with a sharp stick. At one place she muttered, "Aha," knelt, and dug some fat, juicy tubers from the dark earth.

When they came back, Chain Coil had finished with their tent, and was seated cross-legged, grinning, with the pair of rabbits laid out before him like an offering.

Mama Root grinned back at him. "Fetch my bag from the tent, boy," she instructed him jovially, "and then we'll see if I'm not as good as my word."

Green Eyes watched, goggle-eyed, as Mama Root withdrew pots, stirrers, and a host of small sacks filled with exotic spices from her bag. By the time she had everything spread out, Green Eyes was marveling that so much could fit in the large straw pack. It seemed impossible that there was enough space—and the bag looked hardly smaller at all.

A magic bag! Green Eyes thought to herself. How wonderful!

By the time the food was ready, it seemed half the camp had just happened to wander by, noses twitching at the sublime aromas rising from their fire. Even Twisted Tooth am-

bled along, frowning and pausing only to spit, which made
Mama Root laugh deep in her throat.

As they ate, with much slurping, lip smacking, and finger
licking, Mama Root leaned close to Green Eyes and pointed
at Chain Coil. "First lesson, girl. They say the way to a
man's heart is through his balls, but the truth is, the best road
is through his belly. Do you like Mama Root's cooking?"

Green Eyes didn't have to do anything thinking about that
at all. She felt only a slight twinge of guilt, thinking of her
own mama's meals as she said, "It's wonderful. It's the best
I've ever tasted!"

"Why, thank you, dear. Would you like to learn how to
cook the way I do?"

"Oh, yes."

"Then I will teach you."

When they had finished, Mama Root looked across the
fire. "Did you get enough, you great galumph?"

Still licking the last greasy remnants from his fingers,
Chain Coil nodded happily.

"Good," Mama Root said. "Remember, there's more
where that came from. And now you can take the pots to the
spring and clean them."

"Yes, Mama Root," Chain Coil said.

"And tonight you can spread your bedroll in front of our
tent. To make sure we're not disturbed by any . . . animals."

"Yes, Mama Root," Chain Coil said.

"Good. Be off with you, then."

"Yes, Mama Root," Chain Coil said a third time as he
began to gather up the soiled pots.

Green Eyes watched him from the side of her eyes. She
had the strangest feeling that Chain Coil didn't exactly belong to Twisted Tooth any longer.

Later, they sat near the fire and Mama Root reached into
her bag and brought out a wondrous thing, a brush made of
boar's bristles set into a polished wooden handle inlaid with
bits of white shell.

"Come here, girl, your hair's a mess."

Obediently, Green Eyes settled herself in front of Mama Root, who began to draw the brush through her tangled, matted hair with long, sure strokes.

The sensation was infinitely sensuous. Her own mama, whenever she had time to think about it, used a hard comb made of tortoise shell to accomplish the same task, always bringing squeals and yelps of pain as she yanked out the usual burrs and thatches. This was entirely different. The tangles seemed to melt away, and the slow, rhythmic motion of Mama Root's strokes soothed her so much that without realizing it, she began to doze off.

"You have beautiful hair," Mama Root whispered.

"Mmm . . ."

Mama Root began to half hum, half sing a slow song. Green Eyes couldn't understand the words, but the sound lifted her to a different place. It was a place touched by waking dreams, that place partway between light and sleep. She saw a tall, dark hill and a dark-eyed woman, and a man with blue eyes.

The man was smiling at her. She had the feeling he really could see her, from where he was in the dream. But she felt no fear.

"That's enough," Mama Root murmured into her ear. "Time for bed, my girl."

Mama Root took her hand and gently pulled her up, and led her into the tent. Gratefully, Green Eyes lay down on her freshly made bed. She was conscious of Mama Root arranging her own blanket on the pile of sweet grasses next to her.

It was the same tent, now mended, where Old Big Nose had crept in to kill her. But somehow, with Mama Root nearby, it didn't seem to matter. As if by her presence alone she banished those dark spirits of memory.

Mama Root smelled of fresh berries and dried flowers, and it was the scent of these wonderful things that filled Green Eyes's nose as, for the first time since it had all begun, she slipped into a deep and dreamless sleep.

4

The lands about them had changed, gradually rising, becoming drier and more mountainous, by the time Green Eyes's rebellion finally reached full flower.

She'd been distracted, petulant, and fractious throughout the entire day's march. Mama Root's lips were compressed into a thin line by the time Chain Coil finished raising their tent and preparing their fire ring.

As Mama Root worked with the turkey Chain Coil had bagged, her sacks of spices spread at her knees, she looked up at the youth and said, "Chain Coil, go away somewhere. I'll call when the food is ready."

Without a word, Chain Coil rose smoothly to his feet, grinned and wandered away. Mama Root had tamed him well. It was accepted throughout the party, even grudgingly by Twisted Tooth, that the young guard belonged to the girl and the old woman.

Green Eyes understood this was so, even as the idea of it festered like a burr beneath the blanket of her thoughts. She enjoyed having the big, cheerful youth do almost anything she asked him to. And she saw how he instantly sprang to do *everything* Mama Root ordered.

Chain Coil's constant guardianship made her feel even safer, as Mama Root made her feel safe. It was because Mama Root was strong and wise and determined. Whatever Mama Root wanted, somehow that thing came to pass. And yet . . .

In the back of her mind, Green Eyes Blue had been counting her steps. Her steps had been many, so many she couldn't really add them up, even if she'd understood anything about counting beyond the span of the fingers on her hands. But the number of steps didn't really matter. What did matter was that each step she took carried her one step farther away from her mama, her papa, her village, and her life.

She didn't yet think of it as her old life. Everything that

had occurred since the Big Noses had carried her off still felt
to her like a bad dream. With Mama Root around it wasn't
quite a nightmare, but it was bad. Tenuous and filmy, not
real. As if somehow she might blink, shake her head, and
suddenly see the small cottages of her village around her,
feel the familiar dust of its paths between her toes, and hear
her mama suddenly cry, "Why, Green Eyes! There you are.
Where have you been? I've been looking all over for you!"

And she would run to her mama's arms and all this would
fade away as if it had never been. Perhaps it was the change
in the country through which they were passing that brought
things to a head. She had grown up in the overwhelming
heat and damp of the lowland jungles. Now even the trees
had changed. The nights were cooler and during the day,
even in the heat of the sun, the air was dryer. Sometimes she
felt as if her skin were becoming parched and dusty; the sensation frightened her.

And she, who had never seen a bit of ground uncovered
by green, unless it was the fields by the river freshly planted,
now saw in the far north and east great naked points of
stone, dark and brooding. Sometimes she had the feeling
they were watching her, with a kind of dumb, blind, ancient
awareness.

They were mountains, Mama Root told her. And it was to
these mountains she was going, whether she wanted to or
not—although Mama Root had not said as much in so many
word, Green Eyes understood the hidden truth well enough.
So all this had grown in her, bubbling beneath the surface,
until she was unable to think of anything else. Even Mama
Root took on an aura of evil, because Green Eyes had come
to love the old woman, and once having given her love, she
couldn't understand why it wasn't returned.

Mama Root claimed to love her, too, yet Mama Root, who
could get anything she wanted, still led her on toward those
distant peaks, many, many steps farther from her mama. Her
real life.

"What's the matter with you, Green Eyes? You've been a perfect little brat these last two days."

It was what Green Eyes perceived to be the unfairness of this accusation that plucked the cork from her seething anger. Her face grew red. "I *hate* you, Mama Root. I *hate* you!"

Mama Root was rolling out tortillas, the muscles along her meaty forearms twisting like snakes beneath her skin. She stopped.

"You hate me? But why, Green Eyes? I love you."

She said this so simply that all of Green Eyes's feelings, snarled as a nest of snakes and as irreconcilable, welled up in impossible frustration and boiled over. Green Eyes began to weep, the sound of her sobs so deep and heartrending that Mama Root raised her bushy eyebrows in alarm. Then, slowly, the expression on her face softened.

"Come here, dear," she said.

Still bawling, Green Eyes shook her head emphatically.

"Come to Mama Root, little daughter. Let Mama Root hold you in her arms."

Green Eyes could not explain it, but the sound of Mama Root's soft voice suddenly became deeper, softer, and infinitely compelling. It was as if her body listened even while her mind refused.

Mama Root held out her hands, and Green Eyes came to her and crawled into her broad, soft lap. Those arms enfolded her and pulled her against the yielding pillows of Mama Root's great breasts.

"There, there, dearest. Cry against Mama Root." She began to rock, one hand gently stroking Green Eyes's shining hair. "Lean on me and cry it all out. Give it to Mama Root, give Mama Root everything bad and let her take it away from you."

Mama Root's voice was a gentle thunder in her ears, soothing and uplifting at the same time. Something in Green

Eyes clutched at that voice, and eventually her cries lessened into hiccups and gulps, and finally silence.

Mama Root kept on rocking and stroking her. "It's hard, isn't it?" she finally murmured.

Sniffle.

"Yes, I know it is. Your journey takes you farther away from your home every day. Farther away from your mother, your father, your sisters and brothers. And Mama Root leads you on the path, doesn't she? You love Mama Root, but you think maybe Mama Root doesn't really love you, eh? Because if Mama Root really loved you, she'd take you home. That's right, isn't it? If I loved you, I'd take you back to your mama, and make everything the way it used to be for you."

Green Eyes raised her tear-streaked cheeks in wonder. "How did you know that?" she whispered.

"I know lots of things, my love," Mama Root said. But in her voice was a distant, windy sadness. For no reason at all, Green Eyes felt a pang of unfocused fear.

"Well, why can't you? Why *won't* you? Mama Root, I want to go *home*."

"Yes, yes, I know, dear. I know you do. But you can't. Even I can't take you there."

"But you can do anything."

Mama Root shook her head slowly. "I can do many things, my love. But I can't do that."

"I don't understand."

Mama Root exhaled slowly. "Men rule the Middle World, dearest. Men with their heavy clubs. With their strutting and brawling and their big muscles. With their heavy feet and their hardened minds. Men rule our world, Green Eyes. Not women. Not us. It isn't our world at all. Not really."

Green Eyes didn't really understand much of this—she especially didn't understand why Mama Root sounded as if she might start crying, too—so she said nothing. Yet she had the strange and certain idea that she would never forget these words, and that someday she *would* understand them. And they would make her sad, too.

After a time, Mama Root said, "Do you know what a slave is, Green Eyes?"

"Well, yes, of course I do. It's . . . it's a . . ." And then she realized that she really didn't know. Not exactly.

Mama Root nodded to herself. "If you buy a dog or a pig, that's not a slave, is it?"

Green Eyes shook her head. "No. They're just animals."

"Exactly. Are men animals, then?"

"Of course not!"

"What about women, or little girls? Are they animals?"

"No."

"If a man buys another man, is the man he bought—as he would buy a dog or pig—is that man an animal now?"

Green Eyes suddenly had the feeling she was treading into deep, dark waters. Her forehead crinkled. "Well, no. Not exactly . . ."

"But why not exactly, dear? Why is a man different than a dog or a pig, which everybody agrees we can buy or sell as we wish?"

"I don't . . . know." Then something glimmered up in her thoughts and she grabbed it. "Because the Gods love men? They must love us, Mama Root. The Gods made us, and they watch over us."

"If they love us, then why do they allow some men to buy and sell other men as if they were animals? Don't the Gods love those men? Didn't they make them as well?"

Green Eyes felt her tenuous understanding begin to unravel.

"I don't know," she said.

Mama Root stroked her hair in silence for a while, still rocking gently. When she spoke again, Green Eyes had the idea she wasn't talking to her any longer, and that what she spoke had more to do with something other than just one little girl.

"Some say that when a man becomes a slave, and is treated just like a dog or a pig, it is a sign the Gods are displeased with that man, and are punishing him for sins against the heavenly ones. And others say that the man was never truly a man, that he was only born with the shape of a man, but underneath he was a pig or a dog."

"But how can that be?" Green Eyes said.

"Hush, little one. Listen to what I say. It's important."

Green Eyes nodded her head against Mama Root's yielding breasts.

"So many things are said about men, and dogs, and pigs. And slaves. But what about woman?"

Now her voice grew stronger. "Are women pigs or dogs? No, they aren't. But women are not men. For a man to be treated as a pig or a dog, he must believe he is one. Or must be forced to behave as if he is an animal. Men fight each other in wars, and capture each other, and drag each other away from home. Just as what happened to you. And when that happens, those men are forced to act like pigs or dogs, or they will be killed by the men who want them to act that way."

"Then men are evil . . ."

"Be still, dear. Let me finish. Those men have to make a choice. Sometimes the only choice they have is between being killed or becoming like pigs and dogs. The property of other men. Men who own them, who can buy them or sell them, or do whatever they wish to them."

"But that isn't right, Mama Root. Those men are still men. They belong to themselves. No matter what you do to them, they are still men and not pigs."

"Many would disagree with you, dear. Almost all men would. Even here, if you asked Twisted Tooth, or Chain Coil, or Lord Golden Hand, they would say it is true. But we women, dear, we know it is a lie. Do you know why?"

"No, Mama Root."

"It is because we are women, and we are born into slav-

ery. We are not men, with big muscles and deadly weapons.
So we have to seek their protection, lest other men take us
and treat us like pigs or dogs. Yet the funny thing is, in order
to gain the protection of some men to keep us safe from
other men, we have to *pretend* we are like pigs and dogs. In
other words, we are slaves because in the Middle World,
which is ruled by men, we have to become slaves to men in
order to live. And the sad truth is, none of the men even
think of us as slaves. We are women. Not quite pigs or dogs,
but just as malleable, just as much property. Just as much en-
slaved. They don't know it, but we do. At least some of us
do. Strangely enough, there are many women who don't
even know they are slaves. Isn't that odd, Green Eyes?"

Once again Green Eyes had the feeling that though much
of what Mama Root had said was beyond her understanding,
it wouldn't always be so. She did grasp one thing, though.

"Mama Root?"

"Yes?"

"Are you like a pig or dog? Are you a slave too?"

This time Mama Root remained silent for a very long
time, so long that Green Eyes decided she must not have
heard. But just as she was about to ask again, Mama Root
said, "No, dear. I am not a slave. Because being a slave is a
matter of choice. As I told you, some men must choose between dying, between allowing themselves to be killed or
becoming a slave. And as long as you understand you have
that choice, and can make it whenever you like, then you
aren't a slave. Rather than be a slave, you can die. It is a hard
choice, but a real one. And knowing you always have it can
let you live without being a slave, even if you are tied in a
hundred ropes."

"So you aren't a slave?"

"I would die before I would live other than as I choose to
live, dearest."

"So you love me because you choose to? You don't have
to, you really want to?"

"Yes, Green Eyes. Nobody can force my love. Nobody at all."

Now Green Eyes fell silent for a long time. "Mama Root? Am I a slave?"

"Lord Golden Hand paid Old Big Nose money for you. So Lord Golden Hand believes you are his slave, yes."

"Is that why you can't take me home?"

"Lord Golden Hand would kill me if I tried to do that. More likely his factor would, but I would die."

"I want to go home, Mama Root. More than anything. If I can't go home, I don't want to be a slave. I'd rather be dead."

Mama Root pushed her away, until she could see her eyes clearly in the firelight.

"Green Eyes Blue, that is always your choice. And if you choose it, I will freely give you the means to make it happen. But I think you should wait a while before you make your final decision."

"Why?"

"Ah, because you are young, and the world is young, and maybe things will change for you one day. Maybe you will not hate your life as much as you do now, and you will be willing to accept the things you cannot change."

Green Eyes blinked. Then, with a child's clear and unerring instinct for truth, lies, and hypocrisy, she said, "But if I do things I don't want to do, aren't I still a slave?"

Mama Root didn't flinch back from it. And though her voice sounded like the night wind sighing through empty, dead forests, her words were clear and cold. "That is my second lesson, Green Eyes Blue. We are women. In the Middle World of men, we are always slaves. The only difference is, some of us know it. You cannot go home again. As for the rest, it remains your choice."

Green Eyes began to shiver. "Why did this happen? Why did it happen to me? I hate men, Mama Root. I *hate* them."

"Yes, I know." Mama Root paused. "So I will give you

my third lesson. Men are slaves, too. Even the ones who buy and sell other men like pigs and dogs, they are also slaves. And their slavery is all the more binding, because they don't even know they are slaves. And the worst thing of all is they have created the thing that enslaves them. Men are fools."

To Green Eyes, it sounded like a curse and, in fact, it was. But she would not learn the full extent of that curse for many more years.

It was enough now that she finally understood she could not go home again.

5

TO THE STAIRWAY OF HEAVEN

Spring gradually slipped away into summer as the sky overhead lost its hard blue glaze and became vague and milky with heat. The sun was a silent furnace over their heads, and dust rose at their backs and hung motionless in the air for hours after they had passed.

Twisted Tooth took to personally checking the water bags and the gourds everybody carried, making sure that everything was refilled whenever they found a stream or spring. By this time they had passed through several villages, most of them much larger than any Green Eyes had ever seen before.

Often times the caravan would stop, and Golden Hand and Twisted Tooth would parlay with the chief, the elders, and the local priests. In one of these places, Green Eyes saw a wonder such as she'd never imagined before. In the center of the village, where the trail widened out into a broad, dusty plaza, stood a two-story building. Mama Root had led her inside and showed her a rude ladder made of peeled logs that led through a hole in the ceiling. Together they had climbed up, and to her wonder, Green Eyes found herself standing on yet another floor, just as solid as the ground on which she'd walked before.

"Come. Look," Mama Root said, and led her over to the only window. Nervously, Green Eyes peered over the sill, gave a little squeak, and jumped back.

"What's the matter, girl?" Mama Root asked.

"So high . . ." Green Eyes gasped. "I could see the tops of their heads. I was looking *down* on them."

"Of course, child. What did you expect? And why so frightened? Is it any different than climbing a hill and looking down?"

Green Eyes shook her head stubbornly. "This isn't a hill, Mama. This is a house." Her eyes grew large as she slowly twirled around. "It must be the biggest house in the whole world."

Mama Root chuckled. "It's probably bigger than any house in your village, at any rate."

"Oh, yes. Even the chief doesn't have anything as nice."

"I'm sure he doesn't, Green Eyes. But if you think this is a big house, you have a real treat in store for you."

"I do? What? When?"

"If I told you, it wouldn't be a treat. You wouldn't believe me anyway. But you'll see. When we arrive at Tollan."

Mama Root had already explained to her that Golden Hand, her new master, was taking her to Tollan. Green Eyes was still having a good bit of trouble understanding the master part. She could not yet entirely grasp how, one moment, she could belong only to herself, free to run and hunt and play as she chose, and the next be dragged hither and yon against her will by somebody who called himself master.

But Mama Root had warned her not to tax Lord Golden Hand with her questions or her complaints, at least not for the time being. "He likes you, dear. I think it's a good idea if we can keep things that way."

"You mean, pretend I'm a slave?"

A faint cloud had passed across Mama Root's flat, broad forehead at that, but she'd only nodded and said, "Exactly."

But as the days and even the seasons ground past, Green Eyes became, if not reconciled to her fate, at least interested in it. She still had moments, particularly as she fell asleep, when she remembered her mama or her village with a vividness that brought tears stinging into her eyes. She cried herself to sleep more than once. Curiously, after the first few times this happened, Mama Root would not take her into her arms and rock her anymore.

When Green Eyes asked Mama Root if she was angry at her, the old woman shook her head and said, "It's better not to pray to dead Gods, dear. They can't answer, and it takes time from praying to the living Gods."

Green Eyes hadn't quite understood that, either, but shortly after, her teary episodes of bleak depression began to fade—along with her sharp-edged memories of the life she'd led before.

Her life on the road settled into a comforting routine. She walked with Mama Root, and Chain Coil carried their things, made their campsite every night, and sometimes could be coaxed into giving her rides about the camp on his broad shoulders.

Mama Root also took Green Eyes's education into her capable hands. Sometimes, she would spy some special plant off the side of the trail, and they would go into the forest and look, while Mama Root took her by the hand and pointed out the valuable qualities of the flower, or root, or bush. The bark of this, if stripped, heated over a low fire, and then ground between two stones into a fine powder, made a tea that was very good for demons that caused a pain in the head.

Or that flower, if picked fresh and at full blossom, then crushed into a thin paste with this tender weed, made a poultice that would draw the fever demons out of a swollen wound. This one settled into the stomach, and that dark green leaf, if chewed, was good for pains in the chest. The list went on, endlessly, it seemed. At one point, after a particularly informative session, Green Eyes had stared at Mama Root with awe.

"Mama, do you know everything in the world there is?"

Mama Root laughed. "No, dear, not everything. But I know quite a lot. More than many would guess. You should try to learn as much as you can, daughter."

"Why?" Green Eyes was honestly uncertain. What had all her learning done for Mama Root? She was still only an old woman who stood beside the road, waiting for the Gods or fate to bring whatever chance happened along. She was certainly no great lord like Golden Hand, who had enough money to buy any little girl he wanted and make her his slave.

"Because you need to know the world firsthand, dear. To experience it and learn its riddles. So that when you see something you don't understand, you'll be able to figure it out from things you *do* know."

"I'm not sure. Is that a good thing?"

"It is for a woman, dear. Men sometimes don't need anything but a strong back and the thirst to kill. We women are weaker. We need more than that."

Green Eyes nodded, but privately she reserved judgment.

All this continued while they marched endlessly through the changing country, working their way higher and higher. Even the air changed, became somehow harder to breathe, though Mama Root assured her it was normal, and not to worry.

Green Eyes's latest obsession had become Tollan itself. She knew it was their destination, and that Lord Golden Hand intended for her to live there. But she knew nothing of it, and it was one of the few things Mama Root refused to discuss with her.

"You'll see it when you get there," Mama Root would say. "Until you've seen it with your own eyes, nothing I can say would do any good. Now, *after* you've seen it, then we'll talk. I promise you."

Of course, this only inflamed Green Eyes's curiosity, and in recent days she'd taken to asking the same question over and over, to the point that sometimes Mama Root bent down the brim of her great floppy hat, hid her face entirely, and refused to respond.

"How soon will we get there? How soon? How much longer?"

It became a chant, an unanswered riddle, until one cloudy morning as they walked down a trail much wider than it had been before, almost a road, Mama Root pushed her hat back, tilted up her chin, squinted, and said, "Very soon, Green Eyes. Look up ahead!"

Green Eyes skipped off to the side, the better to see around the tall men who marched in front of her. The road continued to widen, and in the hazy distance she saw a pair of stone towers that reached to the sky. Tiny spots floated lazily above their tops, and she had to squint very hard before she finally decided the spots were eagles.

"What is that? What are they?"

Mama Root took off her hat and fanned herself. Even with the clouds—which never seemed to spit rain, only thicken and then slowly thin and vanish away—the day was hot. She stared at the distant pillars and said, "That is the Mouth of the Gods. Inside is the Stairway of Heaven."

Green Eyes goggled at the approaching peaks. "Do the Gods live there?"

"The Gods live everywhere, dear, but I don't think they live *exactly* there any longer. It is an ancient canyon, and when we have passed through it, you will look down on the Valley of Tollan."

Green Eyes clapped her hands together. "Oh, good! How soon, Mama Root? How soon?"

Mama Root smiled. "Not long," she said. "The Mouth is very tall, but the stairs not as high, and we should come to the other side by dusk at the latest. Probably earlier, if nothing happens to delay the march."

But as they drew closer, Green Eyes saw a small structure off to the right of the canyon entrance, made of stone and covered with brightly painted shapes. As they came up to it, she saw a broad, high stone table, its thick, flat top supported by four snarling serpents of such realistic ferocity that she scuttled back to Mama Root and hid herself in her skirts.

Two priests came out of the stone house, which Green Eyes now realized was a temple of some sort. "Is that where the Gods live?" she asked in wonderment.

"Some do, sometimes," Mama Root said. "Watch now."

The ceremony took almost an hour. Lord Golden Hand sacrificed a pig on the table, with the help of the priests. The pig's blood gushed and drained down the sides of the stone to basins designed to catch it. Then the priests strode out onto the road, carrying long, shell-shaped things, raised them, and blew on them. A sound like the moans of a giant Jaguar filled the air and echoed vanishingly up the dark incline.

Thoroughly impressed, Green Eyes held on to Mama Root's hand as they entered the canyon mouth. It was instantly cooler, almost chilly, for the sun did not shine all the way to the canyon floor.

The way sloped steeply upward—and in places the stone itself had been carved into broad steps. Where this occurred, the way was usually guarded by a pair of stone figures, always fanged, always fearsome.

The sound of their footsteps echoed eerily off the bleak and naked walls. Hardly anybody spoke. Once, somebody laughed aloud, but the sound was lonely, and it trailed off quickly.

The light in the narrow vertical notch at the far end slowly changed from white to blue to gold as they approached it. Green Eyes became aware of a stir ahead, and quickened her pace. And so Mama Root was behind her, breath heavy, hurrying to catch up, when Green Eyes Blue reached the final step on the Stairway to Heaven, stepped out upon the Tongue of the Sky, and beheld the vast and changeless splendor of Tollan, the City of the Gods, for the first time.

Chapter Seven

1

The Tongue of the Gods was a broad, flat ledge that jutted out from the narrow cleft at the top of the stairs, ringed with a low stone wall. Green Eyes approached the outer rim of the ledge, her eyes wide with fright, her heart fluttering so badly she pressed both fists against her breastbone to hold it still.

Beneath the ledge a sheer cliff fell away endlessly until it vanished into the green and distant mists far below. Slowly, she lifted her gaze, and felt herself being drawn out into the vast, hazy expanse that was the stone and air and earth of the Valley of the Gods.

"Here, little one, take my hand," a clear voice trilled. She looked up and saw Golden Hand's smiling features and his outstretched fingers.

Shyly she put her hand in his. He led her forward, almost to the low wall, but she dug in her heels and wouldn't approach any closer.

"What's the matter, Green Eyes? Does it scare you?"

Mama Root bustled up from behind. "Of course it does, Lord. It would scare you, too, if all you'd ever seen was a tiny village at the side of the river, and the highest seat you'd ever perched on was the branches of a tree."

She looked down at Green Eyes's shining face. "Don't be frightened, dear. I won't let you fall. Come . . ." She took Green Eyes's other hand. She and Golden Hand exchanged amused glances above Green Eyes's head as they chivvied her to the edge of the parapet. Then all of them stood silent for a long moment, drinking in the glory that was Tollan at the pinnacle of her splendor.

On the left and the right loomed the dark volcanic peaks of the mountains of Tlaloc, home of the Lord of Storms, the

Fallen One, and his many minions. Above them floated eagles and hawks, slipping and drifting like specks of shining dust in the hot updrafts of the evening. These mighty piles of stone, their shoulders clothed with ancient trees, slid down to cup the valley between their feet. To their left, in the west, the sun bulged and swelled as it squatted upon the highest of hills. Fantastic streaks of red and gold painted a thick band of clouds that marked the limits of the World Above.

"Look," Golden Hand said, pointing. "See my city and your new home."

Her gaze followed his outstretched finger. At first she didn't understand what she was looking at. The nearest she could come was a stony river beach she'd once seen, where shells had been cracked open, sucked dry, and left in a carpet of shattered pieces that covered the entire bank.

There was a broad apron of green stretching from the feet of the hills toward the center of the valley, but the green vanished as it approached what looked to her like another such riverbank covered with white shells. Three large white lumps stood out of the shells.

With an inner *click!* her mind suddenly made the adjustment for distance and perspective, and she gasped. Those weren't shells. She didn't know what they were, but they were very far away. They must be huge!

"What . . ." she breathed softly.

"Houses, my dear," Mama Root said as if she'd read her thoughts. "Each one is a house, like the ones in your village. Except some of those houses are big enough for everybody in your village to live together."

Green Eyes looked up at her and blinked, then returned to the endless, coruscating spectacle below. Mama Root must be joking with her. Those couldn't be houses. There weren't that many houses in the whole world. There weren't that many *people* in the whole world.

She forced a small laugh to show that she understood the

joke, but it trailed off hollowly. Neither Mama Root nor Golden Hand were smiling. Rather, they seemed transfixed, their features hallowed by the light of the crimson sun, their expressions high and deep and solemn.

Green Eyes couldn't know her own face looked the same, nor did she know it was always thus, even for those who knew Tollan well and loved her. No man or woman could stand upon the Tongue—whether for the first time or the hundredth time—and gaze out across that limitless spectacle without seeing Tollan for what she truly was: the City of the Gods, the Place of the Reeds, where the Middle World and all that was in it had been born out of darkness at the beginning of time.

In vast and inexorable silence the sun continued its journey into night. Overhead the great arc of the sky turned velvety, and stars began to appear. After a time they shook themselves, as if awakening from a dream, and began to descend.

"Tollan," Lord Golden Hand whispered. "Ah, Tollan."

2

A roadway, switchbacked and narrow, had been cut into the living stone beneath the Tongue. As the caravan progressed down it, darkness fell, and Golden Hand ordered torches lit. Green Eyes walked along with Mama Root, desperately clutching her fingers, fearful of the crumbling edges of the road.

As the stars came out, high and hard in the velvet darkness, their light echoing the flickering torches below, it seemed to Green Eyes that she walked through the sky, and a whisper of old dreams touched her.

All about her she heard the clink and rattle of the march, the sliding shuffle of sandals in the dust, the murmur of voices. It was a moment of magic, a yeasty blend of sights and smells and sounds, and the feel of Mama Root's rough hand wrapped around her own.

By the time the party reached the bottom and marched out onto the valley floor, Green Eyes was sleeping soundly, resting in Golden Hand's tireless arms. He continued to cradle her as the camp rose around him, looking down on her sleeping face with a quizzical smile twitching the corner of his lips.

Mama Root materialized out of the shadows at this side. "Chain Coil has our tent ready, Lord. I can take her now."

He raised his head. "She sleeps so sweetly."

Mama Root laughed. "Of course, Lord. She's a little girl. Men have not begun to plague her yet, and so her dreams are peaceful."

Golden Hand eyed her. "Do you hate men so much, Mama?"

She shrugged. "Hate? I might as well hate these eternal hills, or despise the rain. Men are. Women are. We live with what is, not what might be."

"Yes, that is wise. Do you know my plans for her?"

"No, Lord. It isn't my place to speculate on the doings of a great lord like yourself. You are like the mountains or the rain."

He chuckled. "In other words, I am something to be endured."

"Of course, Lord. What other choice do we little ones have but to endure? We are but feeble reflections of your glory."

"Oh, stop it. I doubt you've ever felt like a feeble reflection of anything, Mama. And this little hellcat in my arms, with her God-marked eyes, she's as untamed as the wind or the sunlight on a mountain stream."

"But you intend to tame her, don't you, Lord?"

"With your help, perhaps."

"To what end, Lord?"

He paused. "I'm not sure," he said finally. His eye patch

was a pool of dark shadow, the outlines of the yellow eye shifting and vague upon it. It gave him a sinister look.

"Just a whim, perhaps. An example of why we endure. And what we endure."

"I mean her no harm, Mama Root. I didn't seek her out. Fate and the Gods brought her to me. She was meant for better than the life she had, growing old and wrinkled in some dung-ridden riverside hovel."

"Ah," she replied. "I see it now. How silly of me not to understand. You want her because the Gods gave her to you. And here I thought you bought her for a lump of gold."

"You have a sharp tongue, Mama."

"Perhaps because I have so much to cut, Lord. I'll take her now."

"No. I'll carry her."

"Whatever you wish, Lord."

They weren't friends. But they understood each other well enough.

3

Green Eyes woke early, a charged expectancy running through her bones. She clambered out of her blankets and crept into the gray light of the morning, then slipped around the back of the tent to do her business. Mama Root was still a brown lump emitting soft, bubbling snores.

Though dawn was only a silver promise tincturing the tops of the eastern mountains, the camp was already stirring. Mostly it was slaves and a few guards up and about, but she could feel their excitement as they built fires and saw to the preparations for the resumption of the journey.

She found Chain Coil leaning on his spear, staring dreamily into a freshly lit fire pit.

"Good morning, little one," he said, yawning. "You're up and about early. Where is Mama Root?"

"Still in the tent. She snores."

"Hah. Of course she does. But you shouldn't wander about unattended, you know. Here, stay with me awhile. I'll see you back to your tent later."

"Why shouldn't I go where I please, Coil?"

"Because . . . because . . ." He shook his head. "There are men . . . well, you should ask Mama Root."

"Men? Oh, you mean men who would try to hurt me? Like Old Big Nose and Young Big Nose?"

"Yes, little one, just like that."

"But, Coil, nobody here would do that. They like me. Everybody gives me sugar cane."

Still keeping hold of his spear, he squatted down. "Green Eyes, you can't always be sure of that, even if somebody does give you sugar. Men are not always what they seem. You must always be on your guard."

She sniffed. "That seems an awful way to be."

"Nevertheless, you will have to learn it. Tollan is a great city, but even in Tollan there are evil men."

The mention of Tollan sent her shooting off on a different path entirely. "Oh, Coil, will we get there today? I can't wait. I couldn't see it very well last night, high up in the air. What's it like?"

He grinned. "Tollan is very beautiful, child. White and gold, and everything painted with every color you can imagine."

"I want to see it!"

"You will. We should reach the Road of the Temples by noon today. Of course, by then we will have been in the city proper for a good time. Tollan is very large, Green Eyes. It takes hours just to walk across it."

But Green Eyes couldn't comprehend a village that took hours to cross. It still sounded like some kind of joke to her, the sort of things adults were always saying to children.

"I know," Chain Coil said. "Would you like a ride on my shoulders?"

"Oh, yes." She clapped her hands as he hoisted her up.

4

Six hours later she was riding on his broad back again as he strode down a wide highway paved with stucco and pressed on every side with wonders. Golden Hand and Twisted Tooth were on his right and Mama Root stumping steadily along on his left. Green Eyes held on tightly, her mind overloaded with marvels beyond anything she could have ever imagined. Had she not had the reassuring presence of Mama Root, Golden Hand, and the others nearby, she knew she would have simply closed her eyes, curled up into a little ball, and refused to look at anything at all.

Their party had set out shortly after the first rays of the sun strengthened into a clear, golden light. The road they were on continually widened, cutting straight as an arrow through vast green cornfields that stretched off toward the foothills on either side. She saw hundreds of bent figures laboring away, swinging hoes or squatting, some so distant they looked like stick figures made of twigs.

The ones up close barely looked up as they passed. "Who are those people, Mama Root?"

"Some are farmers, dear. And some are slaves who work in the fields other men own."

"In my village everybody works in his own fields."

"Yes, but things are different here."

"I don't understand."

"We'll talk of it later."

They continued on. Many of the party began to sing. The song was strange to Green Eyes, but everybody seemed to know it. She didn't understand all the words, but it seemed to be about the Gods and the beginning of the Middle World. The words sounded solemn, but the tune was bright and cheerful, and she felt her own spirits bubbling up with it.

Overhead the sun became a burning coin, and their shadows shrank into bobbing circles about their feet. Finally the fields themselves began to vanish, as more and more buildings appeared alongside the road and blocked the view.

Green Eyes had thought the two-story house she'd visited with Mama Root had been impossibly huge, but now she saw it was a hut when compared to the structures now lining the way.

All of these were taller. These buildings came right up to the edge of the road, but showed only a single large doorway, their facades otherwise blank and windowless. But even their broad walls were a spectacle. Great swirling blots of color covered every inch of them. It was as if a rainbow had melted and spilled red, blue, green, purple, gold, and yellow onto them. She saw pictures of Gods and demons and kings and wondrous animals. There were flowers and butterflies and birds whose wings were so real they seemed as if they must take flight from the silent stones.

And the people!

Men and women came and went from these houses in numbers that made Green Eyes dizzy. They spilled out, laughing, chattering, waving greetings at each other or, preoccupied, bound on mysterious tasks with their heads down and their elbows pumping. Hordes of slaves trotted by, their backs slumping beneath loads almost as big as they were.

At one point a palanquin, a brightly painted wooden box, richly draped with dark blue cloths, approached, and Golden Hand stopped.

The palanquin, its long, ornately carved tongues resting on the shoulders of eight blank-faced slaves, stopped also, and Golden Hand walked up to it.

Green Eyes saw a curtain draw quickly aside, and caught a glimpse of some creature whose eyes were impossibly large. A flash of red lips. Golden Hand spoke, then laughed. The curtain dropped shut, and the litter continued on.

"Was that a God?" Green Eyes whispered to Mama Root.

"No. It was a woman who thinks she should marry a God, though," Mama Root replied. Golden Hand caught her words and turned, a strange expression on his face, but Mama Root only laughed.

The buildings lining the road grew so thick and tall, Green Eyes could no longer see any distance ahead. It was like walking through a river canyon when the banks were too far over her head to see above them. And suddenly she found herself thinking of it that way: the road as a river of people, constrained and channeled within fantastically painted banks, flowing endlessly into and out from the heart of the city.

"What do you think of Tollan?" Mama Root asked as a cloud of screaming children swept past.

Green Eyes shook her head. Mama Root nodded and patted her hand. "Well, the best is yet to come."

But Green Eyes couldn't imagine anything more wondrous than what she'd already seen, and so she said nothing.

5

When it finally came, it appeared as a complete surprise. Green Eye's senses, already overwhelmed, had reduced the city to a series of bright, fleeting impressions, salted with the interminable passage of more people than it seemed possible the world could hold. Chain Coil had set her down, and so her line of sight was even more constricted.

Golden Hand called a halt. On either side of the road stood a pair of towering guardians, eyes bulging, fangs dripping, claws gleaming white in the sun. He turned to Green Eyes.

"This is the Gate of the Two Guardians," he said. "Beyond this point is the Sacred Precinct, where I live. We will be home soon. I'm sure you must be ready for a nap, eh?"

She stared at him and shook her head slowly. She had no

idea what he was talking about, but the last thing she wanted was sleep. Already the great, pulsing rhythms of the city were creeping into her bones. Her ears were full of the muted roar of its many voices, her eyes strained by the endless sea of color. She was nearly exhausted, yet she would not have traded this day for anything. And for the first time she saw how small, how grimy and dirty and insignificant her old village was. She felt a twinge of guilt as she thought this. It seemed disloyal somehow.

"I'm going to put you on my shoulders," Golden Hand said. "I want you to see everything."

She nodded, and he scooped her up. A moment later they swept forward, passed the last of the surrounding buildings, and entered the boundless hive that was the Way of the Gods, the heart of the City of Tollan, and the center of the Middle World.

"Ohhh . . ." she said. "Oh, *oh* . . . !"

6

They didn't traverse the entire length of the Way of the Gods, which was probably all to the good. Had Green Eyes been forced to encompass the entirety of it, she might have gone into hysterics.

Golden Hand strode along, describing in a dry, calm voice the impossibilities that loomed on every side.

"Up ahead, on your right, Green Eyes. See how those temples rise in steps, on wide platforms like a stairs for giants? Beyond them is a great plaza, where traders from all over the Middle World gather to transact their business. And of course you can see the Mountain of the Plumed Serpent. Or at least the top of it."

She goggled, trying to understand. Of course it was a mountain. But a mountain unlike any she'd ever seen, infinitely carved, with a wide staircase extending up the sloping front to a flat top, where she saw yet another great building perched, its facade a series of intricately incised columns looking out over the city below.

But huge as the Plumed Serpent's compound was, it paled before the incomprehensible majesty of the structure looming beyond it.

"That is the Mountain of the Sun," Golden Hand told her. "It is the greatest temple in the Middle World, and the holiest. For it is on that precise spot the Middle World was born, and there also is the exact heart of the City of the Gods." For a moment even he sounded impressed. Green Eyes was overwhelmed. That gigantic thing had been made by men? It seemed impossible.

But before she could gather her wits and her tongue to say anything, Golden Hand directed her gaze straight ahead. "And all the way down there, at the end? That is the Mountain of the Moon, which was the first built in the city. It honors the Goddess Herself, who founded our city with Her brother, son, and husband, the Lord of the Dawn."

Green Eyes began to whimper.

"What's the matter, little one?"

"She's tired, Lord. I think this has all been too much for her. She needs to lie down and close her eyes. It's not much farther to your house, is it?"

"Eh? No, not at all. We're behind the Plumed Serpent compound, near the gates of the Council Palace. How did you know? Have you been to the city before?"

"Many times, Lord. Starting a long, long time ago."

He sighed. "Nothing is long when measured against the lifetime of Tollan," he said.

She only eyed him, her gaze enigmatic, and said nothing.

7

Despite her most vigorous efforts, Green Eyes had fallen

into a doze in Golden Hand's arms by the time they reached the tall, graceful outer walls of his home near the rear of the Serpent compound, hard by the pyramid itself, now lying under its cool afternoon shadow.

The caravan had been falling apart behind them for a good while as factors, junior traders, guards, and slaves peeled away to pursue the necessary business of finalizing their long journey, under the watchful eye and shouted orders of Twisted Tooth.

By the time they stood before the great doorway of his home, Golden Hand's party had shrunk to only a handful: himself, Green Eyes, Twisted Tooth, Mama Root, a couple of guards, and his personal body slaves.

The doorway loomed before him, dark and cool, and then a pale figure moved within it. He stopped and waited for her to come forth. She moved to greet him. Her robe was of the purest, whitest, most expensive weaving imported from the far south. It trailed out behind her as if it were sewn of clouds. Her face was long and narrow and slanted with mysterious shadows, matching her eyes, which seemed to glow with serene welcome.

"My son. Welcome back to your home at last," she said. Her voice was soft and cultured, its accents the pure, liquid trill achieved only by those born in the city, and then only after countless generations of refinement. She paused, looked at the girl in Golden Hand's arms, and said, "What's this? Is she hurt?"

"No, Mother, nothing like that."

"Then why are you carrying her?"

"She's tired."

She seemed about to say something. But she didn't. Her gaze swept over the rest of the group.

Golden Hand turned and passed Green Eyes to Twisted Tooth. "Mother," Golden Hand said, "this is Mama Root. She is the girl's guardian and teacher. I have hired her to watch over this girl, whose name is Green Eyes Blue. Mama Root, this is my mother, the Princess Gentle Dawn."

Mama Root bowed slightly. After a moment's hesitation, Gentle Dawn returned the gesture. Then, with only the barest flicker of her eyelids, she dismissed the old woman and turned back to her son. "I don't understand," she said simply.

"Let's go inside where it's cooler," Golden Hand said. "I'll explain later. Is my father here?"

Gentle Dawn made a graceful, welcoming gesture with her right hand as she stepped to the side, bidding the party to enter. They passed through the doorway and found themselves in a high room about twenty feet square. A skylight had been let into the poles and stucco of the roof, through which flowed a bright spill of light that illuminated a beautifully carved stone catch basin brimming with rainwater.

Drifting ahead, Gentle Dawn led them through more chambers, some dark, some bright with bands of colored pictures running along the stucco floors, around the doorways, and along the ceilings.

Finally they entered a deep, wide chamber, this one brightly illuminated by a flood of sunlight pouring in from the back, which was columned but otherwise open to a broad, square atrium. The floor of the atrium was of painted stucco, and in its center was an altar and a replica of the Moon Pyramid that stood as high as a tall man.

On the top of this miniature pyramid was a replica of the Temple of the Moon, and on top of that, the shape of the head of the Goddess Herself.

Mama Root's eyes narrowed at that, but she said nothing.

Scattered about this large room were low platforms made of stone, topped with thick, feathery mattresses. These were covered with fabrics of incomparable softness and richness, obviously the work of the skilled weavers in the south. Mama Root guessed the price of a single one of them would keep a poor family for a year.

The atrium was sunken, rising at its edges in low steps to reach the columned chambers that surrounded it completely, ensuring privacy for the dwellers in the house.

In the rooms across the way, servants worked with brooms and paints, goaded by the overseer of the house. Gentle Dawn sank down on one of the stone divans, and gestured for her son to take another.

A kitchen slave came hurrying into the room bearing a large clay mug brimming over with some kind of fruit juice. He bowed before Golden Hand and presented it to him. Golden Hand took the refreshment and nodded absently. He ignored his mother's invitation to sit, and wandered off toward the atrium, where he paused and watched the servants at work across the way.

"Your messengers arrived only yesterday. I took the liberty of making your rooms ready."

He sipped at his drink and smiled. "Thank you, Mother. Efficient as always. Where did you say Father was?"

"I didn't. But he is where you'd expect, in the Council Chambers. Some sort of important business came up." She shrugged slightly. "Some sort of business always comes up, of course."

Tiny wrinkles appeared at the corners of Golden Hand's eyes. "Well, no matter. I'll see him this evening, no doubt."

His mother sighed, then looked up at him. "Step into the light, my son. Let me have a good look at you."

Grinning, Golden Hand moved to obey. When he came out of the shadows the sun struck him full on, painting gleaming highlights on his long fall of hair, glinting off the bony lines of his naked skull, and making his single black eye sparkle.

"Well, Mother, do I meet with your approval? Am I different, or still the same? It's been almost a year, after all. How time hurries, doesn't it . . ."

"Your poor eye," she said. "Ah, well. You look . . . harder

somehow, Golden Hand. And of course you're still wearing all that strange metal jewelry."

He rattled his bracelets cheerfully. "Am I the only one, Mother? Does anybody else wear it here in the city?"

"Oh, while you were gone, it became all the rage with the younger people. There's not much of it around yet, but everybody who has some wears it. Terribly vulgar, of course. I suppose you brought a great load of it back with you?"

He strolled back inside, draining off the rest of his cup as he came. "Of course I did, Mother. *Great* loads of it. It will make us all very rich."

"Well, yes, to be sure, but we're already very rich now anyway, aren't we?"

He laughed. "Mother, be glad Father and I are here to take care of you. Without us you wouldn't have a bead to your name."

"Certainly I wouldn't, dearest. How could I? Surely you're not saying your old mother should become . . . well, I can't even think of what I should become. Oh, Golden Hand, I'm so glad you're home."

Mama Root thought that underneath that seamless exterior, Gentle Dawn sounded very tired. And maybe just a hint bitter. She wondered what was wrong.

But Golden Hand only laughed, walked over, and kissed his mother on the cheek. He knelt down beside her, took her smooth, unmarked fingers in his own, and smiled up into her face.

"Mother, about the girl."

"Oh, her. I haven't opened all the servants' rooms in your house yet. She and . . . the other one"—her glance drifted lightly across Mama Root—"will just have to wait. If the girl's tired, she can rest out in the atrium for a while. I'll have a sleeping mat rolled out for her."

"Oh, no, Mother, you misunderstand. The girl isn't a slave or a servant. She'll be living with you, her and Mama Root, too. You see, I need you to teach her. She must learn to become a lady, and who better to instruct her than the greatest lady I know?"

Gentle Dawn's eyebrows slowly rose into her smooth forehead. "I beg your pardon, dear? Did I hear you correctly? I am to teach something to that . . . girl? Whatever do you mean?"

Golden Hand seemed oblivious to the warning signals drenching his mother's soft words, but Mama Root heard them quite clearly. She leaned forward a bit.

"I mean," he said patiently, "that you must teach her—her name is Green Eyes Blue, as I said—how to be a lady. You wouldn't want me to marry a little country savage, would you?"

"What?" said Gentle Dawn.

"What?" said Mama Root.

Twisted Tooth only chuckled.

8

Long Fingers reclined on a raised divan in his private reception room. This room also overlooked the atrium, and was a part of one of the four houses of the compound, together with the family house, the house set aside for servants and slaves, and his son's personal household. This house was devoted to family business, both personal and that of the Clan Water Moon, of which he was the titular head.

He was a short, thin man with an oversized, bald head, a great hooked beak of a nose, large, dark eyes, and strong chin that gave his face the impression of greater strength than it really possessed. His voice was deeper than his son's, but just as clear, though now it was husky with drink.

"Father," Golden Hand said as he entered. "I'm back."

The older man looked up. "So I see. And have already heard, I might add. Your mother is very upset."

Golden Hand came over and gracefully lowered himself

to sit cross-legged on a mat near his father's head. "I know. She's made it plain enough."

Long Fingers sipped his ever-present pulque—in this case from a gorgeously painted flagon sculpted in the shape of an alligator's skull. He smacked his lips and sighed. "Your mother has a strong sense of propriety. Only normal, I suppose. That clan of hers is famous for producing prigs. Not that I mind. Her indisputable rectitude provides a fine cover for my own sad lapses." He raised his mug and sipped again.

"Have you seen the girl yet?"

His father shook his head. "No, I thought I'd better talk with you first, before deciding what to do about your mother. She still thinks of you as a boy, son. And a wild boy at that. But she is a mother, and all mothers have that particular weakness. I don't. I know you haven't been a boy for a long time. Which leads to my next question."

Golden Hand grinned. "The answer to which, Father, is contained in my previous question of you. You say you haven't seen her. I won't bore you with exhaustive descriptions. Suffice it to say that her right eye is green, and her left one blue."

The shadows crawled slowly. The flame in the single oil lamp resting on a stand behind Long Fingers's couch flickered in a sudden draft. The old man lifted his cup and drained it.

"I see," he said. "Pity."

"What's the pity, Father?"

"That you couldn't have found her here. In the city. Preferably in one of the Eighteen Families."

"Surely, Father. Of course, had she been in any of those places, others might have found her as well."

"Yes. There is that." He paused, looked around, then shouted suddenly, "Fat Dog! More pulque!"

The two men waited in silence, wrapped in the shifting gloom and their own thoughts, until the servant had replenished Long Finger's cup and departed.

"Tell me all about it," Long Fingers said finally.

Golden Hand related at length the strange tale of his acquiring of Green Eyes. When he was done, his father groaned softly, and shifted himself into an upright position on his seat.

"You didn't seek her. She came to you."

Golden Hand nodded. "In a roundabout way, yes."

"And with her came the knife."

"Yes, sir."

"Did you perform the correct rituals over the old bandit's body? Nobody can say you stole the knife from him? Everything was properly done?"

"My own priest directed the ritual. The Jaguar Lord Himself appeared to bless the proceedings."

"Lots of witnesses to that, I presume?"

"Yes, Father. I was careful."

"And the brigand's son? You whipped him into the forests?"

"Yes, sir."

"Probably a mistake. You should have had him strangled. You always did have that odd streak of mercy in you. Probably from your mother's side."

Golden Hand didn't say anything to that. His father fell silent again for a time. Finally he leaned forward, his eyes seeking his son's face.

"It was well done. The girl and the knife. I believe any unbiased observer would have to say it was the will of the Gods that brought her to you. And the knife, given by the Old Ones to the girl in the heart of an Old Place, well, I can't see any other interpretation than that it must be the symbol and affirmation of what she must truly be."

"Such was my own thought as well, Father."

Long Fingers tapped the side of his mug. It gave off a soft, ringing sound. "Since you've been gone, rumors have arisen. It is said that King Thunder Girdle is giving some consideration to abdicating his throne four years hence, in

favor of his eldest son, Prince Thunder Shield. I have reason
to believe they are more than rumors. The timing would be
propitious—the culmination of the Thirteenth Cycle—and
Thunder Shield would be twenty-six years old. The same
age his father was when he ascended to the throne."

"And the same age I will also be," Golden Hand noted.

"Have you had a chance to talk to anybody yet? Did you
go out into the Serpent compound at all?"

"No. I haven't left the house. I wanted to speak with you
first."

"When you go, you will find that the market for gold has
risen enormously since you left. Your factor's messenger
was sadly not explicit. He said you brought gold, but not
how much."

"I brought back sixty large bags of nuggets, Father. All
pure. One of the nuggets is as big as my head."

For the first time since he'd returned, Golden Hand saw
his father's thin smile. "I believe we should put it into the
markets slowly, to maintain the price. If we're careful it
might take a year or so, but at the end, we will double our
personal wealth."

"I think we can move more quickly than that."

"Son, I know you are eager, but pay heed to an old
trader's advice. If we sell too quickly, we'll glut the market
and depress the price."

"Normally, I'd agree with you, Father. But if the buyers
should come to believe this is all the gold there is, they
might still pay top price for it."

His father stared at him, the candlelight caught in his dark
eyes like chained sparks. "You didn't," he said slowly.

"Yes, Father, I did. I made agreements with all the Dog
Ear mines to supply only the Clan of the Water Moon with
their gold."

"Agreements. What do the Dog Ears care for agreements?"

"Something, I hope. I took firstborn sons as pledges of

performance from each man I contracted with. I brought back eight hostages. We'll have to find room for them some-where—actually, I promised to see them educated here in the city—but it will be worth it. One could say those boys are . . . worth their weight in gold."

His father burst out laughing. He hacked and cackled and finally ran down into a series of gurgling coughs that Golden Hand had to pound him on the back to stop.

"Sorry. I'll speak to your mother. We'll turn your little wood sprite into something suitable. Does this . . . Green Eyes have anything to recommend her beyond her God-marks?"

"Actually, Father," Golden Hand said, "she's quite won-derful."

Long Fingers's eyebrows rose again, but he let it pass. Surely he must be mistaken. His son couldn't have fallen in *love* with this country bumpkin?

9

Summer was yielding to fall. Nights fell earlier, and sharp, bitter winds began to blow.

On this night the stars were washed dull and flat by a thin layer of haze. A horned moon leered blearily above the tow-ers that gave onto the Mouth of the Gods.

Inside the small temple at the roadside, the two resident priests had barred their door and reclined at their ease before a crackling fire pit. There was a large clay pot of pulque near at hand, and on the edge of the fire, resting in a sizzling bed of coals, the meat of a tortoise steamed in its own upended shell. The rich smell of the meat mingled with the smoke ris-ing through the hole in the roof.

The aroma of the cooking meat was surprisingly sweet. The first priest, a short, very fat man with permanently greasy lips, said, "Smells good. Maybe that farmer wasn't lying when he said he'd caught it fresh this morning. I can't imagine where he found it, though. You just don't see them that big around these parts anymore."

The other priest, as thin as his brother was fat, shrugged and scooped up another gourd of pulque. "He'd know better than to give spoiled meat to the Gods. He'd curse himself even before he entered the city. You saw the blood when we cut its throat. Looked fine to me."

The wind outside their snug room suddenly rose, twisted the plume of smoke, carrying with it the distant mournful howl of coyotes.

They glanced at each other and grinned uneasily. "Smells like storms coming," the fat one remarked.

"Getting time for it," the thin one said. "You barred the door?"

"Yes."

"Then let's see if that turtle's ready yet."

Outside, a thin figure completely muffled in a shapeless black robe, with the hood pulled down so that only his eyes were visible, lurched down the center of the road. The robe whipped and billowed in the wind, so that it was hard to make out any details about this lone wanderer, except that his back was hunched and strangely twisted, and he limped off his left leg.

These deformities resulted in the peculiar and distinctive sound he made as he struggled along, dragging one sandal in the dust. *Ssss-flap. Ssss-flap.* As the traveler drew closer to the temple, his path angled toward it. After a few moments it became evident the temple door was not his goal. He paused before the table altar in front of the temple and stood motionless for a long time.

Had the wind been lower, or perhaps the coyotes not so loud and persistent, one might have been able to hear whatever it was he whispered as he stood at the altar. At any rate, his misshapen body shook with the intensity of the words he snuffled and muttered.

After a while he completed the prayers he'd meant to pray and he limped back to the road. The light of the moon had turned rancid, a clotted yellow color like spoiled cream. That malign light gleamed down on him, but it drew reflection only from his eyes, which gleamed like the eyes of a cat in the weird, luminous night.

He crossed between the two towers and entered the darkness of the Mouth and was soon swallowed. Had one of the priests come out and listened, all he would have heard was the fading shuffle of laborious stride: *Ssss-flap. Ssss-flap.*

And so it was that in sickly light and mournful cries, sanctified before a dead altar, blown by an ill wind, did something broken and remade return to Tollan, City of the Gods, as the brightness of that summer ebbed away.

BOOK TWO

—◦◦◦—

Tollan

" 'Tis the men, not the houses, that make the city."
—Thomas Fuller, M.D.
Gnomologia

"A great city—a great solitude."
—English proverb

Chapter Eight

1

"Ouch!" Green Eyes stared in dismay at the bead of blood welling up on the meat of her thumb. Automatically, she swiped the offending digit across the hem of her white skirt, leaving a bright streak of red.

Seated on one of the atrium's lower steps, Gentle Dusk, the eldest of Gentle Dawn's two daughters, looked up from her own stitch work and made a disgusted face.

"You are such a hopeless beast, Bump Face. Look at you. First you are clumsy, then you are stupid, and finally you are dirty. Do you wipe your bum on your skirt, too?"

Gentle Dusk was four years older than Green Eyes, and her younger sister, Gentle Moon, was two.

Green Eyes looked down at the cloth she'd been working on. Her cheeks burned. The finely polished bone needle she'd been using was tipped with red. She threw it down, trailing a streamer of blue thread. Her thumb was still bleeding. Reflexively, she started to wipe it again, then stopped and popped it into her mouth.

"Oh, look, Dusk," Moon said. "Now Bump Face is angry. She's sucking her thumb like a baby, and look how she pooches out her lip. Just like a real lady. Oh, our Bump Face is such a *perfect* lady now, isn't she? Mother will be *so* pleased."

Green Eyes flung the scrap of cloth aside and leaped to her feet, the high, evil sound of their laughter ringing in her ears.

"Don't call me that!"

"Don't call you what? Bump Face? But it's your little name, dear. We gave it to you. Don't they have names in your dreary village?"

Green Eyes faced them, her fists clenched so hard her

arms quivered. "My name is Green Eyes! Why can't you call me by my real name? Why do you hate me so?"

The two girls, both of them near replicas of their smooth, haughty mother, eyed each other in perfect complicity.

Dusk raised her chin and peered down her nose. "But, Bump Face, we don't hate you. How could we? It would be like hating a dog, or a slave. And that's all you really are, just a slave."

Green Eyes ground her teeth together. Not for the first time she wished she had her old bow in her hands again. From this distance she could shoot an arrow into Dusk's supercilious right eye without a second thought.

"I'm not a slave!"

"But you are, Bump Face. Golden Hand bought you. What else could you be?"

Hot tears burned in her eyes. The words exploded out of her mouth before she could stop them. *"Then a slave is going to marry your brother!"*

It immediately silenced them. Their dark eyes clicked toward each other, then away. Green Eyes felt a sick kind of triumph as she watched their silence. But it didn't last.

Dusk put aside her sewing and stared at her, her stubborn features not giving an inch. Her voice was as cold as the wind that whipped gray clouds across the square of sky above the atrium.

"Mother says our brother will come to his senses. She says that you've bewitched him somehow, or that some spirit demon has stolen his mind. But he will come to his senses one day, when he sees what a disgusting little savage you really are."

Green Eyes turned and ran.

2

"Oh, Mama Root. I hate them. I *hate* them!"

Mama Root was sitting in one of the kitchen rooms, rolling out tortillas. The room, unlike most of the other rooms in the great house, was so hot sweat dripped down the old woman's cheeks.

Ever since the rains of the late summer had ended, Green Eyes had learned she could usually find the old woman here, or in one of the other kitchens. If the sun was at its peak, it was usually warm enough, but if there were clouds, the big house grew so cold Mama Root said her bones ached like bad teeth. Green Eyes could understand. She hated the cold, too. Even at their best, the weathers of Tollan were far cooler and drier than the unending humid heat of her old home.

It was in this house Green Eyes had recently discovered a new and very unlikable thing. She'd awakened one particularly frigid morning, and when she'd gone, teeth chattering, to draw a gourd of water from one of the stone catch basins, she'd found the water covered with a filmy white skin, so hard it had clicked like a stone when she tapped her fingernails on it. Her first thought was that the sisters had worked some kind of black witchcraft to keep her from drinking, and she'd run back and dragged Mama Root from her bed.

"It's called ice, dear," the old woman told her. "When it gets cold enough, water thickens and becomes hard." She paused, musing. "Once, when I journeyed far to the north, I saw a lake in the high mountains where the ice was thick enough to walk on. And I saw snow . . . but that's another story."

Green Eyes listened with half her mind. Mama Root had so many stories, and some of them were so strange and fantastic Green Eyes didn't know whether she was joking or not. She eyed the ice dubiously. "Will it hurt me?" she asked.

Mama Root snorted. "No, dear," she said, and struck out with one brown fist. The ice shattered into small pieces that bobbed like bits of cork on the water. "Dip your gourd. It will be nice and cold."

But Mama Root had decided her days of walking on icy

lakes were behind her, because she sought the comforting warmth of the kitchens at every opportunity. Now she turned and armed sweat off her broad brow. Her hair seemed grayer of late, her eyebrows whiter, and sometimes Green Eyes worried about her.

"Come here, dearest," Mama Root said, and held out her arms. Since that refuge was the reason Green Eyes had come running to the kitchens in the first place, she didn't hesitate. She launched herself in the old woman's embrace with such force she almost knocked her over.

"Whoof! My goodness, you're growing, dear. That's all right, snuggle up. And your hair! It's so nice and smooth now. You look like a real little lady."

This observation set Green Eyes off into a fresh cascade of tears, and it took Mama Root several minutes to soothe her again.

"Now tell Mama all about it," she said. "It's all right. Just tell me, and I'll make it better."

Mama Root was seated on a straw mat, cross-legged beside the stone metate on which she ground corn into meal for tortillas. She moved over a bit and stretched out her legs toward the fire, wiggling her bare toes as she did so.

"Ah, that's good," she said. She hugged Green Eyes, whose fierce howls had now subsided into a muted series of sniffles.

"Tell me all about it, daughter," she said.

Green Eyes did. Because her head was resting on Mama Root's soft, heavy breasts, she couldn't see the way the old woman's face grew stonier as she told her tale.

"I asked them why they hate me," Green Eyes said, "but I know. It's because Golden Hand says he's going to marry me. They're just jealous."

Though Mama Root's expression had become as inviting as massed thunderclouds, her voice was unruffled.

"Yes, dear, they are jealous. Of course they are. Look at how they must see you. They have been the darlings of the family, the center of their mother's love and attention. They worship their big brother. And then you come along, and you are so very different from them. You are everything they've been told they must not be. You aren't ladylike. Don't you think sometimes they must want to burst into song, or run barefoot through the dust? But they can't. They must behave as women are supposed to behave. As they are expected to behave. Or they won't find husbands. They won't please men. Yet they are still girls. How they must hate you for what you are."

This was not precisely the kind of soothing Green Eyes was hoping for. She'd come to Mama Root in search of vengeance, a stout arm raised in her defense. Instead, to her surprise, she found herself suddenly feeling sorry for Dusk and Moon.

She pulled at her lower lip. "Well, maybe. But they hate me, too. They call me names, and pinch me when nobody is looking and make fun of me. They call me Bump Face!"

"They do? Bump Face, eh? Green Eyes, have you looked at yourself in the reflection of the water basins?"

"Yes . . ."

"And your face. Is it bumpy?"

"I don't think so," Green Eyes replied. "There's that little teeny scar by my eye, but I don't see any bumps."

"So are Moon and Dusk speaking the truth when they call you that name?"

"Well . . . I guess not."

"Very good. Now, what if your face was bumpy. What then?"

Green Eyes shifted uncertainly. A bit of familiar irritation with Mama Root was starting to nag at her. It was always like this lately. Every time she went to the old woman for comfort, she got a lesson instead. And not always a very comforting lesson.

"I don't understand."

"If your face had bumps on it, and they called you Bump Face, would it be true?"

"I guess it would."

"So that wouldn't be any reason to get upset either, would it? If you say the sky is blue, the sky doesn't mind. Because the sky *is* blue. And if you say I'm old and getting far too fat, I don't mind because that is true also."

Green Eyes didn't like the direction the conversation was taking. Everything Mama Root said *sounded* true, but it didn't *feel* true. Yet she didn't know the words to explain what she wanted to say.

"But what you're saying is that if something isn't true, it shouldn't bother me, because it's a lie? And if it is true, it shouldn't bother me, because it's the truth?"

Mama Root nuzzled her cheek. "Yes, dear."

She sighed. "Well, all that may be right, but it doesn't make me feel any better."

"Hah. Well, if you think on it awhile, until you really understand it, you'll find that it will make you feel better. Because if you stop and *think* every time something like this happens, you'll discover that most people don't understand what they are actually saying. It's because most people are stupid, and don't like to think much at all. But you'll understand, and you'll feel better because you do."

It suddenly struck Green Eyes what bothered her so much. "But, Mama, it doesn't matter *what* they say, it's *why* they say it. They call me Bump Face because they think it will hurt me. And they want to hurt me because they hate me. And that *does* hurt."

"Ah." Mama Root patted her on the back. "So you have learned something. If you stop and think about the truth of what you see and hear, then you may discover the truth beneath the truth. And that can be very valuable. Did you know that is the way men often think? With their minds instead of their hearts? They never think we poor women can think that way, because . . . well, because we are women. They say our minds can't work as well as theirs can. That we can't see the truth as clearly as they can."

"But you can, Mama Root."

"Yes, dear, I can. And so can you. If you listen to me carefully, and try to understand what I'm telling you, then you can think just as well as I do. Or as well as any man can think."

Green Eyes pushed herself away from Mama Root. "Mama, do I want to think like a man?"

"Yes, you do."

Green Eyes stared at her for a long time. Finally, Mama Root said, "What are you thinking about, dear?"

"I'm trying to see if there's truth hidden beneath your truth."

"Hah ah!" Mama Root reached forward, took Green Eyes's head between her two hands, pulled her forward, and planted a wet, sloppy kiss on her forehead.

"You're learning, my dear. You're learning."

Green Eyes found that she was feeling much better. "I guess I'll go back and work on my sewing."

"Go get a clean skirt, though. Leave that one and I'll wash out the blood for you."

"Thank you, Mama." Green Eyes let her gaze drift to the fire. She stared into it for several moments. "I still wish they didn't treat me the way they do, though."

Mama Root gave her a cheerful swat on the fanny. "Off with you, girl. As for the rest, I'll see what I can do."

"You will?"

"I will."

3

Prince Long Fingers didn't return home from the Council Chambers until late, and when he did, he found Mama Root waiting for him in his reception room.

She had lit the oil lamp and seated herself on one of the stone divans next to it. He didn't notice her when he came into the room, and when he did, he inhaled sharply. In that light her face seemed impossibly ancient and unbearably hard. It reminded him of some of the things he'd seen imported from the south, bits of rough-carved rock, the visages of Gods so old they were now forgotten. It was a stony face, serene it its own bitterness, offering nothing but the judgments of eternity, and in that flickering instant, her face frightened him to the depths of his mortal being.

"Ah. Mama Root. I'm sorry, you startled me."

He went to his own divan; automatically reaching for the mug of pulque his body slave had left for his return. He always drank a full mug before going to bed. Without it, he found it difficult to sleep all the way through the night.

"Prince Long Fingers," she said. He had the strangest feeling that only her lips moved, and that the rest of her was immobile rock. He shook his head slightly and swallowed a good mouthful of pulque.

The room was cold and silent, except for the faint hissing pop of the oil lamp. The night wind had died away. Out through the columns toward the atrium he could see a band of stars above the rooftop—high, green, distant. The uncaring eyes of the Gods. He shivered, not entirely sure if it was because of the chill or something else.

"Is there something you wanted, Mama?" he said at last.

"Yes, Lord, there is. I want to discuss Green Eyes with you."

He fluttered his fingers. "Go on."

Slowly, with no emotion, she related what Green Eyes had told her.

"Well? What do you want me to do about it?" Long Fingers said. "This is women's business, Mama Root. My wife is in charge of the girl and her education. Surely you wouldn't question the Princess Gentle Dawn as to how to teach the girl to become a lady?"

"Lord, I don't blame your daughters. They only follow their mother. Oh, I don't say she tells them to mistreat Green Eyes, but they are her children, and they are sensitive to her true feelings. She can hide those feelings from you. Perhaps she even hides them from herself. But she can't hide them from her girls, and because of that, Green Eyes is miserable."

Long Fingers began to feel uncomfortable. He'd always been somewhat in awe of his wife, though he privately chuckled at her stiff-necked probity. But to discuss her with an ancient serving woman, in secret, as Gentle Dawn slept under the same roof, made him feel vaguely nervous. And so he spoke with more sharpness than he might have.

"How dare you? What can an old country woman like you know of the thoughts of a great lady like the Princess Gentle Dawn?"

Mama Root smiled grimly and raised her head. Her eyes gleamed in the lamplight. "I know this, Lord. When Green Eyes Blue marries your son, she will become the head of his household. And when you die, she will be the head of what remains of your household too. Those two girls will be in her charge, unless they are married off by then. And your wife will be dependent upon Green Eyes's kindness for whatever she may have. So your wife, though she is without a doubt a great lady, is also a stupid one. She isn't thinking with her head, but her heart. She is frightened of Green Eyes, and she isn't accustomed to being frightened. So she turns her fear into anger at the cause of her fright. In her muddled way, she thinks that if Green Eyes becomes too unhappy, then Green Eyes will go away, and the marriage will never happen. And your daughters sense her hopes, even if she never says a word."

Long Fingers stared at her, his jaws slowly dropping. "Maybe she's right, old woman. Maybe this . . . girl won't achieve her desire to marry my son."

"Hah. That girl has only one desire in the whole world, Lord. And that is to leave you, your son, your daughters, and your miserable wife behind forever, and return to the village from which she was stolen. You speak of *her* desires, Lord, as if she had any choice. Would you like me to take her away? I can do that. We could be gone tonight, and then Green Eyes would no longer be a problem to anyone here."

"Ah. Ah . . ."

"Well, Lord?"

"Of course she can't leave. My son is going to marry her. And while I may not approve of everything my son wishes to do, I must respect—"

Her voice cut through his like a sharp blade. "You want it too, Lord. She will be his first wife. You hope in secret that one day she will be something else, too. And you would kill me to keep me from stopping that, wouldn't you?

Long Fingers felt as if she were slapping him back and forth across the cheeks, though she hadn't moved a muscle. He tried to speak, stopped, drained his cup, and quickly refilled it. She watched him silently.

"I will offer you a trade, Lord. Something for something. A deal. You understand deals, don't you?"

He nodded, as fascinated as a rabbit before a snake. Part of him was offended, another part appalled, but a third waited only to see what this amazing woman would say next.

"Very well. Speak to your wife. Explain the truth of life to her. Explain her own self-interest to her. She doesn't understand your schemes. You don't need to explain *them* to her, but make her see what she must do, and how she must do it. She doesn't need Green Eyes as an enemy. If she succeeds in turning the girl into her enemy, she will only destroy everything she holds dear. You know it is true."

"But . . . how could you . . . you can't *know* . . ."

Mama Root's voice ground on, inexorable as an avalanche. "Do you want my part of the bargain, Lord? If so, all you need to do is say yes."

Despite himself, Long Fingers heard his tongue shape the word.

"Good. You have the knife in the house, I believe?"

"What knife?"

"The knife that once belonged to Green Eyes. That was stolen from her by thieves, and taken from the dead body of a thief by your son. Do you have that knife?"

"Um . . . yes. It is here."

"It is hidden in darkness, then."

"Yes."

"Take it out. Let it drink of the sun's light."

"What?"

"It has lain in darkness for a long time. It has grown weak. Now it is thirsty. Feed it, Lord. Feed it the power of the sun. If you do that, when the time comes, it will serve you and your house well. This is my prophesy. *Ignore it at your peril.*"

Long Fingers realized that the fine hairs on his wrinkled forearms were standing up straight. "You are a witch," he whispered finally.

"No, only an old woman. A very old woman, Lord. And one who is tired from all the deal making she has just done."

Just like that, the eerie, creeping sensation of being in the presence of something dark and powerful vanished, and Prince Long Fingers blinked. Now he saw her as she described herself—small, wrinkled, sagging, slumped. Her eyes twinkled out of the darkness at him. A sudden wave of good feeling swept over him, and he chuckled.

"Well, Mama Root, I'll see what I can do. What you say makes sense."

She stood up. "Thank you, Lord. And with your leave, I'll see myself to my bed."

He dipped another gourd of liquor. For some reason he felt even thirstier than usual.

"Sleep well, Mama. You know something?"

"What's that?"

"Send me to the Dark World if I don't enjoy talking with you. You're not like any woman I've ever known."

"What do you mean?"

He grasped for it. "Well, you think . . . like a man. Do you know that?"

She smiled. "Yes, Lord, I do."

4

Golden Hand entered his father's reception room in the middle of the morning. He was wearing rough clothes, and his hair was bound into a tail above his freshly shaven scalp, rather than falling free as was his usual wont in the city.

Long Fingers was seated on a divan, surrounded by accountants and scribes who squatted on mats in a semicircle before him. One of the accountants was running long, knotted strings through his fingers, and announcing the totals as he went in a soft, singsong voice.

Golden Hand came over and stood behind his father where he could watch and listen. The merchants of Tollan used a simple, yet extremely flexible system of accounting that involved different colors of string into which were tied knots of varying types and sizes. By combining diverse sorts of colors, lengths, and knots, the accountants could keep track of very large quantities at any level from the huge to the individual.

The scribes were somewhat different—they were more painters than writers, for the principal written language of Tollan was a glyphic one, capable of reasonable precision, but not as clearly defined as was the numbering system.

There was also a priestly glyphic system based on the Language of Hands, a secret sign language known only to the scribes of the Inner Temples and the highest priests, which was rendered by pictures that resembled flowers. These pictures denoted the various hand and finger positions. This language, both written and signed, was said to be more precise than the common one in general, non-religious use, which was only fitting. It was used to maintain a continuous record of the words of the Gods Themselves, and the secrets of Their priests. Neither Long Fingers nor Golden Hand knew anything about this language, since the penalty for revealing it beyond the Inner Temples, or using it outside their confines, was lingering and painful death.

Golden Hand, like any master trader, could read the knots as quickly and easily as the accountants. He stood with his head tilted and eyes squinted, leaning forward slightly, his ring-bedecked right hand resting lightly on his father's shoulder as he watched the fingers flying up and down the knots.

"Look there," he said. "The yields from our northern fields are down almost a tenth from the last harvest."

His father nodded. "Yes, I see that."

"Hm. Those are the oldest fields we have. They've been in our hands almost since the beginning of the Water Moon Clan. And they've been our soundest and most reliable producers. I wonder what happened?"

One of the scribes looked up. "Lord, I have a report from the chief overseer of that district."

"Well, go on," Golden Hand said.

The scribe sifted through a stack of very thin, flexible panels of wood. The making of this "paper" was extremely complicated and involved a great deal of hand labor. There was a compound of artisans in the foreign merchants' barrio that specialized in its manufacture, using techniques they'd brought down from a far northern country where men lived in adobe caves high in the mountains. Those men were strange—it was said they believed the world was created by a coyote, and rode on the back of a great turtle. They were savage, of course, but since they had a monopoly on the techniques used to make the writing boards, it was said they were very rich savages.

The writing boards were bound into stacks by using leather cords threaded through holes punched along the edges of the boards. The boards were so delicate they would dissolve into mush even if only left out in the rain, but if properly handled they would last for years. Nevertheless it took many scribes to recopy old boards onto new ones. Golden Hand had often tried to think of some way to get a piece of that business, but so far he'd been unable to break the iron hold of the Guild of Scribes, which had strong connections within the Great Temples.

The scribe shuffled through his boards with delicate, practiced ease, found the one he was looking for, and began to read.

"The overseer reported there were two breaks in tributary aqueducts leading from the main aqueduct during the spring planting season. As a result, some of the seedling maize didn't receive enough water during the critical early growing period, and produced both stunted stalks and shriveled ears."

"Ah," Golden Hand said.

His father glanced up at him. "I've been up there for a look around myself. You can't leave everything to the overseers. Anyway, I'm not entirely convinced that it was only the fault of the aqueduct breaks. Some of those fields got quite enough water, and yet still produced undersized ears. The plants looked fine, but the ears were bad. It makes me wonder."

"Wonder what, Father?"

Long Fingers shrugged uncomfortably. "It's almost as if the ground itself was cursed. It happened in spotty patches, not in entire fields. I'm considering seeking help from the temples. We keep up our sacrifices and contributions, of course, but perhaps the Gods are sending us a hint. Maybe we've been remiss in some way we don't know about."

Golden Hand nodded. "An excellent idea, Father. And if more is required, we can certainly afford it." He tipped his head toward the accountants, whose fingers were still working busily on their brightly colored strings.

"Our new gold business has been very good."

His father smiled. "Yes, I'm happy to say you were right. Parading those boy hostages throughout all the temples was an excellent idea. Especially when you explained to everybody who would listen who they were, and what they were held in hostage for."

Golden Hand's dark cheeks flushed slightly. It wasn't often his father praised him, especially in front of witnesses. "Thank you, Father."

But then Long Fingers's eyebrows crooked in a disapproving glance, "Of course, it appears the single biggest customer for these golden trinkets is you, my own son. Must you wear so much of it? When you move, you sound like one of those temple maids, covered with enough strings of shells to start off a major celebration."

Golden Hand shrugged, affirming his father's censure with the soft clink of golden necklaces so thick about his neck and chest he seemed to be made of metal. "If I set the style, others may follow. And if they're buying from us, it seems to me the style ought to be as ostentatious as possible."

"Well . . . perhaps." He glanced at his son again. "Your hair. I'm sorry, I'd forgotten. You've bound it up. Is it today you leave, then?"

"Yes, Father. I'm taking a caravan twice the size of the one from last year, mostly for the gold. We won't visit Pital this year. I'm going straight to the mines. I want to buy some more gold workers, too. The two families I brought back are doing a wonderful job, and they've managed to train some of our slaves and artisans. But their new work isn't quite so fine as the original. So I want to bring more of the skilled ones here, if I can find them."

"Yes, I thought it was a good idea when we discussed it last month. Do you think I'm going daft, boy?"

"Of course not, Father. You're as sharp as you ever were." Golden Hand said this heartily, and he hoped believably, as well. But he'd noted how his father had misremembered his departure, which the older man had known about for weeks now.

Which brought a further twinge of worry.

"Father, can we speak privately before I leave?"

"What? You mean now?"

"Yes."

"Of course." His father turned slightly. "You. All you people. Go away and leave us alone."

While the scribes and accountants scurried to pack up their gear and depart, Long Fingers motioned his son toward the divan opposite. "Would you care for a mug of pulque to speed you on your way?" he said.

"No, thank you, Father." Golden Hand had never developed a taste for the sour, fiery-tasting stuff. Even when it was mixed with honey and water, he seldom drank more than half a measure at a time. Any more made his head spin and he didn't like it when he wasn't in full control of his thoughts.

His father, however, seemed to have no such qualms. He stood up, went over to the ever-present clay jar, and scooped himself a fresh mugful. "Ahh," he said, smacking his lips. "Nothing dries a man out like listening to accountants. After a while they begin to sound like a hive of buzzing bees."

Golden Hand grinned in agreement, waited for his father to take his seat again, then grew serious.

"Father, I've had half my personal fortune moved to your own safe rooms."

His father nodded. No matter how befuddled he might sometimes seem, the talk of money always sobered him. It was this so-far reliable trait that Golden Hand was, somewhat nervously, counting on.

"Before I go, do you have any further ideas, beyond what we've already discussed, as to the proper use of that money?"

Long Fingers sipped his pulque, his forehead wrinkled in concentration. Finally he shook his head. "No, I can't think of anything. You plan to be gone most of three seasons, and arrive back in high summer next year. I will make the appropriate sacrifices at the Great Temples myself, and certain of my most trusted people will handle the bribes at the lesser temples and among the guilds and the free traders. Do not fear, son. I haven't forgotten how to scheme. Or how to keep from getting caught at it."

"Oh, I'm not worried about you, Father. Not in the slightest. Now, are you sure our strategy as far as the Summer Moon is sound?"

Long Fingers didn't hesitate. "Absolutely. My ears are long, and I hear much. The latest word is that, as we guessed he would, Old Thunder Girdle has already begun politicking for Thunder Shield. It's all he thinks about, and he's throwing hard cash down every rat hole he can find that he thinks might aid his cause. But he's besotted, and his son is a dunce. I think his head factor has noticed, too. I have reports there have been mysterious shortages in their accounts. But Thunder Girdle, as far as I know, hasn't taken any notice. So if his factor *is* stealing, he will only grow bolder. Worse, he won't keep *his* eye on business either. He'll be too busy watching his back, and Thunder Girdle's purse."

"If what I've given you isn't enough, tell Twisted Tooth to let you have whatever you need. I'm leaving him here, by the way. I promoted his son, Shank Leg. He's going with me. It's time he had experience running a full caravan. And I want somebody I can trust keeping an eye on my own affairs while I'm gone."

His father peered at him over the rim of his mug. "You mean besides me?"

Golden Hand exhaled sharply in exasperation. "Father, you will have more than enough on your mind. You have our family and our clan to manage, as well as the dickering with the Eighteen. And the Council itself, of course, not to mention your own businesses. And everything else. Twisted Tooth will help. There's no need for you to watch over my affairs, when he can give his full attention to them and leave you free to handle more important things."

"Yes, true. I'm sorry, I didn't mean to take you to task. I sometimes forget you are a grown man now." He sighed. "A grown man soon to be married, in fact. My goodness. Where has the time gone?"

For a moment he looked slightly bewildered, and Golden Hand's heart went out to him. Then, just as quickly, the older man's usual penetrating expression returned.

"Which reminds me. Have you talked to her lately?"

"Who? Green Eyes?"

"Who else? Is there another you plan to marry?"

"I spoke with her not an hour ago. To bid her good-bye."

"She seems like she's finally beginning to come around somewhat. Some of the rough edges coming off. It's your mother's doing, you know."

"I know."

"I talked to her a while back. Your mother. The girl was very unhappy, evidently." He paused, seemed about to say more, then shook his head. "Anyway, I think your mother has done a fine job with her. We'll make a proper lady of her yet."

Golden Hand grinned. His last sight of Green Eyes had been her scampering barefooted over the house altar in the center of the atrium. More like a monkey than a lady. Still, he had to admit his father was right. The girl did seem happier these days, and more polished.

"How soon will you perform the official ceremony?" he asked.

"You mean adopting her as a ward of the clan?" He shrugged. "Most likely a few weeks after you're safely gone."

"You can make sure it's done privately? She will wear a mask, of course."

"Of course. The reason I said a few weeks is it will take that long to bribe the proper people. Things will remain secret, son. Oh, word will get out I've taken a ward into my house, and there may be some talk, but I don't think anybody will learn the secret at the heart of the matter. Not, at least, until it's too late to do anything about it."

Golden Hand rubbed his chin. His dark eyes went vague and distant for a moment. "Even if somebody knew, they might not make the connection. I was so young . . ."

"Well, it was remarked upon at the time. And some may still remember. Better to take no chances if we can avoid them."

Golden Hand nodded suddenly. "You're right. Father, I'm going now."

He stood up, and his father rose to meet him. The two men came together and hugged each other.

"Father, give me your blessing."

His father stepped back, grasped him by his shoulders, and looked up into his face. "You have it, my son. Go with my blessing, and the blessings of all the Gods. I will sacrifice for you."

"I love you, Father."

Long Fingers squeezed hard. "And I love you too, son." They stepped apart. "Have you already said your good-byes to your mother and sisters?"

"Yes, Father. Just before I came here."

"Very well. Off with you, then. Gods speed you, and bring you luck. And, son?"

Golden Hand was already at the curtain that covered the door. He looked back and saw his father's trim form outlined against the bright glare from the atrium. And, clearly limned by the morning light, he saw beyond his father's shape the girl, still clambering about the pyramid set into the center of the atrium. Her body shielded the little temple with its head of the Goddess, but as he watched she moved aside, and he saw a flash of green.

He knew what it was. His father had set it here, without offering any explanation. It was the knife made of green

Godstone. Green Eyes had been inordinately pleased to find it there, and for once had obeyed without argument the warning to leave it alone, and not touch it.

"Yes, Father?"

His father smiled. "Don't worry, son." He raised his mug of pulque. "I may guzzle this like water, but I haven't forgotten how to steal whatever I want from a dolt like Thunder Girdle. He'll never know what happened until it's over and done with."

"Farewell, Father. I'll see you in the summer."

"Gods speed you, boy. I'll be here."

Golden Hand flashed a final grin, nodded, and was gone.

Chapter Nine

1

"Come with me, Green Eyes," Gentle Dawn said.

Green Eyes looked up with a guilty start. For reasons she didn't understand, both Gentle Dawn and her two daughters had begun to treat her with icy politeness instead of their previously open scorn. But this formidable woman still scared her half to death. Without saying a word, Gentle Dawn could raise her head and stare down her nose in such a way that Green Eyes would hear girlish voices shrieking: "Bump Face! Bump Face!"

And though Gentle Dawn had taught her the beginnings of sewing, how to weave fine cloths for scarves, and the proper use of feathers, Green Eyes still had the feeling that Golden Hand's mother thought she engaged in a fierce struggle, trying to make a fine bowl out of pig dung.

"What are you doing there, girl?"

"I'm sorry, Lady. It's . . . I'm making a cup for Golden Hand. As a present for when he returns." She lifted the small brown shape and presented it for inspection.

Gentle Dawn eyed it as if—well, as if it were pig dung. "Very nice. But look at you. Mud all over. Where did you find . . . that?"

She gestured toward the basket full of dried clay sitting next to a brimming pitcher of water. Green Eyes was kneeling on a mat in a sunny corner of the atrium. She'd been there all morning, working on the cup. Mama Root had sent a slave out to find the clay for her, and showed her how to mix it with the proper amount of water to make a soft and malleable lump.

"When your cup is ready, I'll take it to the pot workers' quarter and have it fired," Mama Root told her. "That will make it hard, so it won't leak. We can even have it colored if you'd like."

Green Eyes thought this sounded like a fine idea. She had nothing of her own beyond the few scraps of clothing Gentle Dawn had provided. But because Moon and Dusk had been chattering about going to the markets to buy presents for their brother's eventual return, she wanted to give him something too.

Now, staring up into Gentle Dawn's carefully veiled expression of disapproval, she realized she'd somehow made another mistake.

"I'll go clean off the mud, Lady," she said. She looked down at the crooked bowl in her hands. "Do you think he will like it?"

"Well, I'm sure he will, Green Eyes. Now put it away, clean yourself up, and come to my rooms. We have much to do, and not a lot of time to do it in."

"May I leave this here?"

"Oh, I suppose. Now hurry."

Carefully, Green Eyes set down the cup. It still didn't look quite right, and she was afraid it would dry out and harden before she could return to finish it. She set it down anyway. If this one became ruined, maybe she could make a new one tomorrow.

"Green Eyes, please hurry."

"Yes, Lady."

She rose, bobbed her head to Gentle Dawn as she'd been taught, scurried up the far steps, and disappeared into the shadows beyond the columns. Gentle Dawn looked down at the mess. So crude, so dirty. Sometimes she despaired.

Her husband had taken her aside and spoken, if not exactly harshly, at least with greater sternness than she was accustomed to hearing from him, and the subject had surprised her most of all. She hadn't imagined Long Fingers as having any idea of her trials with the impossible task she'd been given, but it seemed somehow that he'd learned the girl was unhappy. And so he had told her of the importance of bringing Green Eyes along, but doing it in such a way that the girl might come to feel at home, and happy with her new life.

At home? Happy with her new life? Gentle Dawn stared down at a pile of what she considered no more than mud pies, the crude scrabblings of a savage. And in that moment she despaired. What could her husband understand about any of this? She and her own daughters had been raised from birth to become what they were, and in their veins flowed high blood that extended back for generations. But this girl had lived as wild a life as any beast of the forest. There might have been some hope if she could have taken her under her care as a very young child, before she'd been formed in all her bad habits.

But Green Eyes had come into this house nearly a woman. Those breasts of hers were growing larger every day, and without doubt she'd begin to bleed soon. And what then? Long Fingers didn't understand, and Golden Hand didn't either. They were used to a certain kind of woman. Oh, she could paint a thin veneer of civilization over the girl's most obvious faults. It would be little more than training an animal to jump through a hoop. But anybody who had ever seen a real lady of the Tollan aristocracy would know the difference immediately—just as this poor sad cup at her feet was indeed a cup, and it would hold water if hardened in a fire. But it was as far as the endless night sky from the ceramic bowls and cups and pots that filled the shelves in her own kitchen rooms. As hopelessly far as the bridge between Green Eyes and any true high-born woman.

She sighed and poked at the mess with one perfectly sandaled toe. There was something heartbreakingly naive about that crooked little cup. A gift for Golden Hand indeed. How could this untutored wild child begin to comprehend the sort of riches that stuffed her son's storehouses, let alone what filled those of her own husband's treasure rooms?

The answer was, of course, that she couldn't. She came

from a place where a skimpy field, or a good day's catch from the river, was real wealth. Before she'd come here, she'd probably never owned more than a single filthy garment, some laughably coarse excuse for a skirt, in her life. And so she fashioned a lump of mud into a gift, and thought it suitable for a lord like Golden Hand, a lord who would one day be a prince.

She raised her face to the sky and closed her eyes. A great dark wash of anger and grief swept over her. She clenched her fingers and raised her fists. *Why are they doing this to me?*

For one dizzy moment it was all she could do to keep from crying out her rage and shame at the empty sky. But she didn't. She couldn't. She was a princess of Tollan . . .

"Lady?"

"Eh? What? Oh, there you are, girl."

Green Eyes stood before her in a fresh skirt. And she'd obviously tried to wash herself. But the folds around her sadly chewed fingernails were still packed with mud, and there was a small clod dangling at one side of her hair.

Gentle Dawn sighed. "Come with me." She forced herself to extend her hand. Slowly, Green Eyes took it. They left the atrium linked together, yet as separated as the unbridgeable distance between their worlds.

One old woman and the other young, each one utterly different from the other in so many ways, yet sharing a secret cup neither knew how to acknowledge even to herself.

The cup of despair, that men had filled and given them to drink. Because they were women.

2

He trudged along, sweating in the noonday sun, garbed in a shapeless brown robe, a bag slung across his bent and twisted shoulders.

Ssss-flap went his sandals on the dusty street in the foreigners' barrio. *Ssss-flap.*

As always, his hood was up, shielding his head from the heat of the day. Its flaps fell down across his face, but occasionally a passing breeze would twitch them open, exposing black eyes of such opaque ferocity that any who saw them looked away immediately.

Even the packs of heedless children who scrambled and screamed everywhere grew silent as he approached, and stood aside to give him passage. With big, frightened eyes they watched him go, and only after he was a safe distance away did they make the signs that warded off evil spirits, or were supposed to. They didn't seem to have any effect on him, though.

Step by sliding, crooked step he penetrated deeper into the quarter, pausing intermittently to shift his burden from one shoulder to the other. He was tired. He'd been up all night, with nothing to eat or drink, and his muscles cried out for the filthy bed and the rat-gnawed hovel he called home. He ignored the protests of his body, though. He'd learned to do that long before.

As he passed like a ghost down one street and another, he looked around for the signs and directions he'd learned only after days of seeking them. He knew where he was going, though he'd never been there before. He could have investigated, but what was the point? He had nothing to bring. He had no credentials. But now he did, so he examined every spoor with dead-eyed care, and only found himself disoriented once.

When that happened—a corner where two narrow alleys crossed beneath silent walls—he paused. He thought he was on the right trail, but this intersection had not been mentioned. He heard voices around the corner and went in that direction.

He found three men squatting against a wall, playing a

dice game. The men were burly, ill-favored, with low brows, filthy hair, and many scars. He walked up to them.

"Excuse me. I'm looking for the Street of the Weavers."

The largest of the three, a ruffian whose shoulders showed the marks of some ancient whipping, ignored him and cast the dice. Then, without looking up, he turned his head a bit and spat a glistening green wad in the general direction of the stranger's feet.

"Excuse you, eh? Why don't you excuse yourself? If you're such a stupid dog you don't know where you are, you're probably in the wrong place. Eh, mates?"

His friends, still looking down at their game, laughed in agreement.

"Excuse me," the stranger said again.

The burly man froze. He squinted, as if he couldn't believe his ears. Then, grunting, he rose to his feet and turned to face the stranger.

"Listen, you—"

The stranger pushed back his hood.

All the color leaked from the burly man's scarred features. The tracks of his old wounds stood out like spectral tattoos.

"Uh . . . uh . . . uh . . ."

"The directions, please."

Wordlessly, the burly man raised one trembling hand and pointed. "Th-th-that way . . ."

"Thank you."

Ssss-flap. Ssss-flap.

The burly man doubled over, arms wrapped around his flabby gut. "Gah . . . did you see . . ." he managed to gag.

But his two friends had already run away.

3

When he finally found the place, he recognized it instantly from the descriptions he'd been given. The foreign merchants' barrio, unlike the rest of Tollan, was a jumble of different architectures, everything from adobe huts, to tents, to flimsy constructions of poles and ragged thatch. This was a compound of solidly constructed circular dwellings made of red brick with thick and neatly thatched roofs that rose to a sharp central point.

The architecture native to Tollan was simple and consistent. There were no walls around compounds, because compound and house were the same, and the outer walls of the rooms were the outer walls of the entire structure. Tollanese homes were built around the open space of their central atriums, of which many of the larger homes had two or three.

Here, the foreigners built their homes as they were accustomed to in whatever place they'd come from. Some of the compounds had low walls or fences made of wooden logs surrounding them. The compound he faced had a surprising amount of open space—even a few trees—surrounding several of the distinctive round brick structures.

In fact, it looked very much like a small village picked up whole and transplanted from some faraway location. Most of the open space—hard-packed dirt—was toward the center of the group. He saw several heavily bronzed women with slanting brown eyes, broad shoulders, and long black braids working on their knees before low, wide-topped clay jars, busily dying yarn. Their dyes all appeared to be the same dark, sludgy liquid, but when they dipped in the bleached, golden yarn and pulled it out, it came in dark, rich blue, red like fresh blood, green, yellow, and purple. There were a lot of women working, and the amount of dyed yarn hung over wooden racks to dry was great.

Two men, very tall, also with braided black hair, wearing finely embroidered kilts but no shirts, appeared silently on either side of him. Their arms and chests were thickly tattooed with blue ink, a wild panoply of mysterious beasts and arcane magical symbols. They wore wide leather bands around their heavy wrists and well-fashioned sandals on their feet. From their earlobes and their nostrils dangled beautifully wrought examples of the latest fad—the gold jewelry now being imported from the south.

Neither of the two smiled or frowned. They regarded him blankly. "Are you looking for something, friend?" the one on his right hand asked. He spoke the language of Tollan, though with an odd, slightly guttural accent that betrayed his origins as the coastal lands far to the west, below the Great Mountains.

"I come to see . . ." The stranger lowered his voice and glanced around. On his left, behind a brick wall of medium height, somebody was sacrificing at the communal altar. From the right, hidden behind one of the round brick structures, he could hear the rackety-clack of a strap loom whipping back and forth. He whispered the name.

Neither of his two interrogators showed any reaction. Finally, the one who'd spoken said, "Does he know you?"

"No. Nor I him. But I know of him. For some time he's had a task he's been unable to accomplish. And so he has offered a reward for anybody who can accomplish that task for him. Do you know what I'm talking about?"

"Perhaps."

The stranger shrugged. The movement jiggled the sack on his back. "I have accomplished the task. So I have come to see him and claim the reward."

"Oh? You have accomplished this task, which *he* could not?" The man's tone was rich with disbelief.

"I have done that, yes," the stranger said. "I would be a fool to come here and lie to him, in his own place. Wouldn't I?"

The other man spoke for the first time. "There are many fools in this city. Some even come here. They never come again, but perhaps you are one more of them."

"That is possible," the stranger agreed. "Shouldn't you let him decide what I am, though?"

"Maybe. How do you know that one of us is not the one you seek?"

The stranger chuckled softly. "He shows his face in the light of the sun no more than I do."

They were all silent a moment. "Let me see *your* face," the first one said.

Wordlessly, the stranger pushed his hood back a little. Neither man said anything, or showed much reaction, though the first one's eyelids flickered slightly.

After a moment he said, "Wait here," and walked off into the compound.

They stood silently, the stranger watching the business inside the compound, the other man watching him. That man's hand had shifted to the leather-wrapped handle of a sharp knife stuck through his belt, though he did this without any particular ostentation. He might have been merely finding a handy spot on which to rest his fingers. But his fingers twitched faintly every few moments.

"Your homes look rich and happy," the stranger remarked.

"The Gods smile on us. We have been very lucky."

"You make fine woven goods. That helps your luck, I think."

"We've been lucky in other things."

"Yes. I know."

The other man came striding out of the largest structure, threaded his way past the women, and came up to the stranger again.

"He will see you."

"Thank you," the stranger said simply.

"Follow me."

The single doorway into the round brick building was covered with a straw mat that hung from a horizontal pole. Bright strands of wool had been braided into the mat and left to dangle, giving it a cheerful, ragged appearance, like a field full of wildflowers. Tiny clay bells were attached to some of these strings. They made a soft chiming sound when the breeze struck them, or when somebody pushed the curtain aside.

The stranger entered between the two men, and found himself in a circular chamber about twenty-five feet across. In the center was a fire pit, on which a blaze burned brightly. The smoke was carried away through a hole at the very top of the thatched roof. Several women knelt or squatted around the fire, trimming skeins of brightly colored wool. A few others rattled clay vessels as they made preparations for a meal. A very tall, thin shape sat cross-legged on a mat across the fire pit. The mat had been elevated on a wooden platform. The man was naked except for a small clout that hung loose about his skinny shanks. But as the stranger entered, two of the women rose and draped the most beautiful feather robe the stranger had ever seen over the seated man's shoulders. That robe was fit for a king of Tollan. They clasped it across his sunken chest with a fastening made of polished shells. Instead of a collar, the rope continued up into a hoodlike mask, which covered the man's head and face entirely.

This all happened so quickly, and the light was so gloomy, that the stranger didn't get a good look at the other man's features.

The first of his escorts stepped forward and said, "This is the one, Lord."

The man raised one hand and motioned him away. "Come to me, stranger. Sit yourself and be a guest in my house."

The stranger stepped around the fire pit. As he approached, one of the women spread a clean mat on the earthen floor. The stranger glanced at the other man, then sat down on the mat. He dropped his bag and settled it carefully beside him.

Up close, the stranger saw that the top of the robe was not simply a mask, but the face of some strange beast. Fangs made of the beaks of eagles shaped a snarling mouth. Ears made of beaten gold dangled from the sides. On the chin of the mask was a beard that looked as if its pieces had once ridden on living human skulls.

"Why have you come to see me?" the man said, leaning forward and looking down at him. His voice was high-pitched, soft, and so breathy it sounded almost like a muted whistle.

The stranger caught a glint of yellow behind the holes of the mask, like the eyes of a cat.

"You have a competitor named Two Belly Fist. He is of the fierce northern tribes, and he has many men who pay allegiance to him. He came to Tollan about four years ago and set himself up in the barrio of the brick makers. His spirit is strong. He speaks with the secret Gods, and practices black magic. He is a sorcerer and a murderer, and he has grown very powerful."

The fantastic feathered mask nodded. "Yes, I know of this one. But why do you say he is my competitor? That one is an evil man. As you say, a black sorcerer. I am but a humble weaver and dyer of cloth."

"I have heard it said, in the streets and the places where men drink pulque, that even a humble weaver might pay well to find a way to bring down this evil man, this Two Belly Fist."

The man in the feather mask waited a moment. Then he said, in his high, whistling voice, "Yes, maybe I would part with a small bit of my wealth to see this evil man gone. For the good of the city, of course."

"Of course."

"So I ask once again, why have you come? Do you work for Two Belly? Perhaps you can betray him? Tell me how my friends might aid me in cleansing the city of his noxious presence?"

The stranger shook his head. "Oh, no. If I did work for Two Belly Fist, I would never betray him. Nor if I did betray him would I come to you. It is said you are an honorable man. If I came to you with treachery, how could you respect me? How could I respect myself? No, I am no traitor."

"Very well. You aren't a traitor. So what have you brought me? If you have come here with nothing, you have made a mistake. A very unwise mistake."

"I don't come empty-handed."

"Then tell me. What is this information you have that will give me what I want? Come, speak!"

The stranger spread his hands. "I have no information."

"You try my patience. That is not wise either."

"I came to tell you that Two Belly Fist will not bother you any further. Two Belly Fist is dead."

"What! How can you know this when I have heard nothing?"

"I don't suppose it will be getting around for a little while. His unfortunate passing occurred early this morning, just before dawn, when he went out to take a piss. He never returned. Perhaps his friends are still looking for him."

"And how do you know all this, my friend?"

In answer the stranger upended his bag and dumped its contents out onto the platform on which the other man sat. A large, round object landed with a dull thud and rolled crazily across the platform until it bumped to a stop against feather-mask's right foot.

The man in the mask leaned forward and stared at the severed head resting against his foot. On the cheeks of the head were distinctive bright red tattoos.

The man in the mask stared at the head for a long time.

"Ah," he said. He looked up. "Leave us alone," he said suddenly.

When all the women and the two men had gone, he straightened, then reached up and lifted the mask away from his face. He smiled at the stranger. His eyes blazed like melted gold in the dim light. His skin was the color of charred logs. It was curiously smooth and shiny, its damaged angles and planes riven with a patchwork of red cracks, like mud dried on an empty lake bottom.

"I am Black Face, stranger. Let me see you."

The stranger threw back his hood. He had a high forehead, across which trailed a white scar as thick as a finger. His skin was dark gold. In the exact center of his face, between his dead eyes and his thick, pink lips, was a bright yellow beak carved of wood, held in place by a cord that stretched around his head, hidden beneath his hair. Ancient dead scarlet veins, like clawmarks, straggled out from beneath the wooden nose. A thin trail of clear liquid also leaked from beneath it.

"I am called Parrot Beak," the stranger said.

Black Face glanced down at the head, then back up at Parrot Beak. "Are you looking for a home?"

"I am," Parrot Beak said.

"You've found one," Black Face said.

4

It was late in the afternoon when Long Fingers led the small party out of his house onto the stucco pavement beyond. His wife walked on his left hand, her arm in his. Behind them walked their daughters, Dusk and Moon. Behind the two girls came Green Eyes, walking with Mama Root. Chain Coil led the way, bearing a heavy staff that he used to warn people out of the path of the party. Long Snake, now retired from dangerous duty with the caravans, brought up the rear, also armed with a staff.

The Prince and Princess wore robes appropriate to their high rank: over inner gowns of fine white cotton were draped much heavier trains so heavily studded with glittering stone beads and polished shells that two house slaves walked behind them holding up most of the weight, and keeping the tails from dragging on the pavement.

The two girls were less heavily clad, though their garments of light cotton shells covered with layers of quetzal and parrot feathers weighed considerably more than their everyday skirts, and they started to sweat almost as soon as the walk began.

All four members of the noble family also wore headdresses of varying complexity. Prince Long Fingers's was the largest and most ornate, consisting of a light carved wooden shell in the shape of a serpent's head, with polished red jewels for eyes, and a great ruff of white quetzal feathers. Gentle Dawn wore a smaller arrangement that represented a mythical bird sacred to the Goddess. The girls struggled to keep their own headdresses, which were large feathery things draped with strings of beads, from being ruffled by the evening winds that were beginning to blow.

Green Eyes counted herself lucky. Though she was the center of the ceremony to come, she wore no headdress, for she was not a noble. Only a thin circlet of green ribbon bound back her dark hair. Her robe was plain and white, though the fabric was of the highest quality. Around her neck she wore a chain of flowers that, though very pretty, smelled bad, and made her nose itch.

Mama Root stumped alongside, leaning her weight on a tall walking stick, wearing her usual shapeless brown robes, her head covered with the wide, floppy straw hat she always wore.

The Lord of the Water Moon had his residence in a neighborhood of similar large establishments. The streets were wider here than in most parts of the city, though much less crowded because they were within the walls of the Citadel that surrounded the great compound of the Plumed Serpent. Also, since the neighborhood was toward the rear of the Citadel and separated from the heavily thronged marketplace before the Plumed Serpent Pyramid, there was no reason for casual strolling.

Long Fingers led them quickly forward, using both hands

to keep his headdress and robes straight. Green Eyes tried to look at everything at once. She had not been out of the house since Golden Hand carried her across the threshold so many months before.

Once again she beheld the vast reach of the Plumed Serpent Pyramid, this time from the rear. They were so close it dominated the sky, blotting out the much larger but more distant pyramids of the Sun and the Moon.

The entire Plumed Serpent compound, including the pyramid, rested on a vast, stepped platform three layers high that raised the whole thing forty feet higher. A broad stone staircase cut across these levels from the rear, affording entry to the nobles who lived behind the immense compound.

The Citadel and the compound were the commercial and governmental heart of Tollan. In the front of the pyramid was a great plaza that on most days contained the city market. Vendors of every kind plied their wares here, as well as traders who dealt with each other in wholesale quantities. Here farmers brought the fruits and vegetables they grew in excess of what the city took in taxes. Here came exotic, coppery-skinned men from lands far to the north, bearing carved wood and beautiful pots and furs whose like could not be found anywhere in the south.

On days of high ceremony or ritual, the market space was cleared, and nearly half the residents of Tollan could pack into the area. This was not an inconsiderable number. On behalf of King Thunder Girdle and the Council of Eighteen, Prince Long Fingers had overseen the most recent census of the city's population. It was the first one done in more than a generation, and it surprised even the Prince, who had seen the city grow significantly in his own lifetime. It had taken two years to count everybody, and when the totals were presented to the Council, they numbered Tollan as having more than two hundred thousand residents.

Although all the priestly sects had members who pursued knowledge in both the natural and spiritual worlds, it was

those of the Lord Sky Snake who were the greatest enumer-
ators, who understood the innermost secrets of the calendar
of the days, and who studied the bodies of the night sky.

After they reached the top of the stairway they passed
through the rear gates of the temple compound proper and
entered a wide plaza set at the rear of the pyramid itself. The
party halted, while the Prince and Princess sank to their
knees and made proper obeisance. Then, rising, they hurried
off to their left, toward a temple as tall as four men, made of
stone and faced with painted stucco. The motif of the
brightly colored designs was an endless repetition of the
Plumed Serpent in his numberless incarnations. To Green
Eyes it looked as if the great God was crawling all over the
outside of the building.

"Oh, Mama, look," she said.

"Hurry along, dear. They're getting ahead of us."

"Those—what do you call them?"

"Columns."

"Yes, columns. They look like trees. I wonder what it
would be like to climb them?"

Mama Root laughed. "Today of all days, dear, don't think
about such things. Behave yourself. And hurry, as I said."

"Oh, hmph. I never get to have any fun. All I ever see is
the house and the atrium. And now, when I finally get outside, I have to hurry."

But Mama Root was frowning, and they *had* fallen behind. Up ahead Long Fingers had noticed her lapse, stopped,
and turned to look for her. So did Gentle Dawn. Green Eyes
felt a sinking feeling. Once again she was doing everything
wrong! *Why* couldn't she figure out how to do things the
right way? Moon and Dusk didn't even think about it, they
just did it, and it was always right. But she had to figure out
everything, and half the time nobody would even give her a
hint.

Biting her lip, she quickened her steps until she closed the
distance between them. Gentle Dawn gave her a chilly

smile, though Long Fingers looked slightly pink and exasperated.

"Try to keep up, Green Eyes. And put your mask on right away!" Gentle Dawn said.

Long Fingers glowered at her. "For the Gods' sake, Green Eyes. I told you to put it on as soon as we left the house. Don't you ever listen to what people tell you?"

Green Eyes looked down at the colorful, feather-decked thing she'd been carrying heedlessly in her hands all along. "I'm . . . sorry." She turned to Mama Root, her cheeks flaming.

"Can you help me?"

"Certainly, dear. Turn around."

Green Eyes did, and Mama Root tied the cord that held the feathered mask against her face.

"Good. That's perfect," Long Fingers said. "Now remember, you don't take that off for anything. Understand?" He glanced at Mama Root. "Mama? See to it."

"Yes, Lord."

Long Fingers sighed. "All right. Let's get this over with." He leaned closer to his wife and whispered something in the general direction of her ear, hidden beneath her fantastic headdress.

Gentle Dawn turned and peered sharply at Green Eyes's face. "No," she said. "You can't tell anything through the feathers."

Green Eyes had no idea what she was talking about, but Long Fingers seemed satisfied. He nodded, turned, and walked off in the direction of the steps leading up into the temple.

Gentle Dawn said, "Green Eyes, *please* try to remember the correct way to bow when you come before the King." With a final worried glance she nodded at her daughters, said, "Come, girls," and followed her husband.

"King?" Green Eyes hissed at Mama Root. "Did she say *King*?"

"You mean no one told you?" A familiar thunderous expression passed across her features. She muttered, more to herself than Green Eyes, "Of course they didn't. Why should they? You're only a . . . village girl." Then the storm passed, and Mama Root squeezed her hand. "You'll be fine, dearest. Remember, though. Whatever you do, don't take off your mask. Especially in front of the King."

5

King Thunder Girdle was a huge man, with darker skin than usual for a native Tollan, wide and sloping shoulders, the beginnings of a belly, and an air of softness about him. He tended to move slowly, and he was not considered to be a man quick in his thoughts. All of this was true, though it was an example of Mama Root's maxim about seeking the truth beneath the truth. His thoughts *were* slow, but they were deep, and when he made up his mind about something, after long consideration, he was right more often than not. Moreover, he found his own use in his reputation for slowness of mind. Sometimes it even fooled the fast thinkers like Long Fingers, who was Prince Water Moon and his great rival.

"Are they here yet?"

"You mean Prince Water Moon?" his son replied. His son, standing next to him, helping him arrange his ceremonial robes, was Thunder Girdle's equal in size. On first glance he looked tougher and harder. Both father and son shared the long hatchet nose of their clan, and the wide-set dark eyes beneath broad, smooth brows.

Thunder Girdle's hair fell to his shoulders, helping to mitigate, though not entirely conceal, a bald spot. His son wore his own hair in a style similar to that of Golden Hand. He also imitated Golden Hand's fondness for a great number of gold chains, earrings, bracelets, and rings. It was one of these rings that somehow got snagged in a hank of decorative quetzal feathers that fringed the edge of his father's robe.

"Now look what you've done. Pulled them right out. Why do you ape that Water Moon boy with all his silly gold bangles?"

"It's all right, Father. Look. Only a few feathers. Here, let me brush the others over—"

"Don't touch it!" The King made a gesture with one hand, and a courtier immediately hurried over and began to gently smooth the remaining feathers over the problem spot.

They were all gathered in a low, luxuriously furnished anteroom behind the throne room. The walls of the room were fashioned of dark stone blocks, but unlike most surfaces in Tollan, these were unpainted. Instead, every inch of their exterior was carved in partial relief—men, Gods, animals, dates, numbers, symbols, all swirling in an endless riot of minute details. The likenesses of more than a few of the King's ancestors were carved there and, in fact, his own face appeared eight times, next to the dot-and-bar inscriptions that represented the dates of the mighty deeds memorialized. He knew those by heart, too.

"They must be here," the King said, and whispered to a courtier. The man went out and quickly returned.

"They are waiting before the throne."

"I wish this didn't have to be a formal ceremony, but Prince Water Moon asked for it." Thunder Girdle looked around, a helpless expression on his broad features, and then shrugged. "Come on, everyone. Let's get this over with."

6

Mama Root waited with Green Eyes in the back of the huge room. All around them towered gigantic stone stelae,

carved and engraved with the exploits of all the kings who
had ruled in Tollan.

The room was about sixty feet deep, forty wide, and thirty
tall. Green Eyes could not imagine such a huge chamber—
even as she stood in it she could not believe that men had
built it. Surely only Gods could do such work.

Far away, at the other end of the room, her new family appeared as small as dolls as they knelt before the raised dais
that supported the throne. The throne itself was carved from
a solid chunk of the famous Tollan greenstone, into which
had been set innumerable glittering gems. High torches surrounded it, sending up clouds of black smoke to stain the
great painted wood beams overhead.

Green Eyes could not know this chamber had been designed to impress just such folks as she, emissaries from distant and rustic places, who'd never seen the might and
power of a great city, and would return to their homes with
tales of the might and grandeur of the Gods of Tollan.

Today the cavernous chamber seemed curiously muted,
however: usually it was full of courtiers, officers, petitioners, and businessmen, all dressed as brightly as birds, and
sounding as raucous. Now, nearly empty, it breathed a cool
and remote gloominess. Green Eyes shivered, even as she
drank in everything she could with eyes hidden behind the
feather mask.

Suddenly, without warning, a huge figure appeared from
behind the throne, mounted the steps, and seated himself. He
looked around, then stood, while a smaller man rushed up
and placed a pillow under his posterior. Then another gigantic figure appeared, and took up station on the King's right
hand.

The acoustics of the room were so good that although
Thunder Girdle spoke in his usual soft tones, Green Eyes
could hear him clearly from sixty feet away. She thought the
King sounded tired, irritable, and rather too human for what
she'd expected. She'd heard her own father speak in the

same tones after a hard day in the fields, and the similarity was strange.

"Well, Prince Water Moon, shall we get on with it?"

"Yes, Great One. I've come to petition on behalf of my clan, to allow a girl to become my ward."

"Yes, go on," the King replied. Green Eyes thought he sounded bored.

"The girl comes from a far place, and will one day be a part of my son's household. He purchased her as a slave, but wishes her to be written on the rolls of the city as a free citizen of Tollan, with all the rights and privileges accorded, including the right to marry another citizen of Tollan."

The King glanced at his son, who raised his eyebrows. "Where is Lord Golden Hand, Prince?"

"I'm sorry, Great One. He has been gone this month on a trading venture to the south."

"So you are acting on his behalf as well?"

"Yes, Greatness."

The King sat silent for several moments. "Very well. I don't understand this, but bring the girl forward."

Mama Root gave her a slight push. "Remember to bow."

Slowly Green Eyes walked up the long stone aisle toward the throne. As she approached, the others stepped aside. She came right up to the lowest step, stopped, dropped gracefully to her knees, and bumped her forehead gently on the floor three times. Then, hearing a grateful sigh from Gentle Dawn, she rose to her feet and, still facing the King as she'd been told to do, retreated until she stood next to the Prince and his wife.

"Why, she's hardly more than a child, Prince."

"She is of proper age to become my ward, Great One," Long Fingers said. Green Eyes thought he sounded a bit curt, and was amazed at him speaking to the King in such tones.

The King, however, seemed unsurprised. "Oh, very well,

Prince. You have my blessing. And my official seal." The King raised one hand, and the royal scribe, who was also his youngest son, appeared. "See to it, Waterlily Jaguar."

Then he turned back to the group waiting below. "Come here, girl. And take off that silly mask. I know this is supposed to be formal, but we're all friends here. Let me look at your face, now that I've just raised you to the highest nobility in our land. Well, behind my own family, of course."

Long Fingers moved forward. "Great One, my son has requested that she not reveal her face until the wedding." He sounded pained and angry.

"What? He's going to *marry* her? What's this about? Why hasn't anybody told me?"

The King turned back to Green Eyes, who stood paralyzed at the foot of the steps. "Now I really want to see you. What's your name?" A courtier leaned forward and whispered in his ear. "Ah, yes, Green Eyes. One of those country names, I imagine. Come on, let me see your pretty face."

"Lord . . . Thunder Girdle . . ."

"Oh, hush, Long Fingers. Golden Hand won't mind if it's me. I'm the King, after all."

Green Eyes had no idea what to do. The one warning most strictly given to her was that she should under no circumstances remove her mask before the King or any of his court. Yet here he was, a giant of a man, staring down at her, demanding that she do exactly what she'd been forbidden to do.

Her hand rose toward her face, paused, dropped somewhat, then rose again.

"Come, girl, I'm waiting," the King said. He glanced at Long Fingers, who was watching him with stony eyes. "What's the matter with her? And don't look at me that way."

Green Eyes took one corner of the mask in her fingers and

began to lift it. She wished she could somehow disappear in
a cloud of smoke, as spirits were said to do.

Something black and very fast darted in from the far edge
of her vision.

Chapter Ten

1

Whenever White Feather Writer stood in this particular spot, he always found himself struck by the wonder of Tollan. It reminded him that Tollan really was the Place of the Reeds, and the City of the Gods. All around him was splendor that testified to the holiness of the city.

He stood with his back against a high stone platform twice his height. This platform supported the Goddess Altar, one of the two most sacred places in the city. The platform and the Goddess Altar were perfectly centered in the middle of the Plaza of the Moon, around which loomed the fourteen Lesser Pyramids.

He was looking due north, toward the Pyramid of the Moon, whose distant peak towered a hundred eighty feet above his head. From his vantage point the top of the pyramid, with its great temple, perfectly bisected the top of the Mountain of Thunder in the dark range beyond the city. That was no accident. It had been constructed that way by his forebears. According to the secret records in the Goddess Temple, they had exerted great effort in getting the mathematical relationships exactly right.

No matter how many times he saw it—and he'd been coming to the Plaza of the Moon since before he could remember—he never failed to experience a catch in his chest and a curious tightness in his throat at the view.

The Pyramid of the Sun, on the right at his rear, was larger than the Goddess's pyramid. But Her pyramid had been the first to rear its crown high above the valley floor.

The Goddess had come up from the south, bearing the first king of Tollan, Shining Star, and founded the city in this spot, the holiest in all the Middle World. For here was where the Goddess had *created* the Middle World, sending it out from her womb upon the void, and naming this the Place of the Reeds, first of Her creations in the deeps of forgotten time.

He raised his eyes toward the gigantic pile of stone before him. Up and up it rose, stepped back five times toward a flattened top on which rested Her temple. Seen from his location, the great building atop the pyramid looked like a child's toy, and Her head above the temple like a human face seen from miles away.

Sometimes standing here, with Her pyramid before him, and the other huge structures that ringed the plaza rising over him, he felt as tiny and insignificant as an ant. Other times, knowing the secret histories as he did, he felt very near to Godhood himself. Of course that was sacrilege, but he knew men had built these incredible structures, built them as the Gods Themselves would have done, and so through them men partook of the divine glory.

It was quiet. The sun was quartering down the sky toward his left, casting long, slanting shadows across the pavement of the plaza. There were only a few people about, almost all priests of the Lady, bound on Her work. Somehow, their lonely presence made the plaza seem even larger than if it had been completely empty.

Not that it needed enlargement. It was the biggest open space in the city, paved with pure white stucco over fitted stone, and it could easily accommodate every living soul in the valley of Tollan. In fact it did so four times a year, at each of the four Great Festivals.

He noticed a flock of birds wheeling lazily above the image of the Mother that surmounted Her pyramid. He squinted and finally realized they were crows, not the more common hawks that often drifted there.

Black crows attending the Mother. Was it an omen? As he watched, one of the crows flew away from the others and arrowed south along the Avenue of the Gods. White Feather turned to follow its flight, until it finally vanished south of the river, diving toward the compound of the Plumed Serpent.

Black crows were sacred to Her, though they rarely flocked around Her pyramid as they were doing now. And why had only one flown away?

He considered the direction of that flight. Perhaps She was sending some sort of message to the One who was father, husband, and son to Her. It was well understood how closely bound She was to the Plumed Serpent, Lord Sky Snake, whom the secret writings said had incarnated Himself in the human flesh of Shining Star, Her son whom She'd made the first king in Tollan.

He raised his hand and shielded his eyes. Now the original flock of crows was scattering and wheeling away. Automatically he numbered the five long flights of steps that divided the center of Her pyramid, climbing unobstructed to the temple building on the top.

His father was up there waiting for him. The afternoon air hung clear and hushed about the plaza, as if the valley held its breath. The rays of the sun were hot on his bare shoulders. Though he was young and in fine health, the climb before him would be a chore for anybody.

Better to start and get it over with. At least there was the usual consolation, common to both climbing and life. The way up might be hard, but the way down was always easy.

2

It was floating on the warm afternoon thermals when something clicked inside its tiny brain and it immediately slipped sideways and fell away from its brothers.

Now the city rushed beneath it as it dropped in wide, swooping curves toward the glimmering thread of the river. But it knew nothing of city, or river, or pyramid. It was a crow. Its world was a hot, bright, fearful place, where things were either food or predators. It feared the eagles particularly, but there were none of those great shapes hunting the sky, so it continued on its flight without care.

By the time it crossed over the river and veered to its left, it had forgotten about its flock. Its black and beady eyes flashed in the slanting light. Another huge pile of stone reared up before it, but its tail feathers shifted, the sound of its windy passage increased the tiniest bit, and it slid around the Pyramid of the Plumed Serpent like a leaf riding on smooth, invisible waters.

Lower still, and a brightly colored shape appeared below. Another click in its tiny skull. It folded its wings and dived for an opening between two tall pillars of stone along the front of this building.

It flashed between the columns and entered the dark interior. Up ahead, the glint of gold . . .

3

King Thunder Girdle had advanced to the top step of the dais and stood looking down on Green Eyes. He bent forward at his thick waist, one big, soft hand outstretched in encouragement.

With no warning whatsoever a huge black crow came flapping into his face, wings beating frantically.

Haw! Haw! shrieked the crow.

"Ah . . . *oof!*" cried the King, throwing up his hands. Reflexively he raised one foot, then put it down again, but caught his heel on the top of the riser.

The crow flapped and cried. The King, overbalanced, toppled.

"Ai!"

Green Eyes stood frozen in horror as, in a welter of flying arms and kicking legs, the King's huge body came bumping and thumping and cracking down the steps toward her.

Thunder Girdle's undignified and painful descent ended at her feet in a tangled sprawl of limbs. She felt fingers tighten about her arm and jerk her sharply backward.

Confused, she flailed out with her free hand, but struck nothing. "Stop it, girl," Mama Root hissed. "Come with me!"

Before she could catch her breath, she found herself outside the throne chamber, blinking in the bright sunlight, as the old woman dragged her willy-nilly down the steps to the plaza beyond.

"Mama . . ."

"Hurry up, dear."

Green Eyes was amazed. She was young and strong, but she had to run almost as fast as she was able in order to keep up with the old woman's long strides. With each step Mama thumped the butt of her stick on the pavement. The soft brim of her hat was pressed against her forehead by the speed of her advance.

They passed down the staircase between its banisters of wriggling stone serpents without slowing. Only when they were beyond the compound of the Plumed Serpent entirely did Mama Root pause a moment, let go of Green Eyes's hand, and begin to fan herself with her straw hat.

"My . . ." she wheezed. "My . . . my. I'm getting too old to run foot races with young girls." She glanced aside. "Aren't I, dear? I'll bet I surprised you, though. You didn't think Mama Root could move so quick, did you?"

Green Eyes looked up into Mama Root's face and giggled. "No. What a surprise you are, Mama Root."

The old woman's cheeks were rosy as ripe fruit. She wedged her hat back on her head. "Yes, I am a surprise," she said. "Sometimes I even manage to surprise myself."

They proceeded along the deserted streets. "Straighten your mask, dear. You can take it off when we're safely home."

"Mama, did you see the King fall down? Did you see the black bird?"

"It was a crow," Mama Root said.

"I didn't know what to do. Lord Long Fingers—and Gentle Dawn, too—most specifically told me not to take off my mask. But the King *told* me to. I didn't know what to *do*. I hope the King is all right, but I'm so glad he fell down. If that crow hadn't come along . . ."

Mama Root smiled grimly. "Yes, that was a very lucky thing, wasn't it?" They began to walk again, but this time more slowly. "When we get home, I'll show you how to make a *pretty* cup for Golden Hand. Would you like that?"

"Oh, *yes,* Mama."

They reached the door of the House of the Water Moon without further incident. And though Green Eyes didn't know it, she would not step through that door again for nearly two full years. She passed inside it as a girl. When she issued out its portal again, she would be a woman.

4

Prince Water Moon was the first to reach the King, but Thunder Shield was only a pace behind.

"Lord!" Long Fingers gasped as he knelt beside the older man, who was groaning loudly.

"Help! The King needs help!" Thunder Shield cried as he too dropped to his knees next to his father. Gently he slipped one big hand beneath his father's head and lifted him up. He glanced across at Long Fingers.

"He's bleeding."

Long Fingers leaned closer. "Yes, he struck his forehead." He reared up and glared about the room. "Courtiers! By the Gods, where are the healing priests?"

"Get jumping, you worms, or I'll string your guts on every altar in the city!" Thunder Shield roared.

"Urmmmm . . ."

"Father!" the young Prince said, looking down at the head he still cradled.

"Urmm . . . get off me, you great ninny." The older man's eyes popped open and stared up angrily.

"Father, you're hurt, you're bleeding."

The King's dark eyes looked filmy, but after a moment they began to clear. "A bump on the head, nothing more." His eyes shifted, focused. "Fingers, is that you? Help me up, for goodness' sake."

"Yes, Girdle, it's me. Here, Shield, help me lift him."

The King was large, but working together they managed to shift him into a sitting position. Just as they did, a herd of priests came galloping in, led by the High Priest of the Plumed Serpent Temple himself.

They found themselves surrounded by a horde of wild-eyed, shouting men. The King rolled his eyes, then looked at Long Fingers. "Oh, my Gods," he muttered.

Long Fingers grinned at him. "Did you strain anything? Men our age, it's always the back."

The King twisted his torso a little, then winced. "Going to be sore. What do you mean, men our age? I'm at least three years younger than you are, you old dog."

They were now surrounded by a thick wall of nervous, hovering priests, all wanting to do *something*, but all equally fearful of shoving a pair of princes out of the way to do it.

"I'll leave you to their ministrations," Long Fingers said.

"You would, wouldn't you?" Thunder Girdle paused. "Sorry about ruining your ceremony. Where did that blasted bird come from, anyway?"

"It's all right. You got it done before you decided to fly from your very own throne."

Thunder Girdle chuckled, a bit painfully perhaps, but it was still a laugh. Long Fingers felt his knees pop as he stood and let the priests take his place. Thunder Girdle vanished immediately beneath their frantic ministrations.

He turned and saw his wife and daughters standing several steps away. All three of them looked pale and shocked. He walked over to them and took Gentle Dawn's hands in his own. "Are you all right?"

"Just a little . . ." She blinked. "I thought he was dead."

Long Fingers leaned closer and whispered, "No such luck." He looked down at Dusk and Moon. "Girls? We'll go home now."

He scanned the larger part of the room. "Where is Green Eyes?"

Gentle Dawn sounded puzzled. "I don't know. I was watching the King."

Moon piped up. "Mama Root took her away. I saw her."

Long Fingers breathed a heavy sigh of relief. His eyes met Gentle Dawn's and he winked.

"Come, wife, let's get these girls home. I think they've had enough excitement for one day."

Chain Coil and Long Snake and the rest of the servants met them outside on the steps. After they had formed up and set off for home, Dusk asked, "Is Green Eyes now our sister?"

"No, not exactly, but she's our ward."

"Is she as noble as we are?"

Long Fingers looked startled. "Why, I suppose she is. Her full name is now Green Eyes Blue Water Moon."

Dusk nodded thoughtfully, but said no more. Long Fingers wondered what she was thinking. He didn't see the two thin lines that appeared above the bridge of his wife's perfect nose as he spoke those words, and they were almost gone when he did happen to glance at her. He saw something, though.

"What's the matter, dear?"

"Nothing. A little headache, that's all."

"Well, I shouldn't wonder. It must have been a shock."

"Yes," she said. "It is."

Long Fingers didn't catch that, either.

5

Ranged all along the front of the temple atop the Goddess's pyramid were huge stone sculptures of the Gods and the Great Spirits that served Her. White Feather Writer passed by them without a second glance and entered the broad space of the main altar room. He circled past the altar itself, which was a smaller replica of the Great Altar in the plaza far below. His steps sounded briskly on the polished and painted stucco floor. At the rear of the large chamber he went to the middle door that was covered with a plain red curtain. He pushed the curtain aside and said, "I'm here."

Cham Ix, the High Priest of the Goddess, looked up. "Oh, good. Sit down, White Feather. I'm almost done."

White Feather raised one hand in acknowledgment and found a seat on an empty mat near the back of the room. This chamber was much cozier than the altar room outside. A window had been cut into the back wall. It gave a fine view out over the northern part of the city and the valley beyond.

His father turned back to the accountants and scribes who were giving him the daily reports. One of the things laid upon man by the Gods was the duty to know what the Gods had made. The rules were quite complicated and extremely precise, but in essence they boiled down to one thing: count and record *everything*.

It was in that counting and recording—of everything from ears of corn, to stones, to men, to slaves, to stars—that man could learn to know and love the world the Gods had created. And such learning and loving was why the Gods had created man in the first place.

So over the years he had sat just like this, at meetings just like this, while accountants and scribes named the things they had counted and recorded. Some of it was temple business. The temple was the wealthiest in the city, wealthier even than the Plumed Serpent. The Goddess owned many of the fields that covered the valley beyond the city, all the way to the mountains. The temple also had its own traders, priests raised from birth in the arts of seeking, finding, and exchanging wealth on behalf of the temple.

Some of it was city business, for the temple kept track of everything. There had been temple money in the last Great Census, and though common knowledge held that the Temple of the Plumed Serpent had charge of the results, a few knew that copies of those knotted strings also resided in the secret storehouses of the Goddess.

Long experience told White Feather the reports were almost done, but it would be a little while yet. His gaze drifted toward the window. He had grown up with that breathtaking view, for even as a young child his father had brought him here. He'd once said, "You don't understand what you see now, but you will absorb it anyway. Someday you will understand, but for now it is enough that you live in your heritage, as you live in the air you breathe."

White Feather thought his father was the wisest man he knew, and he loved him very much. They didn't look at all alike. White Feather was tall and well formed, with light brown eyes that were quite striking in a world of dark-eyed people. His father was short and round, with bright, black-button eyes. As he sat cross-legged on his mat, his belly bulged into his lap.

Cham Ix had lost most of his hair over the years, and now only a short white fringe remained. Sometimes White Feather thought it was a symbol of all else his father had lost, including his beloved wife and his two eldest sons. White Feather had never known his mother. The Goddess had sent a fever demon for her shortly after White Feather's birth, and he'd been raised by a succession of serving women and slaves. A similar demon had taken his eldest brother, who was his father's pride, and two years later his middle brother had fallen while climbing on one of the statues he was forbidden to climb on.

So from his early adolescence on, White Feather and Cham Ix had been alone together, two men trying to find their way to each other, rattling about in their huge apartment as silent old women tended to their needs.

White Feather saw the aura of sadness that surrounded Cham Ix, though his father was able to keep it hidden from all others. But the sadness didn't put off the boy, either as a child or when he finally reached manhood. If anything, he respected it. A lesser man might have broken beneath so much loss, become embittered and sour, but Cham Ix remained what he always had been: a gentle, loving priest whose faith in his Goddess had never wavered in the slightest.

White Feather surfaced from his thoughts to the whispers and rattles and grunts of men readying themselves to depart. He sat still until the last of them had passed beyond the curtained door, and then he stood up and walked over to the window.

He heard the creak and crackle of aged joints behind him, a soft grunt, and then his father joined him. The older man reached up and put a friendly hand on White Feather's shoulder. They stood in silence, staring out at the eye-boggling panorama.

"It's beautiful, isn't it?" Cham Ix said softly. "Every time I see it, I think of what She has given us."

"Yes," his son murmured. "I, too. She must have loved us very much." He sighed. "And yet many men take it for granted. I have seen the old records. Tollan was not always great. Once, even this pyramid didn't exist. But She raised us up."

"Men forget," Cham Ix said. "And it is our duty to keep reminding them."

"Yes, I suppose," White Feather agreed. "Father, you sent for me. How may I serve you?"

"I have a task for you, son. It is a delicate one, I'm afraid, but necessary."

White Feather had much experience with tasks his father thought delicate but necessary. Usually they were also interesting. His curiosity quickened.

"I am at your command always, Father. Just tell me what you want."

Cham Ix moved away from the window. "Certain things have come to my ears . . ."

White Feather grinned. Many things came to his father's ears. The spying apparatus of the temple was not the largest in the city, but it was perhaps the most effective. Very little passed in even the most secret rooms of Tollan that Cham Ix did not eventually hear about, one way or another.

"What have you heard, Father?"

"There is a mysterious young girl living in the house of Prince Water Moon."

"Eh? What is so interesting about that?"

His father rubbed his palm across his bald pate. "Oh, I don't know that she is interesting at all. What *is* odd, though, is the way Long Fingers is behaving when it comes to her."

White Feather was well aware of the endless tricks of the head of the Water Moon Clan, and he thought he had a fair idea of the direction in which some of those tricks were leading. It was no secret in certain parts of the city that the hand of the King was not quite as strong as it once had been, or that the strength of the Water Moon had waxed as that of the Summer Moon waned.

But Long Fingers, for all of his trickery, was something of a known quantity. It was his son, Golden Hand, that made the exercise interesting, for White Feather understood something that others missed: had Long Fingers been intriguing to secure the throne for himself, he would eventually fail.

It was White Feather's own judgment, which he had related to his father, that if Long Fingers attempted to take the throne for himself, he would fail not because of any lack of personal power and wisdom, but because he was old.

"There are two things that make a king," White Feather

had said to his father. "The first—and of course most important—is the blessings of the Gods, particularly the Goddess. But the second is the agreement of those powers lesser than the Gods, but greater than common men. That would be us, the priests, for instance, the wealthy families like the Eighteen and their adherents, and then the new people. The merchants and the manufacturers. Tollan has become a great factory, almost without anybody realizing it. I have read the old records. Many generations ago, almost all the wealth of the city came from this valley alone. But now by far the largest part of it comes from far outside our own mountain walls. An endless river of things comes here and is changed and remade into other things. We mine our famous greenstone, as always, but where we once traded it raw to those in the south, now we fashion it into fine knives or ax blades or into the shapes of our Gods, and we trade it all over the Middle World."

His father had nodded. "Yes, that is so. And you think all that makes a difference in how the powers are balanced nowadays?"

"Yes, Father, I do."

"Well, not exactly. Take, for example, this new metal that has appeared from the south recently."

"I have seen it. Looks gaudy to me. I certainly wouldn't want any of it."

White Feather grinned. "Of course not. You are old too, Father."

"Hmph."

"Well, think on it this way. You, and your friends, aren't much interested in it, because you don't much like new things. But Golden Hand found it, and brought quantities of the raw metal back to the city. But that wasn't the most important thing he brought back."

"Oh? And what was?"

"He brought foreigners skilled in working the metal, at shaping it and polishing it into rings, necklaces, armbands, earrings. And now many of the young nobles wear the new jewelry."

"Huh. Including young Golden Hand himself. Far too much of it, I'd say."

"He's a wise young man, Father. He parlayed his own social standing into profit. And he understood what he was doing. It wasn't luck. He even changed his own name, so that nobody could speak of him without speaking of his new metal. But the most important thing was those artisans. And if I'm any judge of him, he will soon go back down south and return with as many gold workers as he can find."

His father frowned. "All right, I can understand that, I guess. But back to the kernel of things. How does this peculiar sort of thing make Tollan more vulnerable? After all, even your pretty Lord Golden Hand brings the artisans *to* the city. They are still under our finger. We tax the wealth they create."

"Yes, of course. But think a moment. Would you or, say, King Thunder Shield have thought to build a whole new industry for Tollan out of some soft yellow lumps?"

Cham Ix stared at him. "Perhaps not."

"No offense, Father, but I don't think you would have. I don't think even Golden Hand's father would have. Such doings are for young men, with new thoughts and fresh ideas."

"Well, perhaps. I'll think on it. Does your theory explain why Long Fingers can't take the throne himself?"

"Yes, I think so. It is because the people like his own son won't allow it. In the past two generations the world has changed, and the older generation does not yet understand how much. But the younger generation does. And the power rests with them now."

"The power in the City of Tollan rests with such young upstarts? You must be crazy, boy."

"I don't think so, Father. And I think I know someone who agrees with me."

"Oh? Who is that?"

"Well, you have heard the rumors about the King. That he plans to abdicate in favor of his son, who is Golden Hand's age. Why do you suppose he would do that? He is still strong and healthy. He could rule for many more years. What would drive him to give up the throne?"

Cham Ix had stared at him then for a long time, his black eyes thoughtful. But they had spoken of it no further. Until now.

Now Cham Ix said, "This mystery girl in Long Fingers's house. I believe she has something to do with what we discussed some time ago. I think she is intended to be a pawn in the game Long Fingers is playing, and I would like to know how she can be such a thing. From what I gather, she is nothing more than a rude savage from some village in the southern jungles. Yet he has taken her into his own house, and I am told that today the old pirate plans to become her official guardian. That she will become a full member of the Clan of the Water Moon, with all the rights and obligations of the high nobility."

White Feather raised his eyebrows. "Now, that *is* strange. Today, you say? But I believe Golden Hand is out of the city, on a trading journey."

"Yes, gone a month now. Makes it all the odder. If, as you believe, Long Fingers is scheming not on his own behalf, but on his son's, then where does this girl fit in? It doesn't make any sense. Which of course doesn't mean there is no sense to it, just that I don't yet know what sense there is. Which is where you come in."

White Feather grinned. "I thought I would."

Cham Ix grinned at him. "Long Fingers gave me an opening when he *officially* adopted her. That means she is now a noble lady, with, as I said, all the rights. But she must also bear all the *obligations* of noble womanhood as well. She must be taught the lesser secrets of the Goddess, just as any other noble woman would be. So when I discovered Long Fingers's intentions, I approached him with this."

"Hm. I'll bet he enjoyed that. He doesn't like meddlers in his affairs."

"Who is meddling?" his father asked blandly. "I am merely doing my duty."

"Yes, of course. What did he say?"

"Oh, he was very reluctant. Wouldn't let me see the girl at all. But finally he agreed the law was plain. If she is to become a true noble, then she must be taught. And so he gave in. Grudgingly, I might add, and only after I agreed to certain conditions."

"Ah, what conditions?"

"Oh, absolute secrecy, for one. I am not to reveal anything I know about the girl to anybody. Neither can the teacher I send, who must also be absolutely trustworthy."

A faint grin had been flickering across White Feather's lips. Now it spread into an ear-to-ear smile. "What's her name, Father?"

"Green Eyes Blue."

Green Eyes Blue? White Feather liked the sound of it.

6

They carried the King on a litter to his rooms in the palace behind the throne room.

"I can walk," he said testily, but when they got him on his feet he swayed dangerously.

"Father, let them carry you to your bed. I'm sure you'll be fine after a good long rest, but you look pale right now."

He was still grumbling as they laid him down. "Send them away. Get rid of all those priests," he told his son.

Thunder Shield shooed them all out, then returned to the raised stone divan on which his father reclined atop a thick feather mattress, his eyes closed.

"Can I get you anything, Father? A cup of water? Something to eat?"

"No, I'm not hungry. Did you see that bird? Where did it come from?"

Thunder Shield shook his head. "It must have flown in from the outside. I didn't see it till the last moment, and by then it was too late."

Something in his tone caused Thunder Girdle to open his eyes. He reached out and took the boy's wrist. "I'm not blaming you, son. It was just odd, is all. I hope it wasn't an omen of some kind."

Shield relaxed a bit. "I'll talk to the priests about that if you'd like."

"Yes. What do you think the Prince is up to?"

"Long Fingers? Why?"

Sometimes Thunder Girdle despaired. He fully intended to put his son on the throne in three years time. But he seemed unfledged, still too . . . boyish. He was a quick thinker, but most of the time that only meant he made his mistakes just as quickly as he could think of them.

Thunder Girdle had tried to teach him patience, explain how you had to wait and look and think about things so you could understand how they really were, not just how they looked on their surface. He closed his eyes again. Maybe this would be a good opportunity to give the boy another lesson.

"Son, what did you see out there today?"

Thunder Shield spoke immediately, with no thought whatsoever. "I saw the bird fly in, and startle you, and then you fell down."

"Yes, yes, of course you saw that," he said testily. "Everybody saw that. It was the most obvious thing to see. The King falls down. Quite a show. But did you see anything else?"

Thunder Shield realized, as he had so many times before, that once again, without quite knowing how, he had angered his father. No, that wasn't quite right. His father might be angry, yes, but it was because Thunder Shield had let him down. But he didn't understand how. Nevertheless, he tried to practice what he'd been taught, slowly, patiently, over and over again.

"Uh . . . you mean before you fell down?"

"Yes, perhaps. Think about it. Is that what I could mean?"

This confused Thunder Shield even further. Now he had to decide not only what his father wanted him to say, but even what his father was saying to *him*. It made his head spin.

He took a chance. Sometimes he guessed right, and this time he did. "Yes. Nothing happened after, except the priests came. But before, there was the ceremony. That girl. Prince Long Fingers took her into the Water Moon Clan. He made her a high noble. Officially. That was strange."

Thunder Girdle smiled. "Good, good. Go on."

"Well, uh . . . that's all, I guess. It was strange."

"Why was it strange?" Thunder Girdle was no longer smiling.

A long silence ensued. "I don't *know*, Father."

A vein began to throb in the King's wide forehead. "Long Fingers is the head of an ancient and proud family. And he is as proud as any of them. So if he were to take somebody into his clan, do it officially before the throne, what sort of person would he be likely to do that for?"

"Well, ah, one of the minor nobility. Some small clan, outside the Eighteen, perhaps. Actually, some likely boy, I'd think. Somebody with talent."

"But he didn't do that, did he? Instead, this girl. This Green Eyes. What do you know about her?"

Thunder Shield shook his head. "Nothing, Father. She's a girl."

"Well, I know something about her. She was his son's slave. His son bought her from some traders while he was in the south. And he brought her home."

"That's strange, too, now I think about it," Thunder Shield said. "That he'd bring her to his house. I mean, he could have had her all he wanted, and kept her anywhere."

Thunder Girdle groaned softly.

"Father? Does your head hurt? Shall I call the priests again?"

"No. *Think,* son. You're right. If all he wanted her for was as a consort, he wouldn't have brought her home. Certainly not to his father's house. But he did bring her there, and his father accepted it. Even more, his father raised her to the nobility. So of course there's more to it than the obvious. Do you know what it is?"

Miserable now, Thunder Shield shook his head. "No, Father, I don't."

"Well, this time, don't feel so bad. I don't, either. Now. What else did you see today?"

Silence.

"Well, I guess it's asking too much. We keep coming back to the girl. There was something strange about her, too, besides her background. Why was I standing up, so that the crow could startle me into falling?"

"You were holding out your hand to her."

"Why?"

"You were asking her to take off that . . . oh."

"Yes. The mask."

"Well, I don't see how that's so strange. Young ladies of the nobility often wear masks in the presence of men outside their family. It's only propriety."

"But this wasn't public. This was private. And I am the King. There was no reason. Yet she wore a mask. What do you think, boy?"

A slow warm glow began to bloom in Thunder Shield's mind. Finally he thought he saw what his father was driving at. "For some reason, Long Fingers didn't want anybody to see her face."

This time his father's smile was genuine. "More than that,

boy. Not just anybody. He didn't want *us* to see it. You or me, maybe both, I don't know. Now why do you suppose that is?"

But Thunder Shield was exhausted with so much thinking, and this stumped him. "I don't know," he said finally.

"Do you think it might be worth your time to try to find out?"

"Ah . . . I guess so."

The King stared at him. "Go away, son," he said after a while. "I'm tired. I need to rest."

Chapter Eleven

1

The sun was a fine hot glow on White Feather's shoulders when he arrived at the door of the Water Moon house promptly at the first hour after noon.

He'd never been inside, though he'd walked by the house many times. From the outside it looked like most of the great private homes scattered about this part of the Citadel. Its outer walls were long and high. The thatch that hung over the edges of the roof line was thick and well trimmed. The painting on its stucco surfaces was particularly excellent. A talented artist had been at work here, filling every bit of space with the colorful beasts and Gods and men that had some relevance to the history of the Water Moon.

He grinned as he noticed special prominence had been given to the last man of the clan who'd also been king. This house bore the markings of royalty by right, though that right was from the distant past. White Feather wondered how much longer it would be before new symbols appeared denoting royal power in the present.

A single guard stood at the door, lazing on his spear. White Feather walked up to him.

"I am White Feather, a priest of the Goddess," he said. "Would you tell your master I am here?"

The guard snapped to immediately. "Yes, sir, he's been expecting you. I'll be right back."

White Feather waited, enjoying the feelings of anticipation that seemed only sharpened by the sparkling afternoon.

Green Eyes Blue, eh? he thought. Well, I'll know soon enough.

To his great surprise, Prince Long Fingers himself appeared in the doorway.

White Feather ducked his head. "Lord," he said. "How nice of you—"

"Yes, yes. Come in, won't you? I want to speak with you a moment before you meet my ward."

"Thank you, Lord." White Feather followed the shorter man inside. The interior was quiet and cool. There were fewer servants about than White Feather had expected. Eventually they emerged into the brighter space of Long Fingers's reception room, where the Prince offered him pulque with his own hands.

"No, thank you, sir."

Long Fingers poured for himself. "Ah, well. You're a priest. You won't mind if I do, though?"

White Feather shook his head. He knew about the Prince's drinking habits. He reminded himself not to underestimate the man because of them.

"Sit down . . . White Feather, I believe it is?"

"Yes, sir."

The Prince seated himself across from the priest. "I believe your father to be an honorable man," he said.

"He is, sir," White Feather said.

"I trust him to keep his word. And to keep the secrets he has agreed to keep."

"He will do that, sir."

"And what about you? Will you do so as well?" A stern tone insinuated itself into the Prince's words that might have cowed most men. But White Feather's lineage, in its own way, was every bit as good as Long Fingers's own. He raised his head and deliberately stared down his nose. After all, his family had served the Goddess before the Eighteen Families even existed.

"My father's word binds me as well," he said haughtily. "How else could it be?"

The Prince only nodded, seeming not to notice the hauteur. "Good. No more than I expected, of course."

He sipped his pulque. "Very well. The rules. My ward is

not from the city, as I'm sure you've heard. My son brought her back as a slave from one of his expeditions. When you see her, you will understand why. He intends to marry her when she is ready. You will also understand about that when you make her acquaintance. But here is the critical thing— because you will understand so easily, so will others. And so you must agree not to reveal anything of your understanding to anybody else."

"I must speak of it with my father. We have no secrets between us."

Long Fingers's lips shaped a moue of irritation. He waved his free hand sharply. "Oh, I understand that. Cham Ix and I have already spoken. Other than your father, I mean. Do you agree?"

"Yes, Lord, I do."

"Swear it, then."

"No, Lord, I will not. You have the word of my father, and mine. Which means you have the bond of the Goddess Herself. It will have to suit you."

"Hmph. Arrogant young fellow, aren't you?"

White Feather grinned. "No, sir. But you impugn the Goddess, whom I serve. Surely you don't expect me to let it pass?"

Long Fingers drained off his cup, belched, and set it aside. "Very well. The rest of it, then. Nothing you learn of Green Eyes goes beyond you and your father. You will teach her the Lesser Secrets, so that when the time comes she may serve the Goddess as all noble women must. My wife has charge of the rest of her education, but Cham Ix tells me you may also have knowledge to impart that would help her make her way. If so, you have my permission. Just do me the favor of checking with me first. Do you agree to all this as well?"

"I do, Lord. When can I see her?"

Long Fingers stood and gestured to the atrium beyond the room. "No point in waiting, is there? Follow me."

2

White Feather had no idea why he felt a twinge of nerves as he followed the Prince down the wide atrium steps. He looked around with interest. The place was even larger than he'd guessed, and very nicely kept.

Immediately his eyes were drawn to the altar and pyramid in the center of the atrium. Some unknown sculptor had done great work here. The pyramid was a perfect replica of the larger one, even to the small copy of the Goddess's head atop the tiny temple.

"Beautiful," he murmured.

Long Fingers glanced over his shoulder. "Thank you. It was made for my ancestor, the last man of the Water Moon to be king."

"Ah."

The atrium seemed deserted. He wondered where the girl was. Long Fingers led him around the altar and he saw her on the other side. Her back was to him. She was sitting on a mat, hunched over what appeared to be a box of mud. Black hair that shone like oil on water streamed down her back.

"Green Eyes," the Prince said.

She turned. "Oh. Lord . . ." she said.

"You must call me father," he told her.

She looked up at them, her glorious eyes glowing in the sun.

"This is White Feather," the Prince said. "He is here to teach you the secrets of the Goddess."

Green Eyes nodded seriously, her eyes growing even wider. "Hello, White Feather," she said shyly.

He couldn't answer. He was frozen, struck dumb by what he saw. Surely the Prince couldn't know. Could he? No, of course not. It was at the heart of the Goddess's most secret mysteries. It was never spoken of aloud, only in the language of hands.

At the moment, only three priests knew of it—himself included, but only because he was his father's son. He stared in wonder at her, and felt a bubble of joy swelling in his chest.

This changed everything!

"White Feather?" the Prince said.

"Oh, I'm sorry." He felt his smile stretch like some long string of rubber. "Hello, Green Eyes Blue. I'm very pleased to meet you."

3

The crimson rays of sunset tinged the smoky dusk as White Feather ran up the steps of the Moon Pyramid. He should have collapsed halfway up from the exertion, but such was his excitement that he felt as if his feet had wings. He bounded up like a mountain goat, and when he reached the top, he felt more energetic than when he'd started at the bottom.

He rushed across the altar chamber and whipped aside the red curtain. "Father!"

As usual, Cham Ix was surrounded by priests and servants. The administration of a great temple was a never-ending affair. The High Priest looked up, his eyebrows rising. "A few moments more, White Feather."

"No! I mean . . . Father, I need to speak with you now. It's very important."

Cham Ix's eyebrows rose even farther. "My son, many things are important, even what—"

"Father!"

"My goodness." Cham Ix turned to those ranged around him. "I'm sorry, gentlemen, but evidently my son has lost his mind. If you'd allow me a few minutes alone with him?"

The other priests gathered up their things and departed, some of them with grins twitching on their lips. White Feather might be the son of the High Priest, but everybody knew this gave him no immunity when he overstepped the bounds.

White Feather didn't notice. He watched them go, jittering from one foot to the other as he tried to suppress his excitement. He waited until the red curtain fell a final time.

Cham Ix rose to his feet. "Now, look here, White Feather. I know you're my son, but that gives you no right to come barging in here—"

White Feather raised his hand and interrupted his father for the third time in as many moments. He went quickly to the curtain and peeked around it. He saw nobody within earshot, and let the curtain drop.

"Son!"

He turned around and walked quickly across the room, until he stood by the window. He gazed out at all the richness beyond, at all that tangible evidence of the Goddess's bounty, and thought his heart might explode with the joy of it all.

His father came up to him. "I was joking about you losing your mind, but now I'm beginning to wonder."

White Feather swung around and took him by his shoulders. He pushed close to his father's face and whispered the words he was terrified to speak aloud. Though he really wanted to shout them at the top of his lungs.

"It isn't just a name. Green Eyes Blue. It's the truth. *Her right eye is green and her left one blue! Green Eyes Blue!*"

Cham Ix stared up at him. His mouth fell slowly open as his eyes grew wide.

"Oh," he said. "Oh, my . . ."

"Yes," White Feather replied, somewhat calmer now. "Oh, my, indeed."

4

About two-thirds of the way up the Moon Pyramid, on the rear side, hidden behind a carved stone panel, was a narrow

crack in the facing stone, so thin it was almost invisible. A
wooden door concealed the crack. The door was carved and
painted to match the surrounding stone, and completed the
illusion. If you didn't know about it you could stand a pace
away, stare directly at it, and not realize anything was there.

At night, of course, it was utterly invisible. Cham Ix
found it by touch. "Help me," he said softly.

White Feather stepped closer. Together they lifted the
door aside, moved past it, and then in total darkness set it
back into place.

White Feather heard soft scrabbling sounds. He reached
into the small bag slung over his shoulder.

"Strike the flints," his father said.

White Feather scraped the two fire-stones together, producing a sudden shower of sparks. He did it twice more before one of the sparks landed on the oil-soaked rag that
wrapped the end of the torch. It smoldered a moment. A blue
worm of fire began to crawl. A moment later it burst into
bright yellow flame. His father raised it.

"Come," he said.

The torch set the shadows to dancing crazily on the rough
stone walls of the narrow passage. "Let me light another
one," White Feather said, moving toward a stack of torches
upended in a huge pot just inside the door.

"Hurry," Cham Ix said.

When both torches were flaring, sending clouds of dark,
greasy smoke upward, they moved forward. The tunnel
widened gradually, and was of almost normal size when
they came to a carved stone lintel that marked the end of this
part of the tunnel.

It was very stuffy, though a thin trickle of cool air blew
outward from the darkness ahead. It was here they entered
into the heart of the pyramid, the oldest part, of which the
rest was an outer shell added much later than the original
structure. White Feather knew that though they were almost
a third of the way below the present top of the pyramid, this

level here had once been the peak. It had simply been covered with dirt when the pyramid was rebuilt on a grander scale. Beginning here the tunnel that led inward was crudely walled with naked, dripping stone. It felt more like a natural cave than anything man-made.

They walked along quickly without speaking. Eventually the tunnel ended in a space large enough that the light of their two torches touched the far corners of the chamber with only occasional flickering shadows.

In the center of this chamber was an altar carved of gray stone, and behind it an image of the Goddess that was wholly unlike the one atop the current pyramid. This lumpy figure was smaller, darker, and seemed both hunched and looming. Its flat female face sported fangs, and its thick, squat torso shaded into the hindquarters of a great cat.

This was the image of the Old Mother, a blacker, harder, hungrier version of the bountiful Goddess. On the altar before her were stains so ancient they'd almost faded away, but White Feather knew what they were. This Mother had once drunk greedily. And not only in times past. There were some newer blotches. When needed, the most secret mysteries of all were performed here, beneath the stone gaze of the Old Goddess.

The chamber smelled of dust and blood and time. Stacked all about, nearly to the ceiling, were baskets and pots and bales. Here were records so old only a few could still decipher their meanings, for they predated the time when men could write. Here were arcane pictures, symbols drawn in blood, things carved on sticks or bits of stone. Squat idols, lumpy shapes, crude figurines from a time when the Gods had been closer, and the Goddess had walked the Middle World as She pleased.

About the altar were several sockets sunk into the stone to hold torches. They fitted their torches into them and set to their work.

"It's been years, even for me," Cham Ix remarked. "In

fact, I think the last time I looked for these was when I showed them to you."

White Feather remembered it well. His penis had just begun to spurt the man juice, and his father had told him he was ready to know the heart of the mysteries. So he'd brought him here, on a night much like this one, and dug out the ancient things, the carved logs and the tiny idols that, if arranged in the proper way, told a story.

And so White Feather, still a quaking boy, had been initiated into the most ancient secrets of Tollan, mysteries so crusted with time they went back *before* Tollan, to the first recounting of the Goddess and Her son Shining Star, he of the blue eye, offspring of the Divine, and first king in Tollan by his terrible Mother's grace and his awesome Father's blood.

"Ah. Here we are," Cham Ix said. "Help me with this."

He was hunkered down, pulling out long carved sticks worn nearly smooth by the passage of countless years, and stubby little clay things with pear-shaped heads, thick lips, and huge ears, that looked like deformed babies.

White Feather knelt beside him. Together, they arranged everything into the proper patterns, and then, crouched over, they strained their eyes in the gloom to read the story.

When they finished, Cham Ix leaned back and clapped the dust off his hands. White Feather sneezed. They stared at each other.

"Well, I knew. I just had to check anyway."

White Feather wiped his nose. "I didn't remember all of it. I was young and scared. Some of the details slipped away."

"Yes, I suppose they would have. It's a long story. Even I had forgotten some of it. But it's all here." He gestured helplessly at the ancient records spread out before him. "All of it. So we know, and yet we don't know."

White Feather leaned forward and reexamined one part.

"It says here She came with eyes of black. But the Feathered Serpent took Her, and their son had a blue eye as His mark."

"Yes. She raised the Lord Plumed Serpent from the Underwater World and put Him back in His place in the sky. And She fought the Lord Jaguar and defeated Him, with the Serpent's help."

White Feather shivered. He looked down at the crumbling remnants, knowing they'd been made in the deeps of time by men who'd heard the true words from the lips of the Goddess Herself.

"This is Her city," he whispered. "And Her face looks down on it and guards it. Nowhere else, on no wall or stele, is there a female visage, for She is a jealous Goddess. Only on Her altars, and in Her temple . . ."

He glanced up. "I found Her in the atrium of the Water Moon, at the top of the house altar. It was a replica of this pyramid, and Her face was set upon the temple at the top."

He paused, remembering. "I saw the Goddess first, and then the girl looked up at me and smiled. One eye an emerald, the other a sapphire. Just a girl, not yet a woman."

"Help me up."

White Feather took his elbow and lifted him. They retrieved their torches and made their way out of the chamber. And though the air was baked, as if it were in an oven, White Feather still felt chilled.

They returned to the temple at the top of the pyramid. At this time of night only the two priests who maintained the ever-burning lamps around Her altar were still awake. They nodded to the High Priest and his son as they passed.

"I can't see any way that Long Fingers knows. If he did know, he'd run screaming, not adopt her and bring her into his house."

White Feather shook his head. "He doesn't know, of course. Only you and I know. This tale isn't told beyond the heart of our temple. No, he sees her eyes, and he—or his son—thinks they are important."

White Feather scratched his head. "The God-marks, of course. They probably think that's all there is to it. The blue eye—the mark of the Serpent. The mark of the kings of Tollan. It hasn't shown itself for . . . how many generations?"

His father was by the window, staring out at the limitless stars. "Many generations. Many." Then he paused. "Wait a moment. I'm remembering something. Something . . ."

He snapped his fingers. "Yes. There was a tale, many years ago when Long Fingers's only son was born. They named him Bright Eye . . . because he had the mark. The single blue eye. There was a stir at the time. But the boy had some kind of accident before his second year, and poked out the eye. So of course the talk died away. It had to be a false mark . . . for if it had been a true one, the Goddess would not have allowed it to be struck away."

White Feather said, "The Water Moon have been farmers for a hundred generations. They breed corn and vegetables. They know how things are handed down. Golden Hand must have seen it. The offspring of himself and this girl would likely bear the God-mark. If he produced such offspring, his claim to the throne would be immeasurably strengthened. The Summer Moon, Thunder Girdle's house, hasn't produced a God-marked one in any man's memory."

Cham Ix clasped his hands behind his back. "I'm frightened, son."

White Feather joined him at the window. The night breezes cooled the sweat from his brow. "The old prophesies are plain, aren't they?"

Cham Ix nodded. He spoke softly, in chantlike singsong tones. "When My city faces its greatest peril, then I will send My vessel, and when the time comes, I will fill her. And I will mark My vessel with the eyes of her Father, that all may know her. And I will come to her in wrath, to punish My enemies. So I speak to you, and so you remember. For I am She who brings Light and Death, and I will come again and again, unto the end of Time."

White Feather listened to his father. His own hands were cold, though his face was hot, and his belly was a single cramp of fear. He looked down and saw goose bumps on his arms.

"What's coming?" he whispered. "What has called Her back?"

"She doesn't lie," Cham Ix murmured. "She comes as She has promised. To punish Her enemies."

He looked again at the stars, but found no answer. "Whoever Her enemies are, I don't know. But She will show us."

He shuddered. "Oh, yes, She will show us."

5

"White Feather, why do you look at me like that?"

"Like what, Green Eyes?"

They were seated on mats on one of the steps around the atrium floor. The sun was exactly overhead, and so they were each centered in the dark blobs of their own shadows. White Feather was wearing nothing but a green kilt and sandals. He felt pleasantly sweaty in the heat.

Green Eyes wore a light yellow tunic that fell from her shoulders to the middle of her knees. Gentle Dawn had explained that she was too young to be alone with a man and have her breasts exposed. Green Eyes thought this very silly—in her own village women never wore any more than necessary because of the never-ending heat and humidity. But she'd learned to go along with all of Gentle Dawn's silly wishes. She'd finally learned that her life was much smoother if she did.

But what was much better lately was that her life had become more *interesting*. Ever since she'd officially become a ward of the Water Moon Clan, she had noticed an odd shift in the attitudes of those around her. A little more respect, perhaps. Dusk and Moon still weren't friendly, but at least they were no longer actively hateful.

And, of course, this handsome priest who came to visit with her several times a week. At first, when she'd heard a priest was coming to teach her the mysteries, she'd been afraid. If he taught her the same way Gentle Dawn did, it would be just one more dark spot in a seemingly endless series of dark days.

But he hadn't been like that at all.

"Oh," she said, "I can't really explain it. Sometimes I won't be looking at you, and I'll *feel* you staring at me. And when I turn, sure enough, there you are looking at me with this odd expression on your face. I get the feeling you aren't really looking at me at all. Or you might be looking, but you're seeing something different than me. Something else."

He tried to keep his expression unchanged, and from watching her amazing eyes he could tell he'd succeeded. He knew he walked a tightrope, and that an abyss yawned below, waiting for him to fall.

At first his father hadn't wanted him to return to this house at all.

"It's too dangerous," Cham Ix told him. "I'll have to cast auguries, make sacrifices. We have to learn Her will in the matter. Maybe She just wants us to stay away."

But White Feather shook his head. "Father, if that's what She wanted, She would never have sent you to Long Fingers."

Cham Ix thought for several seconds, sighed, and said, "I see what you mean. I could have sent almost anybody to teach her the minor mysteries—and do a little spying. But I didn't. I sent one of the very few people who would know immediately what she was. It's as if . . . *She* wanted me to know."

"Do the auguries, Father. Make the sacrifices, read the omens. But I think you're right. For some reason She wants us to know Her vessel is among us. And I think there's even more to it than that."

"Oh? What do you mean?"

"Well, after I got over my shock at seeing her—it must have been obvious, by the way, because Long Fingers gave me some very strange looks before he left us alone—anyway, after that I sat down with her and we talked. Nothing important. I was just trying to get to know her a little. You can imagine my curiosity."

"Yes, of course."

"Well. After we'd chatted a while, she told me an interesting story. I may even have been a part of it, in an odd way."

"Go on."

"When the Prince took her to the King for the ceremony of adoption, he told her very strongly that she should not remove the mask he'd given her to wear. No matter what, don't take off the mask."

Cham Ix raised his head. "Ah. He didn't want Thunder Girdle to see her eyes."

"Obviously not. Not before the girl is married, of course. By then it will be too late for the Winter Moon to do anything about it. In fact, if I were Golden Hand, I would try to keep the whole thing a secret until the first child is born. If it's a male, and bears the God-mark, the colored eye, that would have tremendous impact among the Families. Not to mention anybody else who follows the old traditions."

"The old traditions." Cham Ix sighed. "The Gods are all around us. They are in the ground we walk on, the air we breathe, the water that falls from the sky and runs in the rivers and nourishes the food we eat. They are in the animals, and they are in us. Maybe that's why *She* is coming back. Because, with all the new things and what you call the new men, we have forgotten. We call them them old traditions, as if they weren't as new as tomorrow morning, as permanent as the Middle World. Maybe the Gods are angry with us for forgetting. For letting our faith in Them grow weak."

"Is our faith weak, Father?"

"Maybe not yours or mine. But Tollan? In Tollan everything is money and striving and greed. Men plot against men for power, and though they give lip service to the Gods, they withhold their true faith. Oh, the great Families and the King do and say all the right things. They support the rituals and festivals and ceremonies more richly than they ever have. But it is their purses they open, not their hearts."

"Then maybe She knows about this. I think She knows about Thunder Girdle, and about kings. Because I think She protected the girl from the King."

"Eh? What do you mean?"

"On the day you first told me about the girl, I stood down in the plaza and looked up at the pyramid. A flock of crows was circling overhead. As I watched them, one flew away. I turned and watched it vanish, diving toward the Citadel."

"An omen . . . ?"

"More than that, I think. Green Eyes told me about it. As I said, she was taken before the King masked. Obviously so he couldn't see her eyes. But for some reason after the ceremony was over, he demanded that she take off her mask. She told me she was frightened because she didn't know what to do. Her new father had told her one thing, but the King was demanding something else. She'd finally decided to obey the King, and was reaching for the mask, when a black bird flew into the throne room straight at the King's face, startled him, and caused him to fall down the steps from the throne. She told me that while everybody tended to the King, her nanny took her away, and so the King never saw her face."

Cham Ix stared at him. "The crow is sacred to Her . . ."

"Yes."

Now White Feather thought of this conversation as Green Eyes shifted on her mat before him. He knew what she was talking about—about the way he couldn't keep the wonder out of his gaze. It was very hard for him. One moment he would be chattering away with a lovely young girl, and the next he would see her in her deeper, truer incarnation: as the vessel of the Great Goddess, empty yet but waiting to be filled. She was a harmless girl, and at the same time she was a terrible instrument.

He grasped her shoulders and gently turned her until he could look directly into her eyes. "Green Eyes, listen to me. If I look at you strangely, it's because . . . I think you're beautiful. That's all."

Color flushed into her cheeks. She broke eye contact and looked away.

"You shouldn't mock me, White Feather. I've never done anything mean to you, or tried to hurt you."

He had no idea what to say. He'd told her the first lie that popped into his head—how could he tell her the truth? But he'd trapped himself, because he hadn't lied.

He did think she was beautiful.

His thoughts churned in panic. What is happening to me? he wondered.

"There," she said. "You're doing it again."

"What?"

"That strange look."

"Green Eyes, I have to go."

Her lower lip stuck out. "I made you mad, didn't I? I didn't mean it, White Feather. Please don't be mad at me. You're almost my only friend. Please don't go. Please don't leave me."

But he had to get away from her. If only for a while, to gather himself. He touched her hand.

"Look at me, Green Eyes. I'll be back tomorrow. I just don't feel well all of a sudden. Maybe I ate something bad."

Her expression cleared somewhat. "Do you promise?"

"I promise."

"All right. If it's your stomach that's sick, maybe I should call Mama Root."

"Who's Mama Root?"

"She's my other friend. Besides you. She takes care of me. She knows all about roots and berries and leaves, and how to cure sicknesses."

"Oh, she does? Is she the one who led you away from the King?"

Green Eyes nodded. "Yes."

White Feather heard, in the recesses of his mind, the sound of a veil sliding aside in the breeze. "Why . . . yes. Maybe she could help me. Is she here?"

"Yes. She stays with me. She's probably in one of the kitchens."

"Well, then. Why don't you take me to her?"

Her small hand was cool in his own. I do have a fever, he thought.

He wondered why that should frighten him so.

6

White Feather knew her as soon as he saw her, and she knew him.

Green Eyes skipped ahead, leading him into a small, over-heated room, and he saw her hunkered down on her mat, a shapeless brown lump hidden beneath a broad floppy hat.

"Mama Root! This is White Feather, the priest I told you about."

Though the room was hot, White Feather felt a sudden chill blow up his spine as the hat slowly tilted up, revealing a blocky chin speckled with moles, thick, dark lips, and wide, staring black eyes. The eyes pinioned him like a frog on a pointed stick. Her gaze rummaged around in his skull. He wanted to turn away from her but he couldn't. For a moment he felt as if he were trapped in one of those strange dreams, halfway between waking and sleep. When the body was paralyzed and the demons danced in the corners.

"Ah . . . priest," she said.

Green Eyes squatted beside her, chattering away. "He's sick, Mama. He told me so. So I brought him to you, because you can fix anything. You'll make him well again, won't you, Mama?"

One gnarled brown hand crept from the shapeless robe and began to stroke Green Eyes's hair. White Feather couldn't take his eyes off that hand.

"Sick, are you?" Mama Root said.

"I'm feeling much better. Much better. I should probably just go home and rest awhile. I told Green Eyes I would—"

"Child, leave us."

"Mama!"

The old woman turned. "Dearest, if I am to help this *poor sick priest,* I need my privacy. Now go, and you can come back later, when I'm done."

"Oh, Mama."

"Hush, now. Go on with you."

Green Eyes sighed, then leaned forward and kissed her withered cheek. "All right." She stood and turned to White Feather. "Remember. You promised to come back tomorrow."

"I will. I'll be here."

She passed on by him, but paused at the door. "White Feather?"

"What?"

"Do you really think I'm beautiful?"

"Yes, Green Eyes. I do."

She giggled suddenly, and then vanished.

Leaving him alone with . . . what?

Many times he had stood on the top of the Moon Pyramid when the afternoon thunderstorms were gathering. You could see the great, fat-bellied clouds pile over the mountains and spill into the valley. A slow pressure would fill the air, a tension so great it made the chest squirm. And then the lightning would begin, hot, sizzling lances, the Sky Snake rampant, hissing and striking from sky to earth.

You could smell them and feel them. Your hair would stand up, and the back of your neck itch, and your nostrils fill with the stink of the burning air. It was the presence of the Gods. It was unmistakable. He felt it now.

But when he turned to look, it was just an old woman, still seated at his feet. She pointed at the floor.

"Sit down, boy. I think we should have a little talk, you and I."

He was surprised to find his knees were weak as wet rags. He started to lower himself and collapsed the rest of the way, landing on his butt with a dull thud.

"I am Mama Root," she told him solemnly.

"Yes . . ."

"And you are a priest named White Feather." The way she said it didn't sound like a question. Nothing she said sounded much like a question.

He stared at her. "You know, don't you? I don't know how, but somehow you know."

"I know what?"

"What she is."

Mama Root held his gaze trapped in her own, and for one awful, dizzy moment, he imagined himself toppling forward, falling into those deep pools . . .

"You look sick, boy. She said you were. Are you?"

"I don't feel well, but it's nothing you can fix. Answer my question. You know what she is, don't you?"

"Of course I do."

He realized he was clenching his jaws so hard that his skull ached. And the skin on his arms was crawling with goose bumps.

"She's a pretty young girl," Mama Root said.

"What?"

Mama Root eyed him, a puzzled expression on her sagging features. "You act like you've been out in the sun too long. Feverish. I do have some potions that might help . . ."

He felt like a man who'd just run for his life from some dark beast, only to turn and find himself facing a rabbit. His eyes bulged as he stared at her. What had he been thinking? There was nothing frightening about her. She was just an old woman, hunched near a fire to warm her chilly old bones, and there was nothing on her face but puzzled concern.

He sucked in a long breath. "I'm sorry. You must think I'm mad."

She smiled at him. "I'm glad she brought you to me, you know. I've been wanting to meet you."

"Oh?"

"Certainly. She's been much happier since you started coming to see her. She's a lonely child. I feel sorry for her sometimes, but there's only so much I can do." She sighed heavily and gestured at the fire pit. "I'm an old woman. It's hard for me to get around. To keep up with her. The master won't let her leave the house, and so she's cooped up inside all the time. It's not natural, and it's not good for her."

Though sweat was rolling down his face in sheets, dripping from his chin and pooling on his chest, White Feather suddenly realized he felt much better.

"She's a sweet child," he said.

Mama Root nodded. "She's more than that. You told her she was beautiful, eh?"

Now White Feather sighed. He felt like a fool. "Yes. I should be ashamed of myself, I suppose. But she really is beautiful."

Mama Root had begun to rock back and forth. It was a slow, rhythmic movement, not very large at all, but the little brain at the base of White Feather's skull, the brain that was the exact size and shape of an alligator's brain, noted it and thought of snakes. White Feather ignored the thought. He'd had enough of nameless terror for the day.

"I'm teaching her the Lesser Mysteries," he said.

"Yes, I know. She told me. They must have changed since I was a girl."

He stared at her in surprise. "You were taught the mysteries?"

"Oh, yes. But I don't recall my teacher ever telling me I was beautiful. I suppose it must be something new they've added since my day." She glanced at him. "Everything now is changing so fast it's hard to keep up. All the old ways are disappearing."

He felt the flush return to his cheeks and, embarrassed, he dropped his eyes. "I told her that because it's true. I just said it to cheer her up. She seems so sad sometimes. But after I said it, I realized I meant it." He shook his head in confusion. "Sometimes, when I'm around her . . ."

"Priest." Her tone was abruptly cool. It whipped him lightly, and he raised his chin, startled.

"What?"

"Guard yourself. She is not for you. She is betrothed. I know you were told that."

"Ah . . . yes. I was. I thought it a secret, though."

"Nothing in this house is secret from me. Teach her what you will, boy. You serve the Goddess, don't you?"

"Yes, of course." And though he had no idea why he suddenly wanted to impress this old woman, he did want to. "My father is the High Priest of Her temple. One day I hope to serve Her as he does."

She stuck out one hand. "Help me up."

He stood quickly and then hauled her to her feet. He was surprised at her weight and solidity. From the looks of her she would be as light as a bird. But she wasn't. It was like hoisting a bag of rocks.

"Come with me. I'll fetch you something for your illness."

"No, really, it's all right. I feel much better."

"You're sure?"

"Yes."

"Then I'll walk you to the door."

They passed through the maze of rooms and silent, cool halls. All about him the intricate paintings coiled and leered. He could hear the sound of his own sandals on the hard stucco, but Mama Root's footsteps were as soundless as the night. At the front door he paused. "I mean her no harm," he said.

She nodded. "I don't think you do. But as I say, be careful. She is a pretty little girl. But soon she will be a woman, and she is promised to the son of this house. Not to you. You are a priest. Don't forget it."

"No. I won't forget it."

"Good. You'll be back tomorrow, as usual?"

"I will."

"I'll tell her."

"Thank you. And now I really must be going."

"Good-bye, then, young White Feather Writer. Say hello to my old friend Cham Ix for me."

He caught only the barest flash of her twinkling black gaze as she turned away, and then she was gone.

"Hot out today," Chain Coil observed from his post at the door.

White Feather stared at him as if he'd just appeared in a flash of lightning.

"Yes," he replied. "Very hot."

He wasn't quite running as he stumbled blindly down the road. But he was close to it.

Chapter Twelve

1

Green Eyes left Mama Root and White Feather in the kitchen room and returned to the atrium. White Feather's mat was still unrolled next to hers. She rolled it up neatly and placed it with a stack of others, and then returned to her own seat.

She sat silently, her hands folded in her lap, staring up at the blue sky overhead. A few puffy white clouds drifted slowly past. There was something cheerful about them, the jaunty way they floated along, and they raised her spirits.

Did he really think she was beautiful?

It was the first time anybody had ever said anything like that to her. Gentle Dawn never said anything about her appearance at all, except to chide her when she was dirty. Green Eyes knew instinctively that her new mother would think such compliments unseemly. Long Fingers had ignored her since her adoption into the clan. And Dusk and Moon hardly talked to her anymore either. The only thing they'd ever said about the way she looked was the nasty name. Bump Face.

Beautiful? How can I be beautiful? she wondered. My hair seems all right, but I'm too skinny. And my eyes are certainly ugly, not dark and pretty like everybody else's. And no matter how hard I scrub, my fingernails are always dirty.

As she sat thinking about this, she became aware that it was very quiet. The wind had died away. The sun was a silent glare. She realized she was holding her breath, as if waiting for something.

A glint of refracted green light snagged her gaze. She turned her head. There, again.

She stared at the top of the pyramid. The light was striking it just right, glancing off the green knife resting there. Deep inside her mind a slow thrumming began. The knife.

Why had she forgotten about the knife?

The sound in her mind stirred memories like leaves, or a cloud of butterflies, and they came ghosting up. She remembered the feel of the sun on her back that day. The soft fur of the rabbit as she'd pulled its limp body from the crack. The hot, dry tumble of gray dirt, and the scratching, sliding sound the knife had made as it fell from its matrix of earth.

She remembered how cool it had felt. How the grains of soil had been hard and rough as she brushed them away from the smooth surface. How the stone handle had seemed to *shift* as it fitted itself into her palm.

She remembered the sure and certain knowledge that had come to her as she held it for the first time: *This is mine. This is for me. . .*

Her expression was blank and open as a sunflower turning toward the light as she rose from her seat and slowly approached the altar. When she reached it she put her hands on the side of the stone altar table. The surface held the heat of the sun. She sighed and scrambled up on the flat top of the altar.

She stood there a moment as if dazed. The peak of the pyramid was still above her head, and from her vantage point she could no longer see the knife.

She could *feel* it, though. Its deep, tolling cry still echoed back and forth within her bones. She placed her right foot on the first level of the pyramid and stepped up. The beat inside her brain paused, and then resumed, louder now.

Step by step she ascended. Now she could see the knife, resting before the small temple. She stared directly into the eyes of the Goddess on top of the miniature building as if mesmerized. That head was fashioned of greenstone, its eyes blank and empty. Yet she felt its gaze on her, bathing her with slow, expectant watchfulness.

As if it had been waiting for her.

The stone beneath her bare knees felt hot and gritty as she leaned forward, her right hand outstretched. Her dark hair hung in curtains on either side of her face. Her eyes were hidden.

Just before her fingertips touched the knife, she felt her ears pop. It was as if she'd suddenly been enclosed in an invisible bubble, an emptiness separating her from the rest of the world. Only she, the knife, and the Goddess were inside that bubble.

A faint sparkling sensation fizzed in her fingertips just as she touched the blade. Then things changed.

Sometimes, when she stood up too quickly, she grew suddenly dizzy. Darkness would crowd in at the edge of her eyesight and the world would shrink to a small lighted circle in the middle of her gaze. This was like that.

Her fingers curled around the blade. It still felt unnaturally cool, though it had been lying in the sun all day. But now it was all she could see, as a curious emptiness pressed in all around her. Some part of her was still aware of her surroundings—the atrium, the pillars of the rooms, the sky overhead. But those things had become gray and unreal. Only the knife, throbbing in her hand, was real.

Then it vanished, and she saw visions. Everything became utterly silent as she stared into the green blade and then felt herself falling forward into darkness.

A high place. A fire. Above her, a storm. The knife was no longer in her hand. It was . . .

Fear rippled in her belly. Overhead, the clouds exploded with light. In that awesome glare she saw a great dark shape off to her left. A black cloud, full of gnashing white fangs.

A woman appeared. Her face was twisted with rage. She shrieked something, but the storm swept away her words. She held a squalling baby cradled in the crook of her left arm. In her right hand she held a knife.

The knife.

She raised the knife as if to strike the baby. Behind her, the dark cloud writhed and moaned. And then from the sky came a bolt of light. It struck the dark cloud and burned it away, revealing a man.

The man began to burn.

The sight of his burning was hideous. Green Eyes felt her guts twist with nausea. The woman stared directly at her, but didn't seem to see her.

The baby screamed louder, and waved its chubby fists.

"I'll kill the child!" the woman shrieked, her features tortured beyond anything human.

Then a great, clear voice sounded. It held the same slow thrumming that she'd heard before, in another world.

"No, you will not!"

Green Eyes was aware of something vast and white approaching, something of such power that it could not be resisted. It took her a moment before she understood this was also a woman, a small woman in a white robe, its hems flowing with blood. From her hands emanated naked power, a force as strong as the bolts that rained from the sky. This woman raised her hands and the earth began to shake.

The shrieking woman staggered. The knife arced into the air. Green Eyes watched as it fell, sparkling against the gloom, into darkness.

A moment later the darkness covered everything, and she began to fall too.

She awoke, the knife in her hand, and found herself staring into the empty eyes of the Goddess. Her teeth chattered and her hands shook uncontrollably. The knife clattered from her numb fingers and fell with a rattle to the stone beneath.

Panicked, Green Eyes scrambled back down. She slid across the altar surface on her rear and slammed down onto the atrium floor, a jolt of pain bursting from the base of her spine.

She looked up to see Dusk and Moon staring down at her, their expressions thunderous with horror.

2

The fall had also slammed her teeth together on her tongue, and now Green Eyes realized her mouth was filling up with blood. She swallowed. But for some reason she was paralyzed. All she could do was sit there on her behind, her thoughts a confused welter, and wait for whatever horrible doom fate had prepared for her.

Dusk stepped forward, as haughty as only a sixteen-year-old girl born to the assurance of her own perfection could be. She folded her arms and looked down on Green Eyes.

"What have you been doing?" she said. Her voice was cold with triumph.

"I . . ."

"Look," Moon said. "Her mouth is full of blood."

"Of course," Dusk said. "What would you expect from somebody like . . . her?" She turned and glanced at her sister. "I can't imagine what Father was thinking of . . ."

Green Eyes experienced an almost overwhelming urge to scramble forward and sink her teeth into Gentle Dusk's smooth, beautiful leg. But Dusk turned her attentions back to her before she could act on the notion.

"You were on the altar. You climbed up and played with the knife Father put there. We both saw you."

Green Eyes lowered her head in misery. There was no point in denying it. She had done it. And she'd been told not to touch that knife. Why *had* she done it? For the moment the memory of the slow, grinding urge of her summoning vanished from her skull. All that remained was bewilderment. And terror.

"You are a bad, evil girl," Dusk continued remorselessly.

"It is a holy thing. We will tell Mother, and she will have you whipped." Dusk sounded quite unruffled by that idea.

The older girl thought of something and turned to her little sister. "Moon, who knows what the silly pig did with it? Go climb up there and make sure the knife is in the right place, that she hasn't harmed it somehow."

Moon had not been expecting the scene to take this particular turn. "Climb up on the altar?" She shook her head. "I'd better not."

But Dusk was not to be gainsaid. "I said *climb up there,* Moon. It must be done—and I'm certainly too old to clamber around like a monkey. Go on, do it."

"No, she shouldn't," Green Eyes said.

"You be quiet. You bad, bad girl." Dusk seemed to savor each word as if it were a stalk of sugarcane, full of sweet-tasting juice. "Go on, Moon."

Reluctantly, Moon approached the altar.

"Hurry!" Dusk hissed.

Moon stood there, her face pale. Tears brimmed in her eyes. Her lips quivered. "I don't want to."

"Climb up there now, or I'll tell Mother on you!"

Though this threat made no sense whatsoever, it galvanized the younger girl. She hiked up her skirt, exposing a smooth expanse of golden flank, and hoisted herself up. Dusk watched for a moment to make sure her orders were being properly carried out, then returned her attention to Green Eyes.

"Look at you," she said. "Bump Face, with your bloody lips and your scraped knees. You may marry my brother, but he won't keep you for long. Poor Mama can try all she wants, but she'll never be able to turn you into one of us. Never in the world. And Golden Hand will find out eventually, and that will be the end of you. I don't care what Father says."

She nudged Green Eyes with the tip of her toe. "Well? What do you have to say for yourself?"

Green Eyes raised her hand and touched her lips. When she brought it away, her fingertips were coated with blood. She couldn't raise her head. Her anger had drained away. Everything had drained away. She saw how it would be. She would never fit with these people, none of them. Why had the Gods caused her to be taken here? She wanted to die. That was the only way to escape.

I am a slave, she realized dully. But Mama Root promised me. If I wanted to, she would show me how.

A fierce wash of heat roared through her. Yes! I don't want to be a slave anymore! And *they can't make me!*

I can *choose!*

She looked up, feeling the blood trickle down her chin as she smiled.

From above came a sudden dry scrabble, like claws on stone. "Oh . . . oof!"

A hard click. "Dusk . . . I'm—"

Dusk raised her eyes, a different kind of horror on her face. She jumped forward. A moment later Moon's falling, flailing figure slammed into her and knocked her to the ground.

There they all sprawled, staring at each other, as with a hollow *tok . . . tok . . . tok . . .* the head of the Goddess rolled down the steps of the pyramid, bounced across the altar, teetered on the edge an instant, and then fell to the atrium floor. Where it shattered into a hundred pieces.

3

"Who was responsible?" Gentle Dawn asked.

A house slave finished sweeping up the shards of the Goddess's head. Gentle Dawn glanced over at him. "Save all of them!" she said sharply.

She turned back to where the three girls were seated on the steps. "I'm waiting," she said.

Dusk and Moon were sitting close together, Green Eyes a short distance away, her chin on her knees, her eyes closed. There were still streaks of blood on her chin. Dusk and Moon glanced at each other with guilty complicity, but neither said a word. Gentle Dawn saw this glance, and a frown brushed her lips. But she couldn't believe her own eyes.

"Young ladies do not disobey the instructions of their parents," she said. "Young ladies do not disobey their fathers, in particular. Young ladies don't go climbing on sacred altars, and young ladies don't break sacred things." She paused, and then continued ominously. "And if young ladies do these things, then young ladies will be whipped."

Moon let out a tiny whimper. Green Eyes raised her head and stared at Moon. She saw the terror in the girl's eyes. And why shouldn't Moon be scared?

Whipped, Gentle Dawn said. Green Eyes had seen whippings. She'd seen what Twisted Tooth had done.

Poor Moon, she thought suddenly. If she's whipped, it will kill her. And it wasn't really her fault.

Moon began to sob openly now. Gentle Dawn turned toward her, an expression of horrified disbelief on her patrician features.

But Moon only did what Dusk told her to, and she didn't want to do it in the first place, Green Eyes thought. If *I* hadn't climbed up on the altar, none of this would have happened. It was *my* fault.

"Moon," Gentle Dawn said, with a kind of crazed and dangerous serenity. "I want you to look at me, Gentle Moon."

"Mama . . ." Dusk said.

"Be *silent*, daughter. I'm speaking to your sister, not to you."

The sound of Moon's weeping grew louder. Her mother took another step toward her.

Once again it seemed that time stopped, and Green Eyes saw the world plain. She saw the look of dismay frozen on

Dusk's features. She saw the agony of terror on Moon's face. And she saw disbelief crawling in Gentle Dawn's expression. It was as if they were in some kind of horrible dance, chained to each other.

They were all trapped. Worst of all, they were trapped by cages they had built for themselves. The father had decreed something to be bad. And a woman had done that thing. So the woman must be punished. The woman must bleed for transgressing against the word of the father.

There was no mercy in the world of women, for women were slaves.

I am not a slave, Green Eyes thought again. I can choose.

"Gentle Moon, did you—"

Green Eyes raised her head. "I did it," she said wearily. "I broke the Goddess. Whip me."

4

Green Eyes crouched on all fours on a mat in the center of the atrium. Her naked rear pointed at the sky. Her hair trailed in sweaty strands down her cheeks. She felt numb, as if she weren't really there. As if some other girl was crouching in her place, waiting for the bite of the whip. Waiting for death.

In a curious way she felt a kind of release. Soon her misery would be over. A longing so strong it was as if a vise across her ribs clutched her and squeezed the air from her lungs. To go home again. To make time itself stop, then spin backward. To have back again that moment when she first saw the rabbit and drew her bow.

Oh, she would not do it. The rabbit would live, and the knife stay hidden in the earth. And she would walk down familiar paths beneath a kind sun, and at the end she would find loving arms, and none of this would happen.

"Dusk," Gentle Dawn said. "Go to my rooms and fetch me my whip." Her voice sounded weak and trembling.

"Yes, Mama." Dusk sounded even worse.

Do they understand? Green Eyes wondered. For some odd reason she thought of the women she'd seen in her vision. They hadn't been slaves. They hadn't been trapped. Had they?

She heard the quick shuffle of sandals. Then Gentle Dawn's voice close by.

"Green Eyes, you did a terrible thing, and you must be punished. You disobeyed the lord of this house. You must be taught never to do that again, taught in such a way you won't ever forget it."

A wild spurt of laughter clogged Green Eyes's throat. She choked it back. If nothing else, she would die in silence, her dignity intact.

She heard Gentle Dawn suck in a sharp breath, and she stiffened against what was to come. A faint, whickering hiss cut the air. A line of fire traced itself across her back. Once! Twice! A third time!

Then it stopped. Green Eyes waited.

"Get up, Green Eyes."

She turned. "What?"

"Get up, and put your skirt back on. Do you understand that you must never be disobedient again?"

Green Eyes climbed slowly to her feet. Gentle Dawn stood a pace away. She was white as a sheet. Her eyes had a glazed, staring quality. She looked as if she might faint at any moment.

Behind her, the two girls clutched each other for support. They didn't look any better than their mother. None of them could take their eyes away from her.

Gentle Dawn held a long, slender switch loosely in her right hand. Without seeming to notice, she relaxed her grip and it fell to the ground. That same awful gust of laughter threatened to fill Green Eyes's mouth again.

That was a whip? That was the terrible whip? Compared to the dreadful instrument Twisted Tooth had used, this was a toy. Yet the three women looked more shaken than Green Eyes felt. A burst of scornful strength came over her. She wanted to pick up the pitiful whip and snap it across her knee.

Instead, she picked up her skirt and folded it around her thighs. She stood in front of Gentle Dawn, and for a moment it was hard to tell who was the girl and who the woman.

"Do you understand . . . ?" Gentle Dawn whispered, her voice husky and indistinct with uncertainty.

"Yes," Green Eyes said. Her own words were clear. They filled the atrium. "I understand."

She raked the girls with a single long glance, and watched them flinch away from it. Then, head high, she marched out of the atrium.

Poor slaves, she thought. Poor *women*.

5

Hidden behind one of the pillars, a dark shape moved farther into the shadows as Green Eyes strode past.

Mama Root watched her vanish into the far hallway that led to the room they shared.

There was a rude cloth bag at her feet. She stooped over. The *click-clack* of broken shards sounded as she lifted it. After a while she slung it across one shoulder and set off the way Green Eyes had gone.

Behind her, in the atrium, Gentle Moon wept softly.

6

"She did *what?*" Cham Ix said.

White Feather blinked at his father's intensity. They stood at the top of the majestic flight of stairs that led down from the Palace of the Priests to the plaza in front of the Pyramid of the Moon. It was midmorning, and the business of the temple was in full swing. Petitioners, worshipers, those bearing sacrifices and donations, hurried past them, bound on small errands of penance or praise.

A man with a pair of squawking turkeys, their legs tied together and slung around his neck like some huge, feathery necklace, came up to them.

"Good sir, I wish to—"

White Feather pointed toward the palace interior. "See the priest just inside the door. He will tell you where to go."

The man nodded gratefully, tugged at a greasy hank of hair that curled across his forehead, and hurried off.

"You say the girl climbed up on the Goddess altar in her house and broke Her image?"

"It was an accident, Father. She said she wanted to see the sacred knife Long Fingers had put there."

"What sacred knife?"

"In a minute, Father. Long Fingers took me aside and told the story to me when I arrived at the regular time yesterday. Green Eyes had confessed, and Gentle Dawn had whipped her. Long Fingers wanted to make certain that if some evil remained, it would be washed away. He wanted me to perform a sacrifice on the house altar and ask the Goddess for forgiveness and absolution of any curse."

"And did you?"

"He offered a mighty donation to Her temple."

"Ah. Like the man with the turkeys."

White Feather shook his head. "No, the man with the turkeys is afraid. But Prince Long Fingers cannot allow himself to show fear. He makes sacrifice from respect, and the goodness of his heart. He shows the world his piety."

"Do you believe all that?"

"I believe that, underneath, Prince Long Fingers is every bit as terrified as that man and his load of gobbling birds."

His father smiled thinly. "Your wisdom grows, son."

"I have a good teacher. Anyway, I did perform the sacrifice, but I talked to the girl first. She admitted everything. She said it was an accident, and that she would never do anything like that again. But I have come to know her somewhat, and I don't believe she told me everything."

"She lied, you mean?"

"No, not exactly. More like she didn't tell all of the truth. I got the idea that something more had occurred, and I even asked her about it. But she only shut her mouth and shook her head."

Cham Ix nodded. They walked along the top of the stairs until they reached a balustrade in front of the pillars that lined the facade of the temple. It was about chest high, a thick filigree of fantastically carved stone. The top of it was smoothed by generations of human limbs that had rested on it. Both of them automatically rested their forearms on the polished banister and looked out over the plaza.

As always for this time of day, the booths around the edge that sold turkeys and piglets and baskets of fine corn for sacrifice were doing a brisk business. In some ways, White Feather thought, we have become as much a business as any other, sending out our traders, demanding our taxes, stuffing our storehouses with wealth. Are we any different than those new men Father dislikes so much?

"You were going to tell me about this knife . . ." Cham Ix said.

"Oh—yes. I saw it. It is ancient. Made of Godstone. Long Fingers told me it came from the south, from the same place as the girl. In fact, it was the girl's knife. She told Golden Hand she'd found it in what she called an Old Place, just before she was taken."

"Taken? By whom? I thought Golden Hand bought her."

"He did. From some bandits who'd kidnapped her from her village. Evidently they'd found her wandering in the forest alone, and couldn't resist such easy pickings."

"You didn't tell me this before."

"Hm? Oh, I've picked up bits and pieces. She doesn't like

to talk about her past. She says it makes her sad." He stopped. "You know, I do see that in her. A great sadness. It's no wonder, I suppose, after all she's been through. But you can actually feel it about her, even when she's laughing."

"Yes, I suppose so," Cham Ix said absently. "You know, I did do auguries and a sacrifice. The omens were not visible."

"Eh? I didn't know that."

"I didn't tell you. But the Goddess did not speak to me one way or another. It was almost as if She didn't want to say anything about the girl. But now I wonder. Is She speaking to us loud and clear? Except, perhaps, we don't recognize the sound of Her voice?"

"What do you mean, Father?"

Cham Ix's glance was troubled. "Consider these things, son. The girl—that particular girl, mind you, with those eyes, those God-marks whose meaning is known only to the few—is taken from her home in the south. The Goddess came to us from the south. And just before she was taken, she found an ancient knife in what she called an Old Place. I have been in those Old Places, son. Long before you were born I journeyed in the south lands, for that is where our Goddess comes from. At the end of the age of the Feathered Serpent She left there, bearing Her son, to begin the age we now live in. So I went there. Those Old Places are haunted. They are full of spirits so old we no longer know their names. I have seen those brooding stone shapes, half buried in the jungles, surrounded by ruins so worn down they are no longer recognizable."

"I never knew you went down there."

"There's always something for you to learn, son, even about me." He sighed. "Anyway, if that knife—made of Godstone, you say—came from one of those places, it is very old. Older, perhaps, even than our age."

"And you say it may be an omen?"

"This girl appears in our midst, in the house of a mighty

prince, bearing a weapon from the pits of time. The birds of
the air fly to preserve her secrets. She is without doubt a vessel of the Goddess, and yet she contrives to break the image
of the Goddess. I would like to see those shards, by the
way."

Now it was White Feather's turn to look troubled. "You
can't. I mean, I couldn't find them. The Princess told me
she'd ordered the slave who cleaned them up to save them,
and he said he'd left them in a bag near the atrium. But when
we went to find them, they were gone. The slave showed us
where he put them, and there wasn't any reason to think he
was lying."

Cham Ix adjusted his position a little, but didn't say anything for a while. "Something is happening. I don't know
what it is, but something is happening. *She* is among us, and
I can feel Her presence. That girl . . ."

He shook his head. "Keep me informed of everything."

"Yes, Father. I will."

"The knife bothers me. I will search the old records further."

White Feather thought of that cavelike chamber deep
within the pyramid, and its hunched, brooding occupant.
Could that knife actually be *older* than that crude lump of
stone?

"Do you see her today? How is she coming with the mysteries?"

White Feather grinned. "Oh, fine. She's very bright, you
know. Much brighter than the Water Moon Clan gives her
credit for."

Cham Ix nodded gloomily. "In some ways, the Water
Moon is not bright at all. But they are only tools, no more
and no less so than all the rest of us."

7

"Green Eyes?"

"What?"

"Can we come in?"

The room was small, only a few paces squares, but it was high. A skylight let in a shaft of the sun, illuminating the beautiful bands of pictures that ran along the tops and bottoms of the walls. As with all the rooms in the house, the furnishings were sparse. Here were only their two sleeping mats, a beautifully carved wooden box in which Green Eyes kept her few bits of clothing and jewelry, Mama's huge straw bag, and, in the corner, a covered chamber pot painted with cavorting dragons.

The chamber pot had been one of the most miraculous things Green Eyes had found in the city. There were no chamber pots in her village. You just went outside, found a likely spot, and took care of your business. But here, evidently, there was a whole magical process to the thing.

She'd once asked White Feather about it, and when he quit chuckling, he explained. The manure was valuable. And so in houses like this one, a servant called a "honey slave" gathered up all the pots every day and dumped their contents into the honey barrel. Every few days other men came along, rolling larger barrels on sledges that stood atop rollers. Only in the city, on the stone or stucco roads, would these roller carts work, and even so, it took many men to push them along. As one roller popped out the back, men picked it up and hurried it to the front of the sledge. It seemed clumsy, but they could move enormous weights in this manner. Eventually, the night soil from thousands of homes ended up on the fields surrounding Tollan.

"Yes, I guess so," Green Eyes told the two sisters.

Hesitantly, the older girls came inside. They stood, looking around uncertainly.

"You can sit on Mama Root's bed, I guess."

They glanced at each other. Moon still looked pale and drained. Even Dusk had lost her customary hauteur. They settled themselves and then there was silence. It lengthened uncomfortably, but since Green Eyes had nothing to say to either of them, she didn't care how long it took for them to speak. They either would or wouldn't, and it made no difference to her which.

Dusk finally screwed up her nerve. "Green Eyes, why did you lie to Mother?"

"About the altar? The Goddess?"

"Yes."

"I don't know. I thought she was going to kill Moon, and since it didn't make any difference to me whether I died or not, I decided to save Moon. She's not so bad, and it wasn't really her fault."

Dusk stared at her. "I don't understand, Green Eyes. What do you mean, you thought Mother was going to kill Moon?"

"She said she would whip her."

"Well, yes, but nobody ever died from a whipping. I mean, you saw that."

Green Eyes uttered a short, bitter laugh. "How was I to know that? Let me tell you what I knew about the way the people of this house do their whipping."

Then she proceeded, in a low, level voice, to describe in graphic and grisly detail about the two whippings she'd seen Twisted Tooth administer. She finished with a shrug. "So I thought your mother would summon Twisted Tooth again."

Dusk stared at her, aghast. During the telling of the tale, Moon had grown even paler. Now, suddenly, she leaped up and made for the chamber pot, one hand over her mouth.

When she came back, she huddled against her older sister, her eyes red, sniffling every once in a while.

"Green Eyes, I . . . didn't understand." Dusk put her arm around Moon and hugged her. "You must think we are monsters."

"I know you hate me," Green Eyes said matter-of-factly.

"I don't know why, just that you do. I want so very much to
go home, but nobody will let me."

"I'm sorry!" Moon wailed suddenly. *"I'm sorry, sorry,
sorry!"*

Something deep inside Green Eyes's chest cracked open
and spilled a little warmth inside her. She felt it spread as
she got off her bed, went over, and began to stroke Moon's
hair.

"It's all right, Moon. I don't hate you."

Dusk's haughty features looked as if something were
working invisibly beneath her skin, taking out the bones one
by one. She gulped, swallowed, then gulped again. "I'm
sorry, too, Green Eyes," she said, her voice barely audible.
"I don't know . . . you must . . . can we try again? We are
sisters now. Maybe we can try that?"

Green Eyes stared at her. "We can try."

8

The bent, hunched figure moved at a crablike pace across
the deserted plaza. Overhead, a grinning moon leered a wan
and yellow light through clouds stretched across the sky like
torn cotton.

Far above her, torches burned along the front of the temple. She stood at the base, looking up the endless flight of
stone steps, and let out a sigh.

As she put her foot on the first step, the bag over her
shoulder rattled dryly. She ignored the faint sound, and continued upward, one step at a time.

By the time she paused to catch her breath at the top of the
third level, she was exhausted. She limped over to the rail-
ing that guarded the broad balcony extending the length of
this side of the pyramid. She pulled off her floppy straw hat
and fanned her face, waiting for the terrifying pounding of
her old heart to slow. When she felt well enough to continue,

she did not return to the steps leading up, but went off toward the left side of the balcony. At the end, she found a space between the end of the stone balustrade and the pyramid itself, hardly noticeable, but large enough to permit a single human to pass.

She turned sideways and squeezed through. She bumped the sack, heard the sound of broken crockery, and grunted. The narrow footpath chiseled into the pyramid was barely wide enough to place both feet upon. And up here the wind tugged at her shapeless brown robe, threatening to pull her off her feet and fling her down the steeply sloping side.

She pulled her hood closer to her face—the wind was cold as well as strong—put her head down, took a tighter grip on the sack, and trudged onward. In this fashion, step by slow step, she made her way across the side of the pyramid, came to the corner, and continued until her way was blocked by a tall stone screen.

It took her a good bit of heaving and prying to move the heavy wooden door, but finally she opened a crack wide enough to pass on through.

Once inside, she stopped and leaned against the tunnel wall, again waiting for her breath to slow. She coughed suddenly. The sound was without echo, dead in the confined space.

She could smell the dry dust of the ancient earth farther on. She made no effort to light a torch. She knew the way well enough.

When she was ready she straightened her hat and, grumbling softly to herself, she went down the tunnel. She went on for a good while, and then, up ahead, she saw a soft glowing light. She smiled grimly to herself. Someone was at home, then. That was nice. This was far too hard a visit to make, now that her bones were frail as the skeleton of a bird, not to find the One she sought.

The light was filmed with smoky haze. It grew brighter as

she approached, and began to throb. She knew that rhythm—it echoed inside her wheezing chest.

"I'm coming," she muttered.

When she finally reached the hidden chamber, the light was spilling from everything—from the walls, the rotting logs that held up the ceiling, even rising from the floor like swamp glow. But the brightest thing by far loomed over the altar, as hunched as she was, but more terrible. That thing's eyes burned with fire, fire the color of emeralds and sapphires.

She approached the altar beneath the thing and saw that the ancient stains now glistened fresh and dark. It brought another grim smile to her dark lips.

"Angry, are you? Well, I guess *so*."

She slung the sack from her shoulder and let it fall on the surface of the altar. The light abruptly throbbed higher.

"Yes, I brought it back," the old woman grumbled. "It's what you wanted, isn't it?"

She untied the mouth of the bag, opened it, and poured its contents out onto the glistening surface. The witch light covered her now, too. It dripped like honey from her clawed fingers as she raked them through the shards. For a moment nothing happened. "Well, go on," the old woman said. "You know she'll need it later."

The hideous deadlight rose and fell, rose and fell, as something invisible and unknowable breathed softly to itself. Then, one by one, the shards began to move. Fitting themselves back together.

The old woman chuckled. "Good," she said. "Good."

Chapter Thirteen

1

Parrot Beak and Black Face walked along a stony embankment at the foot of the Storm God mountains. Above them rose towering peaks, as bleak and bitter as lost hope. The smell of cinders and ash drifted in the air. A few stunted trees poked up from the arid earth, as twisted as Parrot Beak's spine.

Black Face said to the four guards who accompanied them, "Wait here."

He led Parrot Beak farther ahead, to where the rocks jutted out in a natural promontory that overlooked the fields below. He stooped over and picked up a handful of clinkers. A sulfurous breeze blew down from above and fluttered the edges of his hood. His yellow eyes were hidden.

He gestured toward the fields. "Here is the old wealth of Tollan," he said.

Parrot Beak raised his head. Only the tip of his wooden nose protruded from his hood. He turned his head and spat. "Fields," he said. He raised one hand and pointed. "And the animals that tend them. Look at them."

Both men gazed at the object of Parrot Beak's scorn. The vast checkerboard of green squares extended into misty distance. From here only the great pyramids of Tollan were visible, glittering in the sunlight.

In every field a handful of figures moved and stooped, tending the crops.

Black Face grunted. He flung the cinders away. "I own a portion of all this. I take my taxes from the fat men who count grain and beads. And I have grown fat myself on my portion of their portions."

He laughed, a low sound muffled by the wind. "New times are coming, Parrot Beak. This is old wealth, but the new wealth grows from the makers of things and the hands of the traders. I wish to sup at that meal, but I need strong men to help me."

He turned. Parrot Beak felt that yellow gaze bore into him. "Are you such a man, Parrot Beak? Are you a strong man?"

Parrot Beak felt a thrill of excitement. This was what he'd been waiting for.

"You took me in, Lord. You gave me a home when I had nothing. I have done your bidding ever since. I still do your bidding. So it is for you to answer. Am I a strong man, Lord?"

Black Face stood motionless, his head cocked slightly, as if he were listening to something only he could hear. Suddenly, in his mind, Parrot Beak saw that dreadful face again, as he had first seen it. In his thoughts he imagined it was smiling.

"You never told me," Black Face said, "how you killed Two Belly. In fact, you never actually said you killed him. You brought me his head, though. And the other parts. Did you kill him, Parrot Beak? How did you do it?"

"I killed him, Lord. As to how . . ." Parrot Beak threw back his hood, exposing his own malformed features. He touched the great bow slung across his shoulders. "With this, Lord. I shot him in the heart. Then I cut off his head and brought it to you."

Black Face nodded. "You are a strong man, Parrot Beak. I will make you my right hand." He clapped him on the shoulder. "I can make use of a man who sends death from a distance. I have many enemies, but with your help, soon I will have less of them."

Both men laughed. Black Face gestured toward the mountains that rose like black, rotten teeth beyond. "I am your master. It's time you know mine. Come."

2

Though the night air was cool and soft, it burned in her lungs with a dry fire. Her forehead was wet with fever sweat, and her eyes itched. She could feel the long muscles in her thighs trying to cramp, and she paused to knead them until they relaxed a bit.

Ah, old age, she thought. The Goddess sends us aches and fevers so that when death finally comes, it will seem a blessing.

But her Goddess was a hard mistress and the burden was still hers to bear. There would be no release for her, not for a good time yet, and when that release came, it would be in blood and darkness.

Sometimes, just a little, her faith wavered. Usually, like now, in the darkest hours of the night. But she was used to that, and as she kneaded the cramps out of her withered thighs she spat in disgust at her own weakness.

"Pah. Old woman," she muttered.

The moon had dropped almost to the horizon. Only the frailest of gleams remained to light her way down empty streets, past silent, echoing walls. She grunted and swung her bag to her shoulders again. This time there was no rattling of broken shards. But there was a weight.

She found Long Snake squatting inside the door, his spear upright between his legs. His head was forward, resting on his knees, and he snored softly. She grinned at him as she slipped past, just another soundless shadow in the dark.

She cut through the atrium and paused for a moment, barely able to make out the altar and the pyramid by the last dregs of moon glow. She could sense it up there, small, green, and old, awaiting the morning when it would drink greedily of the sun's power again. She knew what it was, and what it would be. A great store of force, a blade to cut, a key to unlock. Sharper than a snake's tooth, and as dan-

SISTER OF THE SKY

gerous. It wasn't ready yet. But it would be. When the time came.

She licked her lips. It made a dry sound in her skull, like the whir of moth wings. She stood a moment longer, and then moved on.

When she came to her room she entered and seated herself on her bed with care, lest the crackling of her old bones wake the girl. Only the faintest dream of light drifted down from the skylight, yet she could see Green Eyes's sleeping features as clearly as if the moon were full overhead.

Ah, she would be a beauty! All the vessels were beautiful. Of course they were. They reflected in flesh the eternal beauty of the Goddess. She herself had been beautiful once, though that was nearly a forgotten memory now.

It didn't matter. The flesh was transient in the Middle World. She thought her soul might still be beautiful, though not as unstained as the sleeping child's.

I love you, girl, she thought fiercely. As I love myself and as I love Her. She stared a moment longer, overwhelmed by her own emotions. A troubled look crossed her face.

Green Eyes was dreaming already. She'd seen the long vision of destiny, seen the shadows of the vessels that had preceded her, each with its own hard choice, each with its own bitter triumph. After the turtle, the Goddess was first, and She was oldest, older even than Her husband, for She was Mother to Him, just as She was also wife, sister, and daughter.

The Middle World belonged to men, and women were men's slaves. Yet it was in the blood of women that men and their world were constantly re-created. It was a fine riddle. She had no solution. She only knew her part, the part destined for her by a force beyond human understanding.

Dimly, she sensed the battles that were only skirmishes in the greater battle. That great battle was old as time, and renewed itself with each new age. Again and again the vessels appeared, and again and again they were filled with Power.

The same dreadful choice, offered over and over, differing only in detail. But always the Choice, for women were not slaves. Yet the triumph, over and over, was always bitter.

Perhaps only the end of time would bring release.

And I am an old woman, squatting on my bed, thinking maudlin thoughts in the middle of the darkness, she realized suddenly. Most of the aches were gone from her legs, and her chest had cooled. Maybe she would be able to sleep the rest of the night out. And then morning would come, and another day. One more day, of the countless number that had already passed.

She reached over and found her big straw bag. Her fingers were stiff and swollen, and it took her a moment to find the thing and withdraw it from the sack she'd carried it back in.

She held it in her two hands for a moment, imagining she could feel the power in it. But she couldn't, because the power was not hers to feel. It belonged to the future, and to another.

Her time was nearly past. Only the end remained. And all she held in her arthritic fingers was a lump of clay.

She put the head into her straw bag, and put the bag in the corner. Then she lay down on her own bed and listened to the sounds of her treacherous body. The gurgles and creaks, the slow inner groans, the wheezing passage of air into her chest. The sounds of decay.

As she finally drifted off, she heard the heartbeat. She knew it wasn't hers. It came from the bag in the corner. The small brown thing inside, beating like a heart.

It was the sound of time, and it was far more terrible than the sound of death. She slept.

3

"Is this the place?" Thunder Shield asked.

"Hush, boy," King Thunder Girdle said. He looked up at

the blank wall before him, then at the heavily curtained doorway. The street in the Citadel quarter where they stood was empty except for their own troop of guards and themselves.

Summer was beginning to wane. The air smelled constantly of distant fires as the farmers burned the stubbled remains of their crops to enrich the earth for the next season of planting. Tonight there was a thin, stinging haze about. Thunder Girdle's eyes watered as he examined the blank house.

"You . . . guard." He could never remember the names of his guards, though many of them had served him for decades. He thought of them as faceless and interchangeable, like some kind of living furniture.

"Sir." At least his face looked familiar. Thunder Girdle groped for a name, but came up with nothing. He gave up. "Go in and see if they are expecting us."

"Yes, sir." The guard slammed the butt of his spear on the pavement by way of salute, then turned, ducked, and pushed the curtain aside. Thunder Girdle noted that there wasn't any light beyond the curtain.

"Father, this is ridiculous. You are the King, and I am a prince. Why are we sneaking about in the dark like common criminals?"

His father sighed. There were times when even his own faith was tested. Surely the boy wasn't the fool he seemed to be.

After all, his blood comes from my own veins, the King mused. Somehow this wasn't as reassuring a thought as it should have been.

"Son, listen to me. If you wish to meet criminals, you don't invite them into your house. This is a neutral place. I had this meeting arranged so it would be safe for both sides. The man we are meeting can no more afford to be seen openly with me than I can with him."

But Thunder Shield wasn't convinced. He shook his head,

a stubborn, puzzled expression on his blocky features. "Father, you are King. Why do you have to dirty your hands with people like this in the first place? If you want something done, just order it. Order me to do it. I'll see that whatever you want is carried out."

The King clicked his tongue against his teeth in frustration. "Boy, is that it? You think all a king has to do is snap his fingers, and that's the end of it? You think I'm all-powerful?"

"Well, aren't you?"

"I only wish. Son, the priests have taught you history. In olden times, kings sometimes died before their time. You remember?"

"Well, of course. But those were fever demons, or accidents, or sometimes war."

"Not exactly. If a king loses power because the Families, or even the great mass of people, no longer fear or respect him, then that king is vulnerable. And odd things happen."

"Odd things? Like what?"

The King glanced about. This was hardly the time or place to discuss such bits of dirty history, but he wanted to pierce his son's thick, slow-thinking skull with a dart or two of reality. He leaned closer and lowered his voice.

"Do you remember the name of the last Water Moon king?"

"Uh . . . no. But I remember he got a gripe of the belly and he died from it. Some sort of spirit, I suppose."

Thunder Girdle lowered his voice even further. "The gripe in the belly came from a cup of poison one of our own clan brewed for him. When it became evident he couldn't give children, his days were numbered. And the Winter Moon has ruled since."

Thunder Shield's mouth dropped. "But, Father, that's—"

"Sir? They're waiting inside. I checked everything. It's safe enough."

"Very well. Take your men and surround this house. And

two of you come in with me. You can wait in another room. If it turns out they have treachery in mind, kill everybody."

"Yes, sir."

The King turned to his son. "Follow me, boy. Come learn how kings get their power. And keep it."

Without another word he pushed aside the curtain and went on in. After a moment, his brow still creased, Thunder Shield shook his head and followed him.

4

In the center of the deserted house was a large atrium. In the center of the atrium was a huge, round catch basin full of rainwater. On the edge of the catch basin stood a single oil lamp.

There were no altars in this house, for nobody lived here. The owner maintained it for just such meetings with the nobility as this one. Since it was respectably situated in their own quarter, the Citadel of the Plumed Serpent, it was perfect for its purpose. Those who wished to meet with the owner could slip in and out unnoticed, without leaving the neighborhood where they felt safest and most comfortable.

Now the owner stood in the atrium, trailing his fingers in the water of the catch basin. Though he'd cut much meat and drunk much blood with the aristocracy under this roof, this meeting was a first even for him. He felt an unaccustomed nervousness, even a whisper of fear. He enjoyed that. It had been a long time since he'd feared anything but his own voracious needs.

He inhaled deeply of the bitter, smoky air, and considered what a triumph it was for him that a meeting like this could occur at all. Long ago he had fallen from a high place into the deepest, most noisome gutter, and now he stood ready to make a pact with a king.

He offered a small prayer to the Dark Lord of Storms, the

Fallen One, who had raised him up again, as he intended to raise that fallen God, if he could.

A shadow drifted across the atrium toward him.

"They are coming," a voice hissed.

"Two?"

"Yes. Big men."

"Very well. Stay back. But stay with me."

The shadow nodded, and melted into other shadows.

Two large shapes appeared and resolved into a pair of large men. They walked up to him and stopped a pace away.

The owner of the house bowed. Not deeply, but enough for propriety. "I am Black Face," he said. "I welcome you."

Both of the others wore masks. The one on the right said gruffly, "We don't name ourselves. But you know who I am?"

"Yes."

"Good. Then let's get to business. The intermediary who set up this meeting is well known to you, I believe?"

"Yes, he is."

"He has told me of your abilities. That you can do things I might find it necessary to have done, but without any connection to me."

"Yes, I can do such things."

He raised his hand. A shadow detached itself from the shadows where it had been waiting and approached them.

"What is this?" the King barked harshly. "Treachery?"

"Softly, Lord. Only my associate. Don't call your dogs."

"Tell him to show himself! I don't deal with hooded specters."

Parrot Beak stepped forward into the dim cone of light cast by the oil lamp, and pushed back the hood of his robe. The King stared hard at him. His son gagged slightly, and Black Face smiled inwardly again. This King wasn't frightened of ugly faces, but his son was. Interesting . . .

"All right," the King said. "I see him, and Gods know it will be easy enough to recognize his face again. I don't want to see either of you again. My own intermediary will deal with . . . that one with the ugly nose. Is that suitable?"

Black Face bowed slightly, but more smoothly than before. "Perfectly suitable, Lord. We should keep our distance, I think. About your intermediary. Is he trustworthy?"

"Entirely so."

"Excellent. Then I will await your commands, Lord."

"Good-bye," King Thunder Girdle said. He turned and walked from the atrium, closely followed by the other.

When they were gone, Parrot Beak turned to Black Face. "You put me at risk. Unless that one's intermediary is trustworthy."

"Oh, the King thinks he is. It's the one who was with him. His son, Prince Thunder Shield."

"That was his son?"

"Yes."

Parrot Beak shrugged. "Well, just as I am, he'll be easy to recognize. And from the looks of it, easy to kill, should it come to that."

Black Face turned lazily and stared at him. "If it should come to it, kill the father before the son. I have plans for the son."

"As you say, Lord."

"Always as I say," Black Face agreed.

5

Black Face sat on his platform before the fire, nearly naked, surrounded by his women. But this time when Parrot Beak entered the stone house, Black Face didn't bother with any masks. He didn't mind Parrot Beak seeing him. Parrot Beak was almost as ugly as he was. It was another of Parrot Beak's attractions for him.

Parrot Beak came over quickly, threw back his hood, and settled himself on a mat.

"Well?" Black Face said. "Did it go as I thought?"

"Yes, Lord. Exactly as you said. He wore a mask, but it was plainly the Prince."

Black Face glanced at Parrot Beak curiously. There was something about him . . . yes. Some of the deadness had left those cold eyes. A dark flame sparked in them. If Black Face hadn't thought it impossible, he would have guess that Parrot Beak was happy.

"He asks something of us."

"Of course he does. What is it?"

"That we kill a man named Twisted Tooth."

Black Face put one finger on his oozing chin. "Twisted Tooth? Hmm. Golden Hand's Chief Factor, isn't he?"

"Yes, Lord."

That odd happiness seemed to burn more brightly in Parrot Beak's eyes.

"Interesting. Evidently the secret war between the King and Prince Long Fingers is heating up. It's a good stroke, though. Twisted Tooth is the one who delivers the bribes. And the muscle, when necessary." He thought about it a moment. "Well, it shouldn't be too difficult. Assign some men to it."

"I already have, Lord. One man, with your permission."

"Oh? Why one man? What man?"

"Me, Lord."

"You?" He squinted to make sure he was seeing what he thought he was. Yes, indeed. He'd never seen Parrot Beak smile eagerly before. It was not a handsome sight.

"Yes, Lord. There is old business between Twisted Tooth and me."

"May I inquire as to what it is?"

"Just . . . personal business, Lord. I'd prefer not to discuss it."

Black Face felt an unusual surge of curiosity. It would be interesting to know what that business might be. Anything that could bring a red flame to Parrot Beak's raddled cheeks had to be interesting. But it didn't really matter, and if Parrot Beak was touchy over it . . .

"Very well. See to it personally. But be careful."

"They would like his head sent to the House of the Water Moon, when it is done."

Black Face nodded. "Crude, but effective. The old King is a worthy adversary. You'll have to kidnap him, I suppose. It would be difficult to behead him anywhere public."

"Oh, I have a place in mind."

Once again Black Face felt that flush of curiosity. At the same time, he felt a vague twinge of sympathy for the soon-to-be-dead factor. He suspected Twisted Tooth would not enjoy his time with Parrot Beak.

"See to it. Let me know when it is done. I suspect there may be some further task for us. For you, perhaps."

"Yes, Lord. Thank you."

Parrot Beak rose smoothly, turned, and walked out of the house. Black Face watched him go, a speculative look in his yellow eyes. He would have to bind Parrot Beak to the Dark Lord soon. It wouldn't do for him to get out of hand.

6

"Who was that, dear?" Amaranth Blossom said as Twisted Tooth showed the messenger out.

"Nobody. Just a messenger."

"I hope you don't have to go out," his wife replied. "It's almost dark. I was just getting ready to light the lamps."

"As a matter of fact, I will have to leave for a while. I won't be gone long, though."

She nodded, though a worried crinkle appeared at the corner of her eyes. "Shall I wait to serve your dinner?"

He paused, thinking. The messenger had been a new one. Nothing strange in that. Lord Long Fingers had stepped up his secret campaign in recent weeks. Twisted Tooth had found himself hauling bags of shell beads and pouches of golden nuggets around to the oddest places, as if he were some kind of delivery slave. He didn't mind these trips, though he took more personal satisfaction when he was sent to deliver threats rather than bribes.

He did a quick calculation. His destination was in the merchants' quarter, not far from his own home near the Citadel. Call it an hour, no longer.

"Yes, why don't you wait for me? I shouldn't be much past moonrise."

"Very well, dear. Whatever you wish." She picked up the needlework in her lap and took a switch.

He came over and said, "Don't worry, dear. I won't be long. Give us a kiss."

She offered her cheek, and he planted a noisy smack on it. They were both smiling when he stepped out onto the street, the bag of cash securely tied to his belt.

7

The moon was a pale line in the sky when Twisted Tooth arrived at the appointed place, the nondescript home of the typical merchant, smaller than his own.

A thuggish-looking guard stood at the doorway, idly scratching his crotch. I'd lash that one into shape quickly, Twisted Tooth thought, his fingers caressing the whip strapped at his waist.

He walked up to the man. "You! Your master is expecting me. Tell him I am here."

Insolently, the man eyed him up and down. "Do you have a name for my master?" he sneered.

"I do not. I know you're a stupid fellow, but go and do as I tell you. Your master will see me, I promise."

The man paused, then spat deliberately. The glob of sputum landed on the stucco next to Twisted Tooth's right foot. Twisted Tooth looked down and then up.

"It might be interesting to buy you, dog turd. I'd like to find out if you can spit with that tongue torn from your head."

"I'm a free man," the guard muttered, but Twisted Tooth's threat seemed to have shaken him. "Wait here," he said.

"Speaking of tongues," Twisted Tooth shot at his retreating back, "you should learn to keep a civil one between your teeth."

Then he stood there far too long, growing angrier by the second. By the time the guard returned, his rage had ballooned to the point he no longer noticed small details.

"Go straight down the hall, then turn to your right. He's waiting for you in the little atrium."

Twisted Tooth grunted and pushed on past. He missed the fact that the guard had exchanged his short spear for a club.

Once past the curtain he found himself in darkness, with just a dim glow up ahead somewhere to light his way. It only made him angrier. He stomped on ahead, breathing through his mouth, his thoughts churning with what he would say to this uppity would-be swallower of the Water Moon money.

They fell on him just as he turned the corner.

8

He awakened with a grinding headache, a feeling of nausea in his belly, and the awareness that he'd made a potentially deadly mistake. He confirmed this when he tried to move and discovered he was bound hand and foot to a stake set into the floor of the room. He looked down and saw that he was naked.

It was quite bright in the small room, despite the fact there was no skylight—not that it mattered when the moon was gone. Nevertheless, he had the strange feeling of being on display, that hidden eyes were watching him, savoring the sight of him squirming against his bonds in the glow of what had to be at least a dozen oil lamps.

Those walls looked thick, too. On the floor were dark, dried splotches that didn't look like paint.

"Hello!" he cried out. "Who's there?"

No answer.

He yelled again with the same result. A wave of panic hit him, and he began to yank against the ropes with all his strength, while he shouted himself hoarse. A small hope began to grow in him as he struggled. He wasn't dead, only tied up. Maybe it had been a simple robbery, and they were gone. If he yelled loud enough, someone might hear him and come let him go.

But his throat had begun to ache. And he knew he'd rubbed his wrists raw and bleeding against the ropes that bound them.

He decided to save his breath and see what he could do with the ropes. The room grew silent except for the sound of his raspy breathing.

Ssss-flap. Ssss-flap.

His head came up.

Ssss-flap. Ssss-flap.

A bead of sweat dripped from his nose. "Who's that? Who's there?"

Ssss-flap. Ssss-flap.

Despite his ragged throat he managed a shout. "In here! Come let me loose! I'll pay—"

A dark, hooded figure entered the room. He was bent and twisted. His face was hidden. He dragged his foot when he walked.

He limped closer and then stopped three paces distant. Twisted Tooth watched him with wide, bulging eyes. His nuts felt as if they'd shrunk to berry pits.

Parrot Beak slowly pushed back his hood, and smiled.

"Hello, Chief Factor. Do you remember me? If not, do you remember *this*?"

He raised the whip in his right hand. Twisted Tooth began to scream.

It took Parrot Beak almost two hours to finish him, and by the last half hour Twisted Tooth had gone mad. Parrot Beak doubted he felt any pain by then, but he kept on.

He stopped when Twisted Tooth died. Unlike the factor, he had no stomach for whipping a dead man. His dreams were bad enough as it was, and his waking memories worse.

9

Long Fingers paced restlessly across the atrium side of his reception room. Most of the house was asleep, but sleep wouldn't come for him. It had been three days since Twisted Tooth had vanished. He'd done everything he could think of to track him down, but with no luck. And just this afternoon a messenger had arrived from his son. Golden Hand would be in the city one day hence, after resting overnight at the bottom of the stairs.

And what could he tell him? He hadn't originally intended to use Twisted Tooth as much as he had, but the man was, as Golden Hand promised, quite trustworthy. How would he explain it to his son if it turned out he had caused the man's death?

Yet he couldn't even say that. He didn't know if Twisted Tooth was dead or alive. He'd talked to the man's wife, but she knew little. She said he'd left on some errand and never returned.

Long Fingers scooped himself another cup of pulque. Normally he could drink as much as he wanted and never feel dizzy. But it seemed to be affecting him differently now. Maybe it was because he was drinking more of it than usual.

He stood at the top of the stairs, between two pillars, looking down onto the silent atrium, his mind muddled and tired. It would be good to have his son home again . . .

A flicker of movement high overhead caught his attention. He watched the round shape fall out of the night and land on the floor before him.

It made a sound like a ripe fruit falling. Its momentum carried it on a bumpy, rolling path right to the bottom of the stairs. Long Finger's heart began to beat faster. Carefully, he climbed down until he reached the bottom.

The head of Twisted Tooth stared blindly up at him.

"Guards!" he shouted. *"Chain Coil! Long Snake! Guards!"*

10

Golden Hand made camp at the bottom of the stairs, as he usually did, to let the caravan rest before the final march into the city.

As he inspected the camp after the evening meal, he was warmed by what he saw. There had been no losses. He'd brought back every one of the two hundred traders, factors, and slaves he'd set out with. And every bearer and slave was loaded down with bags of gold.

Even better were the five families he'd bought. He paid for them outright, but later he told them that if they labored well for him, he would give them their freedom. Two years, he told them, and they agreed gladly.

Now he was back for good. This had been his final trip. He had more wealth than he'd ever imagined possible, much more than he needed to carry out his plans.

He wondered how Green Eyes was doing. No doubt by now his mother would have transformed her—but even if not, it didn't matter. She would still bear his child, and that would be enough.

He retired to his bedroll as a man brimming with satisfaction and contentment. He awoke to chaos.

"Lord! Your father! Come!"

Still blinking sleep from his eyes, he allowed himself to be pulled pell-mell to the place. There he found Prince Long Fingers lying on his back. An arrow protruded from his right eye like some obscene decoration.

"What happened?" he said.

Chain Coil, his face drained of color, stepped forward. "I don't know, Lord. There was a murder in Tollan. Your factor, Twisted Tooth. Prince Long Fingers and I came out to warn you, before you returned to the city. But just as we came up to the camp . . ."

Chain Coil shivered, turned, and looked up at the cliff face looming overhead. "I think it came from . . . up there."

Golden Hand looked up and realized it was hopeless. Darkness shrouded the cliff and the road. There could be a hundred men up there, or none. Whatever. The deed was done.

Slowly, he knelt at the side of his dead father. He picked up his head and cradled it in his hands.

"Oh, Father," he whispered.

After a time, gentle hands touched his shoulders and pulled him away. "Prince Water Moon," somebody said. "Let us wash him and wrap him. Prince Water Moon, come away."

Prince Water Moon?

But he was dead.

11

On the morning after that dreadful night, Green Eyes woke with a blinding headache and cramps in her belly. She was muzzy with bad dreams she couldn't quite remember.

Overhead, the sun pouring through the skylight hurt her

eyes. She pushed herself up on her elbows and glanced over at Mama Root. The old woman was still snoring soundly.

The pain in her belly was quite bad. She glanced toward the chamber pot. But before she could get up to use it, a sudden flash of heat filled her groin.

She whipped aside her covers and stared at the blood coating her thighs. It was still pumping out, a slow rhythmic gush, dark and red.

"Mama Root," she gasped. *"Oh, Mama, help me!"*

BOOK THREE

Judgments

"Justice is the very last thing of all wherewith the universe concerns itself. It is equilibrium that absorbs its intentions."
—Maurice Maeterlinck,
Wisdom and Destiny

Chapter Fourteen

1

TOLLAN

Pale and yet feeling strangely buoyed, Green Eyes sat in the atrium with Moon and Dusk. A thin haze masked the morning sun, and turned the sky overhead a strange, milky white. The day was already hot. All three of them had sewing work in their laps. Green Eyes had become good enough with the needle that she no longer needed to think about what she was doing. Her days of punctured fingers and loose stitches were long in the past. Now she found the mindless shift of thread and cloth and needle soothing.

"Did you have any pain?" Dusk said. "I remember when my bleeding started, I felt bad for quite a while."

"No, it hurt for just a little, and then it passed. I was sick to my stomach, though."

Dusk nodded. "That's natural. Moon had the same thing, didn't you, Moon?"

Her sister nodded. "Yes, I still do sometimes. And I get terrible headaches." She slipped a stitch through and pulled it tight. "What's wrong with Mama? She stayed in her room this morning. I think she's still in bed. And Papa left the house late last night. He took Chain Coil with him, but he didn't say where he was going. And he hasn't come home yet."

"Maybe he went to meet Golden Hand. You know his messenger said he'd be home soon."

Green Eyes glanced at her with interest. "I didn't know that."

Dusk chuckled. "And with your bleeding starting, you've probably had enough on your mind. Hm. That works out very well, doesn't it? You are a woman now, just in time for Golden Hand's return."

"What?"

"You mean you didn't know? Once you start bleeding, you can marry. It's very strange, you know. Men hate us when we bleed, and make us hide ourselves away, and yet they won't marry us until we start."

Green Eyes stared at her. "I hadn't thought . . . I didn't even realize . . ."

"Oh, yes, my dear. He could marry you tomorrow, if he wanted to."

During Golden Hand's absence, Green Eyes's memories of him had grown dimmer, and she'd nearly forgotten about the fate in store for her. And now, suddenly, it all came rushing back, as if it had been lurking beneath her thoughts all along. But she was a different person now. She was a woman.

"Hmph. And what if I don't wish to marry *him*?"

Dusks's eyebrows shot up, and a splinter of her old hauteur returned. "Well, dear, in the first place I can't imagine you making a better catch than our brother. He will be a prince one day, and you a princess." She leaned forward, forgetting her sewing for a moment. "And anyway, you don't have any choice in the matter. If he wishes to marry you, he will."

Green Eyes's lips thinned. "Yes," she muttered. "Because I'm a woman now. I'm a slave."

"What? What did you say?"

Green Eyes suddenly saw her in an entirely new light. Poor Dusk. For all of her beauty, manners, and haughtiness, she really didn't understand. Though she was a proud woman of a proud family, when the time came she would be handed from one man's house to another man's hand like so much meat. No one would ask if she loved her new husband, or even if she liked him. No one would seek her opinions about any of it, because her opinion didn't matter. She was only a woman. She was a slave.

Like me, Green Eyes thought. I'm a slave too. But at least I know it. Does that make it better? Would I be happier if I was like Dusk, not understanding anything about what I was?

"Oh . . . nothing," Green Eyes replied.

"I'll be glad when Golden Hand gets back," Moon said suddenly. "He makes me laugh. It's been too gloomy around here."

Dusk brightened. "Yes, I have to admit I miss him. My brother can be such a terrible tease, but at least he's cheerful about it. Mama and Papa have been so solemn lately, too. Have you noticed it?"

"Like today," Moon agreed. "Papa's gone, and Mama's in her room and won't come out." She looked up at the sky. "And now it looks like rain. Just what we need. We won't even be able to sit here in the atrium."

She looked at Green Eyes. "I wish Mama would let you come out of the house with us. The city is so much fun. I could show you everything. You'd love the markets."

Green Eyes remembered the Big Noses and what they'd had in mind for her in Tollan's markets, but she let none of that show. She'd learned how to mask her own feelings and reactions. So she only smiled and said, "Yes, that would be wonderful. But your mama says I can't go out until I am married."

"Yes, but that will be fine too. Then you can chaperone *us*," Moon exclaimed. "That would be even more fun. A chaperone younger than me!"

"Well," Dusk broke in, "I'm sure by that time we'll also both be married, Moon. I'm already pledged to that boy in the Harvest Moon Clan, you know." A certain smugness crept into her voice. Moon wasn't pledged to anybody yet.

"I've seen him," Moon said. "You think he's so handsome, but he has big ears. And he's always scratching himself in those nasty places."

Dusk sighed. Her betrothed did have a few faults, but she had no intention of admitting them publicly. She planned to whip him into shape after they were married, anyway. She sniffed. "Well, a lot *you* know about anything. You're not even—what's that?"

The sounds of men shouting echoed from the front of the house. All three girls put down their sewing and turned to look. The shouting grew louder and then stopped suddenly. Dusk glanced at Green Eyes. Moon's face had gone pale.

They heard the sound of heavy footsteps approaching from beyond the far columns. Suddenly Golden Hand appeared.

Moon raised one hand to her mouth. Dusk stared. Green Eyes felt a whisper of fear blow on the back of her neck.

Golden Hand had taken off all his jewelry. His hair was unbound and chopped off to a short, ragged stump. Dark stubble grew on his normally shaven skull. His beautiful skirt was torn and shredded. His face and chest were smeared with ashes. His single eye was dull and rimmed with red.

He stood and stared at them, his mouth working silently. Green Eyes felt a sudden urge to run to him, to stroke his tortured face and comfort him. What could have happened?

When he spoke, his voice was hollow and husky with tears. "Where is our mother?" he said.

Dusk began to stand. "I'll . . . Golden Hand, what happened? What's the *matter* with you?" She sounded panicked.

"Dusk, go find our mother. Bring her here. I have terrible news."

"What?" Moon wailed. *"What?"*

He gave a great, shuddering gasp and wiped the back of his hand across his nose. His good eye spilled over. "Our father is dead."

Behind him other men appeared. They bore a long, muffled shape.

Moon began to scream.

2

There were lamps set about the atrium. They would remain until the time of mourning for his father had passed.
But the deeper darkness would also remain, hidden within
his heart, in the void where the light of his father's love once
had been.

Golden Hand stood beneath the cold gleam of the stars
overhead, the planes of his ravaged face only slightly softened by the glow of the lamps. Pinpoints of golden light
danced in his good eye, and glinted off the yellow outline on
his eye patch. He stood near a mound of fresh earth in one
corner of the atrium. The dirt was piled with wilted flowers
and shards of broken pottery. The turned earth smelled of
must and mold. Flames danced atop four lamps, one at each
corner of the low mound.

He clasped his hands behind his back and brooded. Long
Fingers was down there, in the family tomb, wrapped in
scented cloths, washed and trimmed.

Golden Hand closed his eyes. He could picture him, lying
on his slab of stone, his hands folded across his chest, silent
among the bones of the other dead princes who lay in the
tomb with him. He was surrounded with treasure, each piece
of which Golden Hand knew well because he had piled it
there. As he had sacrificed the two body slaves whose
corpses rested on either side of Long Fingers's own, waiting
to serve him in the Underworld. The World of the Dead.

He raised his fists to the sky. Tears streamed from his
good eye. His lips shaped silent words: *Why? Why?*

But in the back of his mind a soft, mocking voice whispered, *You know why. The question is who?*

And suddenly he felt dull and stupid. And tired of himself.
He lowered his fists, and sniffed until his nose cleared. He
wiped away his tears.

He thought, The why is easy. He died because of me. Be-

cause of his ambition and my own. As to who . . . that's
what I have to find out.

He looked down at the mound again. In four more days
they would come to tamp down the earth, crush the dead
flowers into the dirt, replace the paving stones, and cover
everything with a fresh layer of stucco. He would walk on
his father's tomb just as, someday, others would walk on his.
And life would go on.

He turned away and began to walk slowly toward the
altar. Life will go on. Death, too.

He stood in front of the altar. There were lamps on either
end of it, casting light up into his face, where it pooled in
inky shadows on the hollows of his cheeks. Wilted blossoms
were mounded here, baskets brimming with corn, and in the
fire pit centered on the altar table, the remains of a pig. The
pig flesh was beginning to rot, sending up a faint odor of
corruption. Just as his father's flesh beneath the earth was
rotting, and if he dug it up, it would stink too.

Suddenly he sank to his knees before the altar. He leaned
forward and rested his burning forehead against the cool
stone. He wrapped his fingers around the lip of the altar and
squeezed until his knuckles showed white in the light of the
lamps.

"I vow," he said.

Somewhere a dog began to howl.

"Before, you, Great Goddess, I vow." His throat grew
tight, and he stopped. His head shook silently. "I swear on
Your Holy Name to take vengeance for me and my house. I
pledge . . . I *swear* to you I will never rest until the murderer
of my father dies at these hands that I lay on your altar. I
swear . . ."

A great darkness swirled up in him and he went silent. His
hands felt like blocks of ice on the cold stone. The stench of
rotting meat and dying blossoms filled his nostrils. His good
eye stared as blindly as the hidden one, filled with the pin-
prick gleam of the dancing deadlights.

He turned his face up toward the replica of Her pyramid looming over the altar. High above his head, he saw a faint green glow. He stared at it, and as he did so, he saw that it was throbbing slightly. Beat-beat, beat-beat. Like a little heart of light.

He stood, wonderment filling him. A sign from Her!

But when he reached his full height, the glow was gone. The miniature temple atop the pyramid was dark. Yet he had seen it.

She had heard his vow, and She had given Her blessing to it. All that remained was for him to carry it out. He knew how to begin.

3

Green Eyes said, "Come, Lady. You must try to eat something."

Gentle Dawn stirred on the pillows propped beneath her back. Her thin body barely made a mound in the blankets that covered her. And though it was hot in the room—a fire smoked in the corner pit—the blankets were piled up as if it were a winter day, and she shivered beneath them.

Green Eyes held a clay bowl of steaming broth in her hands. But Gentle Dawn wouldn't look at it. In the past week the flesh had melted off her bones, and what little was left had dried out. Her dark hair was tangled and matted with sweat. There were huge shadows under her eyes. It looked as if somebody had struck her viciously in the face.

Death has, Green Eyes thought. Death struck her.

Since the day of Golden Hand's return, she had left her bed only twice. The first time, when Dusk had fetched her, she'd come to the atrium and listened to the dreadful news. Her eyes had looked like holes thumbed in raw, white dough as her only remaining son told her of her husband's murder.

She had straightened to her full height and pointed at him,

her back trembling, her teeth clenched. "I . . . knew he wasn't coming back. I *knew*!"

And then she'd swallowed once, sighed, and collapsed in a dead faint. The next time Green Eyes had seen her was when Cham Ix and his son, White Feather, had performed the rituals for the dead in the privacy of the atrium. As a prince, Long Fingers was entitled to a great burial, with all the pomp and panoply his large and powerful clan could bring to bear. Even the King sent a messenger with condolences, and his pledge to help carry Long Fingers's body on its final march down the Avenue of the Gods.

Golden Hand must have thought nobody was watching when he spat on the King's messenger and ordered him, in a terrible voice, to leave and never come back again. But Green Eyes, who felt like the only person still alive in the house, had seen it. Golden Hand had swept right by the place where she was crouched, his gaze inflamed, and never even glanced at her.

He refused the honors due his father, and ordered a small and private ceremony instead. Gentle Dawn had appeared, tottering on his arm. She looked a hundred years old, as flimsy and delicate as a discarded, bleached-out rag. She uttered not one word, and when the rituals were done, she returned to her room. She hadn't come out since.

The girls were not much better. Moon wept softly and constantly, and Dusk drifted about the silent house as if she were a stranger. Occasionally she would speak, in bright, brittle tones, but quite often what she said made no sense. The last time Green Eyes had encountered her, she'd smiled and announced with hideous gaiety that "the party will begin tonight. Yes, it will, and I will wear my red skirt." Then she'd drifted on, leaving Green Eyes with the feeling she'd not seen her at all.

Mama Root told her, "I'll do what I can with the girls. They're young, and they don't have any reason to dislike me. You'll have to try with Gentle Dawn. She's sent me away twice. But she needs to eat. I've made some broth that will help her, if you can get her to drink it."

At least she didn't send me away, Green Eyes thought as she extended the bowl toward Gentle Dawn's face, hoping the rich smell might tempt her.

"No . . ." Gentle Dawn husked. "Take it away . . ."

"You have to eat, Lady."

"I'll die. Just let me die . . ."

Suddenly Green Eyes was shaken with vision. It was of herself, trapped forever in these dim and silent halls, the only one left alive in a house of the living dead, a place where the rooms held only madwomen, and the air smelled like the rancid breath of the tomb.

And why? Because a *man* had died. Would Long Fingers have turned into a death-seeking shell if his wife had been murdered? He would have mourned, but would Gentle Dawn's death have destroyed him?

Somehow, Green Eyes doubted it. Because in the world of men, only the slaves mourned the deaths of their masters. She had watched Golden Hand kill two body slaves and place them next to his father's corpse. And at the time the thought had crossed her mind that it might have been a mercy to do the same with Gentle Dawn.

Yet that thought kindled a bright anger in her. She set down the bowl, then reached over and took Gentle Dawn by her shoulders. She pulled her close and shook her. It was easy. Gentle Dawn's bones felt weightless, and she resisted only weakly.

"No . . ." She whispered. "Leave me be."

"I won't! Lady, he is *dead.* But you *aren't*!"

Gentle Dawn's lips crawled like worms. There was a grainy yellow mucus in the corners of her eyes. Green Eyes wiped it away. "Your Lord is beneath the earth," she said. "He is dead. His body is rotting."

Now Gentle Dawn's eyes were awake and full of horror. She shook her head. "No."

"*Yes*! Dead, Lady, dead and moldering. But you are alive. You act like you want to be dead too. Do you?" She gave her a little shake. "Answer me, *do* you?"

"I . . . I . . ."

"Your daughters need you. Your son needs you. But your husband is *dead*. He doesn't *need* you anymore."

Suddenly it was like trying to hold a wild cat. Gentle Dawn writhed in her grasp, broke free, and smashed one palm across her face. "How *dare* you? *How dare you?*"

Green Eyes fought her off. "Because I've come to love you, Lady. And I need you too."

She heard her own words with astonishment, knowing they were true. Yet the truth shocked her as much as it did Gentle Dawn, for both women suddenly froze, staring at each other.

Gentle Dawn's face crumpled like cloth rolled into a ball. She uttered a great, honking cry and collapsed into Green Eyes's arms. "I need to be . . . needed," she groaned, as for the first time since learning of her husband's death, she began to weep.

Green Eyes held her and rocked her and stroked her hair and listened to the horrific sounds she made. There was an undertone, a deep sound hidden beneath her tears, that sounded like a dog howling. It made the fine hairs along the base of her spine stand up, and raked sparkling twitches along the nape of her neck.

Yes, she thought, we are all so needy, aren't we, we women? We are slaves to our need, and our need leads us into slavery.

The sound of Gentle Dawn's anguished animal cries filled her ears.

Women weep. What else can they do?

4

A week later, when she looked up and saw Golden Hand standing in the doorway of her room, it struck her that this was the first time she'd been alone with him since the beginning, when she had been a frightened little girl trailing along with a trader's caravan, stumbling into a future she could not have begun to imagine.

She was seated on her bed, sewing a border on a new skirt of fine green cotton. Her fingers continued to work automatically as she smiled up at him.

"Come in, Golden Hand. Sit down."

She had taken to doing her sewing here rather than in the atrium. The light wasn't so good, but the atrium was big and lonely. The sisters had reacted to their father's death in different ways. Dusk had taken to avoiding the house as much as she could—she would take servants and guards and go into the city early in the morning and not return until dusk. She would eat in her room and say little to anybody about anything. She seemed to be growing brighter and more brittle than she had been. She laughed a lot, sometimes when nobody was around. That was the eeriest—Green Eyes would hear her laughing, and if she walked by her door, she might find her sitting on her bed, staring at nothing, chuckling and giggling.

Moon was still weepy and lost. She was too young to be allowed out of the house much, certainly not without her mother, and so she kept to her room. She had twenty or thirty dolls in there. Not two months before she'd told Green Eyes, with a toss of her head, that she was far too old to play with dolls, and would be happy to give them to her if she wanted them. But now she had taken them up again. Green Eyes would go there to sit with her, and Moon would hold the dolls, dress and undress them, comb their cornsilk hair, and hug them fiercely. Sometimes she would cry and not even know she was doing it. Green Eyes felt terribly sorry for her, but she wasn't able to break through the invisible shell of sadness that surrounded the girl.

It was still a house of the dead.

Golden Hand grinned at her, stepped into the room, and seated himself on Mama Root's bed. Her thick, feather-stuffed mattress gave off a dusty exhalation as he sank down into it.

"You know," he said, "I think your voice is the first cheerful sound I've heard in this house in days."

She paused in her sewing. "I should be sad, I suppose, but your father was not really mine. No matter that he did adopt me, he never had much to say to me. In fact, I can't say that I really knew him at all. I am sad that he died, of course. It is a terrible thing for you and your mother and sisters."

Golden Hand grinned at her again, and the unexpected tick of warmth she felt at his expression prompted her to *look* at him. He was turning back into the Golden Hand she remembered, young, strong, and vital. His stump of a top-knot was growing out again, and his skull gleamed with a fresh shave. The ashes he'd streaked himself with were gone, replaced by even more gold than before. He glittered and jingled and rippled with yellow light just from the movement of his breathing. And, yes, he was still grinning at her.

"Well, yours is the first smile I've seen in a long while, too," she replied.

"Do you disapprove? My goodness. Surely my mother's teachings haven't made such a perfect lady of you already?"

"Your mother is very sad, Golden Hand. You shouldn't speak of her in that tone."

His eyebrows twitched, and his grin grew wider. "Do you realize the girl I knew not so long ago would not even have known those words, let alone been able to speak them with such aristocratic propriety? You sound almost like my sisters!"

She nodded, amazed at how composed she felt. But there

was something comfortable about him. "As you once said, your mother is a good teacher. I feel so sorry for her."

He sobered a bit. "Yes, I know. She's taking everything very hard. Which is one of the reasons I came to see you. I wanted to thank you."

"Oh? For what?"

"For what you've done for her. She seems more cheerful—if that's the word I want—at least not so completely disheartened. She's even begun to speak about resuming her position as head of the household. And it seems that she has come to think a great deal of you. She says you've been a greater help to her than her own daughters. I think she looks at you as one of us now."

Her eyebrow rose. "I suppose that's a good thing. If I have no choice about my bed, at least I can hope it will be a comfortable one."

"Ah. And do you find it so?"

"As I say, I didn't choose it."

He began to chew at a flap of skin on his thumbnail. "That's true. I did steal you away from your home, and I did bring you here. And it must have been very hard for you. But you have changed, and it's too late to go back anyway. So do you hate me now, Green Eyes?"

She decided she owed him at least the honor of giving his question honest consideration. She began to fold up her sewing. When she was done with that, she said, "No, I don't hate you, Golden Hand. I see that you treated me no differently than you would have one of your own sisters. I am a woman, as they are women. Men do not ask us our leave about anything, not even our lives. You will marry off Moon, for instance, to whomever you please, and if you think about it, that really isn't any different than what you did to me. In fact, you were honest, and paid a thief good money to take me. I can see why you might be puzzled if I did hate you. After all, you followed the rules."

There was real shock on his face. He shook his head, as if

mosquitoes were whining around his ears. "You surprise me," he said.

"Why? Because I can think? Really, Golden Hand. Women can think, we've always been able to. It's just that you men have never noticed."

He coughed. His cheeks had begun to glow, and she noticed that he wouldn't hold her gaze with his own. No doubt she'd embarrassed or annoyed him, but he had asked, hadn't he?

"Green Eyes, I had another reason for coming to see you, beyond simply offering my thanks for how you've helped Mother."

She waited.

After a while he blushed more deeply, and then spoke very quickly. "I've decided to marry you as soon as possible."

She felt an odd, singing silence swell inside her ears. "What?"

"I know I said it wouldn't be for a few more years, but things have changed. With Father gone, there is no reason to wait. I need to start a family and get an heir. So I've decided to go ahead with it. What do you say?"

She stared at him, wondering if he had any idea what he sounded like to her. He hadn't asked how she felt about it, or even if she was willing. He just told her what he'd *decided* to do with her life, and then asked her opinion of his decision.

"Your mind is made up, I suppose?" she asked him.

This seemed to nonplus him as well. "I thought you'd be happy. You are a woman now, I know that. I talked with Mama Root and Mother both. You will be my first wife. You will become the Princess Water Moon. This will be your house. You could not find a better life in all of Tollan." He sounded honestly puzzled that she should not find this an occasion for unrestrained joy.

Oh, really? she wondered. Ask your mother about that.

But there *was* something to what he said. There was very little chance she'd ever find a way back to her village. She
didn't even know what direction it was in. And she doubted
that she would fit in there any longer anyway. It had taken
her a while to realize how much she'd changed, how different she now was, not just from what she had been, but from
what *any* other girl or woman there was like.

And this house needed a firm hand. Now, with all the
other women seemingly paralyzed by tragedy, somebody
needed to take hold of things. She knew she could do that.
And if she was the Princess Water Moon, then even Gentle
Dawn would not be able to gainsay her.

She nodded gravely. "Very well, Golden Hand. I will not
say I agree to marry you, because I really don't have a
choice in the matter. But I will agree to try and find happiness in it."

"That's the strangest thing I've ever heard. But you know
something?"

"What?"

"I find it very curious—and sometimes I surprise myself—but in an equally strange way, I think I understand
what you mean."

I wouldn't be so sure, she thought to herself. But all she
said was, "Lord? If it is to be soon, I would like to be able
to go out of the house. Did you know I've never seen the
City of Tollan, except for when we first arrived?"

He stared at her. "I'd forgotten about that. Of course you
can go—hm. Wait a moment. It might not be such a good
idea after all. As you must realize by now, my house—our
house—has enemies. They might try to strike at me through
you."

"Then give me an army, Lord. But give me some free air
to breathe."

His eyes grew hooded. He rose, came to her, and brushed
her cheek with his fingertips. "When I first saw you, I

thought you would be beautiful. I was right, Green Eyes. You are beautiful."

For what that's worth, she thought to herself as she watched his broad, muscled back vanish through her doorway. He is a beautiful thing himself.

Now where did *that* come from?

5

Green Eyes was allowed her freedom—at least some measure of it. It was as if the wedding preparations acted as a tonic on the household, drawing out the sting of death with the promise of hope and renewal. And although it wasn't much spoken of, everybody, including Green Eyes, knew that she would be expected to bear a child as soon as possible.

The idea of that, formless and vague as it was, frightened her on some inexplicable level. But her unease was impossible to pin down, and it evaporated in the frenzy of the preparations. Even Gentle Dawn finally rose from her bed and, though prone to bouts of sighs and distant looks, threw herself into the business of a wedding on the grand scale.

"I am a rich man," Golden Hand told her, "maybe the richest man in Tollan. I want a big wedding. Those who might question my power, and the power of the Water Moon, must see that the power remains. That the new Prince Water Moon is as strong and . . . capable . . . as the old."

His remark took a bit of polish off her sentiments regarding the impending ceremony (he evidently viewed it as some enormous business deal), but it did give Gentle Dawn a wider canvas on which to paint the splendor of the nuptials. And paint she did.

The house became a whirlwind of cloth sellers and factors and gown makers. Golden Hand installed an entire family of southern gold workers in one of the rooms, and they pro-

ceeded to melt, pound, spin, and weave enough golden trinkets to weigh down twenty brides. When Green Eyes saw
what they had in mind for her, she thought it might be necessary to have someone carry her through the ceremony.

When she protested, Golden Hand only grinned and said,
"We'll start a new fad. Gold jewelry for noble ladies. No
reason only the men should buy. Hm . . . do you think you
could find space for a few more bracelets?"

Despite everything, she found herself caught up in the
whirlwind as well. For the first time in her young life she
was the center of attention—every female hand in the House
of the Water Moon was turned to her, every eye, and . . .
every mouth.

She received floods of advice that she had no way to eval-
uate beyond considering the source. The most lurid stuff
came from Moon and Dusk, but Green Eyes suspected they
didn't know what they were talking about. At least she
hoped they didn't.

Mama Root and Gentle Dawn were a different matter, and
she weighed their thoughts and their advice carefully. By the
time the day finally arrived, she was exhausted. But the rest
of the clan seemed rejuvenated. What an odd exchange. She
had finally laid the ghost of the murdered prince to rest, but
not until she herself felt wrung dry.

Nevertheless, she rose with excitement humming in her
veins. By the time the great robe made of three layers of cotton stitched with hammered golden threads, embroidered
with lumps of gold, with polished stones and shells, with
thousands of tiny glittering beads, with a great weight of
white quetzal feathers, was hung about her shoulders, she
was almost ready to run out the door. Of course she couldn't
run. The robe would have dragged her down.

Not to mention the headdress she wore, half as large as
she was, and held up with sticks by servants hidden in her
palanquin.

It took a dozen strong men to lift that palanquin. Golden

Hand, wearing so much gold that men turned away from the sunlight blazing off him, and ever after called him the Lord of Yellow Fire, walked slowly at the side of the litter, his beringed fingers never leaving her own hand.

And so she saw Tollan at last, as it blazed and glowed and glittered in the peak of its glory. Two hundred thousand people lined the Avenue of the Gods and choked the Plaza of the Moon.

She arose from her litter and, aided by two stout servants, ascended the great ceremonial platform with its vast altar in the center of the plaza.

Cham Ix himself presided over the ceremonies and rituals. He took the omens and read the entrails with his own hands. His son, White Feather, assisted him.

When this was over the celebrations and feasts began in the plaza of the Citadel. The markets had been cleared for the day, which only made sense. Golden Hand had bought everything they had to offer the previous day, and even the richest merchants had nothing left to sell.

As morning burned to noon, and afternoon tapered lushly into dusk, everything began to blur together into one endless, softly glowing, pulsating memory of beauty and grandeur—both hers and the city's. Somehow she and it became one, if only for an hour.

Night fell and the moon rose, a perfect round orb behind the Pyramid of the Moon. Against the great white shield the crows still circled above Her temple and Her great head as it watched silently over Her city.

But Green Eyes did not see this. She lay naked in the wide feather bed in her husband's quarters, with only the stars as witness.

"Yes . . ." he murmured.

"Oh . . . yes. *Yes* . . ." she answered him . . . and herself. And in that long, trembling moment her heart cracked gently open, and lay warm and still at last.

6

As the tumultuous crowds slowly shifted from the wedding rituals at the Goddess's end of the avenue south toward the Plumed Serpent's Citadel, Cham Ix and White Feather stood high above the churning masses, arms propped on the stone balustrade fronting the Palace of the Priests. Up here the traffic was less frantic, though still busy enough. Because of the festivities—and the generosity of Prince Golden Hand—it was a free day at the smaller temples around the square, and many of the poorest were taking advantage of the opportunity to pray before the Goddess without having to pay for their sacrifices.

The two men spoke casually, of casual things, and their words were quickly snatched away into the hubbub that filled the air.

But their hands moved lightly, delicately, purposefully. The words they spoke with their tongues were meaningless. What they said with their fingers, in the ancient, priestly Language of Hands, was far more consequential.

Cham Ix was so excited his fingers threatened to run away from him. *"I had never seen her, and when I did, I could not believe it. Her eyes are even more spectacular than you said. She is without doubt a great vessel. She is fit for the Mother Herself! And her child . . ."*

"Yes, if she bears a son to Golden Hand, who bears the God-marked eye himself, though hidden, that boy will be greater than a king."

Suddenly White Feather looked down at his hands, as if surprised to find they had moved. Though only a few could read those finger movements, what he spoke of was so grave a thing it was better not to speak of it in any way at all.

His father seemed to undergo the same realization simultaneously, for he flushed and hid his own hands under his robe. They stared at each other, and it seemed that something twinkling, yet not visible, danced between them.

"A great day," Cham Ix said softly.

"Yes, truly," his son agreed.

7

Indeed a great day, thought the man in the plain brown robe who slouched against a wall nearby, in a place that gave clear and easy view of the two priests—and their hands.

His hood was pulled low over his face. Nevertheless, if one looked closely, one could see a faint flicker of yellow, like candles burning far away in the dark.

After a while the man slipped away unnoticed, his mind twisting with surmise, his thoughts dancing as lightly as the fingers he had watched.

8

The second time was better than the first. She had known what to expect. She'd grown up in a village where babies were made on rude mattresses next to other sleeping babies. Nevertheless, the defloration was messy and somewhat painful, and she was glad to slip into the slow, easy plateau that came later.

They came together again as the moon finally slipped high enough to fill the skylight above them. It turned their flesh to silver. She fancied she could see her breath as a frosty cloud above his gleaming shoulder.

Between them the moisture of their bodies became like warm honey, and the breath in their lungs sweet, languid fire. His lips tasted of berries and dust. She wrapped herself around him as he slipped into her, and she felt the muscles move beneath his back, and in his buttocks slick against her calves she felt his power.

He was a weight and yet weightless, a fire and yet cool. His passage into her loosened and then filled her. She felt her belly shudder and relax, shudder and relax. And when it seemed he would never stop, when her pleasure teetered on the edge of pain, a great white wash of light rolled slowly from her curled toes to her blinded eyes.

She shouted. He cried out.

And when they were done, when he lay next to her with his fingers entwined in her hair, he looked into her eyes and said, "This one will be a boy."

"Yes," she whispered. "A boy . . ."

"And a king," he said.

And as she felt her doom begin to grow in her, she nodded. "Yes, that too."

High above, the moon filled the skylight. Crows flew across it.

In the language of Tollan, the name for crow was *omen bird*.

Chapter Fifteen

1

The wind blew cold and steady. It plucked at their robes, flattening and rippling the cloth against their legs. Their heavy sandals made crutch-crutch sounds as they strode through fields of ash and clinkers, their lungs full of the harsh reek of burning stone. All around them were the dark, faintly luminous shapes of the mountains of Tlaloc, home of the Dark God, the Fallen One. They felt the bleak weight of his scrutiny on them.

A small boy and girl trailed along behind them. Black Face turned and spoke in a honeyed voice. "Hurry, children. Don't lag, or the wonderful surprise will be gone by the time we arrive."

The boy, no more than six or seven, tugged his younger sister's hand. He wanted to stop and pee, and he wanted to go home. He didn't understand what had happened. He'd been playing with his sister, both of them engrossed in their game of colored stones, when two men had come and put their big, dirty hands across their mouths, lifted them up, and carried them away from the hut where they lived. Nobody saw this, for their family was all in the fields working.

He'd fought them as well as he could, but no use. And then the dark man came to them and promised them a wonderful surprise, and when that was done, to take them home again.

The boy didn't know whether to trust the dark man. But his sister was terribly frightened. She was only four. He kept up a brave front so she wouldn't cry. He hoped this would all be over soon.

The way led up and up. There was no path, at least none visible by starlight, though Black Face seemed to know the way well enough.

"Over the next ridge," he said.

The stench of sulfur grew stronger as they climbed. Parrot Beak had no idea what to expect, though he knew this was a great honor. Black Face had promised him the opportunity to meet his own master. Parrot Beak tried to imagine what Black Face might bow down to, but he couldn't. His imagination was vivid, but not infinite.

Yellow smoke suddenly belched from the earth up ahead, barely visible in the weirding light. Then Parrot Beak topped the rise and looked down on hell.

They stood on the lip of a great charred bowl, a natural fire pit a hundred paces across. At the bottom of the depression rock bubbled slowly, a soup of molten stone that had cooked for centuries. Around the sides of the bowl were fissures oozing red magma, wounds in the skin of the earth itself. Black Face paused a moment, sniffing the air, his cracked flesh a mirror of the scene below.

"This way," Black Face said, pointing at a thin trail hacked out of the sides of the declivity, leading down. "Take her hand," he said. "I'll take the boy."

Picking their way carefully, they led the children down into the bowl of fire. About a third of the way down the path widened into a broad ledge, which opened onto the mouth of a great cavern. This cave had been shattered by some ancient cataclysm, and now it yawned naked to the flames beyond. At the rear was a huge altar, and looming above the altar, the shape of something . . . terrible.

The children began to cry. Both men tightened their grips and dragged them forward, until all of them stood before the altar. Parrot Beak could feel the girl's hand shivering in his own.

Above the altar a diseased knot of stone grew like a tumor from the back wall. It took Parrot Beak several moments to discern the shape of it—twisted, coiled, *slumped*, a malignancy that seemed to pulse with the same tempo as the fire bowl beyond.

Black Face laughed. The sound was sharp as broken glass, and it tore at Parrot Beak's ears.

"Here is my Lord," Black Face roared. "Here is the God of Storms. He ruled in this place long before the cursed Goddess, and He will rule again!"

Terror pulped Parrot Beak's muscles against his bones, stretched his tendons, shriveled his belly. And yet as he stared at the monstrosity that belched from the living stone before him, he felt a certain comfort. An awareness. A dark, flowing, secret river that welcomed him, soothed him, offered him the joy of a release he'd never before imagined— if he would just let himself sink into those black waters, let them carry him away.

This Lord would love him, would nurture and cherish him. Would lift him up in service to heights undreamed of. All that was necessary was acceptance, obeisance—and sacrifice.

"Yes . . ." he whispered. "Yes."

Black Face laughed again, the sound a wild shriek that overrode the weeping children.

"You do, oh, yes, you do!" he cried out. His hand flashed beneath his robe and came out as a claw wrapped around a long knife. A wild, fierce joy filled Parrot Beak.

They lifted their wailing sacrifices. Edges flashed like razors, fluids spilled forth, and the sudden silence was good.

"*I bring You meat . . .*" Black Face howled.

The night became unspeakable.

2

They walked alone. Dawn painted a thin gray line across the horizon to the east as they strode through silent fields, returning to the city.

For Parrot Beak the exaltation was slowly draining away, yet enough of it remained to remind him of the pact he'd made. A whisper of the promised reward still clung to him like swamp fire to a rotting stump. It warmed him with a sick, delicious fever, the same febrile lust he'd felt as he whipped Twisted Tooth to death.

Black Face, walking beside him, his hood back and his horrible, splintered features exposed to the morning breeze, seemed less affected. "He ruled here once, before She came, and with our help He will rule here again."

After the titanic experience he'd just endured, it took Parrot Beak a moment to make sense of Black Face's words. And when he did, he was still puzzled.

"Yes," he said slowly, "I understand how we serve Him. But we are mortals. How can we oppose Her? She is a Goddess."

"I have opposed Her for many years, and She has not struck me down. I live in His dark fire, and I trust it. He has placed His mark on me." His fingers rose and scraped his tattered flesh.

"Yes, I see that. But He is powerful and we are not. Not as She is."

Black Face nodded. "A time approaches when that will change. When He will strike Her again. She defeated Him once, but even She could not destroy Him. The tides of the Gods ebb and flow, and all things come round again. Now it is His turn. Now, in the city, the hearts of men are finally open to Him. And this time He will seize them. With our help, of course. And He will be grateful, as only Gods can be grateful, for our help."

"Tell me," Parrot Beak said.

"The Year One Reed is upon us. It is a turning point. And now a king schemes for his son. We will place that son upon the throne for him, with His help. And though His ancient enemy also stirs in the city, we know of Her coming, and we can prepare for it. The old King plans to rule the new King, after all enemies are destroyed. But if the old King dies, we know this soft new King, do we not?"

Parrot Beak began to see it, to see the perfect, beautiful treachery of it. He laughed.

"Yes," Black Face agreed. "And when He, through us, rules the new King, then there will be vengeance long over-due, and new priests in the Temple of the Moon."

At that moment the first crimson brush streaked across the far horizon. That glow bathed their ravaged features as they walked, and laughed, and plotted doom.

Their Dark Lord was with them. They had given Him blameless meat and innocent blood, and He had given them His own strength. How could they fail?

"He will heal us, you know," Black Face said.

3

As Black Face and Parrot Beak walked across the empty fields with dawn fire burning on their faces, Cham Ix woke from an uneasy sleep, the rags of nightmare still blowing in his brain.

He climbed up slowly from the hard mat that lay on the floor of his room in the Palace of Priests. He could have taken a vast suite of rooms for his personal use, but he hadn't. He kept to the old teachings. After all, what did any man need, priest or not, but a place to sleep, a roof over his head, clothes on his back, and food in his belly? He had all these things, thanks to Her. It was only fitting that every-thing else should go to Her service.

There was a great hall in the palace where the priests and all the others who served Her took their meals in commu-nity. The only thing that marked out Cham Ix and the other high ones was the place where they ate—a dais raised off the floor a few feet, where they could look out upon the fellow-ship of the temple. When Cham Ix arrived, his son was al-ready seated on his mat, swiping tortillas through a stew made of roots and pork.

SISTER OF THE SKY

"Good morning, Father," White Feather said.

"Morning. Ah, my joints are cold today," Cham Ix replied as he squatted down, a protesting chorus of pops and snaps ringing softly in his ears. He found a bowl and scooped breakfast from the larger pot around which they all sat, folded up a tortilla, and dredged the stew to his lips.

As they ate they chatted companionably about small things, and when they were done, Cham Ix said to White Feather, "Come see me at the first hour before noon."

4

"You may not know all the details of how I achieved my position," Cham Ix said.

They were alone in his room atop the pyramid, staring out at a hazy, hot day.

"You've never spoken of it. I assumed you followed your father, as you expect me to follow you."

Cham Ix shrugged. "While the high priests are in some sense hereditary, there is room for new blood. What usually happens is if an especially promising lad comes along, the High Priest may adopt him, so that if he should be deemed worthy of the highest position, it will appear in the histories that the line goes on uninterrupted."

White Feather didn't know what to make of this. It had the air of a confession. Surely not . . . ?

"Father, are you telling me you were one such? Not of the blood but adopted into it? Or . . . am *I* one?"

"Oh, no. I am the son of my father and mother, and so are you. But there was another who was taken into our home and called my brother. His name was . . . well, it doesn't matter what his name was. I no longer speak it, nor do any others who know it. Eventually it will be forgotten, and so will my brother."

"I don't understand, Father. Why tell me now?"

"Because I dreamed of him last night. For the first time in many years. And that disturbs me, because of the other signs and omens all around us. So I decided to acquaint you with the story. Knowledge is a weapon. If my dream about my brother has any meaning, then I would see you armed as well as I can."

"I guess I understand. What happened with this brother of yours?"

Cham Ix turned back to the window, his eyes as soft and distant as the hazy horizon he looked at.

"He came into our house in my tenth summer. He was a year younger, and we were raised together. As you have been taught, so we also learned the deepest mysteries, the most ancient secrets, and the Language of Hands. He was a beautiful child and grew into a handsome man, but his soul was evil. I didn't discover this until I was eighteen, and my father was trying to decide between the two of us. Of course, I wanted to succeed my father, but I also loved my brother, and I'd already decided that if my father chose him, I would be content, and serve my brother faithfully in all things. But it seems my brother, who was then called Jaguar Dawnlight, was not as content as I was . . ."

5

. . . Cham Ix awakened in the middle of the night, not from dreams, but from an intense itching sensation that seemed to be concentrated mostly on the nape of his neck and in the small of his back.

He rose from his mat quietly, moving with the sinuous ease of an eighteen-year-old. He had moved out of the boys' dormitories two years before, and now had his own small cubicle adjoining his father's rooms, as did his brother Jaguar. Now he stood and scratched his head, trying to figure out what it was that had awakened him, and suddenly he thought of Jaguar.

He left his own room, walked two doorways down the silent hall, and peered into Jaguar's small chamber. That was odd. No Jaguar. And once again he felt that strange itching sensation. Stronger, too.

Now, where could Jaguar have gotten to at this time of night?

He could not explain it then, nor would he ever, but for some reason he decided to stretch his legs on the huge portico that fronted the temple. And so he walked quietly along empty, twisting corridors until he emerged in the atrium in the front of the House of the Priests, nodded to the two brothers who dozed at their posts behind the columns, passed on by, and went to stand next to the balustrade.

He looked down on the plaza, empty and silent, bathed in a wash of silvery moonlight.

Ah, yes, he thought. Tonight the moon is full, and should be well risen by the shape of the shadows.

He thought of it riding high behind the pyramid, and turned to look. As he raised his eyes he saw the tiniest of red flashes, about two-thirds of the way up, on the far end of the left-hand side of the pyramid.

He squinted. There was nothing up there to catch the light, nothing there at all, in fact, except for . . . a place that should not show a light. Not now, not ever.

His breath catching in his throat, he wrapped his acolyte's white robe tighter around his waist. He hurried down the stairs, across the empty plaza, and began to climb.

The higher he got, the more difficult the climb became, and when he reached the third level, he had to stop and catch his breath. As he stood, bent and holding his belly with both hands, he heard a thin cry.

It sounded as if it came from the . . . chamber. When he felt recovered, he lifted his robe and hurried on. There was no wind, and the moon cast a great white light, almost as bright as day. Nevertheless he nearly stumbled twice, catching himself at the last minute. The second time he looked down the sheer flanks of stone and shuddered.

That thin, wailing cry sounded twice again. When he reached the hidden door, he saw it ajar. A dim red glow, softly pulsing, painted the stone wall beyond. His heart jumped like a rabbit into his throat. He stepped on through. He saw that the torches were undisturbed. He didn't light one either. That hidden red fire was bright enough.

When he entered the ancient red cavern hidden in the heart of the pyramid, he stopped dead, runners of cold terror sliding up his arms.

There before him was an abomination worse than any nightmare he could ever have conjured. Jaguar Dawnlight stood naked before the altar, his arms upraised, an infant clasped in his hands. Hot blood ran down his wrists and dripped from his elbows. His beautiful face was thrown back, his eyes were wide and ecstatic. His muscles stood out as if chiseled into his skin. His penis was erect and throbbing.

All around him quivered a nimbus of red fire. And across from him the hideous, hunched shape of the Mother also burned. Her stone eyes were open and blazing with the effulgence of emeralds and sapphires, and from her fanged mouth She vomited a slow blue fog that dropped and pooled on the altar between them.

There was blood there, too. Cham Ix couldn't tell if it was the babe's, or if the ancient stains had somehow come alive again.

The room was deathly silent. The fires seemed somehow balanced, as if mighty forces strove against each other, but with neither of them able to achieve the upper hand. The tension made his head ache—and yet it was attractive, it whispered to him on some level deeper and older than his brain. He felt his own penis twitch and begin to rise.

The infant let out a last despairing wail, and somehow the sound broke the fist of stasis that clenched him.

"Jaguar! What are you doing?"

The sound of his voice echoed like a whip crack. In the heat of the moment he had no time to think how strange that was, the echo of his terrified voice resounding endlessly in the dead, dank air of the room. It was almost as if he shouted into some other space, wider, older, not really here at all.

His voice struck Jaguar like a lash. Jaguar's back arched as if he'd been physically struck. He half turned, and Cham Ix saw his eyes. They had once been dark and beautiful. Now they were yellow and hideous. Cham Ix quailed before his gaze.

The red corona that surrounded Jaguar began to vibrate, faster and faster, and as it did so, it began to darken. At the same time the jeweled light that emanated from the Mother waxed stronger, as if it would pour itself through some breach Cham Ix could no more see than he could understand.

But Jaguar understood something. He kept on stretching back and back, as if an unbearable weight had suddenly settled on his chest. Without a sound the infant tumbled from his hands, bounced off the altar, and fell to the floor. And with that the red nimbus enfolding him flickered and then guttered out.

Jaguar Dawnlight *screamed*. Blue fire boiled up from the surface of the altar and exploded in his face.

Cham Ix saw his brother's features begin to burn, to melt, to blacken before his horrified eyes. Ugly fissures opened in that tortured flesh and spewed forth blood and viler fluids. Jaguar shrieked, and again Cham Ix heard that impossible echo as something fled down distances he could not perceive.

"You!" Jaguar screamed. *"You . . . !"* He clapped his hands—which now looked like skeletal, twisted claws—across his ruined face and ran past Cham Ix, who could only stand paralyzed and watch him go.

After a time the flames on the altar began to lessen, and the dire glow about the Mother to fade. By the time Cham Ix noticed he was breathing again, the light was nearly gone. The great pounding beat of it had subsided to only the barest of flickers.

He ran forward and picked up the baby. It squirmed weakly in his hands and died. He never saw Jaguar Dawn-light again.

6

"My father searched his room personally. He found certain things, ancient, evil things, that should not have been there. Nobody really knows, even to this day, who or what my brother really was. Or what possessed him. To those few who know anything about it, he is called the Black Priest, but we don't speak that name aloud, either. And later, my father told me that he'd decided to raise Jaguar Dawnlight to his own position, to let him succeed to the High Priesthood of the Temple. Think of that . . ." Cham Ix said softly.

White Feather's eyes were wide as he tried to picture it. A human vessel for something *other* in charge of the Temple of the Moon. No wonder *She* had stirred from Her stony sleep. And what would have happened if his father had not come along to interrupt their duel, to break the balance? "Why speak of him now?"

"Because for the first time in years, I dreamed of him. I believe he was a vessel, just as the girl is. But a vessel for another, darker thing. The talismans my father discovered in his room were things that served the Fallen God, the God of Storms whom She overthrew when She came to this valley and built Her city. She broke Him, threw Him down, and drove Him away."

He paused, then gestured at the ring of black, brooding peaks that surrounded the valley. "Those are His mountains, though, and perhaps She didn't drive Him far. Gods rise and fall, but They do not die. And even if They do, They come again. Always They come again." Cham Ix shuddered.

"Father? What do you think it means that this dream comes to you now?"

His father stared at him, and was that a hint of fear in his dark eyes? "I think it is a warning. I think we are all in terrible danger." He turned back to staring blankly out his high window at the bleak shapes surrounding the valley. For a moment they looked to him like vast beasts, crouched down and readying themselves to leap.

"I believe I will take what precautions I can," he said.

"Can I help?"

"No. These I will have to do myself. You continue to keep watch on Green Eyes. Especially if she becomes pregnant. Should that happen, I believe it will be a signal."

"A signal of what?"

"I don't know," Cham Ix replied. "But I suspect nothing good."

7

"Tell your . . . principal," Parrot Beak said harshly. "Even at her wedding it was kept concealed, but she bears the double God-marks. One eye is green, the other blue. And though you may not know it, the one for whom you speak will remember. Golden Hand, he of the one eye, also bore the mark. Tell him what I have told you. He will know what needs to be done, but he must order it himself. We cannot undertake such a task without his full support."

Thunder Shield was glad he wore his feathered mask. He didn't much care whether this hooded gargoyle knew who he was. He suspected he did anyway. But this message meant nothing to him. All he felt was confusion, and he was grateful the mask hid it. His father had told him never to show weakness. He gathered himself.

"Very well, I will tell him. You should await our instructions, and hold yourself ready to do his bidding."

"Oh, yes," Parrot Beak replied. "We will do that."

His smile was hidden in the folds of his hood. All things considered, this was probably a good thing. Thunder Shield was already frightened enough.

8

Summer changed to fall, and eventually fall's rains dried into winter. And though that first time had seemed enough— Green Eyes and Golden Hand had stared at each other in the night and felt the *certainty*—nothing had happened yet. She knew that the moon bleeding should stop, but it did not.

There was an urgency to their lovemaking, a dedication and regularity that sometimes made it seem like work to her. And yet all these slow and lubricious slidings, the sudden sunlit peaks that seemed to find them both absorbed and unawares, the agreements that flesh makes with flesh in the secret darkness, all of these things became the levers with which she pried him open to herself.

During the day his life was separate from hers. She knew he plotted and schemed, sent out his factors and merchants to do battle, bought and sold men and merchandise with equal facility. But it had nothing to do with her, for he would not let that part of his life touch her.

Yet in the gauzy dark, when he came to her, he came as just a man, not a prince, and that was how she learned of men. She saw his weakness and his hope, his odd crotchets—he liked his ears nibbled and his toes squeezed, and a finger drawn slowly up the cord between his balls sent him wild—and she understood that though even these intimate transactions were carried out within the framework of unconscious mastery and conscious slavery, she saw how he was caught, too. Lust and love. The great equalizers.

She had never had anything of her own, but these secrets, so carefully gathered, belonged only to her. These were her brightest possessions. They were not given to her, like the ropes of golden nuggets or the fine robes. She placed her own value on them, and because she did, she came to love them as well as any miser on his pile of shells and stones. And since he was the source of her wealth, finally, slowly, she came to love him as well.

In the beginning was the act. And in the act she found a curious kind of equality, for he would lose himself in her, and only she could find him and bring him back. Morning would always come, and the Prince always return to himself and leave her behind, but night also came once every day.

Now, slow and sweating, she let him take her once again to the peaks, his chin rubbing the hollow of her collarbone as she encompassed his pistoning force within her muscled thighs. He moaned, and moaned again, and she felt him subside both within and without. After a time he sighed, left her and rolled over on his side.

She brushed back her hair, savoring the smoky scent of his musk mingled with hers on her cooling cheeks. He sensed her movement, leaned over, and buried his nose in her long hair.

"Ah," he said. "So good. So sweet."

She cupped herself against his long flank, feeling the rough rasp of his groin against her buttocks. "I didn't bleed last month," she finally said.

He stiffened against her. "You didn't?" There was a catch in his throat as he spoke.

"No," she replied, feeling soft and warm and lazy. In control. "If it happens next time, then we'll know."

"I'll make a sacrifice to the Mother tomorrow."

She nodded. She didn't think it would be necessary. But

he was a man. Men always wanted to make sure. It took a woman to know how to trust. Or to trust too much.

9

Thunder Girdle had taken a late meal in his private chambers behind the palace with his son. Thunder Shield was doing better, he thought. The boy seemed to have lost some of the gawkiness that had plagued him all through his youth. Maybe it was the responsibility of acting as intermediary between himself and those dark ones who did his bidding.

He chewed quietly as his son told him what Wooden Nose had said about Golden Hand's new wife. Though the boy was ignorant and hadn't questioned it, now Thunder Girdle understood why the girl had been reluctant to show herself at her adoption.

Long Fingers. What a wily old snake he'd been. Not wily enough, though. He was dead. In retrospect, the King suspected that might have been a mistake. Long Fingers had at least been a known quantity. His son was something new. And, unfortunately, he'd turned out to have inherited every ounce of his father's cunning, along with, it appeared, a healthy dollop of his own.

Thunder Girdle found he was now spending almost all of his time defending his fortune, and that of his house, against an ever-increasing onslaught from the Clan of the Water Moon. Golden Hand seemed to be everywhere at once. He struck without warning, and when he struck, he struck hard.

The Clan of the Summer Moon had already lost several major contracts, and some of their supplies of raw materials were now coming under siege. Not to mention the mysterious destruction of certain of the aqueducts that fed vast stretches of maize owned by the clan. When he'd tried to retaliate in kind, he'd found the aqueducts feeding the Water Moon crops heavily guarded.

But the real mistake in killing the old Prince might have been that it warned the new one. He had a standing order for Golden Hand's death—a man's weight in gold nuggets, purchased at great price from Golden Hand himself was the offered price—but even the Black Face one admitted failure.

"He's too heavily guarded. And he never lets down his guard, not even for a moment," was the message Thunder Shield brought to him.

"Keep trying," the King had ordered. But there hadn't been any results yet, and he was beginning to wonder if there ever would be. In the meantime, his plan to put his son on the throne was no closer toward fruition than at the beginning. If anything, it had faltered somewhat, as his own influence waned among the Eighteen Families.

Which made the situation all the more critical. More and more he felt a cold wind blowing through his bones when he awoke of a morning. And lately, as he'd coughed the night's wad of phlegm into his chamber pot, he saw bright threads of blood mixed in with the thick yellow sputum.

He knew what his son was. Yet he loved him, and since he was all the Gods had given him, he would make do. He had set out to put him on the throne while he, himself, still lived. If he were to die without the succession fully decided, somebody like Golden Hand would tear Thunder Shield to shreds. It was one thing, though, when princes vied for thrones. It was another for a prince to challenge a king, and Thunder Girdle intended that long before he passed to the Underworld, his son would be king.

But there was blood in his spit . . . and the girl had colored eyes. She bore the God-marks. And so did her husband, for now he remembered what he'd long forgotten: the little child with the blue eye, and how his own father had cursed it.

"They said you would have to tell them what to do. That you would know, but you would order it," Thunder Shield said.

Thunder Girdle stared at him, wishing the Gods had not

been so hard. He had no idea if the boy would be able to
hold the throne or not. But by the time that test came around,
he would be dead and his duty to son and family done.
Sometimes he felt so tired.

"Tell them to kill the woman," he said. "I will protect
them. But kill her now. By all the Gods, the bitch may already be pregnant."

10

Flames off wavering torches beat a fiery tattoo on the
front of the house. Men raised their voices and cried of distant blazes, of warehouses, of goods spoiled, and of death.

Chain Coil left his post at the front door and awakened his
Lord. In all the unused rooms of the house men stirred,
woke, and grabbed for their knives, their axes, their bows,
and their spears.

A great portion of them left with Golden Hand. He no
longer took any chances. His wife had not bled for a second
month, and now he was going to be a father. He intended to
live to see that birth, and for a long time after.

Green Eyes woke a little and listened to the tumult. Gradually it died away, and she sank back into sleep. The house
grew quiet.

In the servants' quarters an old woman lay awake, staring
at a single star gleaming through the skylight. After a time
she threw off her blanket, rose to her feet, and trudged
slowly out of the room.

11

Long Snake continued his patrol long after his Lord had
gone. Chain Coil watched the door. He walked the perime-
ter. And inside were another half-dozen men, no doubt doz-

ing off by now, but ready to leap to their weapons at the first shouted warning.

The stars wheeled slowly toward their dawn appointments with the western horizon. It grew colder, and an ache began to grow in Long Snake's belly. He stopped, looked in both directions, then moved close to the outer wall of the servants' quarters. He hoisted his skirt and began to make water.

He never felt the blade that slid so sweetly between his ribs and pierced his heart, stopping it forever.

12

Black Face, wearing only a short clout and a soft leather belt, dropped like a ghost from the roof of the servants' quarters onto the atrium floor. It was a fall of nearly twenty feet, but he took the shock in his calves and thighs, and immediately came up questing, a long knife in his hand.

He froze.

As soon as his feet touched the ground, the altar in the center of the atrium began to glow. As he stared at it, a deep green effulgence crept and twisted about the shape of the pyramid, and he knew what he faced.

"Old Woman," he whispered. "I bring the One You fear."

He felt the familiar dark fire twisting up from his own innards as the One he summoned rushed to his aid. The God overflowed in him. He looked down at his knife hand, and saw the red fire dancing there. This time there would be no Cham Ix to break the balance. He began to edge around the altar, giving it a wide berth. He was armored by the God Himself, but there was no sense in taking chances.

He spat as he moved across the stucco floor. "I see you, Old Mother," he hissed. "But you won't halt me this time. I bring your doom."

A shadow detached itself from the altar and moved toward him. "I am here," the shadow said. "You shall not pass."

This one was pulsing with the green witch fire too. He didn't hesitate. He flung himself forward, cleaving viciously upward with his knife of flame. Only at the last moment did he see her weapon: a clear green blade, bright as a star. The old woman moved like flowing water, and his edge whistled on empty air.

Lightning blasted into his brain as the green point burst through his eye socket. He stood up straight. The fire that shielded him vanished. A dagger of clear, bright pain burned inside his skull. Surely it could not end this way, so quickly.

A vast question filled his mind.

He said, "You promised . . ."

And then he fell, but Mama Root never learned what that promise was. As she bent and pulled the knife from his skull an arrow whistled down from the roof and buried itself in her chest.

It felt as if somebody had kicked her, hard, in the center of her breastbone. She grasped at it with both hands, but her strength ebbed away, and a sudden coldness spread outward from her heart.

Just before the darkness reached her eyes she let out a scream. She heard it echo in the silence, and then heard the answering shouts of the aroused guards.

The knife dropped from her dead fingers. It made a small, tinkling sound as it struck the floor.

When the guards arrived they found an old woman and a man ugly as a demon, and a green knife. They found nothing else to indicate that Gods had dueled this night. Nor would they. The altar next to the bodies was once again only stone.

13

When the time came, White Feather attended with the midwives at the birth. Golden Hand paced back and forth before the altar, which was laden with the dregs of many sacrifices. His father's old cup was in his hand, and it was full of pulque.

When one of the old maids came shambling out, flapping her robe as if shooing off turkeys, her hair sticking up in fingerlike scribbles, he said, "A boy? Is it a boy?"

But she couldn't answer. She stammered, "The knife, great Lord. The priest says he must have the knife."

It took Golden Hand a moment to understand what she meant. Then he flung the mug aside and scrambled up onto the altar. He reached to the top of the pyramid and fumbled till he found it. So great was his haste that the edge of it scored his palm, and he handed it to her slick with his own blood.

She took it and rushed away.

It was nearly an hour before White Feather himself came out to meet him. The priest looked tired but calm. He came up to him and handed him the knife. "Put it back, Prince. It served its purpose."

Golden Hand grabbed him by his shoulders and held him. "Gods, man, tell me. What *purpose*?"

White Feather smiled a beautiful smile. "To cut your son's birth cord, Prince. What else?"

14

"He's beautiful," Golden Hand said.

The boy, wrapped in the finest swaddling of white cotton, nestled in his mother's arms and regarded him with unfocused curiosity.

Unlike his mother's eyes, his were exactly the same color.

Nor were they blue or green. They were a mixture, a clear, limpid aquamarine, the color of the sea just after dawn. Green Eyes had never seen the sea, but Golden Hand had. He had stood on a great promontory above Pital and looked down on the boats and the waves, the distant lonely cries of the gulls ringing in his ears. He had seen that color, like no other in the Middle World.

"I say his name is Oceanwater Dawneyes," Golden Hand whispered.

But his mother shook her head. "No, husband, it is Shining Star."

"Shining Star? Why?"

"The name of Her son, the first king in Tollan."

"How can you know that? Even the priests no longer remember that king's name."

She rocked the babe and smiled up at her husband. "I know, Lord," she said. "I do. And he will be a king, too."

15

Green Eyes's joy in the birth of her son was tempered by a deep and lingering sadness at the death of Mama Root. She had no idea what had happened. Nobody did. They had found Long Snake's corpse sprawled against the outer walls, and Mama and her assailant collapsed in a heap together near the altar in the atrium.

Golden Hand had refused to let her see the terrible scene. Golden Hand had said nothing about this to his wife. Later he explained that Mama Root had most likely died trying to defend Green Eyes against an attack by the assassin whose body they had found.

"It was awful, Green Eyes, and it was amazing," he said later. "We're still not sure what actually occurred. Somehow Mama Root managed to get hold of the Godstone knife that was on top of the pyramid above the altar. And then, even more miraculous, she was able to kill the would-be murderer. We found him with his own knife in his hand, yet he never touched her. She died with an arrow through her heart."

He shook his head. "There must have been a second assassin. Mama Root's dying shout awakened the house guards, and that must have frightened off the second man."

Green Eyes looked down at the babe cooing in her arms. A shiver of terror shot through her. "Were they coming for me?"

"I don't know." His face was dark, congested with angry blood.

"Mother of the Gods, husband. Who is trying to do this to us? First Twisted Tooth, then your father, and now this. When will it end?"

"Soon," he said grimly. "I promise you it will end soon."

16

Shining Star was in his third month, growing like a weed, when Green Eyes decided it was time to do what she'd put off for so long. She left the boy with his wet nurse, and walked across the atrium to her old quarters.

The room looked even smaller now. She'd given orders to leave it untouched, though somebody had neatened the blankets on the feather bed.

Mama Root's bag, and her floppy straw hat, lay in their customary place in the corner. She sighed, went over, and lowered herself to the bed. She pulled the bag into her lap and opened it.

At the bottom she found it, took it out, and held it in her hands. The little head of the Goddess stared back at her enigmatically.

She felt an indistinct, crawling sensation in her palms, and dropped the effigy as if it had suddenly grown hot. She had seen it broken into a hundred pieces, and now here it was again, whole and unmarked.

Her first instinct was to break it again. It seemed to whisper to her of things she didn't want to hear. It was somehow both a promise and a prophesy, and suddenly she realized it had been in her dreams ever since Shining Star's birth.

She mashed one fist against her mouth. After a while she got up. She left it where it lay and sent a messenger for White Feather.

Let him take it. It belonged to his Mistress, not hers. She would refuse its dreadful promise, for herself and, more important, for her son.

But from that day on, she began to remember her dreams.

Chapter Sixteen

1

What if She's in there waiting for me? White Feather thought suddenly. He pictured Her as his father had described Her at the fall of the Black Priest, Her dark stone pulsating with God-light, Her mouth open and vomiting power upon Her altar.

He remembered the way Green Eyes's gaze had refused to meet his own. She had sounded calm enough, but he'd gotten the impression she was terrified.

"It's in Mama's room. On her bed. I don't want it in this house. When you see it, you'll understand. It . . . belongs with Her, anyway. I want you to take it back to Her."

"I don't understand," he'd said then.

"Just go. When you see it, you'll know."

When he did see it, he understood. The head, small and brown, lay on the feather mattress, its blind eyes staring up at him. He'd seen it before, on the top of the small temple in the atrium of this house. And he knew the story of how it had been broken, and then the shards had vanished. Now it was here again, and whole. Somehow the aged terra-cotta head had been mended. But when he examined it, he could see no traces of such mending. It rested in his hand, small, hard, unyielding. Its eyes seemed to track him as he lifted it. And as he stared into those stony eyes he knew where it should go. Where it *wanted* to go.

Now, with the breezes of the high air rippling pleasantly through his hair, and the everyday sunlight warming his shoulders, he approached the hidden door that led into darkness. He slipped on past and lit a torch. He walked slowly down the tunnel, the dust of dead ages clogging his nose. His thoughts had become nearly as blank as the expression on the head itself. He felt its weight swinging in the bag in his hand, and the slow sensation grew on him that She was expecting him. There, up ahead in the endless dark, She squatted and waited for him . . .

At his back, the wind sighed softly across the door crack and brought forth a hollow moan. The sound quivered in the air, and gooseflesh suddenly sprang up on his arms and back. The torch popped and hissed softly at his ear. His shadow danced like a black ghost at his feet.

As he reached the threshold of the inner chamber, trapped within the flickering circle of his light, terror rose in him. It slammed shut his throat and roared in his ears. For a moment he couldn't move. The weight of the head grew unbearable. How could he hold it? It dragged him down.

It took everything he had to take another step. Even after, he would not recall how he did that. But somehow he found himself beyond the door. His ears popped. The torch flared up and showered sparks on him, but he didn't notice. All he could see was the altar. And *Her,* crouching behind it, waiting for him.

He became aware all over again how immensely quiet it was in this room. The sound of his halting footsteps as he moved toward Her filled his ears with thunder. He didn't stop until his quivering body was pressed against the edge of Her table. When he raised his head to look into Her eyes, it was like trying to lift a huge boulder.

She stared back at him, remote and enigmatic. There was no light in Her eyes. There was nothing but silence, and Her waiting.

His hand shook as he raised the bag and dumped its contents. The head landed with a sharp, hollow sound, but it did not break. It rolled across the altar and stopped at the base of Her idol, where it rested between Her animal paws.

He stared, transfixed, at the fangs that protruded from Her changeless grin. Then he uttered a soft, choked cry, threw up his hands, turned, and ran.

When the sun was in his eyes again, and the fresh wind tickling his hair, it all seemed like a dream.

"I will never go there again," he told himself.

So great was mortal duplicity before the Gods that by the time he reached the safe, comfortable environs of the Palace of Priests far below, he even managed to convince himself he believed his own vow.

2

"Why didn't you bring the head to me?" Cham Ix asked his son.

They were standing on the patio before the temple on top of the pyramid, looking down the long flights of stairs at the plaza below.

"I don't know," White Feather replied. "I can't explain it. It was as if I knew it was something I had to do. As if *She* wanted me to bring it to Her."

Cham Ix frowned. "Look down there. The plaza is nearly empty." He paused, then glanced up at his son and frowned. "Donations and sacrifices at all the major temples are down by nearly half over the last few weeks."

White Feather nodded and pointed down the length of the Avenue of the Gods. "That's the reason. Right there."

The avenue was nearly deserted from the Temple of the Sun all the way up to the Plaza of the Moon. But farther on, the closer it drew to the River Bridge, the more crowded it became, until past the bridge it vanished entirely beneath a turbulent, colorful sea of people. The muted sounds of the crowd floated in the air like the distant hum of bees.

"Yes. More ball games today. Thunder Girdle and Golden Hand are spending fortunes trying to win the city to their own side. Of course those poor fools have no voice in anything, but the Eighteen pay attention to the moods of the crowds. Free food, free pulque, free games." He shook his head. "And the temples suffer for it."

"But do the Gods suffer?" White Feather asked. "Surely They grow angry. The people are turning away from the proper rites, forgetting their sacrifices, ignoring the priests. It is the doing of those two men, of course. But in their desire for power—and vengeance, of course—they may destroy that which they seek to obtain. If the Gods turn Their faces away from us, what then? Of what value is being king of a sinful city? Even Tollan can fall."

Cham Ix sighed. "I'm not so much worried about the city, as I am the Gods. More particularly, the Goddess *we* serve."

White Feather stared at him, shocked. "Surely you don't fear for Her?"

Cham Ix sighed. "You didn't tell me about the head. And I have kept something from you, but now I think I will tell you. I see a deadly pattern taking shape, and you should know about it too."

"What? What pattern?"

"You recall when somebody made an assassination attempt on the woman, before her child was born?"

"Yes."

"Well, I sent my spies to retrieve the body of that would-be killer, and had it brought to me."

"Whatever for? Some low ruffian, no doubt."

"My spies did recognize him. Evidently he's been living in the quarters for many years, a king of the underworld. A murderer for hire, an extortionist, a thief, a corrupter of women. He called himself Black Face." Cham Ix squinted at the sun and shook his head. "It was an appropriate name for him to take."

"I don't understand."

"I looked upon this man's face. It was split and cracked, and even in death puss leaked from it. But as I stared into his dead yellow eyes, I knew him."

White Feather breathed in sharply. "Yellow eyes?"

"Yes. It was the face of my brother, still as ruined as the day I saw him last. Servant of the Dark God, vessel of the Fallen One. Black Face, the Black Priest who was once Jaguar Dawnlight."

White Feather narrowed his eyes in thought. The scent of rich meats was now drifting up into the higher air from the festivals at the other end of the avenue. A wave of cheering rose with the scent. "But that means . . ."

"I don't know what it means. But consider. The Dark God began to move upon the valley for the first time thirty years ago, in the vessel of my brother. Then I broke him, almost by accident, and he fled. But he didn't flee far away. He stayed here, protected and nurtured by his Lord. Now, my spies tell me he didn't do his own evil work anymore, but hired others. They speak of a right-hand man named Parrot Beak, whose face is also ruined. Yet Black Face tried to strike at Green Eyes personally, with his own hand. Can you see the pattern now? He was a tool of the God, and I doubt very much if the stroke was his own. The God sent him. But why?"

"Because the God sought to strike the Goddess," White Feather said. "What else could it be?"

"Which makes the woman and her child all the more important. Far more important, I think, than this struggle between kings and princes, though I fear that is a part of the pattern too."

"How so?"

"They turn the people away from the Gods. Your new men grow ever stronger. The city splits in two and its people growl like dogs over the bone of money, rather than seeking the food of the spirit as they should. And now the Dark God returns, moving in treachery and murder, as He always has."

White Feather raised one hand. "But, Father, you say your old brother is dead. If he was the instrument of the God, has He not been defeated? I'm told the assassin died at the hands of an old woman. Perhaps her hand was strengthened by something greater than herself?"

Cham Ix sighed heavily. "Then more problems, son. The Goddess moves against the God, and the God moves against Her. And the people have no idea. They turn from the Gods equally, and sink themselves in food and drink. Our city is vulnerable, boy. Can't you see it? Can't you *feel* it?"

And, standing there in the bright sunlight, White Feather felt a shadow move across the sun. A great flowing shade whipped across the plaza like the wing of a giant crow. He felt the breeze grow cold for an instant. "I feel something," he admitted. "What will you do?"

Cham Ix stood straighter. "I believe you brought that head to this temple for a reason. I don't know what the reason is, nor do you. But I will try to find out why. It may be crucial in the struggle to come. And I will begin to speak out openly against this mad competition between the lords, and urge the people to return to the Gods whom they have deserted. And, finally, I believe I shall search the old records for history and omens. If the Dark One stirs again, He was defeated once. I will try to discover how that happened. Maybe we can learn how we should proceed."

"Is there anything I can do, Father?"

His father eyed him with a worried expression on his face. "I hate to expose you to this, but you're the only one I can trust who possesses the secret knowledge. Take our spies and find out more about this henchman of the one who called himself Black Face. I *know* that one was a vessel, but if the Fallen One is stirring again, He may have found others."

"Yes, Father. I'll start right away."

"Be careful. This is not a game. Or if it is, it is one the Gods play, and so it is terribly dangerous for mortals to mix in with."

I'm already mixed in, White Feather thought, feeling a

dismal, creeping fear. But he said nothing of this. "I will be, Father."

"These are terrible times," his father replied. He started to turn away, and then, suddenly, whirled back around. He wrapped his arms around his son and held him. "I love you," he said.

White Feather felt that dread again, even as he hugged him back and said, "I love you too, Father."

Why did their words feel so much like a farewell?

3

Parrot Beak stood naked before it, his back arched so far his ribs stood out against his skin like sticks in a worn cloth sack. He was streaked with the clotting blood of the hideous meal he'd prepared for his master. Gore coated his hands as thickly as a paste of mashed strawberries. It dripped from his elbows and his chin, and drooled from the corners of his mouth.

He had eaten of the same meat as his Lord, and it was good. Waves of burning power blasted through him, a storm of potency far greater than he'd ever experienced with any woman. He threw back his head and howled.

The maw before him gaped wider, dribbling strings of red, ropy fire. The stone itself was curdled and swollen as whatever thing lived in it sought in vain to clothe itself with the flesh of the Middle World. On the altar the remnants of the sacrifice, ripped and torn, lay like scraps on the floor of a butcher shop.

"Fill me, Lord. Take me and fill me up! I am yours! Take me!"

Gobbling, spitting, and drooling, Tlaloc, the God of Storms, the Fallen One, took the vessel before Him for His own.

4

"I will be leaving for the evening," Golden Hand said.

Green Eyes looked up from her sewing. She was seated on a low stool near the center of the atrium. It had been a warm day, and the stones still held the heat. The air felt soft and comfortable. A fire crackled nearby in a wide clay brazier, adding to the warmth.

Next to her, Gentle Dawn and Moon both stitched their own handiwork. Frown lines appeared at the bridge of Green Eyes's nose.

"When will you be back?"

"I'm not sure. Maybe late."

"Lord, is this something . . . dangerous?"

"Oh, no. Nothing to worry about, Green Eyes. If you want, I'll wake you when I get back."

She smiled. "You may not have to. Shining Star's been wakeful of late." Her smile grew wider. "As you well know."

After he had gone, a troop of guards thundering out with him—which still left a small army remaining in the house—Gentle Dawn looked up from her own stitches. She had regained most of her weight, but now her face sagged, and her hair had begun to go white in long, ragged streaks.

"He's lying, you know," she said calmly.

"What? What about?"

"About the danger. He's going somewhere that frightens him."

Green Eyes put down her embroidery and leaned forward, her eyes intent. "How do you know that?"

"I'm his mother," Gentle Dawn said. "I can tell when he's lying. Just as I can tell when he's afraid."

5

Golden Hand strode deeper into the quarter populated by the rich merchants who lived in the areas behind the Citadel. Heavily armed men with torches lit his way. He was surrounded by four men who carried tall, upright shields faced with straw, thick enough to stop an arrow. Golden Hand had not forgotten how his father or Mama Root had died.

Besides the torch and shield bearers, a full dozen of his toughest guards crowded around him, their callused hands on their weapons. The few citizens still about saw the approach of the assemblage and hastily moved aside, cowering against the walls until it had gone by.

Golden Hand saw glimpses of this, and it only made his sorrow greater. Once—and not so long ago—he had walked these streets alone, without fear of any man. But now he lived in a cage of his own making. His wife was never allowed out of the house, and he only left surrounded by an army.

It was no way to live, not for him, not for Green Eyes, not for his son. But what other choice did he have? It was either this or . . . or that? Let King Thunder Girdle place his idiot son on the throne in triumph?

He could not forswear his holy vengeance, sworn on his knees before the Goddess Herself. If he did so, *Her* vengeance would certainly be more terrible than anything Thunder Girdle could devise. And it was probably too late anyway. He and Thunder Girdle circled each other, each dealing and absorbing tremendous blows, neither able to bring the other down. Too much damage had been done for either of them to forget. Or forgive.

Golden Hand felt that, on balance, he was winning. Although he kept his wife at home for the sake of her safety, he no longer kept her secluded. Two or three nights a week they held banquets, glittering feasts attended by one or the other of the great Families. Always, one of the features of these gatherings was the introduction of Green Eyes, who had been a great mystery. But now they could see her God-marks for themselves, and, more to the point, the eyes of the babe in her arms.

Old Turkeywattle Harvest Moon, the leader of that clan, had even remarked on it. "Boy's got the God-eyes, the king mark. Got them twice over," he said, his voice loud and carrying because he was mostly deaf and shouted everything. "It's a good omen. Hasn't been God-marks in the Summer Moon in—I don't know. Surely not since your ancestor was king, young Water Moon."

Yes, Golden Hand had thought. Yes, indeed. Shout it louder, Turkeywattle. And tell your friends. He'd taken the old man aside, into a closed-off room where they could yell at each other to their heart's content without fear of being overheard, and Golden Hand had said, "When the time comes, those who support me will be rewarded."

"Eh? Support you?" The old man's eyes had twinkled shrewdly. "We'll see. I've an open mind yet, but maybe it's time for a change. Even an old line can grow stupid. And maybe the Gods are trying to tell us something. Those God-marks on your boy didn't come from nowhere."

As his party reached its destination, three of his guards peeled off and ducked inside the house while he waited outside.

The captain of his guard returned. "Everything's fine inside the house. That one brought two of his own guards. I left four of ours to keep an eye on them. He's waiting for you in the atrium."

Golden Hand nodded. The captain stepped forward, thrust the door curtain aside, and they went on in.

6

"I am surprised, Lord, that you wanted to see me face-to-face."

Golden Hand scowled at him. "I haven't yet. Your hood covers all. Yet I stand before you, plain-faced and open."

"A good point, Lord. Are you sure?"

"Show yourself."

Parrot Beak threw back his hood. If he'd been expecting some exaggerated reaction to what he'd become in the forge of the Dark Lord's mountains, he was disappointed. Except for a single blink and a slight tightening of the lips, Golden Hand appeared unmoved.

"My commiseration," Golden Hand said. He raised one finger and touched his own eye patch. "I, too, have the misfortune to be mutilated. The Gods can be sadly changeable in Their favors."

Parrot Beak nodded brusquely. He needed no sympathy from any lord. In particular, not this lord. But it did answer one question. Evidently he'd changed so much that Golden Hand no longer recognized him. A glance in the rain basins outside his own house had told him this much, but he'd yet to test it against the memory of someone who'd known him before.

"Very well," he said. "You sent word you wished to see me, Lord. So here you see me. What do you want?"

"No, the question is what would you want?"

Parrot Beak mimed surprise. "I, Lord?"

"Yes, you. What would you want to kill a king?"

7

When Golden Hand returned home the house was asleep except for its guards. He stripped off his clothes, paused a moment over the crib where his son slept, stepped across the

sleeping body of the baby's nurse, and climbed into the piled
feather beds where his wife slept.

A fat moon beamed down through the skylight, painting
her dark hair with snowy highlights. At his touch her eyelids
flickered and she mumbled something muzzy with slumber.
He slid next to her, seeking her warmth, though he hoped
she wouldn't awaken fully. She would sense his mood, and
because he couldn't explain it to her, his silence would only
frighten her.

But how could he speak of the monster he'd just seen?
His face charred as black as night, and a body twisted and
bent as a stunted tree. If anything, this one was *worse* than
the thing they'd found dead in the atrium.

He'd never felt such evil in his life. Yet he'd promised this
man his weight in gold if he would kill King Thunder Girdle. He'd even handed over a down payment. And the
demon in human flesh had offered to murder the King's son
as well, but by that time Golden Hand's gorge was so
swollen with disgust, both at the man before him and at himself for holding commerce with him, that he could barely
speak.

He put his arm around Green Eyes's waist and snuggled
closer. He drank in her warmth gratefully. He felt so cold. So
dirty.

It took him a long time to find sleep. Just before he did, a
thought drifted across his mind. The child. The boy in the
crib with his ocean eyes.

He will cleanse me.

8

Thunder Girdle said, "I told you I never wanted to see you
again."

The man in the hood turned and limped away from him,
showing him his twisted back, and inflaming his ire further.

"The news I bring is too important to entrust even to your . . . messenger. Do you want to hear it or not?"

"How dare you speak to me like that?"

"Golden Hand has hired me to kill you."

They met in the usual place, though the King had left his guards outside the atrium for purposes of secrecy. He himself was hooded and cloaked, just as the man before him. Now panic sliced in his veins. He dropped his hand to the long knife in his belt. But he kept his voice level as he said, "And did you accept?"

"Oh, of course, Lord."

The King opened his mouth to shout as he withdrew the knife.

"*Hold!* Don't be a fool. Of course I accepted. But I have no intention of carrying out the commission. Do you think that if I did, I would do so in this manner? In a house surrounded by your guards, one on one, face-to-face? As I say, don't be a fool. Besides, if I *hadn't* accepted, it would only have warned the Prince."

Parrot Beak uttered a scornful laugh. "Lord King, neither of us has time to play the fool any longer."

"You know who I am?"

"I have known you since the first day we met, Thunder Girdle."

The King teetered on the edge of summoning his guards and having this one impaled on a long spear. But then he slowly relaxed. That might yet become necessary, but not until he'd made use of this man.

"Keep talking," he said.

Parrot Beak had thought long and hard before calling this meeting. With Black Face gone, the offer from Prince Golden Hand had the potential of changing things entirely. All along he and Black Face had planned on betraying the King after the son was on the throne. A single swift stroke, and then the new King would be at the mercy of Golden

Hand and all the others who would smell his weakness like dogs in heat.

So the new King would do anything, pay anything, raise anybody up who would stand between him and his enemies. But what about killing the old King now? Take the reward, let Golden Hand have his victory?

In the end it was an easy decision. Golden Hand was no fool. The day after he ascended to the throne—no, more likely the day after the old Kind died—his orders and his money would go to some other assassin. Parrot Beak had no illusions as to whom the new target would be. He would do the same thing himself.

Only a weak man on the throne would suit his purposes. And the only weak man was the son of Thunder Girdle. So he would keep his word and do his treachery at the same time. Besides, in the end he discovered he really didn't have a choice.

The dark thing bubbling in his skull told him so.

King Thunder Girdle moved closer. "What do you propose we do about this?"

Parrot Beak told him. When he finished, the King threw back his head and laughed. "Why, man," the King roared, "you're a genius. Pity you can't show yourself in the light of day. I'd raise you up myself!"

Parrot Beak remembered those words after the King had gone. He carved the insult into the eternal stone of his rage. And he thought, The time is coming when I *will* show myself.

Unfortunately, old King, *you* will be long dead by then.

9

When he awoke from a restless sleep the next morning, Thunder Girdle found his face throbbing like a toothache.

He groaned softly, rolled out of bed, and went to find his chamber pot.

He eyed the result with alarm. The bloody threads in his spit were thicker. So thick, in fact, it was hard to tell sputum from blood.

And later, when he noticed the shock on the faces of his courtiers as they dressed him for the day, he went to one of the catch basins and looked into the still rainwater.

He drew back in shock. All over his face were livid red bumps, some of them as wide as his thumbnail. He reached up and ran his fingers over them. His fingertips came away slick and sticky with some clear, slightly yellow fluid.

"Priests!" he cried out. "Bring me the healing priests!"

Then he went back into his private chamber and refused to come out the rest of that day.

10

It was trickier this time, though in another way not so tricky. He didn't have to kill anybody tonight. But he had to avoid getting himself killed, and that was no easy task.

Thank the Dark One for the clouds that masked the moon tonight! Parrot Beak glanced over his shoulder from where he lay flat on the roof of the house.

The place was an armed camp. Men paced ceaselessly along all four walls, their spear tips bright and glittering in the light of the torches they carried. He had watched these guards for three hours until he deciphered the rhythms of their patrol. He'd waited another hour before he took advantage of the ten-second lapse he'd discovered, to run to the wall and clamber up it like a monkey to the safety of the roof.

But there was a man on the roof, too. He could see his dim form seated across the atrium from him, at the edge of the thatch. He couldn't tell if that guard was dozing or not, but it didn't matter. He couldn't kill him. That would give too much away.

He reached into his belt pouch and took out a rock half the size of his fist. Being careful to keep his own silhouette below the roof line, he drew back his arm and threw. The rock landed on the far edge of the roof with a harsh, cracking sound.

He watched as the guard stood up, turned, and went to check on the disturbance. Long before the man turned back to his post, Parrot Beak had dropped to the atrium floor.

Now he hid in the shadow of the altar itself. Keeping the bulk of the pyramid between himself and the guard overhead, he clambered up until he could reach the top with one questing hand. He found the knife where he knew it would be, slipped it into his pouch. He felt a faint tingle as he touched the smooth stone, but it quickly passed.

The door at the back of the servants' quarters was guarded by a single man. Eventually he had to piss, and when he did, Parrot Beak slipped out into the night, and was gone.

11

Just as Parrot Beak was putting his hand on the Godstone knife, Green Eyes found herself in the same dream that had disturbed her sleep for weeks now, ever since she'd found the head of the Goddess and given it to White Feather.

It was a dream and yet it felt cursed, more like a doom than a dream. And it felt real. She was aware of herself dreaming it, as if some part of her stood off to the side and watched. Each time she dreamed it, it grew more detailed, and more frightening—as if something was slowly being revealed to her, though she didn't yet understand that.

It began as it always did, her standing on some high place, surrounded by winds that howled in her ears and beat at her robes. Overhead, Lord Sky Snake crashed across the bruised sky, again and again, until the dazzling blaze of His passage nearly blinded her.

She could smell the bitter, iron-flecked chill of His bolts. And now, as always, the great dark thing congealed out of the night, boiling with glints of white teeth, its fetid breath foul with unspeakable hungers.

She had seen this a hundred times. This time it felt different. It felt even more real than usual. She looked down and saw raindrops spitting up off the dark, soaked wood of the platform on which she stood. The hot snap and sizzle of the drops spattering on the coals of the fire brought the smell of damp burning wood to her nose. And through the dazzle of the lightning and the endless crash of the thunder she could hear the harsh breathing of the shaman priest, and she could smell the exotic, dusty-flower scent of the woman who held the baby and the knife.

She held her breath as the moment marched toward its inevitable conclusion. The dark thing boiled closer toward the doom it would soon experience at the fiery hands of the Plumed Serpent. Down below, the woman in white rose another step as the winds wailed in piercing shrieks. And less than a hand's breath away, the madwoman raised the knife.

It was always in this particular instant that Green Eyes felt her greatest moment of fear. Each time, as the knife rose above the tiny shape, the child would turn its head and look directly at her, as if it could see her. She would see its blue eye winking, a tiny living spark in the gloom.

And then the earth would move, the woman fall, the knife flip away into darkness, and the rest of it would come crashing down.

She felt that moment approaching now. The madwoman brought the knife to the peak of its arc. Green Eyes looked up at it and saw that it was glowing with green fire. Dimly, she heard the woman in white cry out with a mighty voice.

That was different.

A great sludge of fear suddenly choked every passageway

in her body, and her mind as well. She froze, caught in the dreadful moment, as the child turned its face toward her.

His eyes. Aquamarine, blue-green, the endless deep hue of dawn-lit oceans. The tiny child slowly opened his mouth.

"Ma . . . ma . . ." he whispered. "Mama . . ."

The knife came down.

She bolted upright in her bed, her heart pounding, sweat boiling from her brow.

Golden Hand was there with her, rising on his elbow, his good eye sharp with concern. "What is it?" he whispered hoarsely. "Green Eyes, you're shaking!"

She couldn't speak. She threw herself against him, burrowed against his warm chest, and burst into tears.

He soothed her. He stroked her sweat-drenched hair and whispered softly into her ear.

"There, there . . . only a bad dream. It's all right . . . I'm here. Only a dream, my love. Only a dream."

But as her choked sobs finally died away, she huddled against him in the dark and knew the truth.

It wasn't a dream. It was a doom.

Death was coming. The death of her son. And soon.

12

Cham Ix looked around the dusty room, bemused that he was here at all. It had been years since he'd even thought of the place, and now he seemed to be spending all his time here. Which was something of a problem in itself, since nobody but his son knew where he was. He was the High Priest of the Temple of the Moon. He couldn't simply vanish without raising more than a few eyebrows. So he'd taken to coming here in the dead of night.

He'd carried a few things up to make the whole miserable process more tolerable. He'd brought in several oil lamps, so that he didn't have to choke on the fumes of the smoky torches. And he'd lugged up a large water jug, and a chamber pot. But his eyes were burning and his nose itching and dripping from the oil lamps, the dust, and other indeterminate smells he couldn't identify.

Moreover, he discovered that something in the room, probably the flaky gray mold that covered many of the more ancient writing sticks and even some of the clay figurines, irritated his skin badly. An angry red rash covered the backs of his hands and extended up his forearms.

He persevered. The histories he knew were mostly oral and visual, handed down in the Language of Hands or through stories whispered from generation to generation of priests. But somewhere, buried in this rotting storehouse, might be further clues. Surely something as monumental as a battle among the Gods might have been noted, if not at the time, at least later by somebody close enough to the events to relate more accurate details than he knew right now.

He brushed a thin layer of silken grime off his knees, reached forward, and pulled down another pile of crumbling records. The tiny figurines presented a problem almost as great as the faded carvings on the record-sticks. Many of them were missing or broken, and he had to guess at the proper arrangement of what was left.

He kept on working, determined to arrive at some sort of conclusion. His instincts told him that something dark and terrible was stirring. It had once been defeated, but he had no idea how. He saw what he thought were pieces of a vast puzzle fitting themselves together in the present day. It was surely no coincidence that Green Eyes, her ocean-eyed son, a knife made of Godstone, the Black Priest, and the general malaise of the city had all occurred within such a short period of time. These things were all signposts, warnings perhaps, and maybe even the outliers of the event itself.

But what? How? He found infuriatingly enigmatic hints here, in the old records, but not enough. Not yet, at least. Yet he wasn't without hope. He'd only opened a small part of what was here.

He glanced around, suddenly struck by the quiet and the looming shadows. He heard a soft scrabbling, scratching sound, and recognized the skitter of rats. Abruptly he sensed a watchfulness, an awareness that seemed to focus on him.

He craned his neck and peered up at the altar. The shadows were particularly thick there, and yet he imagined he could see those eyes. Her stony gaze. Or—dread thought—could it be the eyes of something *else*?

He waited a moment, and gradually the feeling began to fade. After a time it was gone. He shrugged, and continued with his work.

Chapter Seventeen

1

In the darkest hour of the night, with his eyes burning in the lowering glow of the lamps, Cham Ix realized he could no longer make out the carvings on the sticks. The lumps of clay had become shapeless clods, with no pattern, rhyme, or reason he could discern.

He decided he'd had enough. When he stood up from where he'd been sitting, cross-legged and crouched over for the past several hours, his body shrieked in protest. He groaned softly, knuckled his aching eyes, and rubbed the fuzzy fringes of his hair.

One of the lamps guttered out with an audible sputter. It was a soft, sad sound in the silence, and he felt an inexplicable twinge of fear pluck at his nerve endings. For a moment he visualized *all* the lamps, one by one, hissing and popping and dying. Leaving him alone in the dark.

Not exactly alone. He glanced at the altar, with its faded dark streaks, and at the crude, brutal shape squatting above it. He sighed. He loved the Mother, and he'd served Her all his life. But what was hidden away in this chamber was a facet of Her that was older, harder, and far more savage than the one She revealed to Her faithful servants in these faithless days.

For a moment he wondered what would happen if She showed *this* face to the city. *This* Goddess would drink blood with a limitless and divine thirst. There was nothing smooth or soft about Her. He understood. It was in this incarnation that She had fought the Fallen One at the beginning of this age. The Gods had many faces, and wore whichever one suited Their enigmatic purposes. In this incarnation She would be as cruel and elemental as the rains themselves. She was the Goddess of water, the fluid of life

that came from the skies and the earth alike. She could not
have destroyed Her enemy if She'd been any softer or more
yielding than Him.

In his pliant and secret heart he hoped She would never
display this face to Her people again. But he'd seen what
moved against Her. He'd seen the horror of the Dark One,
embodied in His vessel, Black Face. And now was He embodied in another?

He shivered. If the Dark One came again, would he as Her
High Priest have the courage to summon Her in Her most
dreadful aspect?

He didn't know. He wondered if he would. And he wondered if Her cure might not be worse than any disease. But
as he stared at Her timeless stone visage, he understood that
the Dark Lord was worse than Her. He knew that if he had
to, he *would* summon Her, for he was Her priest, not His.
For in the end, that was all he had to lean on, his trust and
hope in Her.

He scratched an itchy spot behind his ear, sighed again,
and trudged out of the chamber. He didn't extinguish the
lamps, but left them behind to burn out on their own. He
might love and serve Her. But he had no urge to find himself alone, in the dark, in that chamber . . . with Her.

He was so tired that he took special care as he traversed
the narrow ledge chiseled into the pyramid, and despite the
coolness of the hour, he was sweating by the time he reached
the landing on the front face of the huge structure. He
paused a moment at the head of the stairs, looking down in
wonder.

The plaza far below had vanished, hidden beneath
swirling white billows of fog. Up here the smell of the river
was suddenly strong, almost unpleasantly so. The air
smelled repellently of rotting wood and decaying vegetable
matter. The fog lay on the plaza like thick, gray soup, un-
stirred by any wind.

He hoisted up his robe and began to descend. About

halfway down, he vanished into the fog himself. Only his footsteps still sounded, amplified by the hollow, echoing character of the moisture-laden air. *Slap, slap, slap*. Downward.

2

Centered on the high stone platform in the center of the plaza, the Great Altar was nearly as high as a man. It had been built in the deeps of the past, constructed shortly after the pyramid itself. The stone was so heavily carved with beasts and men and demons that to fingertips brushed lightly across its surface, it felt like ancient bark. Now the fog kissed it, and the stone turned wet and dark.

On the far side of the altar from the pyramid something crouched in the shadows, waiting. Once it might have been called a man, but not any longer. Now it was something else. An empty vessel, suddenly brimming over. It snuffled softly to itself as it savored the power of the fire boiling in its loins. In its clawed fingers it held a knife, and pressed it close to its pounding heart.

The thing raised its head. It heard the expected sounds, sharp and clear in the ragged curtains of fog that swirled around it. The sounds it had been promised. The prey approaching.

Slap, slap, slap. Descending.

3

Cham Ix reached the bottom of the stairs and seated himself. The long muscles in his thighs, not accustomed to such exertions, throbbed dreadfully. He sat for a moment and rubbed them, praying they wouldn't cramp up on him in the damp coolness of the fog.

His thoughts drifted comfortably to his waiting bed. He mused on safety, warmth, and waking up in the morning to a filling breakfast and the company of his fellows. Then he realized how silent it was. Slowly, his head came up.

The silence was almost a tangible thing, a weight that pressed down on him. The fog had thickened and become nearly impenetrable. He could see only a few feet around him, the damp stone steps on which he sat, a shadowy scrap of painted stucco. Somehow the city had suddenly vanished.

His heart began to slam in his ears, but not so loudly he couldn't hear the thing he'd mistaken for silence. Deep and slow, it rose and fell around him. His pulse yammered and his fingertips turned to ice. He thought he'd forgotten about it, but he hadn't. The memory of that sound had slept in him, hidden for thirty years, and now it sprang from the shadows of his past, as fresh and awful as the dreadful night he'd first heard it.

He'd heard it in the hidden chamber that terrible night so long ago. The sound of breathing, choked and dirty and hot. He bolted to his feet, his mouth falling open as he tried to yank enough air into his lungs to shout. But after a frozen moment he dropped his frantically reaching hands. There was nothing to reach for. His mouth slowly closed. If he shouted, nobody would hear. Nobody but whatever it was that breathed in the misty darkness. And he knew that if he turned and ran, he would never find an end to the fog. There was no edge to it, no safety beyond it, for it wasn't of this world.

"Black Face . . . ?" he whispered, though he knew Black Face was dead. His voice thick with terror.

No answer. Just the slow, endless exhalations.

"Who's *there?*"

He thought he heard the roll of distant, muted thunder. As if a storm were approaching. His knees began to shake, and now he did hear a true sound. The clatter and rattle of his own teeth in his jawbones.

That slow, dreadful breathing grew louder as something hitched itself into the world, drawing ever closer. Coming. Coming for him.

Then, as neatly as a curtain being drawn aside, a pathway opened in the fog between himself and the altar platform. He could just see the top of the altar looming up in the darkness. The stones up there were wet. They gleamed and flickered in the reflection of some malign red glow.

He curled his hands into fists and forced them to his sides. He sucked in deep lungfuls of the fetid air as his clogged throat suddenly opened wide.

All my life . . . he thought suddenly. *I've given Her my life. And just a moment ago I stood before Her and wondered if I would call Her in Her most ancient and terrible aspect. But I would call Her now, O Goddess, yes . . . come to me now, Mother, for I need You.*

The red glow seemed to grow brighter.

Numbly, he began to walk forward. Toward the altar. Toward the light. Toward the *breathing*.

4

The thing savaged him. It fell on him out of the fog as a boiling black cloud, thick with gleaming fangs and claws. It tossed him into the air like a rag doll, and it smashed him to the wet stones.

He burst. His fluids painted great, glistening streaks on the stones before the altar. And when the thing was done, it heaved his torn, twisted remains up onto Her altar.

I bring You meat, Old Bitch. Eat of it if You will.

The thing raised the green knife over the corpse. Its verdant light glimmered only for a moment, and then went dead. Up and down, up and down.

5

In the east, dawn brushed its first pink strokes across the tops of the temples on that side of the plaza. Slow morning breezes blew the last dregs of night fog south toward the river. High above, its black wings catching the light, a crow called harshly.

Maize Two Thumbs paused at the top of the wide steps in front of the Palace of the Priests. He stretched and yawned, then scratched his ribs as he flip-flapped down the steps toward the plaza. He was thinking vaguely about breakfast as he ascended the steps of the altar platform. It was his turn to perform the early ritual and offer the first sacrifice of the day. Under his left arm was a young piglet, pink and squirming.

When he reached the High Altar he stopped. Stopped dead. Then he dropped the pig. Maize Two Thumbs had seen his share of human sacrifice. He'd seen ruined, charred human flesh before.

But the eye that stared so coldly at him was a familiar eye, and the remnants of the face in which it was eternally frozen was a familiar face.

Maize Two Thumbs screamed and ran gobbling back down the platform steps. As luck would have it, a detachment of the royal guards was trooping past at that very moment. As luck would have it.

He managed to slobber out his story before he fainted.

6

"What is your name?" White Feather asked as the guard hurried him along.

"I am Coyote River Moon, sir," the young man replied. His handsome face was bleached and his eyes somewhat staring.

"I don't understand. What's wrong?" White Feather said.

"You must see, sir. I . . . you must see for yourself."

It was plain he wouldn't say anything more. Amid his confusion White Feather felt the first clear drops of fear begin to distill.

They clattered down the palace steps. White Feather saw a small group of guards gathered at the steps leading up to the altar platform. In their midst was a priest. Two of the guards seemed to be holding him up.

As they drew closer, White Feather recognized Maize Two Thumbs, and felt a sudden liquid relief. Probably some kind of accident. But then Maize Two Thumbs looked up and saw him approaching.

"Oh, Lord!" he cried out. "Oh, oh, it's terrible!"

The River Moon lad gave him no chance to find out what was so terrible. He took his elbow and rushed him past the other guards, and thrust him up the stairs. As they reached the platform proper, with the altar looming ahead, White Feather wrinkled his nose.

"What's that smell?"

Coyote's skin was now, if anything, even more pallid. Without a word he continued to urge White Feather forward.

"Wait a minute," White Feather said. And then they came to the altar, and he saw.

For a moment he didn't understand. He simply stood, staring frozen at what appeared to be random pieces of partially cooked meat. Behind him, the guard stepped away, his breathing harsh and hollow.

"What?" White Feather said, his voice unnaturally soft.

He took another step closer. The greasy stink of the burned flesh drifted into his nostrils. He shook his head. He blinked, and blinked again.

The stones of the altar felt hard and gritty beneath his trembling fingertips. The single eye stared up at him, as empty and blameless as an egg. Some different part of White Feather's mind noted the teeth marks, and the handle of the knife protruding from the other eye socket.

"Father . . . ?" he said, his voice wondering. "Father?"
But such flesh does not speak.
"Ah, Father, what have they done *to you?"*

7

White Feather met Golden Hand at the main storehouse the
Prince maintained just off the plaza of the Plumed Serpent. It
was behind the trading area where his factors handled the
buying and selling for him and the other members of his clan.

Golden Hand was chatting amiably with three traders
from the north when he looked up and saw White Feather
enter the large room. He said, "Excuse me, gentlemen," left
them, and hurried to greet the priest. He noted that White
Feather now wore the formal long green robe trimmed with
red that signified his new position as High Priest of the
Moon Temple.

He reached White Feather and took both the priest's hands
in his own. "White Feather," he said. "I am so sorry. What a
terrible thing . . ." He seemed about to say more, but he
trailed off when he saw the look in White Feather's eyes.
The priest's fingers felt limp and cold as dead fish.

"Something's happened, hasn't it, my friend? Come, sit
down, drink some tea with me."

But White Feather shook his head sharply. "No. I've come
to warn you."

Golden Hand put one arm over White Feather's shoulder
and guided him into a corner. "It's quieter here. Keep your
voice down. What did you come to warn me about?"

"I didn't tell you at the time. I didn't know what it meant.
I still don't, but it isn't a secret any longer. His men were
there, and they took it right away. Now he has it, and I think
he'll use it against you."

Golden Hand shook his head. "It? What are you talking
about? What is *it*?"

"The knife. The Godstone knife."

Golden Hand stared at him blankly. "The Godstone knife? I still don't . . . you mean the knife that I . . . that we . . . ?"

"Yes. The knife you brought back from the south, when you brought Green Eyes. The knife used to cut the cord of your firstborn child. The knife Mama Root used to kill a renegade priest. And the knife that has always rested on *your* altar, in *your* atrium. *That* knife."

Golden Hand took a deep breath. "Fine, my friend. Now I know what knife. But what about it? As far as I know, it's still on that altar."

"No, it's not. The last time I saw it, it was sticking out of the eye socket of my dead father's skull."

"What?"

"You heard me. And I've seen that knife. I held it in my own hand when I cut your son's birth cord. I wish I hadn't, because if I hadn't, I couldn't identify it. I couldn't swear where it came from."

Golden Hand's eye turned cold and bleak as the eye of a crow. His lips tightened and curved downward. "Who has the knife now?"

"King Thunder Girdle. It just so happened his guards were on hand when my father's body was discovered. They took the knife and kept it. Now I've just received word he's summoned the Council of Eighteen into a special session. And he has ordered me to appear before it to testify."

Golden Hand took his hand again. "Come with me."

"Where?"

"Before we jump to all kinds of conclusions, I want to make sure about the knife."

"Golden Hand," White Feather said softly, "I told you. I saw it."

"Fine. So let's just go and make sure you saw what you think you saw. Even a priest can make a mistake, White Feather."

"Very well," White Feather replied. But as they hurried out

of the storehouse and across the crowded plaza, he muttered to himself, "I didn't make a mistake. I wish I had, but I didn't."

They arrived at the house less than ten minutes later. Golden Hand had left in such haste he'd forgotten to bring his guards along. White Feather was out of breath from running to keep up with him. Golden Hand strode through his front door without the barest nod in Chain Coil's direction. Chain Coil turned to watch him go, a puzzled look on his face, then swung back to block White Feather's passage with his spear shaft.

"You can't go in," Chain Coil said.

"I came with him."

"Then let him come out and get you. I can't let you pass."

White Feather shook his head. "All right, but at least you can—"

Somebody inside the house let out a deep, angry roar. Chain Coil's gaze slid from the priest to the doorway and back to the priest again. He made up his mind.

"Wait here," he said. He turned and darted into the house.

White Feather shrugged, and followed.

They found Golden Hand in the atrium, crouching on the altar like some animal about to leap on prey. His single eye glittered. His lips were drawn back against his teeth. Suddenly, White Feather realized the Prince didn't look like an attacker at all. He looked like something cornered.

"It's gone," Golden Hand shouted. "It was here, but it's gone."

"I know," White Feather said. "I told you so."

Green Eyes appeared at the top of the atrium steps on the far side, holding Shining Star in her arms.

"What's happening out here? What are you all shouting about?"

8

Golden Hand stood in the middle of the atrium, barking orders as quickly as he thought of them. White Feather stood next to him, astonished at the whirlwind of activity. He'd never seen an entire house packed so quickly for a departure.

Green Eyes came bustling up, still holding Shining Star, who was now wrapped in a soft, thick blanket. Her face was pinched with worry. "Husband, will the baby be warm enough? I packed as much as I could."

He glanced at her. "We're going south. I own a trading post not far from Copan. We can weather this storm there, until it's safe for us to return. It's not far from where you grew up, though it's more mountainous. You know the weather."

"All right. But do we have to leave right away? Surely nobody will believe—"

"I can't take that chance," Golden Hand said. "Thunder Girdle will do everything he can to break me with this. That damned knife! I wish I'd never seen it!"

So do I, thought White Feather. But he said nothing. In a momentary lull, after Green Eyes had hurried away to finish what more packing she could manage, he said, "You know, I didn't want to take my father's robes. When the Inner House of our temple asked me to, I thought about turning them down. But I can be of more help to you as High Priest than as an assistant scribe."

"Help? If you want to help, lie for us. Deny you've ever seen that knife before."

"I can't do that. But I can speak the truth about what I think happened Somebody took that knife and used it hoping to implicate you."

"Well, of course. I don't know how they got their hands on it—probably bribed one of the salves—but what else could it be? I certainly had nothing to do with it."

"And that is what I will tell the Council, when they ask.

But you know the King will try to prove otherwise. This is his chance to bring you down."

Golden Hand snorted. "Proof has nothing to do with it. Bribery, threats, pressure. That's what will decide them, my friend."

White Feather stared at him. "All right," he said mildly. "It's not just you in danger, you know. Your wife and son, too. Maybe even more so."

"What do you mean? She has nothing to do with this."

"Think about it. With you out of the way, what is there to stop Thunder Girdle from marrying Green Eyes off to his son?"

"Gods . . ." Golden Hand breathed. "I hadn't even thought of that."

"As I say, I will wield more influence as High Priest. Get yourself gone, and give me time to do what I can. Maybe we can mend this."

Golden Hand grimaced. "I hate running like a whipped dog."

"What other choice do you have?"

"Indeed." He looked up suddenly. "Is that all? Good. Let's get going. Chain Coil, stay with my wife. I'll lead."

They piled out of the front door into the street, a group of a dozen or so, most of them heavy-laden body slaves. And here they stopped.

Golden Hand stared at the ring of spear points surrounding him. The spear in his own hand twitched once. Then he took two deep breaths and relaxed.

"Prince Thunder Shield," he said evenly. "Good day to you."

Thunder Shield, resplendent in the formal robes of his office, stepped between the spears. "And good day to you, Prince Water Moon."

He looked Golden Hand up and down, a sardonic grin on his lips. "I'm so sorry to interrupt your departure, Prince. It looks as if you are planning to go somewhere. And in rather a hurry, I might add."

"Say what you have to say, Prince," Golden Hand replied.

"Very well. Prince Golden Hand Water Moon, you are under arrest, by order of the King and the Council of Eighteen."

"Really? What's the charge?"

"Sacrilege, treason, and murder," Thunder Shield replied, his voice silky with triumph.

9

King Thunder Girdle had ordered the skylight over his innermost chamber covered, so that the light could not come in. A single oil lamp cast a fitful glow as he sat on an ornate stone divan covered with feathered cushions. He stared down at his hands.

They were thickened and lumpy and oozing with pus, but in the near darkness, they were almost tolerable. He didn't want to think about his face.

Something hot and fierce was eating him from the inside out. He could feel it crawling inside him, twisting in his sagging muscles, worming its slow way through his skull, poisoning his blood.

But he didn't think he was dying. In fact, he was afraid that maybe he *wasn't* dying. That he would live on like this for years, slowly rotting, while whatever it was that gnawed at him grew stronger and stronger.

It had grown worse ever since they'd brought the knife to him. When he'd touched it, it seemed to squirm in his hand like a snake. And he'd had the strangest notion when he touched the blade. The idea came to him that if he refused the knife, if he simply turned away from the plans he'd made with Parrot Beak—*Hah! Can't call* him *ugly anymore!*—then the purulent, disfiguring boils on his face and body would subside, and the thing inside him would go away, defeated.

So for a moment he'd hesitated. But only for a moment. Then he'd smiled, taken the knife, listened to the stories from the guardsmen, and said, "Send messengers to all the princes. And call my son to me."

10

The room was small and dim, but not terribly uncomfortable, though it certainly wasn't what she'd become used to. That thought made her smile. She looked down at her son, who was sleeping on her lap.

It hadn't been all that long ago that this small room, with its single feather couch, a low, three-legged stool, a thunder mug, and a small skylight admitting a thin, sunny shaft, would have seemed like unimaginable luxury to a small girl from a riverside village.

But that girl was gone. Somehow, she'd slipped away, and now a princess sat in her place. A princess and a mother.

"A mother, baby," she whispered. "Yes, Mama, yes."

She thought it had been four days. The first had been such a shock to her that she'd spent most of it sleeping, unable to understand exactly what had happened. And then, like a ghost, something of that little girl had returned to her. That same little girl who'd fought the Big Noses with whatever she had to hand.

That strength had grown in her ever since. And she had other wells of power to draw on also. One day you'll understand, Mama Root had told her.

That day had come. Oh, yes, and it had come when she least expected it. Was this slavery? Yes, no doubt it was. She was caged, not free to go. The burly, silent man on the other side of the black curtain covering the door would not let her leave. She had not been allowed to see her husband, and nobody would tell her anything about what had happened to him.

She didn't even know for certain where she was, except

that she was at the mercy of others. At the mercy of men. Slavery.

Shining Star moved a bit, his tiny fists forming into small pink buds. He squinched his eyes and yawned in his sleep. Pretty little mouth.

The worst thing was having no idea what, or how, to fight. She could find no enemy to strike against. All she had was this room, her child, and her past. She looked up at the sky-light, at the tiny square of blue, and saw black dots floating there. Crows, maybe.

A lot of crows. As she stared up at them, a voice spoke quietly within her.

I am coming.

The voice was soft, as if blurred by vast distance. Yet she had the feeling that it was growing closer, rushing toward her.

She raised her head and looked around. The shaft of light from the sky glinted in her eyes, as if stars had fallen there. In her lap, her son opened his eyes too.

11

"Do you know who I am?" he said.

Green Eyes stared at him. He'd come in the night. She had no idea how late it was. The guard had brought a single oil lamp into her room, and then he'd come.

He was a tall man. He wore a rich robe, embroidered with hammered gold threads and strung with beads made of greenstone. He stared at her, waiting for a reply, and she sensed his gaze as a hot ray, like the heat from a fire. It made her cheeks burn.

His voice was thick and full of phlegm. But it was familiar. And that robe . . . fit for a King.

A king.

She looked up at him. "You are Thunder Girdle."

He clasped his hands behind his back, but not before she

noticed the swollen, leaking pustules that covered them.
And there was a sweet and cloying smell about him, though
it was masked by the scent of heavy perfumes.

"Yes, Princess Water Moon, I am." He dipped his head
slightly. "I believe this is the first time I've had the pleasure
since your adoption. You must have thought me a fool, diving down the steps of my own throne like that."

Trying to ignore her own fear, she thrust it away. Now
was not the time for fear. Too much was at stake.

"Lord, why have you taken us like this? Where is my husband, the Prince?"

He unclasped his hands and raised them. She glanced
away. A single clear drop of fluid glimmered on the swollen
tip of one index finger. "I've come to speak to you about
that, Lady."

"What is there to speak of? If you suspect my husband of
the murder of Cham Ix, you are wrong. And you will find
out you are wrong when you bring him to trial before the
Council of Eighteen."

He stood silently for a few moments, and then he said,
"No, Lady, *you* are wrong. There will not be a trial, because
there has already *been* a trial. And your husband has been
convicted of murder, of treason, and of sacrilege in the eyes
of the Gods." He shrugged. "The penalty is death. Death for
him, and for his family. His family, Princess. That would be
you and the boy."

Everything inside her went dead. A chilly paralysis
clawed at her muscles. She couldn't move at all, but she
could sense that her hands had begun to shake.

He moved toward her, loomed over her, his hand outstretched. She felt his crooked fingernails creep over the
skin on the back of her hand. Seemingly of its own volition,
her hand leaped away from his touch.

He straightened up. "So. My touch disgusts you. Well,
that's understandable, I suppose. Your disgust, Princess,

only makes things easier. I can speak freely, with no more concern for your tender feelings than you have for mine."

"Lord . . ."

"No, hear me out. Here is the truth. I have fought against your husband, and he has lost. So he will pay for that with his life. And in normal circumstances he would also pay with your life and the life of your son as well. But these are not normal circumstances, and that payment need not necessarily be made."

He turned away from her, and wandered toward the door. His heavy feet made soft, sliding noises on the hard floor. The hem of his robe gave off a dry whisper. It reminded her of the wings of certain night insects, muted and dusty.

"No, Lady, you can't save him. But you can save yourself and your child. If you wish to. It seems you have a powerful ally in the High Priest of the Moon Temple. He has suggested a solution that could save your life. Because he is powerful, I have listened to him.

"So here is my offer. Marry my son. Yes, it is true you are a nobody from some mud-hut village, but you have become a princess. And both you and your son bear the God-marks, which are the marks of kings. So marry the boy. You will remain a princess. And your son may one day be a king."

He'd spoken softly, with no more emotion than if he were remarking on the weather. Now he swung round to face her again, and in the lamplight she could see his eyes, glowing like hot tar.

"If you refuse, of course you will join your husband in paying the penalty for his failure. But I will promise you this. Neither you nor he will be the first to pay. I will gut your brat first, right before your eyes, so you will have that to remember on your way to the Underworld."

He leaned closer. His thick, curdled voice churned with some grotesque emotion. "And I will enjoy it, Princess."

He stood back just as suddenly. "Don't give me your answer now. Think about it. I'll come back tomorrow and you can tell me."

12

Green Eyes sat and stared at the lamp until it winked out, leaving her in darkness. Finally she got up from the small stool and returned to her mat. Shining Star lay there. He was still sleeping. She could tell by the way his breath was soft and regular on her hand when she held it close to his mouth.

He was being such a good baby. No more nurse. No more regular feedings. Luckily her own breasts still had a little milk. She was able to give him something when he squalled from hunger. She touched her breasts, then squeezed them softly. *What to do?*

The image flashed through her mind so quickly she barely glimpsed it. The baby, the woman, the knife. The darkness. And superimposed over it, King Thunder Girdle. But the knife was the same, and the darkness was the same.

She lay on her side and pulled Shining Star to her. He half woke, then fell back asleep. She felt him breathing next to her belly. The rhythm of his breathing seemed to echo within her, soft and slow. Like a heartbeat. Like a heartbeat, drifting slowly away . . .

13

She slipped into the dream as neatly as one of her needles into cloth. Part of her seemed still awake. She was aware of her child, aware of the dark room around her, aware of the single green star twinkling in the skylight above her head.

Yet she knew that just as a needle pierces cloth, some other part of her had pierced through a veil and left that room. Left her baby behind. Left behind all the horror of the choice yet to be made.

She floated. In darkness at first, and then light. The light grew all around her, swelling gently, and then with ever-rising intensity. The light had a thick feeling to it, though it was clear as crystal. Clear as water. Clear as running water . . .

Going under. Going under again. The water in her lungs, the light in her lungs. The sudden peace, as if nothing mattered. As if she'd left everything behind forever. As if at last she'd gone home.

She stood on a broad meadow. Beyond the meadow were stands of bright trees, and beyond them dark mountains. She knew she'd seen none of them before, and yet she knew them. Their familiarity permeated her as the pure air of this name-less place filled her lungs. As its pure light filled her lungs.

In the distance, some great beast trumpeted. And then the women came. They marched out in single file, a long line of them that extended from the trees to her. When she looked closer, she discovered that each of them was the shadow of the next, although like no shadows she'd ever seen before. They wavered and shifted, as if seen through water, but they were not dark, as shadows should be. They glowed with an inner light. And she saw how each of them was different, yet the same as the other. All the way back. So many of them.

The first of them reached her, and the line halted. The woman stared at her out of eyes as dark and clear as polished obsidian. Yet her eyes were warmer than stone. She said, "I once said that when the time came, you would know me."

A great slow warmth began to fill her. She realized she'd left behind the ghost of the Middle World. She was no longer aware of the cage that held her child and her own body. And somehow she understood that no matter how real that room was, this place was more real. It seemed like a dream, but it was a kind of High World. And it belonged to these women.

"It belongs to you, too," the woman said. "It is yours, daughter. Don't you know me now?"

That overpowering warmth continued to fill her up. Her fingers and toes began to tingle. A smile twitched on her lips, and suddenly her throat was full of laughter.

"Mama Root! It is you!"

The woman, who didn't look like Mama Root at all, but looked like Mama Root might have appeared when she was young, smiled back at her. "You name one of my names. Now I name yours. You are Daughter. Daughter to us all."

The woman made a swift motion with her hands, raised them, and showed Green Eyes what she now held. "And you are Daughter of this, too. You are the Daughter of this Knife."

The blade gleamed in the soft light that seemed to flow from everything, to everything, and *through* everything. It looked as if it had been chipped fresh from living stone only moments before. It drew her eyes . . .

"Yes," the woman said. "It is ours. We have always had it. It is our greatest power, to cut the cords. All the cords. The cords that bind, the cords that enslave, the cords that feed. We can cut through them all. If we choose to. Daughter, you must choose. Do you choose the knife?"

And now the warmth that had been building in her bubbled over and spilled out onto the ground. She felt herself lifted up, and for a single flashing instant she thought she saw a turtle. But it was in the sky, far away, and it vanished as quickly as it came.

"I choose the knife," Green Eyes said. "I will cut the cord."

The woman nodded. She lowered the blade, and gradually the light flowed away. The world began to darken, to become less distinct. The other women faded. Now they really were only shadows of the one who stood before her.

Green Eyes sought her gaze and found it. As she did, the other woman's eyes began to change. Her dark eyes faded to blue, to green, to aquamarine, to every color of the rainbow.

"The knife will be there," a voice whispered. "When you see it, call for me and I will come. Together we will cut the cord."

Her eyes grew larger and larger until Green Eyes toppled forward, as if from some infinite height, and fell into them.

14

Sunlight slanted through the skylight and burned a bright yellow square high on the wall when the King returned for her answer.

He wore a different mask, but she could see his eyes lurking deep within their sockets. Yellow eyes . . .

"Well?" he said. He stood with his arms folded across his chest. He stood with the bearing of a king of men, though the flesh on his hands was curling and shriveling.

She stood to face him. "You think women are slaves," she told him. "I am not a slave. You tell me to marry your son?"

She spat on the floor.

"I would die first."

King Thunder Girdle nodded. "You won't die first."

He pointed at Shining Star, who lay on the bed and watched him with viridescent eyes. "*He* will."

Chapter Eighteen

1

White Feather stood in his father's accustomed place near the window atop the Pyramid of the Moon. It was still early in the morning. The patchwork of fields below was dusted with mist, here sharp and green, there gray and muted. Overhead the sky was soft and blue, but as the sun rose higher, it was hardening like glaze on a fine pot. He lifted his gaze to the mountains. Their flanks were dark and bleak, though the sun picked glints of light from their wrinkled hides. To the west, a pudding of bruised, blood-tinged clouds bulged above the peaks. An omen, perhaps, of the darkness yet to come on this day.

On this terrible day. His breath drifted in and out, slow and full of mourning. He looked down at his hands.

"I tried," he murmured. He didn't even know to whom it was he spoke. Himself, perhaps. Or was it Green Eyes? Maybe even Her?

If it *was* Her, evidently She hadn't heard him.

A fevered restlessness began to twitch at him. He walked back and forth across the empty room, but simple motion wasn't enough to give him any relief. The room felt like a cage to him. It was empty. No priests would meet with him today. The entire city would be gathered in the plaza at the foot of the pyramid, gathered to gawk and slaver at the ritual of expiation.

Expiation. What a joke that was. It was a ritual of vengeance and execution, and innocent blood would flow on Her altar. He paced back and forth, growing more agitated by the moment.

"But I *tried*," he groaned.

He had gone to Thunder Girdle himself and bargained the

prestige of Her temple for mercy. He remembered that meeting with loathing.

The King had received him in a small, darkened room. It was so gloomy he could barely make out the man's hulking form. And the King seemed to seek the corners, the deepest shadows. There was a sweet stench in the air. For a moment White Feather remembered the stink of his father's own ruin, there on Her altar.

"Why come to me, High Priest?" the King said. His voice had become choked and ghastly.

The creeping sense of horror that lurked in the room filled White Feather with dread. "I am not naive, Lord. I understand what has gone before, between you and Golden Hand. These things happen. And in such contests the loser always pays the price. I don't come to speak for Golden Hand. He opposed you with his eyes open."

"Good," Thunder Girdle said. "Even if you were the Goddess Herself come to beg for his life, I wouldn't give it to you." He paused, and seemed to sink even deeper into the shadows. "But perhaps you seek the life of someone else, eh, Priest?"

White Finger swallowed. His throat seemed to be full of bile. "Golden Hand's wife and son bear Her marks, King. The God-marks that are also the marks of our kings. They bear Her open blessing. So on Her behalf, I beg you to spare them."

"They share the guilt," the King said. But he sounded uncertain.

White Feather plunged ahead into the opening he perceived. "I say they do not, King. You have nothing to fear from them. Spare them and the Temple of the Moon will praise your mercy."

"Ah. The praise of the Temple would be a fine thing to have. So would something a bit more tangible."

White Feather took a breath. He'd hoped not to have to commit himself. "When the succession to the throne is de-

cided, King, then the Temple of the Moon will also openly
support the new King."

There. He'd said it. He'd offered the great force of the
Temple's influence as support for this frightful man's
schemes. All for a woman and a baby.

The slow movement in the shadows ceased. White
Feather sensed a speculating gaze resting on him. The touch
of that gaze was filthy. It made him want to wash himself.

"Very well, High Priest. I will ask her. But it will be her
choice. And whatever she decides, you still pay. You buy her
the choice and nothing more."

"Yes," White Feather agreed miserably. "It will be her
choice."

He knew what choice this monster would offer her. But
wasn't any choice better than death? Even slavery to his
abominable son would be better than the Underworld.
Wouldn't it?

He stopped his pacing and stared blindly at the ceiling on
the temple room. *"I tried!"*

But the thick walls swallowed his words. There was no
echo, only the slow, dead sound of his breathing. Suddenly
he couldn't stand the closeness of walls. He had to get out,
to escape, to breathe open air!

He strode quickly across the outer temple, passed through
the columns, crossed the broad space before the temple, and
came to a stop at the top of the Great Stairs.

Far below, the crowds were gathering already. The plaza
swarmed with thousands upon thousands of tiny, brightly
clad figures. Like some fantastic glittering ant heap. By the
time high noon came around, the plaza would be packed
from edge to edge, and silent as a tomb. All eyes would be
on the platform, and the altar on top of it. And on the sacrifices on that altar.

He moaned softly. *Why didn't you take his offer? Why
didn't you save yourself? Slavery is better than death . . .*

But Green Eyes didn't answer him. Nobody answered
him. He uttered a muffled sob and turned away.

I am unclean, he thought.

He went to cover his squalor with fine robes. Noon would
be here soon enough. Maybe he would even find a way to
live with himself afterward.

2

Parrot Beak hummed cheerfully to himself as he climbed.
He felt just fine. Finer than he'd ever felt before. Today all
debts would be paid.

He wore a gray robe and hood. The indeterminate color
blended nicely with the weathered stone that faced the Pyramid of the Moon. He made his way laboriously up the back
side of it, avoiding the central steps, climbing hand over hand
up the blocks of stone themselves. Up close he looked rather
like a hunched spider, some kind of insect that was all twisting, gripping arms and legs. From a distance he blended so
neatly into the background he wasn't visible at all.

Across his back was a quiver of arrows and his great bow.
His face was hidden within his hood. Occasionally, as he
moved, the hood would draw aside enough to reveal the
bright yellow beak in the center of his face. It was a cheerful color, just like his mood.

The sun had almost reached its zenith when he scrambled
up the final blocks onto a level he judged suitable for his
purposes. He squinted up at the sky, estimating the time.
There was more than enough left for him to pick his spot. He
had to be careful. He doubted anybody would be able to tell,
at least not right away, from which direction the arrows had
fallen. But it was best not to take chances. He planned to be
done with it and all the way down the back stairway before
anybody realized what must have happened.

He moved cautiously along the baking stone until he

found the right place. Then he took his bow off his shoulders
and strung it. He twanged it and listened to the pleasant
sound. It was the sound of death, and for him that would always be a fine music in his ears.

He settled himself cross-legged on the warm stone and
arranged his robe around him. He placed the bow and arrow
next to him within easy reach.

The brat would be first, of course. His master demanded
that. And then the Prince, so proud and so doomed. And then
the woman, the bitch who had ruined him. As he thought of
that, a slow heat began to grow in his crotch. He would
enjoy watching her guts torn out. His only regret was that he
couldn't wield the knife himself. He would have enjoyed
looking into her repulsive eyes at the last moment, and whispering, "Remember me?"

But he wouldn't allow even that loss to spoil his mood.
After this day was done, nothing and no one in the sprawl-
ing city below would deny him any pleasure he desired. He
thought of the treachery yet to come, and his smile grew
wider.

He fumbled beneath his robe and took out a small package. He unwrapped it carefully. One of the women had
packed it for him. Tortillas stuffed with a thick, rich stew. He
raised it and took a bite.

Down below, the square looked full to overflowing. Up
above, the sun slid into the top of its daily arc. He chewed
slowly, savoring each bite.

No reason not to enjoy his picnic while he listened to her
scream. The sounds of death always spiced his appetite.

3

White Feather finished putting on his ceremonial robes.
He had bargained with the King and lost, but he still had to
pay his debt. He would stand there, bearing the power and

majesty of his temple, a silent witness to what would be done this day.

He would say nothing. The people would believe the Goddess approved of the sacrifice offered to Her. And nobody would know the truth but him.

He didn't believe he could live with that truth, but maybe he could. Only time would tell.

He trudged out of his room like a dead man walking. The sound of his footsteps as he descended the Great Stairs was snatched away with the wind that had sprung up. He glanced toward the west, where the wind came from, and saw a vast band of swollen clouds advancing across the sky. But the wind was hot, as if it blew off a furnace.

Storm God coming . . .

His face was set and still when he reached the landing a third of the way down. He paused and then turned to his right. His movements were slow and jerky as he found the familiar path.

The wind grew louder. He didn't notice. He didn't notice anything. In fact, he wasn't really there anymore.

4

When they finally came for her, Green Eyes snapped to with a start. She didn't know how long she'd been sitting there with Shining Star in her lap. She felt a pang of hunger and realized she couldn't recall how long it had been since she'd eaten.

She heard a soft commotion outside, some mumbling voices, and then a man she didn't recognize pushed the curtain aside and came into the room. She thought he looked like a nice man, maybe even a good man. His broad face was smooth and flat, but there were smile lines at the corners of his mouth and his eyes seemed kind.

He stared at her for a long moment and then, with the air

of a man faced by an unpleasant but necessary duty, he said, "I'm sorry, Princess. It's time."

He put out his hand to help her up, but she stood on her own. She was surprised that she felt no anger or fear. She'd been drifting for hours, maybe even days, in a vague half world of dreams and memories. Eventually everything in that world had melted together, so that she couldn't tell what was dream and what was memory, and what was perhaps neither.

She thought she'd seen bright, beautiful women, but she could no longer remember if she really had. She thought she'd been given a promise, and maybe even made one in return, but that might have been a dream as well.

It was so hard to sort it out. At this point it was so hard even to care. She felt numb and listless. Maybe this was a dream too.

"I can carry him for you, Lady," the guard said gently.

"No!"

He withdrew his hands, a troubled expression on his features. Yes, his eyes were kind. "No, of course not." He paused uncomfortably. "Lady, will you walk behind me? Or shall I bind you and have you carried?"

She hugged Shining Star closer to her breasts. He'd begun to waken. She felt his soft lips move on her skin. "I will walk," she said.

He nodded. "Then follow me, please."

He led her out of the room. She found herself in a long, dusty corridor. Two skylights admitted a wan, gray light. There were three other guards there. They formed up around her and, at their leader's soft command, led her on down the hall.

The walk up the Avenue of the Gods seemed endless. She held her head high and looked neither right nor left, though she sensed the silent, wondering crowds that lined either side of the great roadway. She could hear them, whispering and muttering to themselves. Their sound was like a different kind of wind, hidden beneath the wind that tugged at her unbound hair.

That wind was hot. It tickled her ears and pressed her robe against her legs. Overhead the sun had vanished behind clouds so dark they looked as if they'd been painted on the sky itself. Every once in a while she heard thunder mutter in the distance. Flickers of white light danced along the bottom of the clouds, making them glow as if they had lamps inside them.

The crowds on either side grew thicker and thicker, and eventually they spilled into the road itself. Her guardsmen raised stout staves and pushed them back, making a way for her.

She thought of the irony. She walked up this great street with her guards, bearing her child in her arms, surrounded by gawking, awestruck citizens. Just like a real princess. She had never come this far before. The vast, spreading bulk of the Temple of the Sun passed on her right. It seemed impossibly huge. Men had built it, and for one brief moment she wondered why they had.

All the great structures in Tollan had been built to honor the Gods. There were nothing like them in the village where she'd grown up. But here the people built nothing in their hearts to honor their Gods. They built fantastic piles of stone, but their hearts were barren. Nothing like this could happen in her village. There were no kings there, only people.

Only people. The bitter smile within her never reached her lips, but she felt it nonetheless. Only everyday people, with everyday thoughts and concerns, and plenty of room within their hearts for loving and honoring their Gods. And each other.

That was what was wrong with Tollan. Tollan, mighty in its pride, vast in its numbers, had raised up great empty towers of stone. But in the long process these stupendous builders had somehow turned their own hearts to empty stone. And there was no room inside those rocky, shriveled chambers for Gods.

Yes.

She blinked. That voice had sounded inside her head like the single beat of a great drum. But it wasn't her, no, that wasn't her voice. Something else. Some*one* else.

Up ahead, the vast rectangle of the altar platform loomed out of the gathering murk. The leader of her little band of guardsmen pressed close to her, took her arm, and squeezed briefly.

"Be strong, Lady," he whispered.

She nodded, raised her head higher, and marched on. Shining Star squirmed against her chest and began to cry. But her eyes remained dry as bones. She would not cry. Not for them.

5

King Thunder Girdle watched them bring Green Eyes up the steps of the platform and lead her to a place beside the altar. He frowned when he saw they hadn't tied her up, but then he decided it didn't matter. What was she going to do, run away?

On the other side of the altar stood Golden Hand, his back proud and straight, his hands tied. One of his eyes was puffed shut. The Prince's good eye glowed as if it were full of black fire as he stared at Thunder Girdle.

The King tried to ignore his gaze, but it was impossible. He was glad there was no way the Prince could reach him, or reach the knife he held in his hand.

He looked down in surprise, as if he'd just remembered that he held the Godstone blade. The smooth, cool stone still felt dry and scaly in his fingers, though maybe that had something to do with the monstrosities his hands had become. He still had trouble believing his own eyes. The skin on his hands, wrists, even his fingers and palms, had split, cracked, healed partially, scabbed over, and split again so that now his hands looked like the paws of some frightful beast rather than anything human.

Yet as he stared at himself, a slow curl of satisfaction grew in his belly. He might be hideous, but these were the marks of a God. A God had touched him and changed him. A God had lifted him above his enemies.

He raised his head, looked across at Golden Hand, and smiled. "Here come your wife and child now, traitor. Soon we can begin, though you will be last. I promised it."

The look of agony that twisted Golden Hand's features was satisfaction enough. The King glanced around a final time to make sure all was in readiness, and that was when he realized White Feather was missing. Where was that blasted priest?

6

White Feather was just reawakening into the dread heart of the day. He wasn't quite sure what had happened. The last thing he remembered was beginning his descent down the Great Stairs, with the cloud storming across the sky, but the sun still warming his shoulders. Now he was almost to the bottom. Directly ahead, just below him, he could see the top of the altar platform. He saw King Thunder Girdle, standing next to his son. The King glanced around the platform, and finally looked in his direction.

I'm coming, he thought. Although if you'd like to proceed with your murderous charade without me, please do.

But of course it was not to be. He saw the King point directly at him, then turn and say something to those gathered around. Thunder Shield laughed. Off to the King's right, Prince Golden Hand shouted something, and one of his guards struck him brutally across the face. The Prince sagged against his bindings.

White Feather reached the bottom of the stairs and walked

slowly across the plaza. His priests had opened a path for him. He was aware that thousands upon thousands of people crowded close, but he walked utterly alone.

His hands were concealed within the wide sleeves of his ceremonial robe. The robe was soft and heavy with beads and embroidery. It dragged behind him as he walked, and made a dry, rustling sound. That sound grated on his spine and sent hard ridges of gooseflesh crawling up his arms, but he ignored it.

His face felt as stiff as if it had been coated thickly with wet clay and now the clay was hardening. He reached the top of the platform and walked around the altar to the left side of the King, where he took his place between Green Eyes and Thunder Girdle.

"It's about time," the King muttered. "I thought you'd forgotten your promise."

"Oh, no, King," White Feather whispered. "I haven't forgotten. And am I not here to fulfill it now?"

The King stared closely at him. "What's wrong with you?"

"Nothing. I am here to keep my promise. I always keep my promises." Yet as he spoke these words, White Feather had the eeriest feeling that something else moved his tongue, something else shaped his dead lips. Something else spoke of promises.

The King gave him one last look, shrugged, and turned away. A priest dumped fresh oil into one of the sacrificial burners at the center of the altar, and the flames roared up.

The crowd sighed, ripples of ecstatic anticipation coursing through it like wind across a ripe cornfield.

The ritual began.

7

Parrot Beak finished his meal, licked his fingers clean, and stood up. He stretched until his back and arms felt loose.

He was still humming to himself. The gleeful sound was both mad and cheerful. He picked up his bow, drew it experimentally, and sighed with satisfaction at the result. Then he knocked an arrow against the string and moved forward until his view of the altar below was unobstructed.

He squinted. The shot would have to carry a good distance, and the wind might be a problem. He noticed that it had become much stronger, and now that he was peeking around the corner of the pyramid, he could feel its hot strength roaring out of the west at full force. Overhead, it seemed the storm clouds were so low they almost touched the top of the pyramid. Ball lightning flickered within them, but the real show as to the west, above the mountains.

Great, jagged white bolts flashed at the tops of those peaks. For a moment he imagined vast trees of light, their branches bare and burning, growing down from the clouds. The roll and boom of thunder was a continuous roar in his ears.

He didn't mind. He knew where that storm came from, and who was riding it. And he thought that soon there would be an even more impressive sign of his master's return.

He will heal us, Black Face had said.

He giggled to himself as he sighted down the long arrow, aiming first at the Prince, then at the woman, and finally at the babe in her arms.

Yes. He could do it from here. If he chose to.

A nimbus of black fire began to glow around him.

8

King Thunder Girdle stepped down from the dais where he'd been exhorting the crowd. The people howled their approval. He'd promised them expiation in blood for the great crime done to the Mother of their city. He'd reaffirmed once again the power and the glory of the Clan Summer Moon, house of kings. He told them how that great clan had struck

down Her enemies, and now offered blood to Her, so that
Tollan would live forever more, proud and eternal, the center of the Middle World.

He stepped down, turned to his son, and grunted, "Let's
get it done with."

Grinning, Thunder Shield moved toward Green Eyes. She
stiffened as he approached. His grin twisted into something
thin and full of angry scorn.

"I'm not good enough for you and your brat, eh? Well,
you made your choice. Now die with it."

He reached for the baby.

"No!" She shrank away from him, but he only laughed,
then reached forward and tore Shining Star from her arms.
The baby began to shriek. Green Eyes threw herself on him
and clawed at him with her nails. But the guard behind her
grabbed her quickly and held her still. She struggled only a
moment and then, seeming to understand the futility, turned
to White Feather.

"Help me," she pleaded. "Help us. He's only a baby."

White Feather stared blankly ahead. Nothing in his face
moved, nothing at all. He might have been made of stone.

Green Eyes began to sob. The sound of it was dry and
harsh. Thunder Shield ignored her and went back to the
altar. He put the screaming child down on the stones before
the fire. Shining Star lay there naked, his skin flushed, his
fists waving in the air.

Thunder Girdle stepped up to the altar and pushed his son
aside. He paused for a moment, as if waiting for something.
Then he took a deep breath and raised the green knife high
above his head.

"I bring You meat!" he roared. The muscles in his back
heaved as he began the death stroke.

9

As Green Eyes stood with one fist mashed against her lips, her eyes bulging, her heart a continuous hammering roar in her ears, everything began to fade away.

Once again she found herself on a high, dark, storm-driven peak. Once again she saw the black cloud approach, its innards whirling with fangs and claws. Once again she saw the knife rise over the babe.

And once again the babe looked at her with ocean eyes.

Everything stopped. She was enclosed within a bubble of stasis. Time had no meaning here. Down below she sensed the approach of the Woman in White. Overhead the thunder shrieked and the lightning sizzled, but all in silence.

The heart of the world began to beat. She felt herself straining forward, though she did not move. The great dark cloud boiled higher, but it didn't move either.

Only the heartbeat.

The Woman in White, who had been climbing those long stairs through all of her dreams, reached the top. She looked at Green Eyes. She moved closer, the only hint of motion in a vast frozen world.

"I come," she said. "The Wheel has turned again. I come."

Behind her, the line of women stretched endlessly down the staircase.

10

In the wide gray distance to the west the charred foothills began to heave. Runnels of clinkers fountained up and then slid back down in black, shining rivers. Higher up, in the bleak stone pinnacles themselves, walls of naked rock split apart and spewed forth red fire. And in the heart of those dreadful spines, something wrenched itself from the crags and took ghastly shape before a bowl of flame.

With a great, belching sound, the world split apart. An un-
chained wall of burning rock thrust itself up against the sky.

Tlaloc, Lord of Storms, the Fallen One, formed Himself
upon the flames and began to laugh. He stamped His foot,
and the earth shook beneath it.

11

White Feather felt that long shudder and woke from his
dark dream. In the eye of his mind he saw the Fallen One
arise again. He saw a black cloud full of jagged, gnashing
teeth congeal around King Thunder Girdle. He stared at the
knife the ruined King held between his two hands as he
trembled on the lip of the final thrust.

He felt his own hands. Something in his hands. A *fire* in
his hands. He took out the thing he'd been holding, hidden
in the folds of his robe.

Small, dark, hard. But now it burned him, oh, yes, it
burned him terribly. For it was no longer his to hold.

Without any thought whatsoever, except for a pervasive
dumb horror, he took two giant, looping steps and stood before Green Eyes.

He offered the tiny head to her.

"Here," he said. "This is for you."

The earth shook. Thunder rattled the stones again, and
lightning shattered the overheated air. Green Eyes Blue took
the head, cupped it in her fingers, and raised it up.

Even White Feather heard the soft, implacable words.

I come.

12

I come!

Green Eyes felt the veils and membranes and walls between the worlds slip away as if they'd never existed. She stood in many places at once: on a peak distant in time and space and memory; on a wide stone altar platform now beginning to rumble and shift; on a green meadow that had never existed in any world; on a bleak high needle of stone, where a great form turned slowly to look at her; on a frozen steppe a hundred ages ago, where a bent and twisted woman climbed down from her spirit pole and began to fashion amber into a particular shape.

Green Eyes stood in all these places, and in each one, at the same time, she heard the words:

I come.

As soon as the head was in her hands, she began to raise it. It was like trying to lift a boulder. Ecstasy howled in her veins, bright as lightning and strong as love. Every hair on her body twitched and stiffened.

The men that had been holding her screamed and stumbled back. They covered their eyes as they did so, as if whatever they beheld was too bright or too terrible for mortal eyes.

Across the altar from her, as she pushed the head inch by slow inch higher, Thunder Girdle suddenly vanished into a wild and shifting darkness. She knew that darkness. She'd seen its knives, its hungry teeth, before.

As this happened, another voice sounded through the stillness only she could feel. As old, as deep, as infinite as the first, it mimicked though it did not echo:

I am here.

As she lifted the head to the limit of her reach, it suddenly kindled into green flame. She stood there, holding it, trembling beneath it, every ounce of her strength pouring into it.

Directly across from her, draped and hidden within the tooth-roiled dark, Thunder Girdle strained equally, holding up a knife that gleamed with red fire.

The witch light, the Goddess flame, began to expand. Tendrils leaked from it and fell to the pavement of the altar platform. Wherever they touched, stone creaked and sizzled. And then from this fountain arched a single spark that scorched across the space between the head and the child who now lay silent upon the altar table, his eyes wide, staring upward.

He raised one tiny hand, and from it he extended one finger. Above him, Thunder Girdle groaned aloud, every muscle in his body warped and swollen by the gigantic effort he expended as he forced the needle tip of the blade down.

"Anggghhh . . ." said Thunder Girdle. The knife reached a point an inch above Shining Star's nose. His brine-drenched eyes regarded it thoughtfully, as if seeing it for the first time.

Shining Star smiled.

He moved his hand and placed his fingertip precisely on the tip of the knife. Then, impossibly, he spoke. Green Eyes heard him. White Feather heard him quite clearly. So did something else.

"Mine," he said.

A single slow, distinct ripple passed beneath the great plaza as the central peak in the western range blew off its top in a pillar of red fire.

Now blue fire roared from the head in Green Eyes's hand.

The crowd turned as a single beast, moaning a single moan of terror. Far above them the great head of the Goddess Herself, perched at the pinnacle of Her temple, began to weep bloody tears.

They fell from Her eyes, teardrops of crimson flame, and as they did, they changed. The blood changed, became green, became blue, became aquamarine, became all the colors water ever has been or ever will be.

The colors of tears and oceans. Blood into water. The infinite, eternal transmutation. A towering wave began to build at the top of the Great Stairs, far above. A wave of blood and water. The blood, it cooled. The water, it burned.

Thunder Girdle screamed! Fire and water and blood

flowed from Green Eyes to Shining Star, and from the child into the knife. Into Thunder Girdle. Into the thing Thunder Girdle had become.

White Feather saw the flash of light that burned away Thunder Girdle's robes in a single blinding blast. He saw the man-thing beneath, naked, boiling with pus, a thing of sucking wounds, a thing that fed on itself and could never eat its fill.

White Feather thought that, at the end, Thunder Girdle saw it too. For the doomed King raised the knife again, and brought it flashing down. There was no resistance. It slipped into the mass of his guts and ripped them open.

The knife clattered to the altar and fell next to the child. Where the King had stood now loomed a heaving ball of storm and flame. To White Feather, it seemed that from this tempest extended a thin cord of light, wavering and nearly invisible, fleeing off to the west, to the place where the mountains burned.

Green Eyes opened her mouth and *shrieked.*

She threw down the head she held. It shattered into a hundred pieces. White Feather had the oddest feeling it had already been broken, and was only now returning to what it had been. That it had somehow come back together only for this moment.

Green Eyes stepped forward, picked up the knife, and sliced cleanly through the cord that fed the storm.

She spoke very clearly: *I cut all cords. I release you.*

Or had she spoken, White Feather wondered. It almost seemed as if a hundred, or a thousand, voices whispered with her.

The cord writhed like a headless serpent, and then it vanished. And where it had been, the cloud began to shrink. Green Eyes stood transfixed, the knife glowing in her hand.

The cloud grew smaller. The knife grew dim.

And then, suddenly, there was nothing but the thin cry of

an infant, and beyond the altar a steaming mass on the pavement stones, all that remained of a man, a king, a God.

13

Parrot Beak tottered to the verge of the ledge on which he stood. His bow was fully drawn. He looked down on the altar without understanding. Far to the west the volcano was beginning to subside. To the east, he saw a streak of blue-green sky as the storm above began to dissipate.

The King seemed to be dead. He couldn't tell for certain, but other things were plain. The woman still lived, and so did her child. And the Prince.

Yet in his fevered mind he thought it might still be possible to prevail. He held death in his hand. Perhaps he could yet wield it to good purpose. He picked a spot an inch to the left of Green Eyes's breastbone, pulled the bowstring one more inch, and let go.

14

Only White Feather saw what happened next. He had turned away from the smoking abomination of Thunder Girdle's fate, his hand rising to his mouth as his stomach began to heave, when a snicker of movement high above caught his eye.

He saw the stick figure clinging to the side of the pyramid, outlined in black against the clearing sky. He saw the great quivering bubble of green fire trembling on the next level up, and then he saw the bubble bulge and slump down.

The stick figure wavered behind the wall of devouring tears shed from the Mother's eyes. A single arrow, blazing with green light, arced up and out of the mass. It slid along the top of its trajectory, turned down, and White Feather lost sight of it.

He watched, transfixed, as whatever it was up there on the pyramid writhed slowly in the dance of its own immolation. He couldn't actually hear anything, but he imagined he heard an endless, wailing scream, that eventually faded into silence.

When he went up there the next day, he found nothing but a light, ashen smudge on the stone. And a bright yellow wooden nose, which he saved. But now, in this moment, he knew he was watching a death almost as terrible as that suffered by Thunder Girdle.

Thunder Girdle. He swung back toward where the King had been. And that was when he saw the Prince, Thunder Shield, rising from his father's ruined corpse. On Thunder Shield's face was an almost comical expression of shock. His lips were pursed. His eyebrows jerked so high they nearly met his hairline.

In his left eye socket stood an arrow, the feathers on its shaft still smoking.

"Ah . . ." Green Eyes moaned, and toppled forward. The knife fell from her fingers, once again landing on the altar. This time the baby tracked it, groped for it, and tugged it close. His pink lips formed a smile as perfect as a rose. He began to coo contentedly.

Out in the plaza, the first screams began.

Chapter Nineteen

Golden Hand looked older. Green Eyes noticed there were now thin strands of silver in his black hair. But his good eye gleamed brightly, and his smile was as wide and white as it had ever been.

He came across the atrium toward her, his arms loaded with packages. She smiled at him, and joggled the baby in her lap.

"Look, baby. It's your father. Can you wave to your father?"

He hunkered down beside her. She lay half reclined on a wooden frame piled with feather mattresses. The frame had been made specifically for her by skilled craftsmen. She was still too tired to be up and around much, but she didn't like staying in bed all day.

"You're looking better," Golden Hand said. He dumped the packages down and began to snap the cords binding them. "Look," he said. "What do you think?"

"Oh, they're beautiful. Where did you ever find such wonderful materials?"

He grinned as he let the gorgeously woven fabrics ripple through his hands. "In case you've forgotten, Lady, I am a trader. These came from far south of your old home. In the mountains there they weave the finest cloth in the world. And of course the best dyers are right here in Tollan."

A shadow passed across her face. "Home . . ."

He stared at her. "Do you miss it so much then, Green Eyes? Do you still miss it?"

She looked down at her child. "He knows one of his grandmothers. But he's never seen the other half of his family."

He patted her knee. "All right. When you're better, we'll go down there. Things have settled enough here that we can make a slow trip of it. Maybe do a little trading. And we'll bring the house servants. Do them good to walk off some of their fat."

Her face glowed. "Oh, husband, do you mean it?"

"When you're better. Stronger."

He looked into her eyes. His own eye was crinkled. She couldn't decide if it was worry or concentration. He seemed to be listening to something.

"Green Eyes, what happened that day?"

She stroked the baby's silken hair. "You were there."

"Yes. I saw White Feather hand something to you. And then I saw King Thunder Girdle gut himself in front of the altar. I thought I saw light on the top of the Moon Pyramid, but only for a moment. And then an arrow came out of nowhere and struck Thunder Shield in the eye. Right after that, you fainted, and the crowd went wild."

"Yes, that's what I remember."

He took her hands in his, and peered into her face. "Is it truly what you remember?"

She hesitated only for an instant. Now it seemed like a dream. And the dream was drifting into fragments. Had there been a woman? Many women?

"Yes, Golden Hand. That's what I remember."

He held her gaze for one more beat, then nodded. "I suppose I'll never really understand it. One moment we were all near death. The next, everything changed."

He sighed, shrugged, and slapped the tops of his thighs. "Well, you say you like this cloth. That's good. It will keep your fingers busy when you feel up to it."

"I have many fine robes, husband."

He grinned down at her. "That's my other news. You have robes fit for a princess. But not for a queen. Well, a queen-regent, at least."

She gasped. "It happened? The Council made you king of Tollan?"

"Not exactly. It seems that just before he resigned his post as High Priest of the Temple of the Moon, White Feather cast the omens in front of the Great Altar. He told the Council they were very clear: the death of the King and his son was a judgment by the Mother on their treachery. That it was the King who'd stolen the knife from our altar, and hired henchmen to murder Cham Ix."

Green Eyes shuddered faintly. "The King was a horrible man. Did the omens tell who the real murderer was?"

"No, although White Feather tells me his own spies learned a name. Some rogue called Parrot Beak." His face was bland as he spoke those words, although she sensed something.

"Parrot Beak? Somehow that . . . seems familiar. As if I know him."

"Oh, no. Impossible. It is said he wore a wooden nose, and was very ugly. Nobody you or I would ever be likely to know, but if we did, we would surely remember him."

"What happened to him?"

"Nobody knows. Even White Feather's spies say he seems to have vanished."

Shining Star squirmed in her lap. Shining Star. Why had she named him that? She shook her head slightly. She couldn't really remember that anymore, either.

She looked up. "So you say White Feather swayed the Council of Eighteen?"

"Well, it didn't take much. With the Clan Summer Moon pretty much destroyed, that left the Clan Water Moon as the most powerful alternative. The only alternative, really."

"So they made you king, then?"

He smiled again. He pointed at her lap. "No. They made *him* king. I am regent, and you are the queen-regent. Until he grows up. White Feather's last reading of the omens said his God-eyes were a sign. A sign to the city."

As if sensing his own new importance, Shining Star began to squirm. His tiny mouth opened, revealing pink gums and a fat tongue. He coughed, mewled, and suddenly let out a thunderous wail.

"Oh, my," said Golden Hand. "He doesn't sound happy about the news at all."

Green Eyes rummaged in the blanket swaddling the child. "No, he misses his toy." She found it and placed it in his hands. Immediately, the boy subsided, cooing happily as his fingers curled around the blade.

Golden Hand shook his head. "It scares me, every time I see him with that. I always worry he will cut himself."

"No, it's dull as butter. And it's too big for him to get inside his mouth. Besides, he gets so cranky whenever it isn't close by."

"Dull as butter, eh? It didn't used to be."

She stared down blankly at it. It was still smooth as glass, but it seemed warmer now, not as cool as she remembered it. And it was dull. It wouldn't even cut twine.

She wondered what it might have cut that could have ruined its edge like that. And for one instant she remembered, (*it cut the cord*) but then that faded too.

"I think he wants to sleep now. Would you take him back to his nurse?"

He picked his son up, swooped him high overhead, and brought him back down for a loud kiss on the top of his head. Then, the baby securely nesting in his right arm, he leaned over and placed his lips tenderly on Green Eyes's mouth. She closed her eyes.

"It will be all right now, won't it?" she whispered.

"Yes. It will be all right."

Epilogue

That is the end of this tale, for I know no more. As I sit here, feeling my old bones warm in the sunlight on the top step of the Great Stairs, I look down the Avenue of the Gods at the throngs filling every inch of that great road. They are thickest beyond the River Bridge, of course, where the ceremonies will begin later today.

I have promised to be there. Green Eyes and Golden Hand insisted. Shining Star will officially become a man, and his parents' regency will be removed. He will become king in Tollan in fact, as well as name.

I think he will do well. He is a likely lad, very quick in his studies, as practical as his mother and father, yet he has a spiritual side to him.

Long ago I read the omens about him. Some said I lied, and perhaps I did twist the truth a bit. But about Shining Star the prophesies were clear. He was meant to be king in this city, Tollan the Holy, heart of the Middle World.

I believe he will be a great king.

As for me, I am content to grow old with my memories. I am the only one who does remember what really happened that day. But evidently the Gods are shy, and prefer to erase Their tracks. I am mystified at why I've been allowed to keep the true recollections.

Of course, I was the one who swept up the shards of Her broken head. They rest in a bag on Her altar, hidden away deep in Her pyramid. Along with that most odd of mementos, a yellow wooden nose. And I will place this record there as well. Perhaps, in the deeps of future time, when this age ends and a new one begins, someone will need to know.

Someone who bears the God-marks. The marks that are really Hers, and should be called Goddess-marks.

Blood and water, birth and death. Life and light. It all changes, and it never changes at all. The circle is closed, but it turns forever.

I have seen it. I remember it.

Set down by my hand in the Year One Reed
White Feather Writer

Chief Scribe
The Temple of the Moon